W9-BJS-019

HIGH PRAISE FOR PETER TONKIN!

In Its Fatal Grip

Katapult pirouetted madly out of control. She spun into the tanker's wake, outriggers threatening to tear themselves out of the water. The blade of the mainsail swung this way and that, threatening to rip its boom out of the mast. And, with a sound like a whiplash, the foresail tore free and flew overboard until brought up short by the last ten feet still firmly attached to the far end of the forward telescopic boom. The whole mast shivered to come down and only the steel shrouds held it together.

The bulk of the tanker, less than forty feet away now, began to suck at the helpless craft. It had created a vacuum in both wind and water because of its massiveness and already *Katapult* was slewing over toward the suction of the thrashing propeller blade, preceded by the billowing dacron of the foresail. In all too few moments, it seemed, first the sail and then the craft herself would be sucked in and pulled under and chopped to bits ...

Other *Leisure* books by Peter Tonkin:

THE COFFIN SHIP

THE FIRE SHIP

PETER TONKIN

LEISURE BOOKS NEW YORK CITY

For Cham and Guy

A LEISURE BOOK®

August 2009

Published by

Dorchester Publishing Co., Inc.
200 Madison Avenue
New York, NY 10016

ISBN 10: 0-8439-6222-4
ISBN 13: 978-0-8439-6222-2
E-ISBN: 978-1-4285-0713-5

Visit us online at www.dorchesterpub.com.

THE FIRE SHIP

Fire Ship: *A vessel freighted with combustibles and explosives and sent among ships, etc., to destroy them*

First used 1588, *Oxford English Dictionary*

Out of the fired ship—which by no way
But by drowning could be rescued from the flame—
Some men leaped forth
                              and ever as they came
Near the foe's ships, did by their shot decay.

So all were lost which the ship were found—
They in the sea being burnt, they in the burnt ship drowned.

(Slightly adapted by the author)
John Dunne 1572-1631
poet, scholar,
sometime rector of Sevenoaks

CHAPTER ONE

Indian Ocean. Lat. 10° N, Long. 55° E.

She came down from the horizon burning, pulled south across the wind by the current. She came like a ghost through a haze that the monsoon could not move. A haze that twisted her, made her seem liquid, like a slow drop of tar in a furnace running over corrugated iron.

She belched smoke and the monsoon pushed it back along her track. Every now and then it would settle wearily, to lie black and oily on the upper ocean, leaving an ugly, unnatural wake stretching roughly northward, up toward Socotra, mile after mile. Such were the vagaries of that thick wind that the smoke stayed low, as if forbidden the upper reaches, so that from a distance it remained invisible and the one thing to be seen coming over the horizon, looming out of that silver haze, was that implacable black hulk, burning, oozing southward, moved by the current alone.

"There she is!" called Robin, who had the keenest eyes of the four of them. Then, "No, but . . ."

"Yes!" confirmed Richard at once, seeing the burning freighter in the blinding distance.

"Dead ahead," chimed in Hood, shading his eyes with a square, black hand.

"Steady as we go, then," concluded Weary, who held

the great spoked helm, the four of them standing shoulder to shoulder in the cockpit, looking forward.

Katapult skimmed northward like a gull, a thing of the wind, immune, unlike the other ship, to the rogue current running counter.

"Better tell him we can see him," commanded Richard and Weary together, then the Englishman, Richard, turned away with a self-deprecating grin, unused to the fact that he was not in command here. The Australian, Weary, finished the command without pause: "Tell the freighter we have him in sight, Sam."

Sam Hood nodded his understanding, his strong brown fingers already busy at the transmitter. He had broadcast at frequent intervals during their approach, ever since they picked up the first "Mayday!" twelve hours ago, but had received little beyond the distress calls, and, since noon, nothing. "Think there's anyone left aboard?" Robin asked abruptly, her clipped English tones drowning Hood's drawl. Richard shrugged and put a broad hand on her shoulder, sharing her concern in silence.

"Soon find out," answered Weary. "She's coming down on us fast enough."

They were running across the wind, at an angle calculated by Weary to bring them in on this tack. Richard Mariner, a sailor since his late teens and a senior captain these twenty years and more, marveled again at the ease and speed of the craft. *Katapult.* Her name was a play on words. "*Kat*" for her multihull configuration and "*Katapult*" for her speed. But she was neither catamaran nor trimaran—more like something in between. She had a long, needle-sleek hull with two submerged outriggers to stabilize the reach of her mast and the weight of her sails. A computer monitored the course, the angle and force of the wind of those great, ribbed sails, then dictated the horizontal angle of the outriggers to the hull so that *Katapult* always moved with maximum velocity and minimum draft unless the hand at the helm dictated otherwise. She was as experimental as she was beautiful and had fascinated Richard and Robin when they first saw her so entirely that they would have arranged a trial sail in her somehow, even had their holiday plans on Silhouette Island not changed so dramatically.

Hood glanced up at his friend and colleague, the Australian, Doc Weary. "No answer, Doc," he said. "Either there's no one aboard, or they can't hear us."

Weary's massive head tilted back as the Australian squinted up past the curved white blade of the mainsail to the communications aerial, extending the broad aerofoil mast nearly eighty feet above. Of all the high-tech equipment onboard, Doc seemed least happy with that, thought Richard. Perhaps because it was about the only part of *Katapult* neither he nor Hood had built.

"'S all still there," he informed Hood, his flat tone and Sydney accent in marked contrast to the American's. "They must have heard you."

They were an odd pair, mused Richard. Held together by bonds so deep that neither he nor Robin— who was so much better at that sort of thing—had been able to fathom them. They were both big men, but apart from their size, Sam Hood and Doc Weary presented a complete contrast. Hood was an automobile– assembly-line worker from Detroit. He seemed to have little formal education, but his fingers understood all things mechanical and electrical from the simplest motor to the most complex microprocessor. Doc also fitted no conventional pattern. His long fair mane, bound back from his forehead by an apparently immovable sweatband, seemed to enlarge an already massive head. Sitting foursquare on his thick neck and broad torso, it gave an impression of huge physical power at odds with the delicacy of those artistic hands and the fastidious intellect that guided them. Robin had managed to discover, though neither man boasted of the fact, that Weary had earned his nickname because he had been the only Ph.D. in his platoon in Vietnam, where Weary and Hood had first met.

Robin.

At the thought of her, Richard, smiling, turned his gaze across to his vital, beloved wife. She stood, reed-thin, five feet eight inches of vibrant energy, blonde, almost luminescent in the brightness. The intensity of his feeling for her filled him to bursting, as it often did, though Richard, perfectly English in this as in most things, rarely put his emotions on parade. She was concentrating absolutely on the black hulk of the freighter. The sight of the ship was now so important because her radio remained silent. Richard put all other thoughts from his mind and followed his wife's gaze. Were there any crewmen scaling down the hot black cliffs of her sides? Was there wreckage around bearing survivors? Were there lifeboats nearby? Which parts of her were ablaze? Was there anything clearly warning of danger—more than was apparent from her condition? Both he and Robin had painfully acquired experience in this field nearly ten years ago now—they had abandoned the first ship they had served on together, the supertanker *Prometheus*, when it had caught fire in these latitudes on the other side of Africa.

As far as Richard could see, this ship was an utterly undistinguished tramp. She was of the timeless "three castle" design with raised sections fore and aft and a bridge-house midships. She seemed ageless: Conrad could have sailed in her—but no one else ever would. Much of the forecastle head, he now could see, was blown away. Her old-fashioned, nearly vertical bow rose from the restless sea perhaps ten sheer, sharp feet to a wreck instead of a point. Twisted metal reached out as though the forecastle were bursting into flower. No mere collision could have done that. Farther back in the well of the foredeck, black smoke collected, solid enough, seemingly, to be contained by the deck rails and to pile itself up the bridge-front before sliding sluggishly overboard. The bridge-house was a mess. Originally white, it was now a ghastly gray. Behind windows gaping between shards of shattered glass, flames flickered madly. The wind down which *Katapult* was riding pushed the smoke back above it all like thick, oily black hair. The clarity with which that gray death mask was revealed allowed Richard a shock of realization. His generation of Englishmen had been to war only briefly, in the Falklands, but he knew its effect well enough. He called, "Hood! She's been strafed. Check the radar for planes."

"No planes visible," said Robin. "Not that you'd see them in this."

"Not till they hit you," agreed Weary, knowledgeably.

"Nothing up there," announced Hood almost immediately.

"Something down here, though," observed Richard grimly, gesturing with a broad, callused hand. The water between the two vessels was alive with sharks.

"I've never seen so many," whispered Robin.

Abruptly, Hood was beside her. She gasped as he produced a handgun. He leaned over and shot one between the eyes. The gray spade of its forehead exploded. The great fish fell away slowly, turning its empty skull from side to side, as though yet unaware that it was dead. It had enough life left in it to strike back at the first attacker that followed the trail of blood down. The two

creatures writhed together obscenely, the jaws of each
fastened in the flank of the other. More sharks charged
in.

Smooth as a machine, Hood drew a bead on another.

"No!" The cry of disgust came from Robin. The
writhing knot of tearing, torn flesh—all that remained of
the first two sharks—was still in sight and she would will
such a terrible fate on no other living thing. No matter
how loathsome the vicious predators were, she could not
let Hood continue to exterminate them for his own grat-
ification. . . . But she hesitated on the thought, already
suspecting the truth. Hood ignored her. Another shot.
Robin flinched. Richard's arm went round her shoulders
instantly. "It's the only way," he said, giving words to her
thought as he so often did. As though reading her mind.

She understood the American's plan as Richard spoke,
of course, and might have felt like kicking herself except that she still felt in the right. As though a secret
signal had been broadcast, the fins that had been cruising dangerously between them and the ship were now
all heading purposefully toward that place—well astern
now—where Hood had shot the sharks. Abruptly, the
water there heaved itself up, boiling bloodily. Feeding
frenzy had become mad slaughter.

Robin turned and looked forward at the freighter
now towering above them. The rumble of its burning
drowned out the terrible sounds of the sharks' self-
destruction.

"No use looking for anything smaller than lifeboats
after this," said Weary, his voice strained.

"Ain't that a fact," agreed Hood flatly. "No one in
the water would've stood a chance."

He was right, of course. And he had acted not a moment too soon, for even as he spoke, Weary spun the

wheel, taking the way off *Katapult*. In one motion, even before she could begin to wallow, he hit the sail-furl buttons and gunned the engine, guiding her delicately over the last few yards toward the burning freighter. With a quiet whine, automatic motors began to furl the sails safely inside the mast. Two booms, one fore and one aft, telescoped obligingly inward.

If the tramp had seemed sinister drifting, dead, down on them, this was nothing compared to the air of desolation she gave off close-to. There was a taste to her that sat far back in their throats. Smoke clawed at them, so Weary turned to run parallel rather than pass under the reeking shadow of her stern.

This close, it was possible to feel the heat she was giving off. The afternoon was stultifying in any case, but as *Katapult* turned and began to run parallel to her starboard side, their skin began to glow with the added heat she was emitting: the most palpable expression of the danger she presented.

But this close, the sight of her had more horrors to offer. A pocked rash of bullet strikes spread across the darkness of her whole hull. Invisible until now, a ragged mouth had been blown at the foot of the bridge-house. Above the gaping steel lips of this massive wound dangled the pathetic splinters of a lifeboat, destroyed on its davits. Halfway down her length, some of the crew had obviously tried to abandon. A long line angled back, its upper end snagged on the deck railing, its lower end dragging the torn, half-eaten wreck of an inflatable liferaft. More terribly still, hanging vertically from beside the tangled line on the deck rail, was a rope ladder. The last good rung hung a man's length above the sullen water. Beneath that hung another, stained, bitten in half. The dark metal beneath it was scraped and scratched and splattered.

It was chilling to imagine the fate of the last people who had used this route, but if anyone from *Katapult* were going aboard, the ladder would give the easiest access. Used to positioning his craft precisely, even with her unwieldy outriggers, Weary swung the wheel and snugged her stern beneath the last good rung. As soon as he did so, the other three jumped up out of the cockpit and onto the after-section of *Katapult*'s deck. Too large to be a mere lazarette, the after-section contained the lightweight engine and steering gear as well as much of the yacht's storage space. The deck above it was a series of hatches laid flush and tight so that it was easy for anyone surefooted to cross over it. There was, for added safety, a low rail around it.

Richard, Robin, and Hood together made for the stern and paused there. Hood caught the ladder and tugged it. Richard reached his shoulder, then glanced up. It occurred to him at last to hail the ship. Until now they had all been stunned into silence by her.

But he didn't know her name: it was gone off the wrecked forecastle, it was obliterated by the lethal smoke oozing over her stern. "Hello the ship!" he cried up, his voice all but buried under the sullen rumble of her burning. "Is there anyone aboard?"

But even as he and Hood hesitated, a slim, strong body sprang past them. Robin, lighter and far more agile than they, swarmed up toward the deck. Richard automatically, used to her intrepid ways, gave her a hand up and then froze, riven with horror as he remembered— they were onboard *Katapult* instead of scuba diving in the Seychelles because she was pregnant with their first child.

She had informed him on Silhouette, largest of the Seychelle Islands in the Indian Ocean, on the first night of their first real holiday in years. They were here to go diving and it suddenly occurred to her that there might be a risk to the baby if they did so.

They had seen *Katapult* anchored off the island, on the second day. Entranced by her, they had tracked down Hood and Weary at once. The shipbuilders had been conducting trials on *Katapult* almost lazily, after years of scrimping, saving, designing, and planning to build her. They were not really interested in taking passengers for pleasure cruises and had already turned down several offers. But Robin and Richard were different. Not only was it obvious that the sea ran in them; not only was it clear that the powerful Englishman and his dazzling wife were a team of unusual competence— they were completely different from everyone else Hood and Weary had met. And the difference lay in *who* they were, not what. They were Heritage Mariner, one of the largest independent shipping fleets in Europe. Their quiet English tones spoke for enormous wealth, almost unimaginable power in the international shipping world.

And Heritage Mariner had been looking for ways to broaden its base for years. Perhaps by going into pleasure craft, if a suitable design could be found. And now it had. If Heritage Mariner went into production with *Katapult*, Hood and Weary would be wealthy men. So Robin and Richard had put their diving gear into *Katapult*'s lazarette and moved their suitcases into the forward cabin—easily big enough to sleep four—and pitched in with a will. *Katapult* had taken to them: four was the perfect number to crew her. They tested the vessel with increasing awe in a long run northwest across the Indian Ocean. The voyage had been almost idyllic until Hood picked up that first faint "Mayday!" in the dead hours before dawn this morning.

Abruptly Robin's face appeared at the rail above the ladder. "It's not too bad up here," she called. "Better than I expected. Can't see anyone about, though."

"Wait there," called Richard. "I'm on my way up."

But she had turned away before his foot reached the first rung, and by the time he reached the deck she was gone.

Richard paused, looking around. He stood in a well between the back of the bridge-house and the bulk of the sterncastle—a couple of hundred square feet of splintered planking raised here and there into hatches. Aft of the well deck, two sets of steps rose ten feet astride a series of sagging, broken doors. The poop deck was worse, from what Mariner could see—the hatches up there were belching smoke like the bridge-house and the forward areas, but the wind that had brought *Katapult* here was still pulling most of it away to the north. Richard was standing in one of the few areas aboard that were relatively clear. Even so, there was a stench strong enough to bring tears to his eyes.

"Robin?" he called, but his deep voice was lost in the sullen roaring that made the deck vibrate like a drumskin beneath his feet.

"Where she at?" asked Hood suddenly at Richard's shoulder.

"Dunno."

"Hokay . . ." The tall American hesitated, very well aware that Richard's instinct was to go in search of her. Hood never had much of a family life, but he had vivid memories of a quiet father and a strong, cheerful mother who had loved and supported him until the car crash that only he had survived. The rock-solid strength he remembered in his long-lost family he recognized in Richard and Robin Mariner.

Richard Mariner stood six feet four, strong and

straight-backed. His black hair had a hint of gray at the temples—a sign of age belied by the agile vigor of his frame. It was a tanned, fit-looking face, a tan acquired in vigorous outdoor life, not on some sunbed in a health club. And, Sam Hood guessed shrewdly, the flat belly and broad chest resulted, like his own lean strength, from exercise that had purposes beyond mere fitness.

The power of the Englishman was held in check now by the only cause that could make him hesitate: he was calculating the action best designed to help his wife.

Robin Mariner was a woman such as Hood had rarely seen. Keen intelligence coupled with a physical strength every inch the match of her husband's. The beauty of her youth had lasted through to her midthirties. She had the physical grace and inexhaustible energy of a woman in her first flowering. The gamin charm bestowed by the windswept, salt-curled hair suited her exactly even though it hardly seemed to equate with the reality that she was a full ship's captain, with all the papers to prove it.

All in all, they were a startlingly unusual pair. No, not a pair—a unit: two halves of one being, bound together at the soul, like twins. Not even the distance unconsciously created by their Englishness and their total absorption with each other could disguise that.

"She'll be all right," Hood prompted, unaware that Richard's concern was not for his wife as much as for the unborn child she carried. "She knows what she's doing."

Richard started talking suddenly, to cover his anxiety. "She fell off a supertanker once," he said, coming to life again. "Went down to a wrecked felucca looking for a sick child screaming down there. Turned out to be a parrot, not a child at all." He moved forward, ice blue eyes busy, toward the bridge-house. "The felucca was

stuck on the front of my ship *Prometheus*. Collided in
the night and wedged there. She heard the screaming.
She went aboard. Felucca fell off."

He gestured toward the only door nearby. They
crossed toward it knowing it would lead them up to the
bridge.

"She knew what she was doing then, too, but she
was lucky to survive."

He opened the door.

"Saved the parrot; would have saved the child, if
there'd been one."

In front of them was a short passageway leading forward to a corridor. There was a door immediately on
their left, open to an empty room; tables and chairs in
disarray, as though recently, rapidly deserted.

"Like the *Marie Celeste*," observed Hood.

"I don't think the *Marie Celeste* was strafed by air-
craft," countered Richard.

"True." The conversation was automatic. Neither
Richard nor Hood was really attending to it.

They moved forward to the corridor, then followed
it left as it turned into the shadowed, stultifying bowels
of the bridge-house until they came to a stairwell. An
elevator shaft gaped before them, doors wide and car
gone, leaving a pendant tangle of cable lit by fire from
below. The bottom of the stairwell glowed and rumbled as though a volcano were active down there. They
glanced meaningfully at each other and ran on up toward the bridge itself.

The bridge was a deserted wreck. The totality of the
destruction told of terrible carnage. The windows were
gone, blasted in with the helm and all the consoles that
should have stood forward, overlooking the bows. Now
they lay scattered against the torn, bullet-pocked rear
wall. It was difficult to distinguish among the smoking

wreckage on the floor what was oil and what was blood; what was wiring and what was entrails.

There should have been a chart table. There should have been logs. There were only dark-stained rags and smoldering splinters. Twisted lumps of lead slid among the mess they had made. The whole place smelled like a slaughterhouse.

"Have you ever seen anything like this?" whispered Richard.

"No," breathed Hood. "I did two full tours in Nam and I ain't *never* seen nothing like this."

As they searched the bridge they began to reconstruct what must have happened, from the unexpected, low-level airborne attack to the intrepid collecting of the dead and wounded—and the launching of the two largest life-boats onto the deadly, shark-infested sea. Two lifeboats that should be out there somewhere, back along the ghostly, smoke-born track of the dying freighter's wake. By the time they reached the main deck again, they were both determined to do all in their power to rescue the people who had been through this. What sort of officers and crew had the awesome discipline under this wither-ing attack to remove each other, themselves, and all their records so completely? But there was nothing anywhere to give a clue to their identity—or that of their ship.

Nor was there any sign of Robin.

"Risk the foredeck?" asked Richard, at the top of the stairway down to the furnace in the engine room.

Hood nodded. Both men were too well aware that the fire down below was burning more fiercely now than it had been when they first came aboard. But such was the mystery that both were compelled to continue. No ship about legitimate business with a normal crew could ever be as anonymous as this.

* * *

Robin was in the sterncastle: here the crew had left more of themselves. The sterncastle itself was a warren of corridors, quarters, and storerooms, reaching one full level up from the well of the main deck then down three—maybe four decks—to the after engineering sections. These were as fiercely ablaze as the sections beneath the bridge, and Robin was as well aware as the men that the fire was getting worse.

Two decks down toward the dead engines and Robin was drenched in sweat and choking from the fumes. The walls were hot and beginning to blister; the coconut matting on the floor gave off dangerous-looking little puffs of smoke when stepped on. The stairs themselves were far too hot to touch. She would not have risked going farther down even had she thought anyone could still have been alive down there.

Up she came toward main deck level, therefore, contenting herself with searching quarters that must have belonged to engineers. She found overalls. She found rags, scarves, and kaffiyah headcloths. She found a copy of the Koran.

It had been a Muslim crew then; Muslim engineers at least. But who would attack with such savagery a ship full of Muslims in the northern waters of the Indian Ocean?

Who and why?

She paused, lost in thought but uneasily aware that she was taking an unjustified risk. A personal adventure, away even from Richard for a little. Perhaps her last like this forever, right at the edge where she loved to be once in a while, with nobody at risk but herself.

Except for her unborn child.

That was the rub. She had started planning names already for the eight-week-old fetus lying so comfortably inside her, a pastime that warned her that she would soon have to give up the only drug she had ever really enjoyed—adrenaline.

Ah well, she thought wistfully, time to move.

She was in one of the cabins overlooking the after-deck. There was a small window, its glass crunching under her feet, overlooking a small drop onto the wood outside, and then, forty-odd feet away, the back of the bridge-house. Beneath the window was the deck on which the Koran had lain, beside it, a bunk. At the foot of the bunk, a cupboard covering part of the wall and at right angles to that, the door out onto the stairway.

And even as she turned to exit, tapping the holy book tucked safely in her pocket, the stairwell exploded into flame.

The door had opened outward: the force of the explosion slammed it shut, then set it rattling thunderously in its frame.

All this happened so suddenly that Robin took a step backward, surprised, then walked toward the door with no real sense of danger. Even the noise it was making seemed hardly real. It was only when she touched its metal handle and burned her fingers that she really registered the fact that the stairwell outside was full of fire.

Still far from panicking, she crossed to the desk and looked out of the window. Yes. She could get through that. And suddenly the need to do so was borne upon her most forcefully. The farthest port of the hatches in the deck before her suddenly erupted into flame.

The window was big enough for her to get out of but it was fanged with stumps of thick glass. And it was early in the day, she reckoned, to deliver little Charlotte or William by cesarean section. Still, that was easily taken care of. She tore the mattress off the bunk and bundled it through the hole until it folded down over the glass. She should be able to slip through quite easily.

Over the chair and onto the desk she moved, only to
pause. It would be safer still if she had something outside to step down onto. Had she time to arrange that?
The practiced eye of a fearless tomboy youth informed
her that it would be an easy jump. Was she fussing too
much? How roughly could you treat an unborn infant
almost two months old?

She turned to look for something that would fit
through the window and still be solid enough to step
down onto. That was when she noticed the blue flames
licking in round the corners of the wooden door and
the realization finally hit her that if she didn't move
fast, then she could die here.

The forward deck was just as much of a mess as the
bridge had been. The planes had come in low and the
forecastle had taken the brunt. Richard and Sam picked
their way through the mess quickly and carefully, eyes
everywhere for clues. They stopped at the gaping top of
what must once have been a safely battened hatch. The
first few feet of ladder going down into the hold were
in much the same condition as the last few feet of the
ladder going down the side. Hood crouched down to
check it and Richard found an instant's leisure to look
at his watch, the battered old steel Rolex given to him
nearly fifteen years ago by Rowena Heritage. Rowena:
Robin's elder sister—Richard's first wife. It was twelve
minutes since Robin had disappeared. He went cold,
fearing he knew not what.

Then Hood interrupted: "Okay. Let's go," and the
two of them went down together.

Richard stepped down off the ladder into water. It
was not deep—just enough to flood his canvas dock-
sider shoes—but it was hot. It was absolutely dark down
here, the ship's lighting having died with her generators

long-since. Sam Hood's deep drawl came out of a nearby shadow, "We don't find a flashlight in five seconds, I'm outta here."

There was one clipped to the ladder at shoulder height. Richard switched it on and they found themselves surrounded by wooden crates stencilled in a range of scripts from Cyrillic through Roman to Arabic.

"See anything in English?" asked Sam.

"Not a thing."

"What d'you reckon?"

"Open one quickly. . . ."

Both men were bellowing over the roar, choking with every deep breath on increasingly acrid fumes. But the boxes were important. They had to be. Nobody strafed an unimportant ship. Therefore the planes were after the crew or the passengers. Or the cargo.

It was the cargo. The first crate they opened proved it. "Heavy ordnance," opined Sam.

"Beyond me. Never seen anything like it."

"Dangerous stuff." Sam was ferreting in among the packing now. "Damn! Richard! This's a *guided missile*."

Richard was in action at once. The markings on the box, in Cyrillic, made no sense to him but they formed a recognizable pattern. It was repeated. Many times. "What d'you think, Sam?"

"I think we'd better get out of here, fast."

"Let's just check for documentation first. Anything on paper!" But an increasingly rapid search produced nothing. After five minutes the hot water was halfway to Richard's knees and he had had enough. "Okay, Sam. Time to go!" And find Robin on the way, he thought to himself; though please God she was safely off already.

Behind the tiny cabin's smoldering door, wedged into a corner, was a tall cupboard that had not yet really attracted Robin's interest. She crossed to it now, how-ever, her mind racing. There might be something—anything—to help her get safely through that window. She tore the door open and a box the size of a child's coffin toppled out toward her. She screamed and jumped back, allowing it to fall with a hollow thud down onto the floor. Her muscles refused to move until her sud-denly sluggish brain had worked out what it was. It was nearly five feet long and two square. There was a hemp rope loop at each end. There was a catch padlocked shut halfway along it. It looked like a gun box to her.

It would do. Without further thought, she took the rope at the nearest end and pulled it toward her. The box lifted easily but proved to be heavy and unwieldy. Only desperation gave her the strength to get it up onto the table so that it leaned on the mattress. Then it was easy enough to slide it up onto the window frame and guide it down onto the deck outside. She leaned out of the window and invested a few more seconds in tilting the box until it fell safely onto its side.

She had followed it up until she was standing on the desk and she turned sideways now, hesitating no longer. She hunched herself over and slid astride the window frame, putting her full weight onto the mattress. There was a tearing sensation on the back of her right thigh. Something scraped across her shoulders. She could sense the glass cutting its way through the bedding toward her as she reached down for the box with her foot.

Then she was free, pausing, her full weight on the box, swinging her other leg down, looking back in through the window—but only for the briefest second. The cabin door exploded in, burned through. The ward-robe vanished. A cloud of flame roared hungrily along the ceiling. In her haste to avoid it, she leaped back and stumbled onto the deck. On one knee by the box, she saw that it had burst open when she dropped it. Inside there were four long guns, magazines, and ammunition boxes.

At once her hands were busy closing the box. Then she grabbed the handle again and began to lug it toward the ladder.

Behind her the whole sterncastle burst into flame, but luckily, most of the force of the explosion went up. A breeze from hell itself seemed to waft around her, then she was free of that, too, and racing forward.

"Robin! What on earth!"

Richard and Sam Hood came tearing out of the bridge and sprinted toward her. They were close-by and yelling, yet she could only just hear them. "What is that?" called Richard as he neared. His shoulder came by hers, his strong arms reaching back.

"Rifles," she said. "Russian . . ."

"Kalashnikovs?" Richard fitted his guess seamlessly into hers.

"Probably Czech," chimed in Hood.

"With ammunition . . ."

"That's cool. Let's take them."

"What on earth d'you think I'm trying to do!"

So the three of them ran the case of rifles over to the ladder. Hood went down first, then the other two lowered the long box to him.

Then, even as Richard and Robin stepped aboard, Weary gunned the engine. While *Katapult* thudded into a cross sea, slowly pulling clear, they stowed what they had found in the lazarette. Moments later, Hood was helping Weary to set the computer. The sail motors whined as the huge sails extended themselves fore and aft out of the gleaming blade of the mast, then the Australian spun the wheel, letting *Katapult* lean into the first strong gust of evening wind. She came alive at once and began to skim away. The four of them breathed a sigh of relief, looking back at last.

Sunset was turning the haze from silver to gold but the incessant spume spun up by the monsoon made the air still heavy. The lingering afternoon heat made the sea seethe and boil even now. They seemed to be sailing through a gargantuan alchemist's limbeck where the base metal of the nameless ship was being magically transmuted into gold. And even as they looked back, the long mystical spell reached fruition and the black bulk of the freighter vanished into the white-gold heart of an earthbound sun, like a great bubble of tar exploding into flame.

Struck dumb by the unexpected ferocity of it, they could only gape at the blinding rift in nature where the freighter once had been. Incredibly fast, the power of the explosion overtook them: the light first, moving fastest, dazzling even tight-closed eyes; the sound next, a cataclysmic detonation, flat, almost solid, like an ax blade to the ears. Then a maelstrom of power as the force of the explosion, twisting through the air, tearing through the water, brought the first flying detritus, the first great wave to them.

Then, for an immeasurable space of time it was as though they were in the grip of a typhoon, pitched this way and that, battered by solid air, rocklike water, steel-sharp wreckage.

They could do nothing other than crouch on the floor of the cockpit, clinging to each other, with Richard protecting Robin, waiting for it—one way or another—to end.

CHAPTER TWO

The roar of a Bell 126 throttling back to alight on a helipad at the Kharg airstrip drowned out what he was saying. John Higgins, captain of *Prometheus II*, flagship of the Heritage Mariner tanker fleet, turned away, driving his fist in rage onto the teak rail that stood along the front of the port bridge wing. The thunder of the jet helicopter's engine was a boon: he had been shouting and this would cover it. He was losing his temper far too much of late. And captains who found themselves yelling at anyone in this heat—especially at their own first officers—would be lucky to stay the course, let alone be posted senior captain, effective admiral of the fleet, as John planned on being.

The helicopter, a blinding speck in the dazzling haze, settled away onto the great gray black monstrosity of the refinery-island, dragging its noise with it, sluggishly over the Gulf. John turned back to face the subject of his ire, Lieutenant Cecil Smyke, R.N. (ret.), first officer, *Prometheus*. Behind the captain's immaculate shoulder, fifty feet down, the main deck of the tanker stretched away to the forecastle head. The green, pipe-covered expanse of it was crawling with G.P. seamen in white overalls and officers in white uniforms all working in concert. At a tank top halfway down the deck in the ineffective shade of a Sampson post clustered a group of figures with cylinders and backpacks. Around them, in pattern, stretching across and along the deck, more men looked earnestly into the black dots of open Butterworth plates, down into the empty tank.

John could sense the intensity of preparations for getting his ship under way. It filled the furnace air all around him. He knew where each crew member was and what he or she was doing. The activity seemed almost anarchic, but in fact it was not. One team was completing a thorough internal check of a troublesome empty tank—a matter of some urgency as *Prometheus* had mysteriously been moved to the head of the line of empty tankers waiting to take on a load of oil. She would begin loading tonight. The others—deck and engineering officers alike—were preparing to receive the oil aboard. Only those on watch were at tasks unrelated to the cargo's reception.

Only those on watch and First Lieutenant Cecil Smyke. Cecil stood, pale as a ghost, copper ringlets tarnished with sweat, round brown eyes narrowed by more than the glare, aristocratic face lined by more than centuries of breeding. Of all the times to get hung over to the point of incapacity, he had chosen the very worst.

"I warned you," began his captain once again, his anger just under control now, "I warned you last night, Number One. If you want to play your stupid, juvenile games aboard my ship, be *sure*, be *certain*, they do not interfere with your duty!"

Smyke wavered slightly, a tall, thin figure in a silk dressing-gown. He kept his thin lips pressed closely together, all too aware of what might happen if he allowed them to part for an instant.

"Now look at us," stormed the captain. "We still

haven't finished checking that blasted tank. We're expected to move to the head of the queue, preferably without bumping into any of those poor beggars who have been stewing here for the better part of a month, and begin to take on a full load of crude in twelve hours' time. With all the attendant paperwork. We have as a matter of *some* urgency to get stocked up for a return journey to Europort—a journey that is likely to start in a couple of days' time. With all the damn paperwork that goes with it. And I have a first officer who cannot even *stand up straight!*"

This was, perhaps, a bit unfair, thought the captain wryly: the idiot was making almost heroic efforts to stand up straight. John Higgins prowled around him exuding outrage.

"*You* should be going down number-four tank but you're sick instead." The list of difficulties this caused began to wash over Smyke altogether. He closed his eyes. He had never seen the easygoing Captain Higgins—a common little oik, thought Cecil, for all his seniority—so enraged. Never believed the captain could become so enraged. Whole new vistas opened up before him as he really took stock of John Higgins for the first time. Richard Mariner's right hand, they said, blessed with some of the great man's genius. Little John, they called him—and never mockingly; as though Richard Mariner were Robin Hood reborn. Smyke hadn't really credited it. Until now.

What if Little John could see beneath the bravado to the real reason Smyke was not on duty this morning? What if this suddenly formidable man realized his first officer had got himself into this state precisely so he could avoid going down into the tank today?

Suddenly the ship's emergency siren exploded in three short blasts: trouble in the tank. John Higgins forgot all about his useless first officer and burst into the cool of the bridge at a run.

And behind him, on the bridge wing he had just vacated, Lieutenant Cecil Jolyon Carruthers Smyke, R.N. (ret.), first officer, *Prometheus* (ret.), opened his mouth to call out and threw up all over himself.

As he ran onto the bridge John looked down, automatically setting the stopwatch function on his wristwatch. He knew the bridge so well, and dictated the positioning of everything on it so precisely, that he did not need to look where he was going. The zeros flashed up, the hundredths spinning. Four minutes to go and every instant crucial. John's mind was working as busily as the figures on his watch dial. Smyke was bloody useless. Everyone else was extra busy and would be slower because of it. Should he send Don Edwards, his third lieutenant? No, he'd better do it himself. *Hell!* it never rained but it . . .

He was through the bridge, past the collision alarm radar, round the central bank of instruments, and out into the bridge-deck corridor before the thought was completed. Kerem Khalil, senior general purpose seaman aboard, and unofficial chief petty officer, was standing by the lift holding the doors open. Shoulder to shoulder they leaped in. The little car was in motion almost before the doors were closed, while Kerem's broad finger was still hovering over the A-deck button.

"Who's called . . ." The words were torn from John like a curse. No one should be using this lift except the crash team. But it was Asha Quartermaine. She had called it from C deck where her cabin was. "Sorry," she said, pushing her doctor's bag in first, then straddling it. "Caught me with my pants down."

Literally, thought John, his mind sidetracked to her for a moment. Unself-consciously, she stood in the elevator next to them buttoning up a white cotton boiler suit under which there seemed to be nothing but her powerful body. She must have been in the shower when the alarm sounded so she just leaped into the suit and some shoes and ran. The shoes were unlaced, the cotton suit threatening to go transparent where it was wet.

Asha swept the red mane of her hair out of her startling russet eyes. Her gaze met his and she grinned: an irresistible flash of strong white teeth. Then she was down on one knee tying her laces. She was the most extraordinary ship's doctor John had ever sailed with but he could not imagine any other he would prefer to have with him now.

The lift reached A deck and the three of them burst out at a dead run. They sped out through the bulkhead door onto the main deck. Here for the first time they hesitated for an instant beside a rack of adult-size BMX bikes. Had the emergency happened farther away, they would have used these to speed down the quarter-mile of *Prometheus*'s deck. "No!" John made the decision at once. "Quicker to run!" He was off first but the other two kept up with him even though Asha still carried her doctor's bag.

John checked his watch at the open tank top—*ninety seconds and ticking*—as the waiting seamen strapped oxygen tanks to their backs. Then his hands were in motion again, adjusting the face mask and holding the tank's raised metal rim as he swung his brawny leg inside it, pushing his foot down onto the first step. Little more than two minutes left to find the second officer's team and the chief engineer who was with them, and to find out what was wrong and to put it right. In any ship's hold a difficult task; in one of this ship's tanks almost impossible.

The midship tank her captain was now entering, like an ancient miner going down some massive subterranean gallery, plunged nearly one hundred feet sheer to the keel. It was half the ship wide—more than one hundred feet again—and nearly one hundred fifty feet long. One and a half million cubic feet: volume enough to contain a modest cathederal. And, like a cathederal, it was divided into aisles, chapels, and choirs by great walls and buttresses of steel designed to stop the cargo from moving with too destructive a force; designed to stop it from tearing the ship apart. The buttresses reached in from the sides of the tank, broke away to become full columns here and there, plunging to the dark serrations of the floor where partial walls arose in series like giant pews facing invisible altars bow and stern, steel pews, eight, ten, twelve feet high. Each pew was pierced by holes but such were the demands of their dangerous, restless cargo that none of these could be made big enough to admit even the slimmest body wearing an oxygen tank.

One hundred seconds and counting. John hesitated on the first balcony—scarcely bigger than a table—and glanced up from his watch. Asha was climbing down above him. He turned away; tore himself away: he could not pause to gaze up at her now. He crossed the platform with one stride and stepped out over space. The crash team followed him one by one. They were well practiced. With the exception of lifeboat drill, this was the most regularly rehearsed emergency. And the one everyone was most terrified of doing for real.

These thoughts served to take him across to the relative security of the steps down the tank's sheer side, across the yawning gap he hated most. Pausing with the familiar slick steel so warm and reassuring by his right shoulder, he paused for a micron to look back, then ran on downward with what he had seen still imprinted on his retina.

The ladder came vertically from the tank top to that tiny platform six feet square suspended impossibly in that cavernous vastness, lit simply by the vertical spotlight of Gulf brightness plunging down until it was dissipated by the darkness far above the tanker's serrated floor. Out from that platform, moving at once into darkness, reappearing under increasingly vague pools of illumination from the open Butterworth plates— bright moons fading to faint stars in the vault of the roof beside the hard-edged sun of the tank top—came the one delicate arch of the steps he had just crossed. Light and dark they curved, like ballistic motion frozen in steel, down to the platform he had just vacated. Fifty feet—sixty, allowing for the slope—of steel step and steel rail looking like thread and seeming to sway as Asha began to cross toward him.

Two mins. thirty and counting . . . He was only a third of the way down to the tank floor—and that floor was fifteen thousand square feet of sludgy, echoing maze with walls made out of steel. He plunged down the steps, running his right hand along the slick wall while his left held the banister, like a frightened child. He was gasping oxygen at a dangerous rate, almost feeling sympathy for Smyke, who needed oxygen for quite different reasons.

". . . Dr. Quartermaine here. On platform two, descending. Over . . ."

Hell! He had forgotten to check in. He bloodied his knuckles on the transmit button of his built-in radio. "Captain here. Past platform two, descending. Ten seconds ahead of you, Doctor."

"Khalil here. On platform two. Five seconds behind Dr. Quartermaine, descending."

"Dr. Quartermaine here. Who's down there?"

"Deck here, Doctor, Cadet Perkins . . ."

"Captain here. All right, Mr. Perkins. I have the list." He was relieved to be able to say it—it put him back in charge somehow. It was written on a plastic-coated notepad dangling from his oxygen tanks, both pad and tanks like those used by a deep-sea diver. It *was* very much like going diving, in fact, for the environment down here could be every bit as deadly as the most dangerous deeps of the ocean.

John did not pause on platform three, halfway down the staircase. Instead, prompted by Asha's question, he scanned the list while he hurried deeper into the tank. Four familiar names registered in a flash. He had held the board so that he could see his watch at the same time and when he hit the transmit button by his left ear his voice was betraying increasing tension. "Captain here. Past platform three. Three minutes and counting. Doctor, about that list . . ."

A vagary of wind—the huge tank had its own microclimate—made the flesh stir on his naked forearms and abruptly he envied Asha the protection of her semitransparent cotton. No one could ever be quite sure what the air down here contained. It could be poisonous, corrosive, explosive—anything. Normally, under power, the empty tank would be full of inert gas from the ship's engine pumped in here to smother the faintest possibility of a spark. And even that nonexplosive gas, protecting them from explosion, was nevertheless quite deadly. But there should be no inert gas in the tank now. Now they were at rest. Now the tank was full of air while the work on one of the automatic cleaners went ahead; of air and God knew what else.

John had expected to be waiting for days before *Prometheus*'s tanks were filled. He had taken the chance to pump the gas out of this tank, fill it with air, and send down the team to fix a faulty washer in it.

Air was in many ways the most dangerous thing of all to allow down here, for it contained oxygen, and that could combine with the hydrocarbon gasses oozing from the ever-present oil sludge to create the most lethal cocktail imaginable. It hung invisibly all around them in the darkness. It could lie low, like ground fog at sunset. It could sail high, deadly clouds floating under the night-black sky of the tank's roof. It could form bubbles, discrete, absolute, where the concentration went from 0 percent to 100 percent in a millimeter. He had seen gas readers jump from SAFE to DEADLY in a step. And once you were trapped in one of those bubbles, you would be lucky to break free; the stuff clung like gaseous glue. But no matter what circumstances you started breathing the gas under, you had only four minutes of life left unless a crash team brought you oxygen. Yet it was impossible to work down here for any length of time wearing heavy breathing equipment. The team he was racing toward would have had breathing equipment with them but they would have been breathing the air unprotected as they worked.

The malfunction of the automatic tank washing unit had shown up on Smyke's computers during routine checking yesterday. Now it was important to get the unit fixed and clean the tank before loading a new cargo—hence the visit by more than a normal survey team: the first name on John's crayon-written list was that of the irreplaceable American chief engineer, Bob Stark.

God! He hoped Bob was all right. They had sailed together regularly during the last five years, and their

current lazy, friendly rivalry for the attentions of Asha
Quartermaine hid a deep affection.

His feet skidded, thick rubber soles suddenly failing
to find traction. He looked down, surprised to find himself standing on the tank floor, virtually up to his ankles
in black ooze. "Captain here. On tank floor. Beware
thick oil scum."

He glanced at his watch again and Asha was at his
side. Four minutes clicked up. Kerem joined them.
That was it. One man remained on platform 3 looking
for lights. Bob's team should have been signaling since
they radioed for help, to guide the crash team in. Omi-
nously there had been no lights: that darkness over by
the suspect unit made John fear for his chief engineer's
life.

He turned toward the first of the seven steel walls
between them and their goal, only to bite back a shout
of fright. Straightening into the beam of his torch came
the figure of the man he feared dead. And, behind him,
the rest of the team. Alive, unconcerned, all of them
breathing the air.

John tore his headset off, gulping in the oil-tainted,
nonlethal atmosphere. "Bob!" he stepped forward, hand
thrust out, almost overcome with relief. Stark's open,
cheerful countenance folded into a look of concern as he
took in Asha's presence. He swept one hand back through
the tousled gold shock of his hair, letting the farmboy
cowlick fall to his narrow blue eyes in an unconscious
gesture.

"What's this?" he demanded. "Some kind of exercise?"

"Didn't you broadcast an emergency?"

"Us? Nope. Clear and clean. Fixed the unit. No
problem."

"Then what . . ."

"Captain!" Distant voice from the headset in the helmet in his hand. "Deck here. Capt . . ."

They set off at a run, everything else forgotten but the urgent need to answer that panic call from above.

John didn't even think to switch off his stopwatch. It had just clocked up eight minutes when he stepped up out of the tank top to stagger a little, stunned by the humid heat and brightness, across his silent deck. He sensed rather than saw Asha, Bob, and the others come up behind him, for all his attention was focused on what was going on in front of him.

Every officer, cadet, and crewman in his complement stood assembled here in shocked, silent lines, hands on heads, under the guns of a dozen figures dressed in camouflage fatigues and bright checked kaffiyah headdresses that hid their faces like masks.

Such are the vagaries of shock that John was overwhelmed at first, not by this act of terrorist piracy, but by the stunning cleanness of the air. And yet there was a familiar scent there too, terrifyingly out of place. He felt suddenly cold and stepped forward after the merest instant of hesitation. At once one of the guns was leveled at him and he saw a tiny trickle of smoke oozing from the muzzle. And he recognized the smell as cordite.

Then even as this jumble of sensation fell into place in his mind he noticed something else. There, at the terrorist's feet was Cecil Smyke, sitting, apparently at his ease, against a vertical deck pipe. But even as John recognized that languid, silk-clad body, it rolled onto its side like a stuffed toy and slumped over until its sick-stained chest was hidden from view. Only then could everyone see the gaping bullet wound where the back of his head used to be.

CHAPTER THREE

England.

Six hours later, three thousand miles west, a black Bentley Turbo Mulsane came off the M6 just south of Penrith, in the north of England, crossed the river and the railway, and began to climb Edenside toward Croglin and Cold Fell. It rode up the slate-dark Cumberland country like a thunderbolt heading for the opening of *Macbeth*. A gray summer's day was drawing to its haunted, misty close and the precipitous, heather-mottled hills were beginning to resemble slag heaps from the Black Country farther south.

Bill Heritage loved this landscape—Wordsworth country—more than any other, and, as chairman of the largest privately owned shipping company in Europe, he had traveled the world and knew them all. And he loved Cold Fell, the great, frowning fourteenth-century border reivers' castle-cum-home that had come to him as a dowery with his wife nearly fifty years before when he had been young, ambitious, and poor, and she— Lady Fiona Graham—had been the most sought-after debutante of the last social season before the War. Their marriage had lasted thirty happy years before her abrupt and mercifully brief, fatal illness. It had been perfected in the birth of two beautiful daughters, both married in turn to Bill's senior captain and business partner, Richard Mariner.

The elder, Rowena, had been killed on the eve of her divorce from Richard. She had driven a wedge between Mariner and Heritage that only the younger daughter, Robin, had been able to remove. But at a price. During the years when Richard had worked away from the sea—and in bitter separation from Heritage Shipping—Bill had come to rely on Robin as his strong right hand. And now, the reliance he placed on her, the closely personal nature of the relationship between father and daughter had been fundamentally changed by her marriage. Bill and Richard were far too similar, though a generation apart, and the products of vastly different backgrounds and experiences, but essentially they were of a kind. In that strange way that men have, each had seen Robin as belonging to *him*, and not even that extraordinary woman could share herself between them.

Now, with Robin on the far side of the world, Bill had found himself a new right hand. Her name was Helen Dufour and she sat in the deep seat at his side now as he throttled the Bentley up the sheer mountain road toward Cold Fell where they would spend the coming weekend as secret lovers.

At the exact moment that Bill turned on the headlamps, sending great white beams into the gathering dark in front of them, the car phone started ringing.

Helen's gray eyes flicked across to him as her long right hand rested questioningly on the handset. This weekend was strictly off the record, exploiting the August bank holiday to get away from the city so that she could come to know Cold Fell before she became its mistress. As far as anyone knew, she was at her family home in Grimaud, beneath the shadow of its castle overlooking the Gulf of St. Tropez; both Bill and Helen were too worried about gossip columnists to risk anything more public yet.

Bill shook his head and gestured—they were approaching a parking area. He swung onto the graveled surface and parked, already too deep in thought to be aware that the headlight beams reached out above a sheer drop as though trying to bridge the valley with light. Night was filling the steep-sided chasm with misty shade. Far below, the river thundered in summer flood; far above, a ragged rent in the cloud cover gave a first glimpse of the crescent moon.

Part of Helen's mind took all this in as Bill reached for the phone, pushing her hand off it. "Yes?" His voice was strong, even at his age; virile.

The handset gabbled.

Helen lay back, stretching, every sense tensely alert beneath apparent sleepiness. She herself had left "emergencies only" notes for both of them with the weekend secretariat; this had to be a major problem. But it soon proved to be much worse than anything that sprang to her pragmatic Provençal mind and the beginning of her part in the nightmare most of them would be lucky to walk away from.

"Piracy!" The quaintly archaic word was the first he could manage to say after hanging up. He turned to her, face expressing both rage and disbelief. "They've seized *Prometheus* with her whole crew. John Higgins, Bob Stark, Asha Quartermaine . . ." .

"Why?" She had no French intonation. She spoke English as though she had spent all her life at Oxford, her accent a direct reflection of her mental acuity and academic education.

"God knows! Arab terrorists, apparently. Nobody knows any more than that, except . . ."

She waited, knowing better than to prompt him.

". . . except they say they've executed a senior officer to prove how serious they are."

"*Dieu!*"

"We have to contact Robin and Richard at once!"

"Impossible, unless they have radioed in to the office. No one knows where they are."

"We've got to go back to London. Now!"

Even as he spoke, he was swinging the Mulsane out onto the empty road.

They were back in Heritage House on Leadenhall Street in London before midnight. A sleepy doorman checked them through security and they rode up in the lift together. The top floor was electric with tension, the twenty-four-hour secretariat supplemented by those executives Helen had managed to contact on the car phone while Sir William was exceeding the speed limit by a factor of almost two, racing down the empty M6 to London. Into this tense atmosphere they stepped, deep in conversation, and unconsciously undid all the careful secrecy that had obscured their true relationship until now. Security had buzzed up. Everybody was waiting for them, many agog to know how two people apparently spending the weekend at different ends of the continent could manage to turn up simultaneously. But such speculations were almost forgotten as everyone bustled into the quickly overcrowded chief executive's suite of offices. It was the natural place to go, under the circumstances. Such was the nature of Heritage Mariner's senior management that there were three suites of offices here: Bill Heritage's, the Mariners', and Helen Dufour's. Officially "retired" for some years now, Sir William's position as chairman of the board gave him a small suite that he used only occasionally.

Robin and Richard, as joint managing directors, shared
a large, fully equipped complex, which consisted of their
own offices, two secretaries' offices, a bedroom, and a
bathroom. But all that was closed off now. So it was
natural that everybody gather in Helen's office because
she was the senior executive present, chief executive
until Robin and Richard returned, the one with her
fingers currently on the pulse of the business.

Her desk was not made of teak or mahogany like the
others', but of molded plastic: more like the console in a
spacecraft than anything else. The central writing area
was surrounded by dials and video display screens controlled from a keyboard designed to slide in and out like
a central drawer. Phones, each one with its own molded
perch, nested round the upper edge; all programmed to
contact over one hundred numbers worldwide, just in
case Helen's computers could not get enough online information directly from the computers of her contacts.
Her fingers were busy the moment she sat in her chair;
simultaneously she began interrogating all the staff members who had been there since the first bulletin. As she
talked she tapped in urgent requests for information and
was answered at once through her electronic mail system. The screens filled with messages. The printers in her
secertary's office chattered discreetly into life.

But no new information of any use was currently
available. As the small hours ticked slowly by, it became
clear that there was no machine-generated or -stored
information for any of them. Bill Heritage, content to
take a back seat and reexamine those files Helen had
finished with at greater depth, began to get restless. He
understood the high-tech information-gathering systems Helen used almost as well as she, but he also knew
they had their limitations. Reaching the limits of his
patience, he scowled at his watch and crossed to his

own, unimpressive office. The new computer networks were stymied for the moment: it was time to try the old-boy network.

They were at school together, went up to Cambridge together, joined up together in 1939. After demobilization, the thirty-year-old Captain Bill Heritage had gone into shipping. Commander Justin Bulwer-Lyons had joined the Diplomatic Corps. He had been Bill's best man—and might be again, sooner than he knew—and was Robin's godfather. Neither man was in his wonted position of absolute power any longer, but each kept his finger on the pulse. Bill and Bull had been famous for their all-night activities in their youth and neither of them slept much now, either. Bull answered the phone on the third ring.

"Bull? Bill Heritage here."

"Been expecting your call, old man. What can I say? It's a nasty business. One dead so far, I understand."

"Yes, that's what we hear. Any word at the Bureau as to who it is . . . was . . ."

"Nothing." Bull was one of the chief advisers to the International Maritime Bureau, the Interpol of the sea. There was little that escaped him if it happened in shipping. And his specific area of expertise was the Middle East—so if anyone outside Heritage Mariner might have helpful information, it would be he.

"Anything on the general situation coming through the Office?" Bill meant the Foreign Office.

"Nothing. The Corps is quiet, too." The Diplomatic Corps.

"Intelligence?" It was a faint hope.

"If they know anything, it hasn't filtered down to us yet."

There was an uncomfortable, almost threatening silence for several long seconds.

Then, "Any projections, Bull?"

Bull was prepared for the question: "Right. The situation as I understand it is this. Your tanker *Prometheus* has a complement of about forty. English and American officers; Hong Kong Chinese stewards; mixed bag of general purpose seamen—everything from Palestinian to Pakistani. Mixed bag of hostages; lots of governments over lots of barrels."

"Right. Most of the G.P. seamen are Muslims, though."

"The same religion as the terrorists, you mean? Unlikely to be much help. I assume most of your people are conservative, ordinary Sunni Muslims. The terrorists are likely to be Shi'ite fundamentalists. Very different kettle of fish: like looking at Ireland and saying Protestants and Catholics are both Christians."

"I see what you mean. . . ."

"Right. Anything else about the crew? Any specific diplomatic levers so to speak? Oh yes, Bob Stark, your American chief engineer."

"His father is John Stark, senator from . . ."

"I know. But I was thinking of his uncle, Walter. Officer commanding the U.S. Navy's Sixth Fleet, currently on maneuvers in the Gulf of Oman."

"That make much difference?"

"Not in the short term, but you never know. They're forbidden in the Gulf at the moment, for diplomatic reasons though. Can't go past Hormuz except in the most exceptional circumstances unless the President gives them the direct order. And anyway . . ."

"Yes?"

"As I understand it, your ship is still off Kharg Island. This puts her firmly in Iranian waters. There have been no pronouncements from Tehran so far, but I would assume both our chaps and the Americans will play it safe until someone fairly senior over there makes the position pretty clear."

"And that means?" There was a frosty tone in Bill's voice: he could see where this was leading.

"If Khadaffi had them, then you might stand a chance. But I really can't see anyone getting too gung ho with the Iranians, especially at the moment; I understand there's the usual power struggle going on between various branches of the Irani armed forces. But even if there weren't, one has only to think of President Carter. . . ."

That uncomfortable silence fell on the lines again.

"But you think it's random, Bull?"

"Don't quite follow . . ."

"Were they after *any* ship or were they after *our* ship?"

"Have you had any demands? Any contact?"

"Nothing."

"Probably is random in that case. I mean, it's possible you have enemies that powerful, I suppose, but I'd say that unless you hear anything specific, assume you're the victim of a sort of diplomatic traffic accident."

The background noise on the phone lines whispered; Bill remembered reading somewhere that people had contacted the dead down unused phone lines.

Then Bull tried to lighten things a little, "But what does my goddaughter say? I can't imagine either Robin or Richard short of ideas. I was just saying a couple of days ago, when the Bureau next goes shopping for advisers . . ."

"They're out of touch, Bull. Gone off the face of the earth."

"Not like you to be so fatalistic, Bill. Getting a bit tired?"

"Maybe just a tad. They left for the Seychelles last

week. Silhouette Island. Went sailing on some kind of yacht three days ago, that's all anyone knows."

"Well that's all right then."

"I don't follow you, old man."

"If they're at sea, they're bound to be fine. Directly descended from Neptune and Amphitrite, those two, the oceans love them."

Unconsciously Bill touched the wood of his desk. Bull had always believed in pushing his luck to the limit; Bill was more careful. "Even so," he countered, "they're not much help at the moment."

"I take your point. Look, if they were there, I suspect at least one of them would get the first flight out to the Gulf they could. It's the obvious thing to do. It's what I would do. Leave someone in charge of the office and see what things are like on the ground. Got anyone there you can trust?"

"Helen's here."

"God! That's lucky. I thought she was in Grimaud this weekend. There you are then. Get out to the Gulf yourself. You'll feel better in the thick of it anyway, if I know you. Now I know you've got your own offices out there, but the High Commissioner in Bahrain's the son of a very dear friend. . . ."

Sir William was back in Helen's office a few minutes later. "Yes," she agreed. "It's the obvious thing to do; and you're the obvious one to send. If anyone's going out, it has to be someone with seniority to make decisions, someone with enough contacts to be sure of what's going on, someone with weight . . ." She trailed off, exhausted. She hated being right. She hated knowing that he had to go. Talking herself into letting him.

He stood, helpless. There was nothing he could do but wait for her to finish. He didn't like it any more than she did. He was long past boys' own adventures now, in spite of what Bull had said. He could have done with some peace and quiet. They both could. He checked his watch. Coming up for four o'clock. They should have been wined and dined and well tucked down in his great four-poster bed at Cold Fell. . . .

"There's a flight at ten from Heathrow," she said at last. "It'll get you to Muharraq airport at eight tonight, Bahrain time."

Muharraq. He paused at the top of the Boeing's steps, shocked as always by the brutal impact of the heat. It was dark—had been for hours—and the yellow security lights of the international airport gave everything a sulfurous glare that went well with the temperature: it was like a minor hell. In the distance, beyond the buildings on his right, he could see the great flares blossoming from the rigs out on the Gulf. The whole world seemed to have ignited around him. He breathed in the thick atmosphere and it seemed to fill him instantly, pushing a trickle of sweat out of every single pore in his body. Even with his jacket off, he was nearly overwhelmed by it. Within two steps he had to move the carefully folded garment—the flesh on his arm beneath it was prickling with the heat. Thankfully it was only a short walk through the oil-smelling, shower-humid evening to the blessed coolness of the air-conditioned arrivals area. Once again, shock. Just as he had forgotten how hot the real air on this island could be, he had also forgotten how inhumanly cold the conditioned air felt in contrast. He quickly donned the soggy jacket that had been such an encumbrance only a second or two ago and buttoned up at once. Even then, he shivered as though in the grip of a Cumbrian winter.

Passport, baggage collection, and customs were formalities that hardly distracted him. He was through into the great new arrivals hall within minutes, looking dazedly around, his thought processes slowed by exhaustion and jet lag, not knowing who—if anybody— would be there to meet him. Bull's man from the High Commission, most likely, though the Diplomatic Service was kept pretty busy out here, what with receptions and parties and dinners and functions. . . .

Heritage Mariner maintained an office in Manama, but it was one of three in the United Arab Emirates and the one man who ran them all—Angus El Kebir—was in Dubai at the moment.

Perhaps he had better get a cab.

Lost in memories of times long past when he had first got to know this island, when Muharraq was primarily an RAF base with a few little independent airlines shuttling supplies from one airfield to another, when old Neville Shute—Neville Norway, his real name— was out here working on his novel *Round the Bend*, when there had been a real sense of adventure to the Gulf, Bill Heritage drifted out into the stultifying night, carrying his own case, looking for a cab. He failed to hear his name being called over the announcement system. He paid no attention to the limousine with its CD license plates that had actually come to meet him. As he had done countless times before, he raised his hand to the driver of one of the great yellow Cadillac taxis and it pulled over to the curb beside him. He opened the back door and slung his baggage in before the driver could offer help. He climbed in after it. "Manama, please," he said. "The Hilton, on Government Road . . ."

But even before he could finish his directions, the door he was closing was torn open again and he had one stunned glimpse of a shadowed body in battle fatigues with a bright checked kaffiyah folded across its nose and mouth looming over him.

Beirut. He *had* to be in Beirut. That was all he could think. There was nothing in the room except the bed, a table, and a rickety chair. There were no identifiable sounds from outside. Nothing except a continuous, muffled, distant roar, but it sounded like traffic. Or artillery.

Perhaps when someone came he would learn more— but he doubted it. He had awoken in this dark room some unspecified time ago, in his shirtsleeves and trousers but with no shoes, no braces or belt, no watch, no luggage. It was dark, but only because there were no windows. He had groped his way to the bed, the table, the chair, the door. He had stood on the chair and searched high up on the walls. He had stood on the table and discovered nothing but an unyielding ceiling. He had listened at the door. Again he had heard only the distant roar. Now he lay on the bed and thought. He had been kidnapped. Certainly by Arab terrorists. Probably by the same Arab terrorists who held *Prometheus*. Which made it all look less like Bull's "diplomatic traffic accident" after all. Yet he was not onboard *Prometheus*. He was not on a ship at all—there was no hum of alternators, no movement over the sea. And he was still in the Middle East; the temperature told him that. The heat confirmed it.

Christ! He hoped Helen wouldn't worry, too much.

Better not to think about that. Better not to think too much at all, actually.

Beirut seemed the best guess then. No doubt he would have plenty of time to test his hypothesis further.

CHAPTER FOUR

Indian Ocean. Lat. 13° N. Long. 55° E.

"Give me the binoculars," Robin demanded, her voice suddenly tense.

Richard didn't hear her. Just at the moment she spoke, a sound, something more felt than heard, rumbled in his ears, distracting his attention from her and from his watch. He moved his head, concentrating on the sinister vibration in the air. Was it distant thunder? Was it something nearer, more threatening? He didn't like it, whatever it was. He glanced up along the spotted skin of the fully extended sail to the blast-damaged wreck at the masthead: perhaps there was something wrong there. Weary hadn't trusted that masthead even before flying debris had destroyed it all those hours ago during the destruction of that nameless ship, wrecking their communications equipment, necessitating the careful watch Robin and he were now keeping, perhaps doing more dangerous damage besides. Then Robin called again and he concentrated on her instead. "What did you say, darling?"

"Give me the binoculars. There's something out there."

He reached down into the rack where the field glasses were kept and gritted his teeth as the ache in his swol-

len elbow, like the damaged masthead a relic of the
freighter's death, flared into pain.

"Here." He handed them up to her. She slung them
round her neck, then gripped the glass windscreen by
his head to steady herself. She carefully rearranged her
stiff body until she was kneeling, painfully twisted to
allow for the angle of *Katapult's* deck.

Richard strained to follow the direction of her gaze,
but he could see nothing. The ocean continued to come
at them in an unvarying series of waves, each one banded
like the one before with the faint, curving slick of oil
they were still following. About ten yards wide and God
alone knew how long, it stretched back like a ghostly,
humpbacked road into the haze.

"Anything?"

They were speaking in hushed monosyllables not
only because of fatigue. Robin had been sitting up on
the cabin roof watching for hours in silence. Richard
had the helm because he could stand easily where she
could not. Hood and Weary were asleep below, Hood
with a cracked rib and Weary with a great welt across
the back of his skull. None of them had come through
the explosion unscathed. Even crouching all together
on the cockpit's floor they had each been hurt in one
way or another by that hard, hot rain of debris.

The subliminal rumble, half sound, half sensation,
came again. Richard checked the damaged topworks
once more. Letting his eyes follow the curved sails down,
along the blade of the mast to the ball-and-socket joint
where the whole mast sat in its steel mast-foot, just below the swellings that housed the retractable telescopic
booms, three feet above the deck. He knew the mast
was stepped in a ring of steel embracing the central hull
at this point. Could there be anything wrong there? He
frowned, trying to pick up that sound again.

Robin screwed the eyepieces of the binoculars into her eye sockets; they seemed to magnify the blinding dazzle without helping her to see farther at all. She dropped them and brushed the sweat out of her eyes with unaccustomed anger. Somehow, during the mayhem that had come so close to destroying even *Katapult*, all the men had ended up in a huddle on top of her. Their wounds were due to flying debris—her painfully twisted knee was due to their clumsy attempts at gallantry. She didn't know whether she was more vexed with them for hurting her or with herself for being so ungrateful.

Katapult smashed into a breaking crest and leaped playfully with what sounded like a roar of joy. She flexed automatically and gasped in pain. God! What a bunch of schoolboys! Here she was, perfectly capable of looking after herself, trying to maintain the last of her independence before motherhood shackled her down, and she found herself surrounded by a would-be James Bond and the Macho Twins. Great!

She pushed the binoculars back under her brows and suddenly forgot all about her rage. There it was—in full view, surprisingly close at hand. She fine-focused automatically, her breath suddenly short with excitement. Oil-smeared, battered, perhaps empty, certainly showing no sign of life at the moment, but at the near edge of the oil-track, thank God, it was less than a mile away.

"Richard, come starboard a point or two. There's a lifeboat less than a mile ahead."

"Any sign of life?" His excited voice lost in the rumble of a wave against *Katapult*'s flank.

Robin was scanning it carefully now. The ravaged lifeboat was low in the water, floating at a strange angle. One gunwale of the boat was lower than the other so that it showed one side, but not its contents. Beyond

that, nothing seemed wrong. Perhaps there was someone lying over on the lifeboat's port side. Several people,
their weight distributed unevenly, might make it ride
like that. But Robin wasn't convinced, her initial feeling of excitement killed by her common sense. More
likely it was the wind playing tricks with an empty
hull. Robin noticed the wind was freshening, pushing
Katapult over more. Her starboard outrigger sank deeper,
the narrow delta of the aquadynamic composite down
deep enough to gain a green tinge from the founda-
tions of a glassy wave. The threatening wind made
Robin glance down from the lifeboat to consider the
craft she was riding on. *Katapult*'s two outriggers curved
out and forward athwart the raked mast plunging past
hinges, where the shrouds were tethered, to enter the
water on either side of *Katapult*'s lean central hull. Deep
below the surface, the outriggers spread into two Concorde shapes that cut through the sea as efficiently as
that great airplane hurtled through the sky, their angles
controlled by the computer controlling *Katapult* herself.
At the moment the electronic system kept her steady in
the face of the freshening wind and the threatening
chop.

Robin suddenly felt at risk up here on the deck. She
swung round, licking the salt off her lips, hissing in
sudden pain as she put her weight on her damaged leg.
One step along the freeboard and she hopped in over
the coaming down into the cockpit beside him.

"Shall I call the others?" she asked. "We may need
their help."

"Not yet." His voice was distant.

"Rick . . ." She said his pet name almost shyly. It was
something she almost never did in public and she
sounded confused even in her own ears. Had her vexa-
tion taken her too far? Was he really angry with her?

She found herself embarrassed and unaccountably close to tears. She dashed the back of her hand across her eyes as though brushing sweat away, and looked back toward the lifeboat, disguising her momentary weakness, even from herself.

Katapult lurched. Automatically she held on to the cockpit's coaming, her left hand reaching out for Richard's shoulder. The white, oil-blotched hulk of the lifeboat was still half a mile distant, but *Katapult* seemed to be picking up speed extremely quickly. There was a sudden series of clicks as the computer was forced to reset the outriggers and trim the sails, the clear mechanical sounds making it shockingly obvious just how much the noise of the wind and sea had grown in the last few minutes. Instinctively she tightened her grip on the thick, hard triangle of muscle behind his collarbone. *Katapult* lurched again and this time she felt something— a slap of wind on her cheek. The trimaran gathered even more way as though she were a racing car with the turbo kicking in. She heard the wheel slap into the palms of his hands and she felt his whole body tense. "God, Robin, she's pulling hard. There's something . . ."

"What is it?"

"Damned if I know. *Aach* . . ." He made a peculiarly Scottish sound of disgust, left over from his Edinburgh schooldays, and put the wheel right over, taking the way off her. The sail motors automatically gathered the sails in. *Katapult*'s mast leaped upright and they staggered into each other's arms as the deck came level— surprised by how much heel there had been on her. As her speed decreased, so the wind seemed to pick up even more. "It's probably nothing," he said softly as he let her go. "Maybe a squall coming. I don't know . . ."

Robin glanced away from the lifeboat and looked around carefully, but the depressing haze swirled round

Katapult, almost willfully concealing everything. It was impossible to make out any cloud formations or see the telltale darkening of air and sea that foreshadowed changing weather. She glanced down into the black bowl of the dead radar—along with the radio and the masthead it was another casualty of the explosion.

The unusual movement of the air stopped.

Richard turned away and reached down to push the start button of the engine. Robin directed her gaze back to the lifeboat. Something was very wrong. Perhaps distance had disguised it. Certainly that errant freak of wind and the swirling haze had camouflaged it. But when one looked carefully, it was obvious that the boat was not sitting correctly in the water. It was angled up and away almost as if it were willfully trying to hide something from them.

Richard pushed the starter button, the engine coughed into life. *Katapult* began to slide forward again uneasily over the choppy water in that slightly ungainly fashion she had if anything other than the wind impelled her.

Without any good reason, Robin suddenly felt reluctant to get any closer to the lifeboat. She swung round toward Richard, half expecting him to be sharing her foreboding, but he was concentrating absolutely on guiding *Katapult* across the wind. He was half in love with the sleek vessel and worried about soiling one square inch of her dazzling white hull with the black taint of the dead ship's lifeblood. The lifeboat was at the outer edge of the oil-slick and clearly Richard wanted to follow its track round, keeping clear of the oil, bringing only *Katapult*'s nose alongside the stricken boat. Someone would have to be out there on the farthest point of the bow to grab hold of the boat and secure it to *Katapult*.

The thought of being out there, so near the boat and so far from the others, frightened her. In near panic, she found herself halfway to the stairs leading down to Weary and Hood. And yet it was that very fear that stopped her. She knew fear of old, knew it as well as most; and unvaryingly she met it and faced it. If she was frightened of doing something, she did it: that was the sort of person she was.

Let Hood and Weary sleep. She would take care of this. Robin walked back and snapped a boathook free of its retaining clips along the lazarette; then she used it as a sort of crutch to support her as she stepped back up onto the sloping foredeck. Forcing herself not to limp, she moved along the hull to the needlepoint bow. She had been here once or twice before, but only briefly and never alone. And it struck her forcefully how small the forepeak was, how terrifyingly close to the dangerous ocean.

Katapult's forward deck sloped down as well as in so that the low deck-railings seemed mere inches above the water. Waves were supposed to ride up over the sleek porpoise shape when the vessel was in full flight; *Katapult*'s designers had not worried about crew who would have to accept blue water washing over their feet as well as that vertiginous feeling that the tiny forepeak was a thin ledge at a very great height. It seemed impossible to Robin that she should become dizzy with vertigo when she was a foot or two above the surface of the sea, but her imagination left her in no doubt whatsoever that if she slipped she would fall—and fall and fall. The foresail was designed to furl or unfurl from the aerodynamic blade of the mast along a telescopic boom just as the mainsail did. They were both tucked safely into the mast now and the foredeck was innocent of any protrusion whatsoever. Even the motor winches and the anchor, the retracting bowsprit designed to take a spinnaker, all the forward equipment lay contained below on a second foredeck just beneath her feet. There was nothing between her and the hungry sea but that derisory little safety rail. Around this she locked her left fist as though she were a cowhand astride a bucking bronco. Only then did she look up and out.

The side of the lifeboat winked at her from twenty feet away. Pitching over the waves, rolling in the gusts of wind, it nevertheless refused to show her what it contained. She heard only the roaring of the wind across the blade of the mast behind her, the tumble of the waves at the stern of the lifeboat, the sucking hiss of them at her feet. Then thunder—abruptly she looked up. The haze roiled weirdly in the distance dead ahead. It was growing thicker and darker there. Had the thunder come . . .

—the thunder of the wind across the ruined masthead eighty feet above her, real, tangible, putting her mind at rest.

She looked back down at the boat again. It was much nearer now, fifteen feet almost dead ahead and at last there was something. . . .

The high white side rolled down suddenly, a freak wave running across the rest. It was a momentary thing, over in a flash, but surely she had seen . . .

"Hey, hello the boat!"

. . . yes, she was certain she had seen . . .

"Hello the lifeboat, can you hear me? *Hey!*"

. . . two or three figures. The outlines of some heads and shoulders clinging to the side.

Why didn't they answer? Perhaps they were too exhausted. But she was certain of what she had seen. With rekindled excitement she let go of the safety rail and began to pull herself to her feet. It took her two painful attempts to unlock the damaged knee, but as *Katapult*'s head creamed over the remaining ten feet toward the lifeboat, the glassy swell washing over Robin's feet began to darken with oil-tar so she pulled herself to full height. Then she began to maneuver the unwieldy length of the boathook out toward the white gunwale before her.

But then another wave ran counter and for all her fortitude she began to scream.

It was full of corpses. They lay toppled on the bottom in a twisted pile in a range of attitudes that suggested they were reaching out in their last instant of life. And what they were reaching for remained. At the far side of the boat, frozen in the act of climbing aboard were five more men, their hands still entwined with the dead hands in the boat. Five figures, stark against the dazzling blue of the ocean, all of them clustered along the port side, their weight enough to give the boat its list, reaching with both arms inward, the gunwales snugly under their armpits, their dusky, bearded faces mottled, bloodless, as gray as the bridge of their stricken ship had been. Eyes staring blindly, mouths screaming silently. All but one looked straight at Robin; they had been dead for a day at least but were still howling for help. The last one, the stern-most of them, was looking away, staring down into the water behind him. What little Robin could see of his face wore the most terrible expression of all.

He was staring down, horrified, frozen, in apparent fascination at the fact that his body ended just above the waterline. Another wave slammed into the far side of the doomed lifeboat, lifting the hanging figure high enough for Robin to see all too clearly where a shark had taken him off at the ribs like a chain saw.

She let the boathook slip into the ocean, turned, and

ran. All thought of challenging the fear was gone: nothing mattered except the overwhelming need to escape the horror of the sight. She sprinted back down *Katapult*'s deck, her wet shoes miraculously finding a clear path between the gathering hump of the cabin side and the low gunwale; her knee holding up uncomplainingly until she was back in the cockpit.

At her first cry, Richard cut the engine and spun the wheel back, taking *Katapult*'s head—and the person on it—away from whatever threatened. He was half out of the cockpit on his way to help when she brushed past him. He followed for a step or two, but she made it plain she needed no help. He returned to the starboard, therefore, to see what was to be done.

He had not put the wheel far enough over. *Katapult* had not moved away from the lifeboat, but collided with it at a glancing angle and gathered it to herself, collecting it like an errant chick under the wing of her starboard outrigger. Richard froze with horror; nausea threatened to overcome him and he turned away, haunted by the gentle *thump, thump, thump* of the lifeboat.

The afternoon closed down on them in a dreadful silence; all sound and motion were driven from the face of the sea. *Thump* went the boat, and everything seemed to stop.

A rumble of thunder, much nearer than any other.

Thump went the lifeboat.

A faint whisper of wind came and grew in intensity. Something completely different from the monsoon they had been following so far. This was a dangerous wind, a wind with a purpose.

Katapult heeled over. The lifeboat rattled and thumped between the hull and the outrigger. The dead men lying in her stirred; the dead men hanging at her side danced merrily, holding hands as though they were playing a ghastly children's game. Then the spray-mist that had hung over them for days began to clear, vanishing down-wind as though rushing off to see what the wind was going to see.

Richard and Robin came out of their trances, both of them suddenly very cold indeed. Their eyes met and they were in action at once, everything else forgotten. Something was very wrong here and this was no time to be sqeamish: they had to search the lifeboat and then get *Katapult* away from here as quickly as they could.

Richard gave her a hand as she hopped up and out along the runway again. By good fortune, *Katapult* had snagged the boathook as well as the boat, so Robin concentrated on that, on the bright orange buoyancy handle at its end with its wrist-loop for safety. She plunged her hand into the icy ripples and caught it first time. Then she pushed its bright hook into the stern of the restless little boat and leaned back, holding it still, keeping her eyes closed tight.

It was only now that Richard seriously thought about calling the other two. Searching a twenty-foot lifeboat containing more than ten dead bodies was not something one person could do efficiently or quickly. And the need for speed was suddenly impressed on him. The stern-most of the upright figures seemed suddenly to move. Richard looked up, shocked out of his meditation, in time to see a battered cap fly off the figure's frozen head and spin away, carried by the same eerie wind through which the ripples were running and the oily spume was beginning to fly.

Whatever was happening, whatever squall was coming down on them, he would awaken the others only when he was ready to get *Katapult* under way. Either he looked in the lifeboat now or nobody would ever look in it. He had hesitated for less than a second and he moved.

Even as he stepped down into the floating charnel house of the lifeboat, one thing became obvious—this boat had also been strafed. Strafed from wave-top level. The scene came vividly alive in his mind's eye: the huddle of men trying to pull their shipmates aboard, the bullets going among them, the remorseless sharks coming. His face expressionless, Richard secured a line to *Katapult*'s low rail and began to check more carefully. There were no documents, no radio or navigation equipment in sight. But the corpses were clustered—piled—in the bottom of the lifeboat, their arms reaching upward like the tentacles of sea anemones, seeming to wave in the rising wind. If he wanted to check further and get at any of the lockers, he would have to undertake the grim business of moving them.

The most obvious place to start was at the stern, where the fewest corpses and the largest lockers were. He began to move down the boat and found his attention caught not by the corpses but by Robin, toward whom he was moving. The sight of her called to him and he made his way toward her carefully. At the stern, he paused, holding the lower end of the boathook and looking up along its length at the beloved figure standing mere feet away tense and strong, her eyes closed, her face blank. A feeling of love and pride overwhelmed him and, had she not been beyond his reach he would have held her tightly to him.

Then something forced his eyes to look past her, downwind, to the place toward which the haze and spray were rushing. In that instant, the mist was plucked away.

And the monster was revealed.

"Oh, my God!"

He shook the boathook and she jumped awake.
"Robin! Get below! Get Weary and Hood. *Now!*"

Jesus! How could he not have known? How could he
not even have suspected? The wind, the mist, the
spume, everything, not blown but *sucked*. Sucked into
the roaring, thunderous gyre of it. Sucked to whatever
eternity awaited at the other end of it.

Robin dropped the boathook on the cockpit sole and
started to run below—when she caught her first glimpse
of its broad white shoulder whipping into its flat black
cloud-base head. With wondering eyes she traced the
sinuous, sinister curve of it down, down inexorably to
the broad foot, wreathed in madly dancing spray. And
suddenly she became aware of just how *solid* the air felt
streaming so rapidly past her; and how swiftly and forcefully it was taking *Katapult* along with it.

"Dear God!" she breathed and hit the cabin door.

It was dark and hot, quiet and still—a numbing contrast to the increasing bedlam above. Once through the
door she had to force herself to further motion. An out-
rageous idea came that she could just curl up down here
with the men she had come to fetch, pull the blankets
safely over her head, and hide . . .

She hit the light switch.

Both men had collapsed on the long bench-seats on
either side of the central table without even bothering
to open out the bunks. Neither one stirred at the sudden brightness; they were insulated by exhaustion from
light as well as from the ungainly motion of the yacht
and the growing din of the wind. Weary was closest.
Without further thought, she ran across to him on suddenly unsteady feet.

He was lying, fully dressed, on his back with his
arms crossed on his chest, laid out like a dead man. Two

strides took her up the length of him and she grabbed him by the shoulders. "Wake up!" she called. His head-band was crushed into his long right hand like a child's security blanket. His curly hair fell forward in a cow-lick into his restless, sleeping eyes. "Come on!" she in-sisted, shaking him with all her might. "Wake up, damn it!"

And his eyes flew open.

She had never seen anything like it in her life. The eyes opened, deep blue and every bit as fathomless as the waterspout outside, sucking at something inside her with the same relentless intensity.

His hands were on her shoulders just as hers were on his, shaking her as she was shaking him. And he was screaming at her as well, screaming as his body shot upright. She had never seen such a look in anyone's eyes. "Who am I?" yelled Weary at her.

There was no knowledge in those eyes, no recogni-tion. Nothing. They were the eyes of a terrified child, one who does not even know why it feels fear. "Who am I?" Weary screamed. And Robin was stunned, ren-dered completely helpless by the shock of it.

Weary was sitting completely upright now, shaking his head from side to side. The hair flew out of his eyes to show his forehead, high, white, pinched in impossi-bly at the temples.

No. Not pinched in. Crushed in.

She was unable to tear herself away from his de-mented gaze. The last thing she saw before Hood hit her, out of the corner of her eye, was Weary's left tem-ple, caved in to a shadowed hollow, starred with bright red scar tissue.

As soon as Robin leaped into action, Richard turned, too. The lifeboat began to pitch severely as soon as the boathook was free, hurling itself back against the bow rope like a willful puppy fighting a leash. The movement made it hard for him to work, but he refused to give up even now. Brutally, for time was too short for him to show proper respect, he heaved the sternmost bodies away, uncovering the lockers. His eyes still busy among the filthy, oozing, twisted pile for any scraps of information, any telltale personal possessions they might have brought with them. More than one dead fist clasped a worn Koran, but that was all. He heaved them aside and tore the doors open. The stern lockers revealed nothing more than a bilgelike well reaching down to the keel, full of seawater, blood, and excrement. He straightened.

The great white whiplash of the waterspout seemed to leap toward him as he moved. The wind howled louder, plucking back stinging spray from the white horses that suddenly surrounded him, its strength roaring up the Beaufort scale with inconceivable rapidity. Hell! Where were Weary, Hood, and Robin?

He turned, spreading his feet to gain stability, and then a hand grasped at his leg.

Hood hit Robin in a sort of American football charge, knocking her back onto the seat. Then he was sitting opposite Weary where she had been. He was saying something in a repeated, gentle monotone, voice lazy and hands busy. "You're Doc," he was saying. "It's okay. It's cool. You're Doc and you're all right." As he talked his fingers loosened the Australian's grip on the sweatband, easing the bright elastic toweling free.

"It's fine, Doc. No sweat. You are Albert Stephen William Weary, born Sydney, Australia, November fifth, nineteen . . ."

As soon as the sweatband was clear, he began to

stroke Weary's hair back as a mother does with a child, as a horseman soothes a frightened foal. The forehead he revealed was huge, bone white, almost false.

Jesus Christ! thought Robin, it's . . .

And then it was gone. Hood was fixing the sweat-band round Weary's head, hiding the hideous scars at his temples, concealing the huge bulge of that forehead. And suddenly there were two voices reciting the simple catechism, "Albert Stephen William Weary, born Sydney, Australia, November fifth, nineteen forty-eight." And Hood was turning toward her while Weary's hands went to that huge, wounded head of his.

"What's up, doll?" The light normality of his tone shocked her back to reality more quickly than anything else could have done.

"Waterspout, dead ahead," she said.

Richard actually cried out aloud with shock, his own left hand reaching down at lightning speed, closing over a cold, hard hand. One of the corpses, moved by the rocking of the boat, had tangled its rigid fingers in Richard's clothing. The material of his trousers twisted through a frozen, insensible grasp. The very movement of something as cold and clammy as this caused him to step back with revulsion.

The last body tilted over, raising its hand in a bizarre simulation of a cheerful wave. The next man to him, unseeing eyes fixed on Richard's, seemed to revive too, as the whole boat, unbalanced by Richard's abrupt movement, rocked. Richard fell to his knees. And the moment that he did so, something caught his eye. At the bottom of the pile of corpses lay that of a slim figure—almost a boy, hardly a man. Most of his head was missing, but his body was unmarked. It was hunched over, with its back to Richard, but it suddenly stood out from

the rest because it was wearing a uniform jacket. Not a
deck officer's or an engineer's, Richard tugged the khaki
shoulder, but the corpse refused to move. Richard
glanced over his own shoulder, suddenly desperate. The
waterspout was getting too close for comfort and there
was still no sign of Robin, Hood, or Weary. He tugged
again at the dead man's shoulder.

The body abruptly turned over as if giving up the
fight. In the sodden breast pocket was a blotched white
radio message. Richard knelt carefully, angling his
body to give maximum protection from the wind, and
opened it to look at once. It was written in sinuous Arabic script, as impenetrable as the writing on the crates
in the dead ship's hold had been. But the layout of the
flimsy form was familiar enough. There was a space
where the name of the ship should be entered. A space
for the time. A space for the message. He glared at that
first space with almost manic intensity, willing the
strange curves of the writing indelibly into his memory.
It was nothing more to him than a pattern of lines and
dots. But it had to be the name of the doomed ship.
The radio officer on every ship he had ever heard of
filled in these forms in exactly the same way. This *had*
to be the name of the ship. Then another thought
sprang into his mind. If this was the radio officer,
then . . .

He crumpled the message into his fist and leaned
forward; at last he was rewarded. Under the boy's legs,
right at the bottom, providentially wrapped in plastic,
was a radio. Richard leaned over, muscles in his legs,
back, and belly jerking to keep him upright in the restless boat, and caught hold of it.

Just as he made this move, the next corpse at the
boat's side followed the other toward the waterspout,
pulling the radio operator's corpse upright as it did so.

A cold dead hand clutched at Richard's face, stiff fingers driving at his eyes as if attempting to protect the precious radio. Richard reacted without conscious thought, driven by primitive instinct. He clutched at the icy forearm and pushed it away, grabbed the slimy shirtfront, and heaved the corpse overboard. It was only then that he realized how he had been betrayed; tricked by the dead men. The radio message had been wadded in the fist he had used to fight off the dead radio operator. As he released the shirtfront, so the flimsy paper slipped through his fingers, too, and the greedy wind snatched it immediately, whirling it away into the stormy sea.

Richard was up at once. He had had enough. The message was gone but the radio was still here. He grabbed it. Five steps down to the lifeboat's head. Massive twist of his body to swing the bulky radio onto *Katapult*, followed immediately by his own chest and legs. Even as he scrambled aboard the rope snapped; the instant his feet kicked free, the lifeboat turned and began to pull away.

He fell into the cockpit clutching the radio just as the other three arrived. "Jesus Christ!" yelled Hood, staring at the fast-approaching waterspout. "Where did that come from?" Then Weary grabbed him, pointing to the lifeboat scudding broadside-on to the wind away from them. The fierceness of the storm swept over it at once and turned it turtle. Then no one was watching it any longer: they all had too much else to do.

The black storm cloud that had spawned the waterspout covered half of the sky; the sun was somewhere behind it. Out of the sinister overcast came a huge white funnel. It fell vertically at first but after a hundred feet or so it twisted off line and writhed increasingly wildly out of shape until it planted its foot firmly on the sea in the midst of a thick column of gyrating mist, dangerously close, dead ahead. The eternal mist was being sucked in, spewed up, and replaced at once in an incredible process by the wind. Such was the power of the thing that the sea dead ahead sloped up quite steeply. The spout sat on its own great hill of water, which appeared and disappeared as the first stinging downpour swept across their line of sight.

Richard had been in storms before but he had never experienced anything like this. The wind was solid around him as he finished stowing the lifeboat's radio. He faced the storm briefly—and it nearly drowned him. He turned his back, choking, and was lucky enough to catch a breath before the air in front of him was sucked away. There was no gusting to it, no variation except for its gradual intensification. And it had all the power of a fire hose. And as the air was sucked in toward the spout, so everything seemed to stream along with it. The sea was steep-sided, dark, and vicious. Spray from the wave tops spewed back in solid chunks of water and the rain was abruptly torrential. Richard staggered forward and clung on. The wind pressed wet clothing to chilled skin so forcefully that the pattern of the material marked it. He suddenly realized there were bruises on his chest caused by his buttons.

Weary, his mind now clear, took charge. Obviously, *Katapult*'s engine was not going to be powerful enough to help much. No. If they were going to get out of this then Weary would have to *sail* them out of it. Hood had no problem with this. Richard was a man of action and would have preferred to be in charge; but he was also a fairweather yachtsman and knew a master when he saw one.

Robin, however, had serious reservations. Less than

five minutes had elapsed since the man now wrestling with the helm, the man in whose enormous hands their lives now rested, had been mindless, screaming, apparently insane. Hood knew this, and when she came toward him, he fell in beside her and as they worked, he talked. It was hardly an idle chat. Some of it was formless, almost meaningless, a series of disjointed phrases and half-sentences projected just a little louder than the screaming wind. Sam Hood was no fool. He knew Robin needed an explanation before she would trust Weary and obey him again—and he was acutely aware that any hesitation by anyone might easily prove lethal.

So, as Weary punched in the manual override and the systems belowdecks prepared to answer his dictates on heading, sail angle, outrigger angle, and all the rest, the others began to batten down everything, and to check every single line, strut, and joint that might fail fatally in the near future. Silently the telescopic booms moved out and the tall sails filled to bursting with the wind.

Richard started at the far stern. Hood and Robin started at the bow. All of them worked back toward the relative safety of the cockpit as fast as they could, for Weary wasted no time. Within thirty seconds of his arrival on deck. *Katapult* heeled to starboard, took the hurricane blast under her solid, experimental skirts— and was off on a wild roller-coaster ride toward the very heart of the thing.

"You know anything 'bout Nam?" yelled Hood as they worked shoulder to shoulder.

"Bit."

"Tet Offensive? Khe Sanh?"

"Some."

"I met that asshole there. That was, what? February 'sixty-eight? *Long* ago . . ." The wind snatched at him, he staggered, and some of his words were lost. "He was in a Huey of all things when I first saw him. I was in the jungle in back of Khe Sanh, pinned down, rest of the unit gone. We was part of D Company, First Battalion, Twentieth Infantry, Twelfth Brigade of the American Division. Mean mothers; born to kill."

The bow disappeared under a steep white horse. The foam hesitated, not knowing whether to splash back over them or to break forward with the brunt of the wind.

"Never found out precisely what unit Doc was with. Some gung ho elite volunteer Australian outfit. He don't know more than that now, that's for sure."

"Wh—"

"Let's get back along here a piece. Hell, girl, this's getting dangerous!" Real, almost boyish excitement in his voice.

A moment or two later, "So . . ."

"So I was pinned down and lookin' to die when suddenly this Huey full of Australians comes along. Picked them up a ways back and taking them down to our lines. But the pilot saw me and came down. Brave mother, I thought. Found out later they made him do it: Doc and the rest. They came down and I went for it like a jackrabbit. That line tight there? Jesus, listen to the sound of it! Back a ways more, Miz Mariner: we'll get some protection from the outrigger."

Hood was having a good time. To tell the truth, so was Robin. The simple sense of fun kept the very real—momentously increasing—danger at bay.

"I almost made it to the Huey when I fell. Thought I'd tripped: been shot in the leg, ten maybe fifteen yards short. Then there's this kid. He just jumps out of the side and comes for me. Big, strong guy. He used to work out with weights in them days. Don't do much

these days. Do ya, Doc?" he yelled at Weary, slapping
him on the shoulder as Robin and he tumbled into the
sloping bucket of the cockpit.

Weary made no direct reply. His massive, golden
body was like a statue as he forced his will through the
wheel to the delicate, intricate machine he had built.
As if he had not heard what they were saying, he yelled,
"I may need some help here."

"Richard's stronger than me," shouted back Hood
cheerfully. He had lost at arm-wrestling to Mariner a
couple of nights ago and was happy to take his revenge
by sending Richard over to help with the wheel now.
But Richard welcomed the challenge. While Robin and
Sam Hood had been working at the bow of the boat, he
had been working at the stern, and, satisfied now that
everything there was as safe and secure as he could make
it, he was looking for something else to do in any case.
Weary moved sideways and Richard covered the Australian's hands with his own. The impact of trying to
control *Katapult* under the circumstances, the elation of
it, nearly made the Englishman shout aloud.

Hood continued telling Robin his story. "Weary
lifted me up by the shoulder straps and ran me the rest
of the way. Like I was a feather!" he shouted. "Up to
the Huey in a couple of seconds and hefted me in. The
others grabbed me and pulled me up. Sort of rolled me
over as they did so and my arm hit him in the head.
Knocked his helmet off. Now I was wide awake at the
time and my fucking leg was really starting to hurt so I
can be damned sure about what happened next. I c'n
still see it if I close my eyes. Hell, I don't even have to
close them. He jumped in beside me—well, half on top
of me really, and I was just fixin' to say thanks and sorry
about the tin hat or something, when this bullet goes
right through his head. I mean I saw the sucker—saw it

go in and saw it come out. Like it was slow motion, you know? And the whole front of his forehead from his hair down to his eyebrows just sort of flapped open. Like it was a door or something. Just opened like a door. Like a trapdoor. It just flapped open and there was all his brains and shit fixing to fall out all over me."

"What did you do?"

"Never moved so fast. I just gathered that piece of skin and bone in my hand and slapped it back in place. He sort of twisted round till his head was in my lap and lay there looking up at me. I mean—he was wide awake and all, hardly blinking. Didn't say nothing. Just lay there looking up. After a while my hand starts shaking. I am holding this man's head together, you know? and the guy is lying there watching me do it. So I starts looking around for some bandages or something but there's no goddamn medic in sight at all. But one of them Aussie guys there with him is some kind of beach bum and he's got this sweatband on his head so I says to him can I borrow it for the kid. And he says sure. So by the time we get to the medical men in Khe Sanh, he's sitting there looking like some hippy, hardly even bleeding, wide awake and sort of grinning and all that's holding his head together is that sweatband. Never been parted from it since.

"We ended up in the same medical facility in Khe Sanh. Trapped there for a while. So I got to know him. Felt kinda responsible. And the more I found out the worse I felt. I mean the guy was only nineteen. Same age as most of ours. Wasn't much older myself. But what this kid had done! He was this high-flying scholarship student. Straight A's. B.A., summa cum laude from his home school. M.A. from somewhere else—he'll tell you if you ask, he remembers that. And the Ph.D. from Oxford, England. All this by the time he's nineteen years old! I mean there was no end to the shit this guy knew. And most of it was spread over the inside of a Huey helicopter—because he tried to help me.

"But he wasn't Mongoloid, you know? There was no imbecility. No, like, brain damage." He said the two words in a slow voice and paused to make sure Robin got the message. "He was either totally switched on or totally switched off: Kid Einstein or some kind of cabbage. The doctors told me that's how it'll always be. It's a miracle he's even the way he is. They were going to put him in some kind of institution but I said no, I'd look after him. Least I could do. You see, he don't know who he is. Not really. Not deep down. Not anymore. Every time he goes to sleep he forgets. You got to tell him every morning, 'You're Doc.' Then things kinda fall into place. He's got a family back in Sydney. Nice folks— nothing special, but nice. Might as well be strangers. Show him pictures, he never met them. His home up in Paddington? Never been there. Hell, show him Sydney Harbour Bridge, he'll ask is it the Golden Gate? Show him the Sydney Opera House he'll say, 'What is this?'

"But ask him about Hamlet—it's like they were brothers. Ask him about quasars or black holes—now there he has lived. Beethoven? Mozart? Now that's his family. It's weird. And boats. Nobody seems to know where he picked up this stuff about boats. . . .

"But he did. Oh, brother, did he ever pick up a shit-load of stuff about boats. . . ."

They were sitting on the bench at the back of the cockpit by the time he finished speaking. They had been talking there for about three minutes. In all, perhaps eight minutes had elapsed since Weary took the helm; certainly no more than ten. There was nothing else for them to do: their lives lay in the hands of the two men at the helm and, perhaps, in the laps of the gods.

Robin was overcome by a massive wave of emotion—a helpless desire to protect Richard and preserve her family at any cost. But she was all too well aware that there was nothing she could do, and suddenly she was afraid. Her fist closed on Hood's arm and he looked down at her, surprised. But her face was calm, slightly flushed. Her golden ringlets, soaking, clutched her head despite the wind. Her eyes were sparkling—and how could he know that the light in them came from unshed tears? On the surface, she looked like a girl about some excitement. He half grinned, suddenly feeling less tense himself.

Weary's hand moved gently out from under Richard's and the Englishman closed his fist on smooth wood, shifting his feet unconsciously, bracing himself as the wheel tried to hurl him overboard. His concentration was absolute, overriding even the pain in his swollen elbow. His eyes never wavered from the course they were following, at a speed he had never imagined any yacht to be capable of. And yet that speed was increasing steadily. Suddenly the wheel kicked viciously. The angle of the mast clicked nearer upright. And again. He looked up automatically. The angle of the sails had varied slightly too.

Had *Katapult* been alive before, now she became frenetic. Richard could not credit the intensity of what he was feeling. He had never sailed like this before, never known—never dreamed—that it could be like this. Weary was pulling every knot of speed and power possible from his creation, using the outriggers ruthlessly to force the closer-hauled sails into the rushing torrent of the wind. Then he was back at Richard's side again, eyes busy on sails and instruments alike, pushing down on Richard's right hand firmly, bringing them over a point or two, sailing across the main thrust of that terrible force, looking for an outer edge.

"*Hood!*" Weary's bellow was snatched away and hurled forward into the great white spray-wall bearing down on them like an avalanche. Richard's eyes were drawn inexorably toward it. There was very little else to look at now. It curved up and out, more than two hundred feet high, a dancing cliff of the stuff, the overhang at the top of it shadowed and dark. The heart of it—it was translucent, like a cliff of ice—danced madly as though a column of black fire burned there. But the surface drew the eyes and threatened to numb the mind with its insane activity. Although it had unity and form, it was made up of individual things, all in wild motion. Dots made by fist-size chunks of water hurling round the vortex left-to-right across their port quarter at hundreds of miles an hour. And more than the water. Suddenly there was the hull of the lifeboat, dead men dancing out of it, there for an instant, plainly visible mast high, imprinting itself forever on Richard's mind, then gone as though it had never been.

He crashed forward onto the helm and thought it was a fluke in the wind—but no, it was Hood hammering at his numb back, moving up to replace Weary at his side. Then Robin was there, too, wedging herself between Hood and himself, hot as fire against his wind-chilled side. He glanced down to see Weary, crouched in the lee of their bodies, calculating the finest points of how to sail them out of this.

But even as he did so, the stresses on *Katapult* began to go beyond her limits. Inch by inch, against the dictates of helm and outriggers both, her mast came past the vertical and began to lean in. And slowly, inexorably, moved by a power beyond that of the four arms at the helm, her head started to come round. The port outrigger sank deeper beneath the streaming, wind-torn surface. The other threatened to break free of the surface and hurl them all to destruction. They began to climb up the hill of water toward the lethal heart of the thing. Richard closed his eyes, his concentration absolute, moving as one with Hood, never giving an inch, fighting the good fight. Robin was yelling something to him, lips hot against his ear, breath sweet on the thick salt air. Her meaning clear but her words gone in that awesome, overwhelming noise.

Then Weary was there, at their left, his hands closing over their left hands, forcing upward with all their combined might.

And the helm spun over. Hard. So hard they lost control of it and let it whirl like a Catherine wheel, hands clear, before they caught it again, the four of them, moving as one; caught it and held it and prayed.

As the blade of the mast, socketed in its mast-foot a yard above the deck, turned, turning the long line of the fore and after booms, turning the close-hauled blades of the straining sails against it, turning the whole screaming construction across the howling wind, and *Katapult* came round on the opposite tack, her head swinging right as though she had been punched, using the massive momentum the wind had given her to break free of its grip and mash through to the far side, away from the thing.

For that one split second they grazed the foot of the spray wall itself; then it was gone. The hurricane that had been roaring into their backs blasted into their faces, tearing their eyes, bulging their cheeks, filling their lungs like balloons. But *Katapult*'s sails were close-hauled now, giving no surface for the air to catch, and she continued to beat across the wind straight and free while the waterspout diminished astern.

How long the four of them stood in that closely entwined knot at the helm they would never know. It was not something to be measured by clocks or chronometers. The moderation of the wind, the calming of the sea, the passing of the clouds, the rebirth of the sun. These things measured that time on a scale beyond mere minutes.

And when they came back down to earth from the almost mystical plane of their concentration, they found themselves in the heart of a crystal afternoon, fresh and bracing. Long blue seas ran down calmly toward Africa. The heart of the whispering breeze smelled of salt and ozone. The light was dazzling in its purity, glancing off a million mirror surfaces all around them from the rime of salt crystals caking everything on *Katapult* like ice.

But before they took even the first step toward cleaning down and tidying up their brave, strong vessel, they had one overwhelming duty to perform. Richard ripped the plastic sheeting off the radio, turned it on, and pressed TRANSMIT.

"Hello, hello, Dubai . . . Damn! I hope this thing is working after all this. . . . Hello, Dubai. This is Richard Mariner reporting from yacht *Katapult*. Can you hear me, Dubai. . . ."

And the radio suddenly crackled into life. ". . . Heritage Mariner office, Dubai. Angus El Kebir reporting. . . . Hear you strength four, *Katapult*, over. . . ."

"This is Richard Mariner reporting from yacht *Katapult*, Indian Ocean. Uncertain of our position at this time. All well. Please inform Sir William Heritage Richard and Robin both well, over."

"This is Angus El Kebir at head office in Dubai, Richard. I'm afraid I have some extremely bad news. . . ."

CHAPTER FIVE

Dubai. United Arab Emirates.

Angus El Kebir sat back from the radio at last and switched the power to OFF. In spite of the efficiency of his air-conditioning, he was running with sweat. In spite of its airy brightness, his Dubai office felt dark and cramped. It perched like an aerie atop one of those new dark-glass skyscrapers, towering against the hard blue Gulf sky, which overlooked the frenetic activity of the Creek. Part boatyard, part port, part market, the Creek was the heart of the city and the state. Heritage Mariner had offices here as inevitably as they kept their head office on Leadenhall in London, close to Lloyd's at the heart of the Western world's shipping industry.

Angus shook his great lion's head, all russet beard and ruddy curls, and brought his clenched fist down on his desktop. Never had he heard Robin so upset or Richard so enraged. He had known them both for many years—he had been at school with Richard at Fettes College in Edinburgh—and not once before had he heard such anger, such desolation, in their voices.

Rising, he strode across to the long window of his office and looked down across the busy maritime spectacle of the Creek, but for once the lively view failed to thrill him; the bustle of commerce failed to bring ela-

tion to his part-Arab and part-Scottish soul. Here was a
bad situation brewing, showing every sign of growing
worse—and here were his oldest and dearest friends
trapped and raging like bears at a stake in the midst of it.

And himself, powerless to help more than he had
done, feeling all that baseless burden of guilt belonging
to the bearer of such bad news. His breath hissed between his tight-clenched teeth as he shared the overwhelming rage of his employers and friends, so far away,
so helpless. If only he could have between his powerful
hands something—or someone—whose destruction could
ease his rage.

A timid tapping at the door intruded itself into his
dark brooding. "Enter," he snapped.

The quiet youth who was his assistant down here appeared, clutching a bundle of files. Angus thrust his hand
out and the young man surrendered his bundle and
fled. Still lost in rage, Angus crossed to his desk, threw
them down, and hurled himself into his chair.

He had been dreading this moment almost as much
as he had been dreading having to break the news to
Richard and Robin. It was cruel that, after so many
hours of waiting, the two moments should have come
so close together. That now, while he was still gripped
by the feelings arising out of talking to *Katapult*, these
files should have arrived, giving full details of all the
men and women he had just been discussing, lost on
Prometheus.

The force with which he had thrown them down
had caused the top few to spill their contents, and it was
in many ways apt that he should spend the next few
minutes disentangling the lives of John Higgins, Asha
Quartermaine, and Bob Stark.

They were the three on *Prometheus* to whom he was
closest. He and John were old friends. They had first

met many years ago in the wake of the affair that had overtaken the first *Prometheus*. Looking at the photograph of the solid, dependable Manxman, Angus was forcibly reminded of his modest charm, his open friendliness. The black hair, neatly parted; the level, intelligent gaze from those calm brown eyes. The pipe, inevitably, at its jaunty angle, emphasizing the strength of the jaw. Little John, they called him, like Robin Hood's Little John.

Bob Stark was a different kettle of fish. With his American film-star good looks, his Ivy League education, and his New England old-money family background, you expected to find him following in his father's footsteps into politics. Or at least his uncle's into the American Navy. But no. A love of marine engines and some vagaries of maritime chance had brought him to Heritage Mariner and he was content, for the moment, to remain. His photograph looked up at Angus quizzically, almost as though its subject had been surprised when it was taken. His blond eyebrows met the straw-colored cowlick, his eyes held an expression almost of incredulity. You expected a long straw to be dangling from the corner of that wide mouth, held firmly by a combination of those dazzling teeth and that square, impossibly wide jaw. Even from a far-faxed Polaroid, the charm of the man leaped out at you.

And Asha. He had known her only briefly, but had been as severely smitten as the other two. The facts in her file were scanty enough, names of parents in Dahran up the coast. Date of birth. Mention of a twin sister, Fatima. Education in England. Medical qualification in Edinburgh. Marriage to and divorce from Giles Quartermaine, the famous journalist. Russet eyes looked up at him from under hair as red as his own, but darker, richer. He threw the file away across the desk, unable to stand having her gaze upon him when she was in trouble and he was powerless to help.

And the action brought to his attention something that he had failed to notice until now. At the bottom of the pile was one extra file, fatter than the others. Without further thought, he opened it and confronted himself with a photograph of the man he most respected in the world, after Richard Mariner. Sir William Heritage stared out of the old monochrome picture as though carved in granite, thin hair swept straight back, thin mouth uncompromising under the white clipped mustache. Proud eyes staring out of the photo, unflinching.

Angus drove his fist down again, and was surprised to discover that he was now holding a paper knife in it. The blunt brass point stabbed through the leather of his desktop, through the backing, glue, and mahogany. Oddly, the desk had been a gift from Sir William many years ago and the fact that he had defaced it now, for such a reason, was the last straw. Had his anger been hot before, now it was incandescent. And it was the merest candle flame, he acutely suspected, beside what Richard and Robin would be feeling.

Without further thought, he leaned forward and lifted the phone beside the still-quivering handle of the upright paper knife. "Get the international operator," he ordered. "First I want to speak to New York. Then I want Beirut."

CHAPTER SIX

Off Rass al Hadd.

They raced northeast at full speed, almost blind in the haze at the northernmost edge of the monsoon. Then Weary spun onto a new tack and they exploded out of a silver mist-wall into clear, calm air, straight under the bows of the USS *Mississippi*.

It was stunningly sudden. One moment the multihull was hurling forward at incredible velocity in the deafening, blinding maelstrom. The next moment, even as the new tack began, the air was still, crystal, and furnace-hot around them. The sea was choppy and mercuric, as though contained, boiling, in the crucible of the desert. And, approaching them at flank speed across it, warning sirens howling, came the great gray leviathan Iowa-class flagship of the American Sixth Fleet.

Weary froze, looking up at it. Richard, providentially beside him, drove the wheel to port, sending *Katapult* skipping out of the battleship's way, over the confusion of wavelets toward Rass al Hadd.

The *Mississippi*'s cutwater sliced past *Katapult*'s stern. The sea heaved around the warship's massive flanks and threw *Katapult* out of the way, then spread in a widening chevron, the largest waves in the choppy sea. In series to the east of her reached the ships under her command, all of them racing in perfect formation dead south, whence *Katapult* had just come.

And even as the four of them, frozen in the cockpit, stared, the American Sixth Fleet vanished into the haze they had just emerged from, and, but for the patterns in the water, it was as though the lean warships had never existed. As though *Katapult* had always been alone here, drifting northeast across the restless chop in the humid heat, slack sails searching for a breath of breeze in the thick, hot air.

"Christ!" blasphemed Weary, disgusted. "That was too close!"

Hood's hand slapped down on the radio and it suddenly jumped to life, emitting a frenzied shriek, which, had it come scant seconds earlier, would have warned them of their danger. The radio had been fading in and out for some time now. They had given up trying to regain contact with Angus El Kebir but had been relying on it as a makeshift substitute for their damaged radar and communications equipment by picking up any strong signals from ships in the vicinity. A reliance obviously misplaced.

Weary took the wheel back from Richard and swung *Katapult*'s eye a degree or two north. At once, almost as though his casual action had summoned it, a sluggish breeze kicked in behind them and an air of purpose returned to the sleek craft even as she wallowed over the last heave of *Mississippi*'s wake.

"We should have stopped her," observed Richard, half seriously.

Robin nodded, following his thoughts with ease. The American admiral, officer commanding that fleet, was uncle and godfather to Bob Stark, *Prometheus*'s kidnapped chief engineer. But they already knew, from Angus's increasingly faint messages over the last thirty-six hours, that even closer family ties than that had failed to influence State's current policy of noninterference in the Gulf. Bob Stark's father, senior senator from Massachusetts and close friend to the President himself, had been met with charm, sympathy, and cold comfort at the White House.

A brittle calm descended on *Katapult*'s cockpit, compounded of reaction to the shock of near-collision, a corrosive feeling of helplessness and—in contrast—a sense of having taken one small step toward some as yet undefined goal. It was a strange, undecided sensation that accorded well with this unsettling sea.

Away southwest across the inshore traffic zones, the great red cliffs of Rass al Hadd wheeled aft as *Katapult* swung in toward the coast away from the busy deep-water sea lanes, and the long black hull of a supertanker, low and fully laden, loomed over the northern horizon, more like a force of nature than a man-made thing.

Then, "There's another one dead aft as well," called Robin softly, and all except Weary glanced back to see the still-shimmering mist-wall part like a curtain as the mountainous jut of another, unladen, tanker's stem thrust out toward them, surprisingly close at hand. Awed by the massiveness of it, they watched as the VLCC gathered itself inexorably out of the haze. The first twenty vertical feet of its side, nearest the water, was dull rust red and banded with vague lading marks up to the sickly green of the Plimsoll line. The next forty feet were dead black, a basalt cliff thrusting through the sea. And when her bridge solidified out of the blinding mist, like a pallid block of flats seven clear stories above that, even the eighty sheer feet of *Katapult*'s mast was dwarfed.

At once the wind died, blocked by the massive bulk, leaving them to wallow once more, telltales drooping dejectedly, in the doldrums of its huge wind shadow. Richard found himself shivering. From down here the sheer size of this machine—whose length could be measured in quarters of miles and whose height above the waterline could be counted in skyscraper stories and whose displacement could be weighed in quarters of millions of tons was simply terrifying. He thought of the story he had so glibly told Hood about the felucca found wedged across the bows of his own tanker, the first *Prometheus*, and he remembered how they hadn't even felt the impact of collision.

They were all so lost in their thoughts and the sheer scale of the tanker that they paid scant attention to the helicopter buzzing busily toward them low over the swells of its wake. Skipping over the sea it came, sullen sunlight blazing off the domed perspex of its windows. Only when the purposeful line of its flight path became obvious did Robin stir. "Hey," she said. "Richard, are they coming over to us?"

"I believe they are . . ." Richard glanced over at Weary and Hood. They were both standing beside the wheel though neither of them had a hand on it—*Katapult* dead in the water until the tanker passed and the wind returned.

"Ahoy, *Katapult*." The cry was almost lost in the helicopter's own engine noise. None of them replied. The helicopter dropped its pert nose and arced toward them like a guided missile, darkening the water with the wind of its passage.

"Better get the sails off her, I think," said Richard. Weary's hand moved. The whine of the sail-furler began and was lost at once.

"AHOY, *KATAPULT*. IS CAPTAIN MARINER ABOARD?"

"HERE!" cried Richard and Robin together. They

both held captain's papers. They both waved. The helicopter bore U.S. Navy markings—perhaps they were going to talk to Admiral Stark after all.

Within moments the helicopter was hovering little more than mast high above them, *Katapult* stirring uneasily in the downwash of the rotors. But the chopper had ridden over on the first breeze from behind the tanker and Weary let her head fall away until the wind was dead astern and the craft was sitting more comfortably.

Then, abruptly, there came a whine from the helicopter's side high above. Something was being lowered toward them.

Richard leaped up onto the after-section of the deck and stood there, looking up, his eyes shaded against the glare. It was a harness on a long line. He caught it easily and strapped it around his torso with practiced ease. Then he paused.

Robin knelt on the bench looking back at him, thinking inconsequentially how romantic he was in his whites, legs spread against *Katapult*'s action, shirt collar up, crisp cotton molded to his lean, firm body by the wind, hair tousled wildly by the thundering gale of it. He grinned wolfishly at her—his first smile since the news had come in. He simply couldn't resist: this was his idea of really good fun. For a moment it had managed to overcome that huge anger she had felt growing in him day by day since Angus had broken the news about her father and their ship. Emotion brought tears to her eyes and when he opened his arms she ran to him thinking only to hug him to her as tightly as possible.

He said something to her the moment their bodies met but his mouth was full of her hair and it sounded simply like, "Syrup."

Syrupy or not, she thought fiercely, I love you, Richard Mariner; and she hugged him until her shoulder joints popped. There was a click and a sudden pressure in the small of her back.

"Stand in the *stirrup*," he yelled again, and, an intrepid horsewoman since her youth, she kicked her foot into the dangling metal automatically.

"Okay!" bellowed Richard, and they swung up and out.

She glanced down once, understanding, to see *Katapult* falling, spinning away on the silver, white-webbed sea. Then she buried her face in Richard's chest and waited to be pulled aboard the helicopter.

As soon as the harness was unbuckled, Robin was off. She loved helicopters and, while Richard was content with his licenses to drive cars and command ships, Robin also held current licenses to fly small planes and helicopters, too. "Okay if I go on up?" she asked the bemused Navy man who had pulled them aboard. He nodded, still helping Richard with the straps and buckles, but she was already gone to crouch between the pilots' seats, eyes avidly scanning the instruments and the view.

The monsoon closed around them at once, buffeting the little craft, causing it to swoop and dance, wrapping it in dazzling mist. Automatically Robin pulled out her sunglasses—a battered pair of flyer's glasses with silvered mirror lenses—and slipped them on her nose. She didn't even notice that the pilot and copilot wore identical protection. She crouched between them for all the world as though she really belonged there, a part of the crew herself.

Unlike Robin, Richard was glad to jump out of the helicopter onto the blustery afterdeck of the *Mississippi*. The sheer size of the old American warship almost tamed the monsoon seas she was steaming across, but every now and then a trough would take her head and she would dip and roll, pitch and heave in a corkscrew motion, shouldering off a great hissing glacier of foam. It was quite enough to unsettle some of the nearby sailors, who glanced almost enviously at the rock-steady progress of the nearby tankers, but not enough to complicate the landing or to slow the Mariners as they ran after their escort up toward the steel-gray mountain of the bridge-house.

Admiral Walter Stark received them in his office. The three of them had first met five years ago in Cannes where his California-class cruiser *Baton Rouge*, then part of the Mediterranean fleet, had been welcoming visitors aboard. But they had known each other for much longer—ever since Bob Stark, his favorite nephew and godson, had joined the Heritage Mariner fleet as an engineer.

"Robin. Richard." He rose and strode toward them from behind his tidily piled desk as soon as they came through the door. "This is a bad business in every way!" His square, craggy face was lined with concern. His intelligent, deep-set brown eyes full of sympathy. He had known Sir William Heritage since soon after the Second World War. His involvement in the affair could hardly have been more personal.

"Walt," Richard said, shaking the American's broad hand while Robin went on tiptoe to kiss his weathered cheek. Then the admiral's eyes met those of their escort and the young officer was gone at once.

"Sit down, sit down. My steward'll be in with coffee in a moment. I'd like to invite you to lunch, but if I did, God knows it'd be a long flight back to *Katapult*."

Richard sat, suddenly almost overcome by the sensations of being back aboard a great steel-sided ship. *Katapult* for the last few days had been all rush and hiss, the slightest vibration of sleek multihull through water, the rumble of her sails and the song of the wind in her stays. *Mississippi* was all throb and thrust—that corkscrew stagger in place of *Katapult*'s leap, the distant, unvarying rumble of the engine, the insistent, immediate throb of everything around him.

A sharp tap on the door preceded the entry of a lean young man bearing a trayful of cups and saucers. He swayed easily across to the admiral's desk as *Mississippi* shuddered, apparently quite at ease while she dipped and heaved back; but when Robin accepted her coffee, she noticed a drop or two had been spilled and the simple fact of this brought to her mind Twelve Toes Ho, chief steward on *Prometheus*, a man who had never, to her knowledge, spilled a drop of anything he had ever carried. A man now, with all the others, held captive like her father. Perhaps even alongside her father. Her cheeks flushed with ill-contained rage. Her hands shook.

"Right," said Admiral Stark as the steward closed the door. "Update. No change in your situation that I'm aware of. Helen Dufour at Heritage House in London still has no news of your father, Robin. Nobody has, not even the Archbishop of Canterbury, and he has his ear pretty close to the ground, so I'm told. Nobody knows where Bill is or who's holding him. Beirut still seems the best bet, but the PLO isn't talking and not even the Shi'ites are claiming any responsibility. We just have to hang on in there and wait."

"But it has to be tied to the taking of *Prometheus*!" exploded Robin. "Nothing else makes any sense!"

"I agree with that," snapped Richard. "We've been over and over this endlessly. It has to be part of a concerted effort. Blackmail of some kind."

"But who by?" asked the admiral, his quiet drawl gentle, soothing the English couple's too-evident anger.

"And to what end? What have you got that someone wants that badly? Who wants to hurt you and your company like this?"

"It could be anything, it could be nothing." Robin now, reiterating parts of conversations shared with Richard, Hood, and Weary during the long haul north to Rass al Hadd. "If it was just one of them—either *Prometheus* or my father—then it might be bad luck. Nothing aimed specifically at us at all. But both together—there has to be a pattern."

"Any more news about *Prometheus*?" asked Richard as soon as Robin fell silent.

"Nary a word. She's been moved down the Gulf away from the shipping at Kharg Island. The last report I had was that she was in that little bay just north of Bushehr. Anchored in five to ten fathoms, according to my charts." He gestured to the desk and Richard suddenly realized the chart was laid out there, ready to be consulted. But he had a chart of the Gulf in his head as accurate as any on paper. As he got up, he said, "That's what, two hundred miles due north of Bahrain?"

"One hundred and eighty-five miles due north of Manama Harbor," said Robin, already at Walt's shoulder, poring over the chart that was so much more up-to-date than the one in *Katapult*'s cabin: and it did have *Prometheus*'s present whereabouts precisely plotted on it, observed Richard as he joined them. Just on the edge of the bay there, under the eyes of the little Iranian airport—though there was no proof of any Iranian involvement or even suggestion of it, so far. As the admiral had said, anchored in about fifty feet of water.

Unladen then, almost certainly. Sitting high and hard to get aboard. Damned hard for armed men to board unsuspected . . .

He glanced up and found both of them watching

him, gray eyes and brown eyes alike alive with speculation. *Mississippi* corkscrewed. Foam thundered back
along her starboard foredeck. Spray splattered onto the
porthole glass beside him and foam hissed away into
the scuppers. "If we could get aboard *Prometheus*, then
we could begin to find out what is really going on," he
said. His voice was flat. Level. The throb of his rage
just held in check by an iron effort of will.

Richard was fiercely aware that they were actually
discussing a kind of war. A small war against an unknown enemy, waged by himself and such warriors as
he could summon, fought with such weapons as he and
they could find, against such armaments as the terrorists might hold, and to be fought on the decks of the
flagship of his tanker fleet with more at risk than he
dared to calculate.

"My hands are tied," warned Admiral Stark. "No
men or matériel. Not a gun. Not a round."

"Radio?" asked Robin. "Our first meeting off Rass
al Hadd should prove to you what a danger to shipping
we are in our present state."

"Done!" Stark grinned. His eyes, the image of his
godson's, sparkled with fierce joy at being able to help
after all. "And now you come to mention it . . ."

Half an hour later, Walter Stark's desk was piled high
with the sort of equipment the enthusiastic, safety-
conscious admiral thought to be essential for the protection of *Katapult* in her present condition from the
dangers of shipping in the Arabian Sea and the Gulf.

A powerful, reliable radio. A portable switchboard
with several portable VHF radiotelephone handsets. A
sextant, very nearly the work of art that Richard remembered John Higgins always kept aboard *Prometheus*,
and the admiral's own since boyhood. A full range of
charts, notices to mariners, and updates.

Stark surveyed the pile, then looked up cheerfully, catching the eye of the President's portrait on the wall above the desk. Richard and Robin followed his gaze. "You know," said the admiral, "I've a feeling he's watching us fairly closely. Maybe I should have turned his picture to the wall . . ."—he rubbed his great, hard hands gleefully—". . . but I'll be damned if I think he would mind!"

"So there are four of us," Richard was summing up after two long days' worth of arguments. "Although for the life of me I don't see why you and Doc want in on this, Sam."

Hood, down in the cabin, hunched over his new toys, simply shrugged. Doc pretended not to hear, his eyes on the far horizon, the helm easy in his great hands.

"We've enough equipment to navigate to the moon . . ."

"Mars, if'n we want," interjected Hood happily.

". . . and back. One experimental trimaran, almost fully functional . . ."

"We can fix the radar easy given the equipment and the time," said Weary. "Rest of the stuff's fine."

". . . and six Kalashnikov AK-47 assault rifles, old but unused," Richard persisted.

"Fine guns," said Robin. "Tough. Reliable."

"And with this we propose to engage an unnumbered quantity of armed terrorists, possibly the whole of the Palestine Liberation Organization and conceivably the Iranians to boot."

"So what else do we need?" asked Weary.

Richard opened his mouth, but it was Robin who answered: "*Help!* All the help we can get."

It was thirty-six hours since *Mississippi*'s helicopter

had dropped them back onto *Katapult*'s lazarette. Thirty-six hours filled with an urgent drive to reach the Gulf as soon as possible. After one long, fast day's sailing, they had anchored briefly in the anchorage area north of Muscat off the Omani coast. They had left on the dawn breeze this morning and a fitful southerly, sucked north by tremendous heat beginning to build in the desert fastnesses of Iran, had pushed them slowly another hundred miles up the coast. It had been a hot, hard, frustrating sail. Now, as the heat died, the darkness gathered, and the faltering wind began to ebb away, they were coming onto longitude 57 degrees east from Greenwich, latitude 25 degrees north of the equator, some fifty miles out from Fujayrah in the Gulf of Oman. Here, too, they proposed to anchor, if their still functioning echo-sounder could find them a bank or shoal a little nearer the surface than the deep water they had sailed all day. Then they could rest up for the long run through the Strait of Hormuz and into the Gulf tomorrow.

The sun was setting on their port beam, bleeding down out of a lower sky gilded with flying sand. Even this far out, the wind blowing from Oman and the Emirates carried enough fine grains to itch scalps, gum eyes, tickle noses, and crunch between teeth. The air should have smelled of salt overlain with hints of sage and tamarisk from the desert. Instead it smelled of oil. The air here, all the way from Rass al Hadd to Shatt al Arab, always seemed to smell of oil.

Another huge tanker pushed inexorably past, long and low in the water ten miles to starboard heading south, her upper works a blaze of rose and ruby. A fleet of dhows, gull-winged, passed farther north, heading for the bay of Khawr Fakkan on the coattails of the wind that had deserted *Katapult* already.

"That's it." Weary drew his hand back through the riot of his hair above the sweatband on his forehead. Even in the beautiful sunset light, his face looked like his name: weary. And for once there was nothing about the evening he found to be new and exciting. "We either anchor here or go ahead under power. Hood? What does the sounder say?"

"Deep water," came his reply from the cabin.

"Hell," said Weary, not really wanting to do anything more. They were on the last of a low flood tide, however, drifting gently north anyway, with nothing seaborne in sight except the distant dhows and the vanishing tanker.

"You want me to take her, Doc?" asked Richard gently. "We can motor over toward Fujayrah. Maybe find an anchorage in ten miles or so."

"We'll see," answered Doc. "Let's get the sails off her first." He hit the button. Slowly, jerkily at first, the motors turned. The booms telescoped in and the massive sails vanished into the mast, kicking off clouds of sand as they did so. In the heavy calm, the fine grains showered straight down, starting everyone sneezing except Hood, who was belowdecks. And so it was that he had to call up several times before he could be understood.

"Doc. There's something registering. Doc. It's dead ahead. A shoal of some kind I guess. Maybe a ridge. I don't know. Doc? You asked for an anchorage. This looks like it."

Half an hour later it was full night. The sky was low and heavy laden with massive stars. Above the distant desert visible through the portholes lay the promise of moonrise, its pale coolness mocking the heat of the air. All the ports and ventilators along *Katapult*'s sleek sides stood wide, but no hint of breeze came through to ease the humidity in her main cabin as she lay idly at anchor there, as though painted under her riding lights. They had dined lightly off cold tinned meat and canned fruit, but most of it still lay unconsumed on the table before them. It was too hot to eat. It was too hot to do anything much except lie back across the bunks—now doubling as bench-seats around the table—and continue their discussion desultorily, already on the edge of sleep. Only Robin seemed to have any energy, and she was trying to interest the others in some serious planning of tomorrow's course and what action lay beyond.

As Hood's charts had been packed away, she pulled out the one she had brought back with her from the *Mississippi* and, using a plate of melting corned beef and a bowl of warm canned peaches, she spread it flat. "Look," she said as she did so, "here we are, anchored about fifty miles off Fujayrah . . ." Her fingers traced the eastings and northings Hood had written in the log until they met at *Katapult*'s position on the chart. And suddenly she stopped speaking.

The others were slow to notice her silence. Weary and Hood were dozing. Only Richard was paying any kind of attention, and that was pretty scant. "Off Fujayrah. Yes? So?"

But Robin didn't hear him. She was replotting their position on the chart carefully with rapt concentration, her blonde curls low above the paper. Richard frowned and sat forward, sensing something at once, even as her eyes, suddenly huge, met his across the blue- and sand-colored diagram. But it was not to Richard that she spoke.

"Hood," she asked urgently, "how old was that chart you were using?"

"Dunno," Hood answered without opening his eyes. "Part of an old set we got in the Seychelles when you came aboard and we took off north. All our really new charts are of our home waters. Why?"

Richard read, upside-down, partly obscured by Robin's finger, DANGER. EXPLOSIVES DUMPING GROUND. The words were written in urgent purple beside a dotted circle. A circle at whose heart they were now anchored.

"Maybe we should get the anchor up," he suggested.

Hood and Weary both leaned forward, pulled out of somnolence by something in his tone. Suddenly they were all on their feet. Hood scooped the plates off the table and hurled the food through the porthole. Everything else went into the bunk beside him and the table was folded away. Then they were up the companion ladder and into the cockpit.

There was light coming from her instruments, through the portholes from the lamps below and from her riding lights above: enough light to see by, even out here. Richard ran easily down the length of her to the anchor chain at her head. It was a fine chain reaching down to a small flanged anchor a hundred or so feet below. Down to that innocent little anchor among all those dangerous, discarded explosives, he was thinking. There could be all sorts down there. In theory, they should all be carefully logged, recorded, made safe, placed in strong containers, and dropped deep. In fact, there was no real control. God alone knew what could be down there, in what sort of boxes, of what sort of age, in what sort of state.

He leaned out over the edge, reaching down to feel the chain, sitting snugly in the hawse hole by the extra deck just beneath him, where the winches were. It told him little enough.

"Engaging anchor-chain winch," called Weary warningly.

"Clear!" Richard called back. Then he knelt up, holding the low rail at her head, straining to feel her anchor lift safely free of the seabed below him. He felt *Katapult* come round and heard the water chuckling against her as the winch took up the slack. He heard the chain begin to gather in, link by link. He waited for the rush, the steady rumble of the anchor being winched up.

But he waited in vain.

"Caught fast," he called to Weary at last.

"Anchor caught fast," agreed Weary. "I'm slacking off to try again."

The second attempt was no more successful than the first. Weary slackened off once more and engaged the propeller, moving *Katapult* to a new position before engaging the winch. It made no difference. The anchor refused to budge. Richard returned along the length of the hull and jumped onto the lazarette. The top of the first rear hatch lifted easily enough and there was a torch handy to shine down past the case of Kalashnikovs to where the diving equipment was. He had swum in the Gulf and knew about the sharks and the seasnakes there: he was suiting up and going armed. But he was going: someone had to. A half-hour swim, after all, might free the anchor, resecure it safely on the reef, put their minds at rest, and let them all get a decent night's sleep. On the other hand, if they lost the anchor, it would be watch and watch from here to Bahrain, and no real sleep for days. At the moment, it seemed well worth the risk.

He was suited up and ready to go within minutes, the mouthpiece pushing cold air over his clenched teeth, his left hand holding a submarine torch and his right hand a spear gun. Secured round his waist was an assortment of crowbars looped over his weight belt and cinched tight by Robin's robust strength. Weary tied the end of a long, strong line just above it and Richard duck-walked to the edge of the cockpit. They hoisted him up and turned him round. He held his face mask in place as well as he could and tumbled backward into the oil-dark sea.

It was slack water. The currents around him were as still as the breezes above. It was no problem to hang in the water and test his torch, orienting himself carefully until he could see *Katapult*'s hull. Then he followed it to the anchor chain, careful to swim outside the sleek sweep of the starboard outrigger.

Once more he hung in the water, holding on to the chain with his right hand, half exasperated with himself for bringing the spear gun, which was in the way already, flashing the torch out into the threatening blackness all around. Nothing moved. Satisfied that he was alone for the moment, Richard upended himself and began to follow the chain downward, head first.

Five minutes later his torch beam revealed a narrow trench into which the chain plunged, amid a jumble of boxes, seaweed-covered, barnacled, apparently danger-ously ancient. He jerked to a halt, just in time. As he came upright, his flippers grazed the topmost box of the whole crazy pile. A stingray, disturbed by his ar-rival, lifted itself into lazy visibility and floated elegantly into the darkness.

Richard settled to the seabed and began to look around. It seemed that he was on some kind of hilltop, though his torch beam would not go far enough for him to be sure. A thin ridge scarcely wider than *Kata-pult* herself coming and going into the darkness on ei-ther hand. On either side of it, hillsides plunged down within scant feet to depths he could not begin to esti-mate. Diagonally across this ridge ran a thin crack, perhaps a yard wide, apparently infinitely deep. Into this the anchor had fallen, and here it had wedged.

All he had to do was to slide his crowbar into the trench and he should be able to get the anchor free. There were some heavy-looking rocks farther down that would hold *Katapult* against the night's calm and sluggish tides. He put down the spear gun, concerned that it might get tangled up in his efforts, took the steel crowbar from his belt, and moved forward. Already planning what to do with the rocks and the anchor—should he prove strong enough to carry it on his own—and wondering whether he should check those nearby boxes as well, he thrust the crowbar down toward the hook of the trapped anchor, only to hurl back, shouting with surprise as the eel attacked.

What sort of eel it was, he never knew. He was no expert and could have made no distinction between types. He remained ignorant also of its precise size, but he related it easily enough to the scale of his own body. Its head, jaws fastened onto the crowbar, was almost the size of his own head. The body that uncoiled with breathtaking rapidity out of the shadows seemed as broad as his thigh, perhaps as his waist. And it was longer than he was.

The power of the thing was awesome. Only his shock-strengthened grip kept him attached to the steel crowbar as the two of them tumbled backward end over end. His only clear thought was an overpowering command to his brain to keep breathing regularly. His lungs obeyed but the demands of galvanic action taxed their calm rhythm severely. Time ceased to have any meaning for him. His left hand, torch dangling from its wrist-strap, grabbed the far end of the bar, forcing the eel's head away from his own, and they rolled back into the darkness, face to face as though the eel were a rabid dog at his throat. He felt its length whip round him and begin to squeeze. Wildly he wondered whether these things could crush you like anacondas. Then his shoulders crashed into angular solidity and he had the strangest feeling that he was tumbling down stairs and the image was so overpowering, so disorienting, that it took him a second to realize what had actually happened. The eel had pushed him against the pile of discarded explosives boxes under *Katapult*'s keel.

He thrust forward with all the power at his command, feeling the unsteady pile crumbling around him. The momentum of the eel's attack was gone in any case and so he found himself moving back toward the crack where the monster lived—and not a moment too soon. As they rolled across the ridge, so the pile of boxes collapsed, some of them disintegrating to spill their contents out onto the seabed. Invisibly in the darkness, a small black disk, some four inches in diameter and two deep, flew lazily toward the crack in the ridge. It was well wrapped in clear plastic, which should have kept it waterproof, but as it landed, so the plastic ruptured, and instantly a thin trail of bubbles coiled upward. On the next bounce, a second later, the disk attained the black cleft and tumbled in. Two seconds later it exploded.

One instant, Richard was aware only of his blind test of strength. The next there was a flash of light and a detonation that made his ears ring. And the eel was gone. Dazzled and deafened, he fell to his knees on the thin ridge, pulled the torch into both fists, and swept its puny beam around in a tight arc.

Nothing.

The eel, more sensitive than he, had been more affected by the explosion and had swum away. No sign of it remained.

He stayed exactly where he was, on his knees, breathing slowly and regularly, waiting for his heart to slow. Waiting for the jumping in his limbs to still. Waiting for the next explosion.

Nothing.

The line around his waist, tangled around much of his body now, jerked suddenly and set his recovery back somewhat. He jerked in return to let them know he was all right, then waited. It took some time, but at last his heartbeat steadied, his breathing became normal and his limbs still. He untangled himself carefully and returned to the trench.

His torch beam showed him the mess the eel and he had made of the boxes. That crazy pile was now strewn willy-nilly across the seabed, but it looked as though only two were open. A cursory inspection revealed many boxes to be the same as the two that had burst, some distinguished by having a large X marked upon their sides. Both burst boxes contained flat black disks wrapped in clear, strong plastic. The look of the things was familiar.

Sidetracked into rummaging through his capacious memory, Richard was paying scant attention to the scene in front of him where the stem of the anchor protruded from the cleft in the narrow ridge, but suddenly a movement there pulled his distracted gaze into sharp focus and he realized wryly what the eel had done: it had run home. And its home was beside the anchor. If he tried to free it again, it would attack again. This looked like a stalemate.

Abruptly a shrill whining filled his head and an instinct trained into him years ago at diving school whipped his left hand toward his face plate. The luminous display on his diving watch was flashing at him. Four minutes and counting down. He should simply give up and return to the surface now.

But he would be damned before he would let himself be beaten by a fish.

Then, because he was thinking of something else entirely, he remembered what the black disks were. They were thunderflash grenades.

He didn't think beyond that. He didn't bother to weigh the implications. He knew what they were. He knew that they worked. He knew how to get rid of the eel—perhaps even without hurting it. Now, where had he put the spear gun?

It was easy enough to attach the grenades to the spears. They were wrapped in plastic just loose enough to push the spear points through. The first two he tried proved disappointingly ineffective. Neither detonated, though he was certain he had armed them correctly. The third was much more satisfactory. Almost as soon as he thrust the spearpoint through the plastic and twisted the top of the disk, a thin line of bubbles burst into the torchlight. He took careful aim and fired again. The spear sped straight and true. Richard curled his arm over his eyes. A second or two later there was a detonation from deep within the trench. Richard never knew whether the eel survived, but it was certainly absent when he moved to free the anchor.

Partway through the process, the line around his waist jerked urgently again.

And that, in the end, was what made up his mind.

CHAPTER SEVEN

The Gulf.

"Thank you, Rass al Kaimah. Multihull *Katapult* leaving Hormuz inshore traffic zone now . . ." Hood consulted the piece of paper Weary had just passed to him. "Position fifty-six-fifteen east, twenty-six-twenty north. Time logged at . . ."

"One-thirteen, local," announced Robin, her clear eyes on the chronometer.

". . . thirteen thirteen hours local time. Inbound on a heading of . . ."

"Due west," called Richard, who held the con, his gaze flicking back up from the compass to their course as he spoke.

". . . due west for Bahrain Island. ETA at Manama Harbor . . ."

"Eighteen hundred tomorrow," said Weary without even glancing up from the chart table where he was plotting their course with practiced ease.

". . . eighteen hundred hours tomorrow. Are there any special warnings or standing orders in force, over?" Hood drew an ebony hand down over his smooth, perspiring face. His short, black curls were jeweled with moisture.

"Good afternoon, *Katapult*, this is Rass al Kaimah,"

said the radio clearly. "We have you at fifty-six degrees and fifteen minutes east, twenty-six degrees and twenty minutes north on an inbound heading due west for Manama harbor, Bahrain Island, with an ETA at eighteen hundred hours local time tomorrow. There are no special warnings in force at this time. We expect the weather to remain as it is, though the wind may strengthen from the south during the day due to the unusually low pressure over the center of Iran. There may be light northerly winds during the hours of darkness. On your heading, you will pass south of Fate but north of Jesirat bu Musa. Beware of oncoming tanker traffic beyond Fate. You will enter the Iranian advisory zone at Jesirat bu Musa. I assume you have already contacted Bandar Abbas, over?"

"*Katapult*, affirmative, over."

"Good. Then you should proceed, *Katapult*. Oh, and post a lookout. There may be mines in the waters south of Fate."

"Say again, Rass al Kaimah?"

"*Mines* in the waters south of Fate."

"Robin," said Weary over the top of the radio message. "You're on watch. Up and out."

"I read you, Rass al Kaimah. Watches have been posted. Will advise you of any change. *Katapult* over and out."

Hood flipped the radio to general receive and turned it down to a background babble. "Mines," he said, his voice disgusted. "Jesus! Is there anything in these waters that doesn't burn or blow up?"

Keeping watch was not Robin's idea of good fun. Kneeling on the foredeck gingerly, careful not to burn herself, she tried to get comfortable without obscuring

Richard's view. His face was behind the small windscreen at her left hip. Once in place, she tried to concentrate on scanning the sea all around the multihull. But it was hard, because of the heat. The Arabian Sea and the Gulf of Oman had been nothing compared to this. The brisk south wind brought no relief from the power of the sun. It was not moving as English breezes seemed to do, with a cool will of its own, but because it was being sucked sullenly from one hot place to another. And it was so humid that the sails dripped with moisture. Robin's hair, already perspiration-soaked, curled wildly, and her heavy clothing stuck to her. It was, literally, like a sauna—and in the overpowering heat of it, she was wearing jeans, a long-sleeved pullover, a scarf, and a hat. The fact was that any flesh left bare to the sun would blister in seconds and burn in minutes. Sunstroke was a very real danger. They had started taking salt-tablets at dawn—which had caused her morning sickness to extend itself until midday.

In the agonizingly clear distance, sharpened to uncommon focus by the activity of the south wind, a tanker loomed, superreal. Robin could see every detail of it, every line and plane and surface.

She shifted position slightly, trying to get some shade from the sail, while resisting the temptation to start thinking about cold drinks. It was less than half an hour since she had had one and she was parched already. Instead, she thought back, past that horrific hour over the explosives dumping zone to that one word she had said when they were discussing what they most needed in order to take back *Prometheus* and get word of her father:

"*Help!*"

It had not been a cry in the wilderness, of course. It had been the beginning of a series of practical maneuvers.

For they could summon help if they needed it. Help was as close as a call to Angus El Kebir. Robin allowed herself a brief indulgence. Of all Richard's friends, Angus was her favorite—apart from C. J. Martyr and Salah Malik, both of whom shared the unassailable distinction in her eyes of having saved Richard's life. In her mind, she called Angus "The Red Beard," for all the world as though he were a heroic figure from a novel by P. C. Wren or an operetta by Sigmund Romberg.

As though it were yesterday, she remembered their first meeting nearly ten years ago when she had gone to his Dubai office trying to get aboard Richard's ship, the first *Prometheus*. How well she remembered the steely glare of his pale, Scottish eyes, the twining of his fingers in his red Rob Roy beard. And the cold disdain with which he raised that eagle beak of a nose and thinned those perfectly sculpted desert prince's lips. On first meeting they had fought like cat and dog. They had been the best of friends ever since.

Angus's mother had been a Scottish nanny flown out to Dubai to tend the royal offspring, but one of the Sheikh's cousins had married her instead. It had been a strange match but a successful one. Angus had attended Fettes College in Edinburgh and there he had first met Richard and there the two had started their own friendship. Now Angus kept offices in Dubai, on Za'abil Street, near Sheikh Ahmad's palace overlooking the Creek; and in Manama City, Bahrain, on Old Palace Road near the Soukh. He had set them up first as an agent for Crewfinders, the first company Richard had ever founded, but now he maintained them as Heritage Mariner's agent as well.

Just as Angus had been the first to contact them with the news, so he was the first they had contacted when starting to form their plan.

"Richard! At last! Yes, I hear you five by five. I was growing concerned, old friend. I thought you had been taken, too. Only your radio! Well that is good news at least." How well Robin remembered that first transmission as they neared the Gulf at last.

"No, there is no more news from here. I have messages for you from all over the world, but no real news at all. Helen Dufour and Sir Justin Bulwer-Lyons have raised nothing other than sympathy from the Foreign Office in London. Eric Ellen's people at the International Maritime Bureau may have more, I expect to be hearing from them again soon. Chris and C. J. Martyr in New York pass on messages from Bob Stark's father: nothing doing in Washington either. They're all too nervous of the situation in Iran. Apparently, the Navy and the Air Force are at each other's throats there. It's a powder keg."

"All right, Angus," Richard's clipped tones echoed in Robin's memory, bringing an unconscious stirring of lust to her heavily-wrapped body, which was beginning to behave a little oddly now, gripped by the hormones of early pregnancy. Nine weeks down, thirty-three to full term. "Here's what I want you to do. First, I want you up in Bahrain—we'll coordinate from there. It's nearer *Prometheus* and more open. It has the international airport at Muharraq.

"Then get Martyr. He can leave Chris to run the New York office and . . ."

"Martyr's already moving, Richard." Angus's calm pronouncement still made the short hairs on Robin's neck stir. Ten years before, the events on the first *Prometheus* had made a friendship between these people more like that of a combat unit than of business associates. They still held a reunion dinner every year. They called it "Separation Day" to commemorate the night their ship had broken in two. Richard, Robin, Sir William, C. J. Martyr, John Higgins, Twelve Toes Ho, Kerem Khalil; all who had been aboard that night and lived to tell the tale. At first, also, Salah Malik, the great silent Palestinian ex-PLO man who had been chief petty officer on that fateful night had attended, mysteriously appearing and disappearing. But of later years, Salah had effectively vanished, returning to the continuing tragedy of his beloved Beirut, impossible to contact any longer.

Of all of them, Salah was the one they most needed now. Perhaps he even knew the men holding her father and her ship. The realization seemed to hit her like a blow in the stomach. Her thoughts grew murderous. . . .

She jerked her mind back from that dangerous path and returned them to yesterday, to that moment when Angus had told them Martyr was moving.

Of course he was. They all would be. Richard didn't even need to contact them. They would know. From all over the world they would come like the crew of a fishing village's lifeboat when the alarm sounds, leaving their families, their work, their lives. All they had to know was where Richard and Robin were heading for and somehow they would be there. Except for the man they needed most.

Except for Salah.

Her thoughts now full circle, she shook her head and brought her mind right back to the present. Richard still stood at the helm, though with *Katapult* slicing steadily across the wind on automatic setting he was there only to take evasive action should Robin spot anything. The other two were below, going about some business of their own.

And now they were just coming under the shadow of

Fate. The massive oil platform, Fa'at to the Arabs but
Fate to Westerners, rose out of the choppy sea on four
great rusted legs like some ancient iron monster. Like
some latter-day Colossus of Rhodes, she thought, striv-
ing to straddle Hormuz as the original had straddled
Rhodes Harbor. It was an anachronism, out of place; deserted, unused, mysterious. It looked as though it had
been built for the North Sea with a high platform raised
further by cliffs of deserted prefabs clustered around its
central derricks. The other platforms that studded this
sea were flimsy by comparison, relying on small waves
and tideless waters. But Fate was different. Alien. Almost eerie.

Who had put it there, when or why, Robin had no
idea. Why they had abandoned it and left it deserted to
rot like the *Marie Celeste* or the *Flying Dutchman* at anchor, she had never been able to discover. Yet there it
stood, four strong legs rising out of that shallow sea, each
one a hundred feet in circumference. Fifty feet high to
the first level, a hundred to the flat tops of its buildings.
Perhaps an acre in area, packed with emptiness, ruin, and
despair. She had never been up there and knew of no one
who had, but the atmosphere of the thing reached this
far with ease. It was avoided alike by the small craft running south of it, hugging the coast superstitiously, by
Abu Dhabi and Dubai; and by the tankers running north
pushing the deep-water lanes dangerously close to the
Iranian naval stations on Jezireh ye Qushm, ten scant
miles beyond.

A sharp double click jerked her mind back aboard.
While she had been daydreaming about Fate, Weary
and Hood's mysterious industry had moved from the
cabin to the afterdeck. They had opened the lazarette
and brought out both the box she had rescued from the

burning ship and the other one, marked with a big X, they had also pulled up on the end of Richard's line from the explosives dumping ground last night. And, surrounded by plastic-wrapped thunderflash grenades, they were stripping and checking the Kalashnikovs.

CHAPTER EIGHT

Richard lay at his ease on *Katapult*'s foredeck while the multihull lay safely at anchor. He was luxuriating in the illusory coolness of night while Weary worked below. Darkness was really little cooler than daylight here, but at least it allowed the freedom of partial nudity. Like Robin, he had spent each day since they had passed the Quoins and entered the Gulf wearing far too much clothing as protection from the sun. Now he lay on the cooling foredeck wearing only a pair of swimming trunks and perspiring freely. He remembered Noel Mostert's description of darkness in this place, "Like sitting in the heat of a black sun." Damn right, he thought. Sleep would have been out of the question, even had he not been waiting.

Katapult had arrived in Manama and anchored at sunset. Robin and Hood had gone straight ashore, leaving Weary and Richard anchored out here, far enough away from the harbor itself to be fairly sure that the Bahraini customs would not ask what they were carrying. Bahrain remained a favorite landfall of his but he was well aware that not even that island state's courteous authorities were likely to overlook six fully loaded Kalashnikovs, several thousand rounds of ammunition, and four dozen thunderflash grenades.

So Robin had gone ashore like any innocent tourist

to take a shower and collect Angus El Kebir. Hood had gone to report officially about *Katapult*'s part in the explosion of that mysterious, nameless, burning ship and to turn over the radio and the copy of the Koran they had found aboard her. And to see what gossip could be collected in the port and in the Soukh. Not much, Richard guessed, and nothing at all that Angus would have missed.

So now he waited, watching the night around him and taking what he suspected would be his last welcome rest until this thing was over.

Katapult's "eyes" looked north, and so did Richard's across the width of the Gulf toward Bushehr on the coast of Iran. Toward his pirated *Prometheus*, if Admiral Stark was correct. It was full night—had been so since half an hour after sunset—but it was not really dark. Before him lay uncounted oil rigs, as numerous, almost, as seaborne stars; each rig with its bright gas flare belching sooty yellow flames, each fiery flower indistinguishable from its reflection in the glassy surface beneath. In series, giving a kind of depth to the night, the flat galaxy of them spread away before him, flickering and dancing one and all, though moved by what forces Heaven alone knew. Certainly not by wind.

Above them, some real stars lay strewn across the sky, pallid in comparison. These were brightest overhead but faded into the distance until they were lost in cloud. For over Bushehr—above *Prometheus* herself perhaps—there was a thunderstorm. He could see the electrical power of it: flashes of brightness so dazzling in their intensity as to make him wince, even at this distance. The occasional discrete blue-white bolt arcing downward, burning itself into his retinas for seconds afterward. It was stunningly impressive—and the more so for being silent. There were few night sounds around him in any case. No wind, not even enough to hum in *Katapult*'s rigging. No sound of humanity, for he was too far out to catch any bustle from the bright glow of Manama. There were no other boats near at hand. No rigs. Nothing. Apart from the slapping of wavelets on her hull, and an occasional unfathomable sea sound, *Katapult* lay at the heart of a total silence into which crept occasionally only the faintest echo of a hint of a whisper of distant thunder, so quiet it might almost be a dream.

Richard knew these desert storms of old. Spectacular pyrotechnics, mind-numbing cacophony if one was close by. And, strangely, no rain at all. Dry desert winds whirling damper cloud-bearing air to colossal heights, begetting the most stunning of tempests, and yet, no matter how heavily those clouds poured, every drop would have evaporated hundreds of feet from the parched ground. Just another little joke of the desert.

But the quiet and the solitude gave him time to think of more than climatology. The relative inaction of the last few days had weighed more heavily on him than even Robin suspected. *Katapult* had begun to seem like a trap; the failure of the radio was the last straw. He was far too sensible to blame himself for any of this—though Robin, he knew, her moods made strange by her pregnancy, was suffering pangs of survivor guilt. It was nothing more than coincidence that all this had happened while they were so far away from base, so completely out of touch. Or seemed to be nothing more at the moment. He regretted poignantly that he was not at the center of things in London. But then again, for all that he had been a passenger so far rather than a prime mover, he felt he was nearer the heart of things here where he was now. Certainly, if he had been in London, he would have been bound with red tape. Doing more, but achieving nothing. Never in his wildest dreams, if

he had been at home when it all blew up, would he ever
have considered what he was planning now. Buccaneer-
ing across the Gulf armed to the teeth with illicit Russian guns and thunderflash grenades.

Suddenly there was a thump on the deck beside his
head. He sat up, swinging round to see what was going
on. Weary was standing behind him, by the mast. Richard looked down. Lying on the deck close at hand was
one of the black disks he had just been thinking about.

"Don't know what made me think of it," Weary's
tone was conversational. He might have been talking
about the weather. "Because they'd all dried off, I guess.
When we were packing them away I thought I'd better
try one. Can't take anything for granted. And now seems
as good a time as any."

"Of course. Good idea. We're far enough out. Try
one now."

Weary nodded. "Fact is, I have tried one, Richard.
I've tried several. Brought this one up for you to try."

Richard knew then, at once, and he actually gasped
with shock. But he picked up the heavy little disk anyway, twisted the top, and threw it into the sea, counting to three as he did so. The water closed over it, and
he recognized the mysterious sea-sound he had been
listening to just now.

And nothing else happened. No explosion. Nothing.
Like two out of the three he had fired at the eel.

"Looks like it was a mixed batch you found," said
Weary. "Some disarmed. Some not. We pulled up the
wrong box. Bad luck."

"Okay," said Richard quietly. He tried always to
meet crisis with calm. "First, let's see if there's any way
we can check the rest without detonating any live ones.
Then we'll have a think."

They went through the boxful in silence. It soon

became obvious that each grenade, like the box they came in, had been marked with the letter X. And, it seemed, X meant they had all been disarmed. They were all useless.

They heard the buzz of the inflatable some time before it came alongside and so they had time to dress in flannels and shirts, and to be waiting silently on deck for the others to arrive. Hood jumped aboard cheerfully. Robin climbed up in a cloud of silk and soap, and Richard at once felt grimy as well as frustrated. What luck! he seethed silently. Angus boomed aboard sparking with energy and all thoughts other than those of action were driven from Richard's head. After the briefest of pleasantries, they retired below to plan their next few moves in detail.

Richard chaired the meeting automatically, as a matter of course. "What we need," he said as soon as they were all seated, "is a careful plan of campaign. Angus, you've been at the center of things so far, what've you arranged?"

"You want contacts made, action taken, or events expected?" asked Angus calmly, as though this were some humdrum board meeting and not a council of war.

"Start with events expected."

"Okay. First, Martyr flies in from New York later tonight. He should arrive at Muharraq in two and a half hours' time."

"We'll meet him," decided Richard.

"I tried to contact Salah Malik but with no success at all. He may even be dead for all we know. Beirut . . ."

"Yes," said Richard, a little too quickly, his eyes on Robin. "But we can keep trying. What about news?"

"Still nothing. It's incredible, I know, but there has still been no word from anyone about either situation. We can't even be certain that they are connected. But we've been working on the assumption that they are . . ."

Richard's eyes stayed on Robin as Angus detailed the conclusions he had reached with the help of Helen Dufour, Heritage Mariner, the International Maritime Bureau, and all their worldwide contacts. The same conclusions Richard and Robin had arrived at alone.

She sat, pale, tired, yet completely intrepid. The shower had gone some way toward restoring her but what seemed to be making the most difference was the white robe she had bought this evening in Manama. It was silken and flowing, covering her from neck to ankle—and so, obviously, perfect protection from the sun—but so light as to give an overwhelming impression of coolness. She had also bought a little hand-carved wooden fan and, as she waved it gently by her left cheek, she filled the whole cabin with the scent of sandalwood.

"Right," he snapped again as Angus completed his report. "Action taken. This one's mine, I think; have you taken any specific action I don't know about, Angus?"

"No."

"Okay. What we have is this. Thanks to the U.S. Navy, we have the communications system we need to mount a concerted attack on *Prometheus*. We have the transport we need. Armaments . . ." He broke off. Leave the useless grenades out of the calculations for the moment, he decided. "We have two trained soldiers: Sam and Weary here. Then we have me. Robin. You, Angus, and finally Martyr, when he arrives. I don't envision us all going aboard, however. We need a backup system as well as a strike force, remember."

"So, do we go in blind?" Angus leaned forward, part of the plan unhesitatingly.

"Not if I can help it. Fast, yes. Blind, no. I need to know exactly where *Prometheus* is. Admiral Stark has helped there, but his information is several days old. I need an update. Ideally we need to know how many terrorists are aboard and where they are likely to be. . . ."

"We can surmise a lot of that information," chimed in Robin. "There are places where they would have to be . . ."

"That's right," said Richard. "And we could do with knowing what they have done with the crew. Are they just locked in their cabins or are they all together in some central location. . . ."

"Depends on how many terrorists there are," opined Robin. "They need men on the bridge. In the engine control room if they want to use the generators. They need patrols. Lookouts. If there are as few as, say, a dozen, the crew would have to be locked in some central location. They'd need more than twenty to police the cabins efficiently for any length of time."

"A terrorist unit of more than twenty?" Hood's tone was skeptical.

"Right. It's likely to be a smaller unit than that. Twelve people, tops," agreed Robin.

"So, *Prometheus*'s crew are likely to be in one central location," said Angus. "Now where would that be, Richard?"

"If it was me," Robin answered slowly, clearly having been thinking about this already, "I'd put them in the gym."

Prometheus, like most modern tankers, had a full range of leisure facilities. After all, she did not dock like a cargo ship and release the crew for shore leave during loading and unloading. She simply moved from terminal to terminal, hardly ever going nearer to the shore than ten miles out, filling and emptying her holds through great pipes in the sea. Crews aboard had no end of voyage to look forward to, simply a turnaround leading to a return journey. Time after time. Under these circumstances, a library, a cinema, videotapes, radios, televisions, a swimming pool, and a gymnasium, as well as the more traditional haute-cuisine dining facilities and inevitable bars, became absolute necessities— bulwarks against the stultifying boredom that could dangerously blunt the edge of even the most able and experienced crew.

"Yes," struck in Richard again. Caught up in the urgent practicalities of planning action, their minds unconsciously clicked into unison. Their words and phrases wove around each other like braided rope until there was neither one mind nor the other, but a union stronger than either. "The gym."

"It's the biggest usable room aboard."

"Apart from the cinema."

"But the cinema's full of seats."

"That's right. Clear the equipment out of the gym. . . ."

"Easy enough to do . . ."

". . . Chuck it overboard if necessary . . ."

". . . a waste, but it'd give you plenty of room."

"Move in some tables and chairs."

"Beds?"

"Bedding on the floor."

"Right!"

"And you should be able to hold forty people in there. Easy to oversee. Easy to guard."

"You've the boxes from the stage if you want some height."

"And the parallel bars up the walls."

"You could just take out the stewards in teams to get food and clear up."

"Seamen to see to anything else that needed doing."

"And some officers to oversee them, holding the rest as hostages against good behavior."

"It'd work!" concluded Robin, face aglow with excitement, until she remembered she was describing the hell being suffered by some of her closest friends. More soberly, she added, "Well, I can't see any other way . . ."

"Nor can I." Richard sat back, massaging tired eyes.

"But you're assuming," said Angus, "that these people are well organized. Intelligent. That they know what they're doing."

"Yes," said Richard. "I think we have to assume that."

"So," said Hood slowly, "your worst-case scenario goes like this. Ten or twelve heavily armed hostiles. Forecastle head watch. Bridge watch. Engine room watch. Two more watching the bulk of the crew in the ship's gymnasium. Two more to oversee the cooking, tidying, toilet, what have you. Maybe two more to oversee the seamen if need be. Two backups. Leader or coordinator. Whatever. Yes; it'd work real sweet with twelve."

"Twelve looking after forty," chimed in Weary. "Not much rest. Damn little sleep. They'll be getting tired. Jumpy. They've got to move soon or they've lost it. Fish or cut bait. I wonder what they're waiting for?"

"God knows. But you're right about moving soon," said Richard. "And it's the same for us. If we're going in, we have to do it quickly, while they're at their most exhausted and we've got our fresh troops. And before they get any fresh troops."

"We can up anchor whenever you like. We'll have the south wind behind us," said Weary. "If we go with the dawn and it holds through the day, we'd sight her tomorrow evening. Go in tomorrow night."

And it lay there on the table before them, like the corpse of some foul thing. Within twenty-four hours, if they chose, they could be creeping aboard *Prometheus* to face twelve desperate, heavily armed terrorists to try to release their shipmates without getting everybody killed.

Tomorrow night.

"No," said Richard at last. "It's too risky. Especially without the grenades." Now that he had had them and had lost them, he realized how much he really needed them. The dud grenades would have to be replaced. "And it's too soon. We'd be going off at half cock. We need another day. Maybe two. And we still need that extra edge. Damn!" His hand slammed down on the tabletop. "Three days."

"What?" For the first time tonight, Robin's mind was not on the same wavelength as his. But she was still trying to come to terms with the news about the faulty thunderflash grenades.

"Three days' hard sailing. Back to Fujayrah and then back here. With one of the other boxes. Doc, could you do that?"

"Yes."

"Right. You go at first light. With Martyr. He knows about munitions too. For God's sake, test them there this time. Angus, Robin, you and I will go ashore now. We'll meet Martyr off the plane. And tomorrow we'll hire a small coastal craft. Do some fishing off Bushehr."

"Find *Prometheus*," whispered Robin.

"Find out what we can and get back here within three days ourselves. Meet up for a final briefing. Go in then." He looked around the table. "It's Wednesday night now. The better the day, the better the deed: we go at dawn on Sunday."

CHAPTER NINE

Once again Weary stayed aboard, checking the multi-hull from stem to stern now that he knew they had seventy-two hours' hard sailing ahead. Hood came with the others to get provisions for the return run to Fujay-rah. Although the Soukh would have closed its gates at sunset, he hoped to get all he needed at Manama Port. Richard and Robin were going to meet Martyr's plane. Angus was going to find them a small coastal craft.

Hood took control of the little inflatable's outboard and sat on the full rubberized side at the back. Richard sat at the other side of the little motor, the two big men balancing each other, but raising the inflatable's round bow well clear of the water. Angus and Robin sat on the slatted wooden seat that divided her halfway along her stubby length, facing backward so that the four of them could talk.

"Guess you have all known each other a good long time?" Hood's question, coming over the buzz of the motor and the slap of the waves, was apparently inno-cent, and yet Richard had been expecting it. He had seen the calculating, careful light enter those calm brown eyes even as Weary had thrown himself and *Katapult* wholeheartedly into Richard's plan. Hood needed to be convinced that this was the best way. That this was the best team. Richard had no doubt that Robin and he passed muster with the careful American, but why should Hood take their word for the quality of the rest of them? The flamboyant Angus might easily prove to be less than he appeared at first sight. The mysterious Martyr all reputation and no reality. As for Salah Malik—all they had established about him was that he worked for the PLO, he might be dead, and he probably wasn't coming. Not very confidence-building. Richard could see that.

"Look," he said. "Angus and I were at school together. I've known Robin since she was sixteen. I was married to her sister. But what you really want to know about started ten years ago."

"It was an insurance fraud," struck in Robin, the business manager.

"It centered on the first *Prometheus*."

"The one you fell off," Hood said, grinning at Robin, "trying to save a parrot."

"You told! You rat!" said Robin to Richard.

"That's right. Well, *Prometheus* was due to sail from Kharg to Rotterdam with a full load of crude," continued Richard, riding over her protest.

"But the plan was for her to slip into Durban, sell her oil illegally, and then sink so the owner could claim insurance on both hull and cargo," completed Robin.

"That was the plan. Then an industrial accident killed off most of the officers aboard before she could sail, and we went out to replace them. I was running a crew-finding agency in those days."

"Crewfinders," said Hood. He knew about that, too: it was the best in the world.

"They knew nothing of what was planned," added Angus. "Then you went aboard later, Robin."

"The cargo changed hands several times on the international spot market," said Robin. "My father owned it at one point. I went aboard then. They need a new third mate in any case."

"A whole set of officers replaced and then they needed a new third mate! Sounds like a death ship to me." Hood's quiet comment stopped the rush of information for a moment.

Then Richard picked up the thread again. "We knew nothing about anything illegal. We were just trying to bring her home. But some of the old crew were still aboard and one of my own Crewfinders people was up to no good. The long and the short of it is this: the original plan still went ahead behind our backs. . . ."

"But these guys, Martyr and Malik, they were Crewfinders men, right?"

"No, they were part of the original crew," said Richard. "But it was one of my own men doing all the damage anyway. He poisoned the food. He tried to kill Martyr after the bomb went off."

"There was a bomb? On a supertanker? And you all walked away?"

"We only brought half of her home. But it's a long story. Martyr and Malik were only on the fringe of the original plan, each one there for his own good reasons. Once they realized what was really going on, they changed sides and helped us."

"Saved us," said Robin earnestly. "Saved our lives. Literally."

"What we went through then still binds us," said Richard. "It was like war. Do you see what I mean?"

"Sure," said Sam easily. "You guys are like Doc and me. All we got in common is Nam. But that's more than enough. Thicker than blood."

Robin nodded, her bright curls outlined by the lights

of Manama. "That's it," she said. "That's exactly the right phrase. Blood is thicker than water—and this is thicker than blood."

They tied up at a low wooden jetty and climbed up a short dark flight of steps into the dazzling light above. And out of the heart of that brightness stepped a slim figure, to stand, legs slightly apart, precisely blocking their path. It was a young man, perhaps thirty-five, slight of build but giving the impression of stature in his erect, military bearing. He wore a meticulously pressed khaki uniform topped by a peaked cap. The peak, worn low over his eyes, gleamed like patent leather, as did the straps of his Sam Browne. As did the open flap of his military holster.

"Captain Richard Mariner?" The calm voice spoke perfect Oxbridge English, as clipped as his pencil mustache.

Richard stepped forward. "Yes?"

"I am Mohammed Suleiman, captain of police. Would it be convenient for us to have a word or two in private?"

Captain Suleiman's office was as precise as the man himself, a modest room lent size and style by its Spartan neatness. Richard, his mind racing, stood a little apart from the others, awaiting events. As he did so, he looked out of the captain's window with veiled eyes, apparently paying complete attention to the view. The office faced the other half of the port, the south side. From here he could follow the curve of Old Palace Road past the school until it disappeared down by the walled fortress of the market known here as the Soukh. Beyond that lay low buildings, square and flat-topped for the most part, overlooking the profusion of boats on the black water that stretched away toward Sitra, invisible in the distance.

There were a number of ways in which the Bahraini police could be involved in this. There was the matter of Sir William's kidnapping at the airport itself. Or the port authorities might have caught some wind of what *Katapult* was carrying. Or it might have to do with Hood's report of this afternoon about the sinking of the arms ship. Or it could all be as innocent as a question or two about the passenger list of the incoming flight from London.

It started with Sir William. "Mrs. Mariner, let me first say how deeply I myself, and indeed, the whole Bahraini people regret the kidnapping of your father from our soil."

"Thank you, Captain. Is there any news?"

"I regret not. We do not even know who is holding him or where." Abruptly he swung toward Richard. "Captain Mariner, I assume that is why you and your representatives have been in contact with terrorists and terrorist organizations?"

"I beg your pardon?" Here it comes, thought Richard.

"Salah Malik. He is an associate of yours, I believe?"

"Yes."

"You cannot be unaware of his standing in the Palestine Liberation Organization."

"I haven't seen him in some years. I know nothing of his current standing."

"Then it will be a matter of indifference to you that he has dropped out of sight. That he is moving. And with such a man, his slightest movements are—how shall I put it?—observed. Scrutinized."

Angus coughed. The captain swung round to look at

him. Their eyes locked for a moment, as Angus thoughtfully tugged at his full red beard. "I may have got a message to him," he admitted at last. "I tried, but I can't be sure . . ."

"So. Captain Mariner?"

"As you say, Captain Suleiman. Of course, I take full responsibility."

"But this is stupid," exploded Robin, suddenly up out of the chair, confronting Suleiman eye to eye. "My father is in the hands of some kind of terrorist group. Of course we would try to contact the one man who might be able to give us a little inside information. I hope your people are trying to do the same!"

"Very well, let us leave terrorists aside for a moment." He paused for a heartbeat. "Let us discuss the murderers you have invited into my country."

Richard was in no way surprised that C. J. Martyr's reputation should have preceded him. The two men had been close friends for ten years now, and this was by no means the first time that such information had traveled from one authority to another. In at least one country Richard could think of, the taciturn New Englander had been slammed into jail within half an hour of landing. It was the old story.

"He's been to court," Robin cried, suddenly. "The jury called it justifiable homicide. He got commended by the judge, for God's sake! Your computer has the charges, not the verdict!" Martyr was more than a shipmate, more than a friend. The tall, strong, lath-thin ex-engineering officer had become almost a second father to her. Since leaving his last berth, he had run their New York office for them with the help of his daughter Christine. Moved beyond words by the injustice of the situation, Robin swung round to Richard, agonized appeal in her tear-bright eyes.

But he was already speaking. "Look, Captain Suleiman, the story's simple enough. Martyr married young. Had a daughter, Christine. Then his wife took up with another man. They kept Christine but Martyr visited. Then Christine vanished. Mother and stepfather were helpless. They had tried everything they could but had got nowhere. Martyr jumped ship, turned detective, and tracked her down. When he found her she was in a bad way. Hooked on hard drugs, working as a prostitute, and making pornography to support her habit. When he took her back, her pimp of a boyfriend tried to stop him. Brought in some pushers for support. Martyr brought her back over their dead bodies.

"But it didn't end there. He put her straight into a private clinic. But he hadn't the money for both Christine's treatment and his own defense: he couldn't risk going to jail, or she would be out on the street again. So he stayed abroad, taking any job, sending all the money back home to her. It was all he lived for. Then he risked it all for me. Risked his life and Christine's future to save me and my ship, *Prometheus*, nearly ten years ago. Since that time he has worked for me. Heritage Mariner paid for his daughter's treatment, and for his own defense. And it's all cleared up now. He runs our New York office with Christine as his executive assistant. All legal and aboveboard. Exonerated of all charges."

Aware of the increasingly bitter irony in the last few phrases of this passionate speech, Captain Suleiman allowed himself the slightest shrug of apology. "Very well, Captain Mariner," he said. "We will consider the matter closed. If you vouch for the man. If he is passing through."

"Thank you."

"But I warn you, I warn all of you, I will not be so

indulgent if Salah Malik appears on the scene! Good night."

As he guided Angus's Mercedes across the causeway toward Muharraq, Richard thought about Captain Suleiman. The captain was no fool. He struck Richard as a careful career officer making his way successfully through a complicated system. And the fact that he had taken such a line with people who habitually dined with the Sheikh was very worrying indeed. Oh, this was not like some states where the ruling family considered themselves above the law and would destroy importunate officialdom at a whim, but the fact remained that if Richard and Robin had been here in any official capacity at all, they would certainly have been invited to the palace once again. And Suleiman must have known that. Yet he had still warned them off in no uncertain terms.

Richard suddenly went cold at the thought of what might happen to them if they ran afoul of less patient, less courteous authorities. Of the Iranians, say, for whose waters they would set sail in a few hours. So far they had been carried forward by their need to react to the twin situations confronting them. They had perhaps been seduced by the freedom of action their unique position allowed them. Were they getting seduced into a situation that they had no chance of controlling, no chance of escaping? They could all too easily end up in an Iranian jail. Executed, like that journalist last year. They could well end up dead, all of them, just a pile of corpses to be dumped over the side of *Prometheus* by victorious terrorists, who would then start taking reprisals by executing the very people they had set out to save.

And Sir William. They could so easily cause him to

be discovered in some gutter in Beirut with a note pinned to his clothing and a bullet in his brain.

"Penny for them."

"It's all so damn dangerous, Robin. It could all go so terribly wrong." His tone robbed the words of weakness. He sounded like a doctor delivering a diagnosis.

"I know, darling. But what alternative do we have? Meet the plane, say hi, then send Martyr home? Get Angus to send another message to Beirut, 'Thanks all the same, Salah, but we've changed our minds'?"

"There's got to be more to it than face and inconvenience. We have to have a better reason for going on than that it would be embarrassing to turn back!"

"Okay. Look at the alternative. We give up here. We go home. We put *Katapult* into production if we can find the backing after all this bad publicity. We run Heritage Mariner. Only we send no more tankers to the Gulf. We can't risk losing another one. So we run out of the few customers for crude-carrying we still have. And in the meantime, all our insurance payments go up until *Prometheus* is safe. Heritage Mariner really begins to lose big money. But we still have Crewfinders. Only there is no one left on the Crewfinders books because all the officers and crew who might have come to us know we can no longer guarantee their safety. Christ! We can't even protect the chairman of the board! So we start closing down Crewfinders and try to put Heritage Mariner into liquidation while the costs begin to spiral way out of control. We move someone else into Father's office and we wait for word of him. Like they're waiting for word of all the other hostages still in terrorist hands. Year after year after year . . ." Oddly, it was the lack of emotion that gave her words so much impact. If he had sounded like a doctor, she sounded like a pathologist announcing the cause of death of somebody else's business. Family. Life. In this as in all things, they were the perfect team. They leaned on each other unreservedly in any crisis, and their strength together was greater than either of their strengths alone. "So what have we really got to lose?" she whispered, as he silently turned the steering wheel and guided them into the parking lot outside Muharraq International Airport.

Even at this time of night, this was a busy place. For the first time in weeks Richard did not feel hot, for after a walk through the suffocating atmosphere outside, the chill of the air-conditioning on the concourse and in the shops was like a drug. Here, during the short time they had to wait, Richard emulated his wife's good sense by purchasing clothing much more suited to the climate than his Western shirt and trousers. By the time C. J. Martyr had cleared passport control and customs, Richard looked more like a sheikh than a sailor with his long, white fine cotton djellabah, his kaffiyah, and his dark mahogany tan—though he still kept his old clothes, together with some other new ones in the bright bag marked KHAM SIN, TAILORS.

When Martyr came striding out of customs and into Robin's waiting arms, it was 11 P.M. local time. In his head it was 4 P.M. New York time precisely, and he was still full of fizz. His lean body seemed to spark with energy. He towered over Robin, sweeping her off her feet into an exuberant bearhug, and even topped Richard by an inch or two. If anything, over the last ten years he seemed to have grown younger. His sand gray crewcut had gained not one more fleck of white, his bony frame had gained not one more ounce of flesh. But the stark lines that had marked his hatchet face when they had all first met were gone, replaced by laugh lines at his eye corners clustering thickly between long fair lashes and great jug-handle ears.

"Richard!" he boomed.

Richard strode forward, thinking how different this was from their first hostile greeting all those years ago. He took the proffered hand, feeling again the old strength still lurking in the long, hard muscles. The old power in the grasp of that great, hard-knuckled fist. They embraced the instant Robin was put down and stood, thumping each other on the back like long lost brothers.

Then, over Martyr's shoulder, Richard saw another, slighter figure close behind. Golden hair drawn back into a simple ponytail that emphasized the beauty of the face and the elegance of the neck, though it was not designed to do so. Straight, slim nose between broad cheekbones. Generous mouth emphasizing her wide jaw. Enormous emerald eyes, as cold as her father's were warm and smiling. Skin like honey, glowing and dusted with gold. Square shoulders, full breasts, slim waist, broad hips, legs that went on forever. The impact of her almost stopped his heart.

It was Christine.

He stepped back as though struck; then he paused, his mind a whirl of speculation and this time Robin acted, behaving as though this had always been part of their plans. "Christine!" Her voice echoed Richard's thought even as he thought it and suddenly they were side by side, Robin's blonde curls dulled by comparison with Christine's flowing tresses. Beside the American beauty, Robin seemed shorter, plumper, coarser. Almost the ugly-duckling schoolgirl he had first met nearly twenty years ago. But it was only in comparison, for the effect had nothing to do with Robin and everything to do with Christine's shining perfection. And after the first breathtaking impact, the first unflattering comparison, it always warmed his heart to see how Robin simply enjoyed Christine's company though she was as well aware as anyone how plain she looked beside her friend.

And, as it always did, Richard's heart twisted with affectionate sympathy for the exquisite girl before him, living her lonely life. He strode forward, therefore, and swept the pair of them into his arms, hugging fiercely and protectively.

"What's the plan?" was Martyr's first question as they pulled their cases from the carousel. Richard silently shook his head and glanced meaningfully at the pair of khaki police uniforms patrolling nearby. Martyr's eyebrows rose fractionally; then he became preoccupied with identifying his luggage.

As the four of them crossed the reception area, Robin earnestly began to discuss with Christine the advisability of emulating her own choice of clothing, but the American girl seemed content with what she had brought. Robin was for once caught off guard by her friend's unconscious sexuality. Knowing Hood and Weary as she did, she really felt that Chris's reliance on bikinis and SPF 7 was going to prove a challenge to all concerned. But how on earth could she put it in a way that Chris would accept?

Abruptly her mood swung and for the first time ever in the nine years of their friendship, she really did feel fat and dowdy in the presence of this vision of beauty. Fat and dowdy and pregnant. She caught the tail end of a strange man's glance at the pair of them and knew he hadn't even noticed her. Oh, why had C. J. brought his daughter now? Now of all times! Her head began to buzz with depression, fatigue, and sickness.

The automatic doors hissed open and closed behind

them. The night air swirled chokingly around her. The shadows attained substance and crushed against her like burning bodies. The stench of the oil, the tar, the car exhaust washed into her throat nauseatingly. The noises fell away as she became giddy with the shock of the heat. She tottered apart from the other three, and not even Richard noticed her distress. Her head spun. Her whole body was suddenly awash with sweat. This is very bad, she thought. Her knees gave. She fell.

And one of the shadowy bodies became real. One of the distant sounds said her name. Her moment of weakness was saved by steely strength and she found herself looking upward like the heroine of a popular romantic novel into the lean, proud face of a familiar desert warrior.

"Salah," she whispered, and fainted into his arms.

CHAPTER TEN

Angus had found them a tidy thirty-footer, one of those craft Richard insisted on calling a "dhow" and everyone else called a launch. This launch was named *Alouette*. She had been built in the boatyards of the Creek at Dubai untold years ago and the only thing certain about her history was that she had once been owned by someone who had given her a French name. Her body was strong and watertight; shipshape, under her peeling paint; neat and tidy, if elderly. She had a high bow, falling in an exaggerated, elegant curve from a near-vertical bowsprit to a fine, sharp cutwater. Her forecastle was only a step or two above her maindeck, but it sloped up steeply toward her head. Her stubby mainmast stood at the center of her deck, along which lay the long crosspiece bearing her dull red sail. They would have no need of this, for, belowdeck, behind the mast, her engine room boasted a gleaming, perfectly maintained Perkins 4-236 diesel engine, complete with Hurth box transmission. At Richard's first command from the bridge-house above the sterncastle, it kicked into steady motion and, as Robin spun the mahogany wheel, Salah and Angus cast off and they were away.

They set forth at dawn the next morning, the stuffy, overpowering darkness hesitating into lifeless gray for a moment; the gas flares paling in their flat galaxy north across the water whither *Alouette*'s head was pointing. The sky became the palest blue arcing overhead, down to the shadow-line at its junction with the pallid water. The whole of the Gulf seemed to hold its breath with only the little launch throbbing purposefully through the stillness. Then the sun came up out of the sea, filling the water with fire. A tidal wave of light seemed to wash over them, its crest brushing the dome of heaven itself, and it was day: day as though the night had never been.

But the night had existed all right, and had been a busy one at that. They had not paused to greet Salah at the airport but instead rushed him and the still-fainting Robin to the coolness of the air-conditioned car. Once inside, she had revived rapidly as they sped south again, with Richard concentrating fiercely on the road ahead. As he tried vainly to come to terms with the local style of driving, so Robin began to describe the plans to the new arrivals.

It was more than five years since Salah Malik and C. J. Martyr had last seen each other and, bound though they were by the events on the first *Prometheus*, they had grown into virtual strangers. Chris automatically mistrusted anyone until he had earned her respect and affection. This process had taken Richard and Robin some years. The fact of Salah's natural magnetism simply complicated matters for her. The American girl's nightmarish youth had inverted all her priorities. The slightest attractiveness in a man brought out a legion of defenses in her. Which was why, Robin thought, it had taken her so long to accept Richard. She glanced affectionately at the back of her husband's head and something about the way his hair curled made her tingle with desire.

Salah's arm lay across the back of the front bench seat

and his knees swung in toward the gear shift as he turned to look back. Martyr sat behind him, and the women behind Richard. His eyes met Robin's first and he smiled his old smile.

"I never thought you'd come, Salah," she said. "It's so dangerous for you."

"It's no problem. After Beirut, even death will be a relief, I think. I suppose that's why there are so many so willing to die."

His tone was difficult to gauge. Was it world-weary? Cynical? Merely ironic? All of a sudden, Robin became aware of the gap that had opened between them during the last years during which they had drifted apart.

"I thought you were a peaceful man," said Martyr abruptly.

"And so I am, Chief." Salah slipped easily back into the old ways. Martyr had not been a chief engineer for ten years.

"Then what are you doing in Beirut?"

"Looking for peace."

"Have you looked for my father?" Robin asked. She had meant to be subtle, to come at it indirectly, in the diplomatic, English way. But her burning sense of urgency abruptly outweighed all her background and social conditioning. She realized that all that had held her back from hysteria since the news of the kidnapping was the pointlessness of indulging it.

"I have looked," he answered gently. "Sir William is not there."

"What?" Richard glanced across. "Are you certain?" He had taken his eyes off the road for a second at the worst possible moment, just as they came down off the causeway onto the first great roundabout in Manama. A yellow Chevrolet taxi sped past on the wrong side and turned across their path, horn screaming. Richard swore and stamped on the brakes. Half a ton of German steel stopped dead in the road. They were thrown around like puppets inside, but Salah had a firm grip on the seat back and a hand on the dashboard too. "Go!" he snapped and Richard did to the accelerator what he had just done to the brake and they hurled into a transient hole. "Hit the horn," suggested Salah mildly, "and you'll fit right in." Richard did, and the car, mercifully unscathed, blended perfectly into the shrieking mass of traffic. So that the gaze of the policeman Salah had been watching passed incuriously over them, apparently noting nothing unusual.

The Palestinian repeated his assertion quietly in Angus's office ten minutes later. "Sir William is not in Beirut. I know where the other hostages are and I am doing all in my power to help them. But no one in Beirut has Sir William, or has any part in this that I can discover. I am afraid we may have to look farther east."

"Iran," whispered Robin.

"It is hard to tell at the moment. Things are so confused there."

"So you are not sure?" Angus tugged at his beard, lost in thought.

"No, I am not. You have tried asking questions in the Soukh?"

"I have. Nothing."

"The Creek, of course? The boatyards there have always been full of gossip."

"The Creek—indeed the whole of Dubai—has nothing to say to me. And as for Kor Rass al Kaimah, the Mujara, Ash Sharq, Al Khalida, it is the same: all the markets, ports, and docks on this side of the Gulf are silent on the subject."

"But damn it!" exploded Robin. "Someone must know something."

"Agreed," answered Salah mildly. "But who? And where?"

"What I know is this," grated Richard. "We have precious little time to sit around and wait for news. Our first job is to get *Prometheus* back. If the two incidents are connected we will then have a counter to bargain with. If they aren't, we will have freed both Crewfinders and Heritage Mariner from their present position and can get on and find him no matter what it costs."

"That's right!" Martyr could sit still no longer. He was up and pacing, seven hours less exhausted than they, like a sober guest late at a boozy party. "So we go after *Prometheus* first. When and how?"

"Dawn Sunday. We need some time to prepare."

"Right. What does your preparation entail?"

Richard explained the situation: They needed better intelligence. They needed more arms.

"Intelligence?" rapped Martyr.

"Team one. Robin, Angus, Salah, and me. Angus found us a dhow . . ."

"Launch."

". . . A launch, thank you, Angus. We will go up to Bushehr. We check on *Prometheus*'s position. See if we can get close enough to learn anything more."

"And if she's not there anymore?" asked Robin.

"Back here at once and pray for news of her."

"Okay," said Martyr. "That's team one. Team two?"

"On *Katapult*. You, Chris, Hood, and Doc. You'll pick Hood up with the supplies and go out to *Katapult* when we're finished here. Your job is to run down to Fujayrah. When you get down there you'll find an explosives dumping ground. It's marked as deep water on the chart, but there's a ridge. Here, let me show you. . . ."

The run up to Bushehr was 190 miles. *Alouette* was capable of eight knots. She had a gently following wind and no currents of the tideless Gulf chose to run against her. They made the crossing in twenty hours, therefore, arriving at 02:00 next morning, four hours before dawn.

Since crossing into the Iranian and Iraqi exclusion zones, Richard and Robin had kept watch and the others had slept, ready to be roused at a moment's notice in case of trouble. It was easy enough to find the place, even at 02:00 in the dark with rudimentary navigation aids, because Bushehr Airport remained active on their starboard and Kharg, on their distant port, was all abustle. The coast from Rass osh Shatt, round the bay to Bushehr itself, was flat and shelved shallowly into the sea. Nearly five miles out they hit the ten-meter mark on the sounder, chucked the anchor over, and went to bed. Things were likely to get busier after dawn, so some rest was needed now.

The brightness woke Richard an instant after sunrise and he opened his eyes to slits. He found himself lying on *Alouette*'s teak decking, curled round Robin. Beyond her still-sleeping form, he could see an apparently thin strip of water, then the desert, reaching from the tide line to seeming infinity away in the heart of Iran. There was no scrub or grass visible, no vegetation at all that he could see—simply an ocher slope of sand rising gently out of the water until it attained a low plain that stretched monotonously away. There were mountains in the far distance, he knew, the southern ranges of the Zagroz with Shiraz at their heart, but they were far out

of sight. All that seemed real was that distant, featureless plain, dominating the land and dictating the nature
of the sea. A morning wind stirred, bringing the brim-
stone stench of it to his nostrils, together with enough
fine sand grains to start him sneezing. So he sat up, took
the headdress he had been using as a pillow and wrapped
it round his head and face like any Arab would. When
he stood, no eye on earth could have distinguished him
from a million men dressed alike in a long white shirt-
like djellabah and a bright checked kaffiyah. It was only
when he called out excitedly in English that the illusion
was shattered.

"Robin! There she is! My God, how could we have
been so close without knowing?"

Prometheus lay at anchor less than a mile away. They
were dead astern so that the length of her was eaten by
perspective, but there was no doubting her scale. Even
here, the clifflike hugeness of her was so overpowering
that Richard was surprised he had felt nothing of it
during the night, or while he was looking away across
the desert just now.

She was sitting high, the great fin of her rudder alone
enough to dwarf *Alouette*—perhaps even *Katapult* herself. Behind it, idle but boasting massive power, stood
the blades of her twin propellers, like the rudder rising
out of the still water to reveal only part of their true
scale. Then, above these, the hull itself, rearing up and
back in a colossal overhang. And on it was written clearly
in white across her stern: PROMETHEUS II LONDON.

Instinctively, not a little awed by her, they spoke in
whispers—they would have taken care in any case after
Richard's first, surprised exclamation, for they did not
want English accents to carry across the still water.

"Well, there she is, just where Admiral Stark said she
would be," said Richard, first to gather his thoughts.

"No sign of life aboard," observed Salah.

"And she wasn't showing lights last night or we'd have seen her," added Robin, her voice heavy with disapproval.

"That's dangerous," said Angus, angrily.

"Bloody lethal. Lucky we weren't a mile farther that way last night or we'd have sailed straight into her. Stupid sods." Robin was not at her best in the morning. After having delivered herself of this opinion, she vanished toward the low sterncastle.

"But what to do next," mused Richard. "What to do."

"You're the boss," said Angus. "We do what you say."

"That's fine with me," said Salah. "But I know what I'd do. I'd try to get aboard."

"Yes," said Richard. "That's obviously our next objective now we're here. But how to start . . ."

"What would we do if we were just a bunch of fishermen out from Bushehr?" asked Angus.

"Sail right up and say hi?" ventured Salah, voice wavering between doubt and excitement.

"Damned if I wouldn't!" said Richard decisively.

"You mean just sail right up to them and see what happens?" Angus seemed less pleased with the simple plan.

"At least it has the merit of the direct approach," observed Richard. "And it'll save a lot of time."

"We're here to save lives, not time," countered Angus. "Starting with our own lives."

"True. So, we'll have to think this through carefully, step by step. Now, could we actually have come from Bushehr?"

"In a smallish launch?" Angus said. "No reason why not. It's why we settled on this type of craft after all."

"But not," struck in Salah suddenly, "in a launch with

a French name. Not from Bushehr. The Iranians aren't calling boats by any names the mullahs mightn't like at the moment. And they aren't writing them in that sort of lettering."

Out of nowhere at that moment, the name of the burning ship on that lost radio message sprang into Richard's memory. It was amorphous, slightly out of focus, a serpentine puzzle of lines. But he thought he might be able to put it on paper fairly accurately. Salah might know what it meant. But he thrust the thought away as soon as it occurred to him. They had more important matters at hand. "Right," he said. "So we're not from Bushehr, or anywhere else in Iran. Where are we from?"

"Not too close by," decided Salah. "We didn't see them last night, but they might have seen us. We were carrying lights, remember."

"Okay," agreed Angus. "Then where's closest on the *far* side of the Gulf? Somewhere in Kuwait, I guess."

"Mina al Ahmadi and Al Mish'ad are both a hundred and fifty miles away," said Richard, his eyes closed, consulting the chart in his head. "Nothing closer of any size."

"Well, I can speak with a Kuwaiti accent," said Angus more happily. "That's no problem. But what are we doing here?"

Robin came rushing back at that moment, her vivid eyes alight with pleasure. "Have you seen them?" she asked at once. "Aren't they lovely?" The others had no idea what she was talking about, so she took them back to see.

The head was at the stern, sticking out over the back, a simple wooden seat with a hole in it secured in a secluded spot. Depending on the disposition of its occupant, it could command quite a view. The view from the stern rail above it was breathtaking this morning. Some time just after dawn, a fishing fleet had arrived. Between *Alouette* and the distant shipping lanes, some twenty dhows had gathered, all of them busily trawling with lines or nets.

"Perfect!" Richard's fist thumped onto the rail. "Now we just need to check where they're from."

"Radio?" inquired Angus.

"No need," Salah flung over his retreating shoulders. "Glasses should be enough." He was back in a moment with two pairs. He gave one pair to Richard and pressed the other to his own eyes.

Richard inspected the busy fleet brought closer by the magnification. The boats varied from twenty to forty feet. None had their sails up—all were using their diesels. Hardly surprising—there was no real wind to speak of. On their open decks, figures toiled industriously but he only glanced at them, searching instead for the names of their vessels. He found several very quickly, but they were all in Arabic and defeated him every time. He spoke a fair smattering of Arab dialects, but—much to his chagrin now—had never learned to read it.

So it was Salah who after a moment said, "Jackpot, I think. They all seem to be from Mina Al Ahmadi. There's even another one with a foreign name. *Seagull*. You see it there? The bright red one? It's written in English."

But Richard was no longer looking. That feeling was creeping over him that this was a good day. A lucky day. They had wanted to find *Prometheus* and here she had come with the dawn like a gift. They had needed an excuse to hail her and here was that excuse. They wanted cover and here it was. Today they could do nothing wrong.

"Salah, you steer and stay on the bridge. You're the

only one not dressed correctly." Salah wore olive camouflage battle fatigues.

"Robin, you're the cabinboy or whatever. I'm a general dogs-body. Angus, you're the fleet coordinator.
You're an important man in Kuwait. You've decided to
hail this tanker in the middle of your fishing grounds to
find out just what the hell it's doing here. Okay?"

"Fine. On the radio?"

"No. Your radio doesn't work too well." Richard gave
a lean smile, apparent to the others only in the narrowing
of his eyes; his mouth hidden behind the folds of the
kaffiyah. "You'll have to sail right up and talk to them."

"Right," said Robin, catching Richard's growing
excitement. "Let's get the hook up."

The pair of them oversaw the winching up of the
anchor, as befitted their lowly position. Salah and Angus went onto the bridge. Once the hook was up,
Richard and Robin went below to oversee the starting
of the diesel, and Salah swung *Alouette*'s head slowly to
starboard until she was pointed straight at the silent,
sinister tanker.

"Wouldn't we be fishing?" Robin asked Richard
tensely as they began to draw closer to her. They were
at the very prow, with only the ornamental bowsprit
between them.

"No. We're too important. It's our job to find the
fish and direct the rest."

They fell silent then as *Prometheus*'s overhanging stern
rolled toward them like a thundercloud. Her after-rail
and bridge-wings remained empty.

"Would we be using binoculars?" The tension was
beginning to tell in Robin's voice.

"I think we might risk them." He did so and within
moments added, "You know, I'm damned if I can see
anyone at all."

Abruptly Angus joined them. "Richard, she looks empty to me. Deserted."

"I'd have thought there would be watches on the bridge-wings," said Robin.

Richard heard her only distantly, his mind back at the discussion they had had in *Katapult*'s cabin the night before last. They had reckoned on intelligent terrorists. But what if they were stupid?

Or brilliantly cunning?

He wiped his mouth through the kaffiyah with the back of his hand. Angus took the glasses and he relinquished them thoughtlessly, mind trying to weigh up the odds. But what were the odds in a situation so completely unknown? It was all guesswork. Blind guesswork, at that. All at once, he did not feel so confident about the luck of the day.

And then they came into the tanker's shadow.

Salah took them up *Prometheus*'s starboard side. At once the massive length of her became apparent. Fifty *Alouettes*, nose to tail, might just have been as long as she was. What numbers of that sturdy little thirty-footer piled atop each other might have reached her bridge-house, God alone knew. But what struck Richard immediately was not her scale, but her silence. Nothing stirred aboard her. Were they close enough to hear the grumble of her generators? He strained his ears with no success. Not a footstep. Not a voice.

Beneath the bridge-wing they lost way as Angus cut the diesel. They drifted out in silence. More of the bridge came into view—empty.

"Ahoy, the tanker," bellowed Angus, the Kuwaiti accent thick. First in Arabic and then in broken English— the Arabic easier to understand. Richard was surprised by the power of his friend's bellow. But then an errant memory jerked him back to the Hay Market ice rink in

Edinburgh and the climax of the Scottish Country Life curling competition with himself brushing feverishly in front of the stone while Angus yelled a mixture of direction and encouragement across the ice as they guided Fettes to victory.

"Ahoy, the tanker! Is there anyone aboard?" Again that stentorian voice in Arabic, then English.

Not a whisper of an answer.

"Let's go on down," said Richard quietly to Angus. "There might be a forecastle head watch."

Angus gestured to Salah and they rumbled forward again. Halfway down, they all looked up wistfully, at the accommodation ladder snugly tucked away some thirty feet above them. There was no way they could get aboard here. Getting aboard at all might prove difficult, even were she completely deserted. The least they would have to climb to gain the deck would be thirty feet, with no hand- or foothold. Nowhere even to secure a thrown rope. Well, thought Richard grimly, they could cross that bridge when they came to it. If they came to it: there had to be a watch on the forecastle head.

Nothing but the cry of a startled gull answered Angus, and in that instant the whole situation changed. Salah kicked in the idling motor and guided *Alouette* around the huge torpedo-head protrusion at the base of the bow. Above them at her head, where the figurehead should have been, was the Heritage Mariner logo, H and M overlapping as the iris of an eye painted there. So *Prometheus* watched them motor round her head to her port side where her anchor plunged down to the shallow sea bed.

The links of the enormous anchor chain fell almost vertically, pulled forward a little and curved slightly by such poor forces as dared disturb her massive inertia.

Each link, an oval five feet from top to bottom, was divided in the middle by a solid crosspiece. The links were still slippery with dew because the morning's heat had yet to reach them. The moisture made the weed with which they were coated slick and dangerous. The chain would be difficult to climb, but by no means impossible. As *Alouette*'s head snugged into the angle between the chain and the water, Salah cut the engine and left the bridge. Still looking speculatively upward, Richard reached for the nearest link. He had to slip his arm through it to hold *Alouette* still; Salah had judged the approach so perfectly that there was no way left on the little launch and he had no trouble holding her head where it was while Robin secured a line to *Prometheus*'s anchor chain. There was no time for a council of war. If they were going up, they would have to move fast. "I'll go first," said Richard and began to climb at once. There was enough tension to keep the chain firm even under his added weight, and so he swarmed up it without too much difficulty, even in his long, unwieldy robe.

At the top of the chain he paused, peering warily in through the hawse hole onto the forecastle head. The sun was shining strongly onto the green deck plates now, so that the air was full of the smell of hot iron and the glare hurt his eyes. Wherever the terrorists were hiding, there were none on the forecastle head. Hanging precariously, Richard gestured to Salah, then he turned back and dived through the oval opening onto the deck of his ship.

Like a parachutist making a textbook landing, he rolled for the nearest cover, hoping that the flash of his white robe would not be visible from the bridge.

He was still certain that someone—someone prepared to answer a hail or not—had to be on bridge watch. But it was early. It was bright. Any lookout would have to look straight into the low sun to see him. He reckoned he stood a good chance of remaining undetected.

A low whistle made him turn and his heart almost stopped. There was a terrorist crouching behind him. Only at the last instant before he launched himself into the attack did he realize that it was Salah. He had been concentrating so hard he hadn't even heard the Palestinian come aboard. His shock put things in perspective for him, however, and suggested the next step. Salah was wearing the international terrorist's uniform. With luck he could creep down the deck and see what was happening. As long as he was careful, it was quite feasible that he could get an accurate idea of everyone's whereabouts without arousing suspicion. Information that would be invaluable on Sunday when they came back with the Kalashnikovs and the thunderflash grenades.

Rapidly, whispering despite the fact that they were a quarter of a mile from the bridge, Richard checked that Salah was happy to risk a quick exploration. He was. Then, with a slap on the shoulder he was off, vanishing from Richard's sight among the forest of pipes running the length of Prometheus's deck.

Still taking care to remain concealed from any prying eyes on the bridge, Richard wormed forward from shadow to shadow until he had a clear view of the deck. Between himself and the bridge there lay an expanse of green-painted metal twice the size of a football field. The deck itself was simply green metal stretching from deck rail to deck rail where it folded down to become the tanker's massive sides. Partway in from the rails was a series of tank tops standing five feet high, carefully clamped closed. There were small lateral pipes running

from side to side between these, but by far the largest
feature on the deck was that central sheaf of pipes
stretching lengthways from just in front of him right
down to the bridge itself. Five pipes each side measured
six feet in diameter. Eight more beside them measured
from two feet to four. The whole complex of thirty-six
pipes was topped by a walkway running the length of
the deck. Immediately beneath this, along the narrow
tunnel between the pipes themselves, safe from all eyes,
Salah was running silently. It seemed so quiet, so safe,
that Richard was tempted to follow—but prudence
dictated that he remain where he was.

As the minutes ticked by, however, the wait became
well-nigh unbearable. He knew better than to look at
his watch—that would only make things seem worse—
but he counted his steady breathing unconsciously,
as though he were diving. So he knew well enough
that nearly ten minutes had elapsed before a tiny flash
of movement warned him that Salah had entered the
bridge-house.

During the next few minutes, while nothing further
happened, he almost convinced himself that the two of
them were in fact completely alone aboard.

But then his hopes were dashed and his darkest fears
revived as the first flat rattle of automatic gunfire rang
out.

CHAPTER ELEVEN

The run back down to Fujayrah was a disaster almost from the outset. *Katapult* got under way as soon as Hood returned with the Martyrs and Richard's orders, pausing only at an all-night fuel-supply dock to load diesel for the engine. Weary, still unhappy to be continuing with the top of the mast damaged and so many of his instruments out of commission, nevertheless acquiesced to the plans and took the con while Sam went down to get some rest. Martyr, still full of vigor, still half a day behind them in the need for sleep, kept that first watch with him and they struck up a working relationship—if not a friendship—during the long night watch.

Christine went below with Hood and took her dunnage pointedly through to the small, forward cabin Richard and Robin had hardly bothered to use. Hood's dark eyes followed her, clouded with confusion, and, as though aware of them, she first closed the door, and then she locked it.

So the first eight hours passed until the sun rose next morning. Martyr was near exhaustion now, and Doc, too, needed some rest. They simply changed watches: Hood took the con and Christine came up into the cockpit with him while the other two turned in.

The day was incredibly hot and, for all that, *Katapult*

was skating across the wind on a strong port tack, seemingly airless. Christine was a sailor—and her father's daughter to the last inch. After her release from the detox clinic, they had rebuilt their battered relationship during long summer days aboard his sloop *Chrissie* off Martha's Vineyard. She was at her ease here on *Katapult*, therefore, almost at home. "You don't need me for this," she observed to Hood, quite correctly. He would not require any help until they reached the end of this tack up near Queshm, where they would have to come about and head down past the Quoins out of the Gulf.

Because she was so much at her ease, so far from home, and so far from her memories, she did something she hadn't done in years. She simply slipped off her dress and lay back on the lazarette in the shadow of the sail, rubbing Ámbre Solaire onto her long, golden body. Her high-fashion bikini was a statement of new life for her: not since her father had brought her home had she dared wear anything like this. Heavy jeans and baggy shirts had been her fashion since—anything that would cover up her body and protect it from the eyes of men.

Even when she had come to work in the Heritage Mariner offices, she had followed a subtle variation of the same stratagem. Her hairdresser, enormously expensive but willing to follow orders, cut her hair carefully but unflatteringly so that it seemed as sexless as the clothes she wore, as the front she presented to the world.

Until now. In fact, she was an amazingly strong person. She had been through experiences that should have destroyed her but she had not allowed them to do so. Little by little, inch by inch, with her father's help but mostly through her own inherent strength, she had adjusted. Recovered. To such an extent that she could now, more than ten years later, dare to wear a bikini.

Hood glanced across at her, a pretty girl oiling herself up to sunbathe. And he froze. He had been looking at her out of the corner of his eye since they had first met. There was something disturbingly familiar about her. And now the memory clicked into place. A memory he had hoped was gone forever.

Back home in Detroit one last time before joining Weary in Sydney, he had attended the wedding of one of the members of his old platoon. It was a typical wedding, he supposed, except for the bachelor party. The best man had taken his duties far too seriously. There had been three strippers, oceans of alcohol, and stag movies galore. Most of the evening had passed in a thickening haze. None of the college-boy highjinks had appealed to him, but he had followed along rather than break things up. After a few hours, in a motel room out on the interstate partway to Grand Rapids, he had gratefully fallen asleep.

Some hours later he had woken again to find himself still in that crowded hotel room facing the TV set. On the screen in front of him, clear as crystal, writhed a maze of naked bodies. A hollow maze. A circle of bodies, at whose center lay a bed. On the bed, alone, a girl lay, stretched out and tied down with ropes. And as Hood had watched, something leaped over the writhing bodies and up onto the bed with the girl. The girl's face had reared up and he had reared up in answer to destroy the screen and spoil the party after all. But he had acted too late. For he would never forget that face beyond the rapist's shoulder, nor its expression. Try as he might. For the rapist had not been a man.

Like many seafaring men, he liked reading sea stories and he had started one last year. It had turned out to be less about sailing than he had hoped but he had enjoyed it well enough. One of the characters in the book had been a pornographic film star and a line of hers had been the last thing to trigger that most unwelcome memory. "If you're fucking people, you're still okay," she had said in this book. "But if you're fucking animals, then you're dead."

And glancing back, up out of the cockpit he saw again, but in real life this time, the face he had seen on the screen that night in the hotel room. The girl from the pornographic video.

He looked away at once, simply too stunned to know how to react. Then he heard her move. How carefully he must have been listening to hear anything at all over the sound of the wind in the sails and the rigging. The thought twisted his face with self-disgust. And that was the expression he was still wearing when he turned suddenly to find her standing immediately behind him. Her expression was impossible to gauge. Hood, normally supremely confident with women, felt out of his depth now. He schooled his face and tried to control his eyes. But the cool lotion had brought her honey skin out in gooseflesh. The points of her breasts showed plainly through the silken bikini top.

"You've seen some of my early work, I think?" The dry tone, so formal, so chilly, so Four Hundred, Vassar, Bryn Mawr. And what was she talking about? Pornography. Filth.

"Yes, ma'am, I believe I have." He kept his tone as dead as hers. As though he were talking to the Queen of England. But the atmosphere crackled around them.

"Magazines? Movies?"

Lord above! Did she really want to know? But there was a ritual air about the inquiries and he suddenly saw the hand of a psychiatrist here. Confrontation. It would

be a good way to go, if you had the strength. Every
time you saw that expression on someone's face, ask the
questions. Bring it out into the open. Deal with it.

"I saw it on a video, ma'am. At a bachelor party. I
smashed the set and then I left."

A fractional movement of her head. Almost a nod.
She turned and went below. Her back was long beneath
broad shoulders and her skin so pale as to allow the
down of fine hair that covered her thighs to gleam like
gold dust. He watched the way her bottom moved as
she swayed slowly down the steps.

And then he felt dirty.

And then he asked himself how he would have felt if
he hadn't seen the video. He would still have watched
her, probably, enjoying the sight of her. As though she
were a centerfold. But then the fact that she *had* been a
centerfold of the most degraded sort came and smacked
him in the face. Made him feel even more dirty. And
he began to wonder how much of this was his fault—
and how much of it was hers.

Doc didn't need much sleep. He could get through a
full, active day on two hours' shut-eye if he had to, but
he preferred four. It was when he slept too deeply or for
too long—or woke up suddenly—that his memory went.
This morning he still knew who he was when he awoke
and strolled into the cockpit just after nine.

"You alone?" he asked as soon as he saw Hood standing morosely by the helm.

"Looks like it."

"Where's the sheila?"

Hood was so preoccupied that for a moment he wondered what Weary was talking about—there was no
one called Sheila aboard. Then he remembered the

name was Australian slang for any young woman. "Gone below."

Weary's wide eyes narrowed. He picked up on the atmosphere at once and he didn't like it. "Anything I should know about?"

The confrontational method again, thought Hood, unable to get Christine out of his mind, discovering the unwelcome fact that everything seemed to revolve around her now. But he couldn't bring himself to tell Doc the truth. It wasn't actually his secret. Nothing to do with him at all, really. "No," he said. "Nothing."

Weary nodded, his bright eyes still speculative. He knew his friend well enough to trust his judgment. If Hood wanted to let it lie, then that was okay. He forgot about it and went to take the wheel, checking the feel of her through his fingertips as she self-steered toward the top of the tack. She was running gleefully across a steady breeze, every line of her alert. Not stretched yet, it took quite a wind to stretch her, but she was tail-up, and running like a hound to a strong scent. And as sometimes happened, Doc was overcome by an enormous sense of love for his creation. It overwhelmed him, and he enjoyed the feeling too much even to try to control it. He stood like a child awed by the strength of his creation and the emotion she brought up in him. He did not know it, but he was transfigured in that moment. The natural good looks of his open, cheerful face attained a kind of masculine beauty as though lit from within. He seemed to gain stature. The sun glinted off the wind-tumbled profusion of his hair and his dazzling eyes became luminescent.

When he looked down, unaware of how much time had elapsed as he stood in his reverie, he met the eyes of the girl he had just been discussing with Hood. She was standing in the companionway looking up at him. She had pulled her hair back and tied it in a ponytail. She was wearing an old pair of jeans and a baggy plaid shirt. Her face was devoid of makeup and looked as though it had just been scrubbed. He couldn't read the expression in her eyes but he was so overcome with a feeling of the goodness of life that he simply beamed at her and said, "G'dday."

And she smiled back. Against her will and better judgment by the look of things, but a smile nevertheless. "Good morning," she almost whispered, as though she couldn't trust her voice.

"I would've thought you'd have brought a bikini. To catch a bit of sun."

"No." Her voice was stronger. She came up into the cockpit. Beneath the rolled cuffs of her jeans she wore a well-used pair of topsiders, the same as the brand he had on himself. Sensible girl, he thought. "You want some coffee?" he asked. "Sam's getting some from the smell of things."

She shook her head and went over to the weather side of the cockpit where she perched on the coaming, looking away forward toward Queshm. The wind made her ponytail frisk about her shoulders and molded the shirt to her body, but Weary didn't notice. Twenty knots! He was thinking. With this rig. In this breeze. Christ! What'll she do in a decent blow. With the spinnaker up.

But this thought darkened his mood a little. They still hadn't had time to repair the top of the mast. If they were going to put a spinnaker up at the moment, he'd have to climb up there with a block and tackle first.

"Coffee, Doc," said Hood, coming up into the cockpit beside him. And as he did so, that strange, unsettling atmosphere returned. Weary looked earnestly down at his friend. But Hood had eyes only for the girl.

So that was it! thought Doc: old Sam had fallen in love.

"Hey!" he said, good humor returning to his voice. "You'd better get onto our nice new Navy radio and tell Rass al Kaimah that we're just about to come back out!"

They rounded the Quoins soon after midday, having come out faster than they went in, but here their progress slowed dramatically. They had been slicing across that unseasonal southerly, but now they had no choice but to run straight into the teeth of it. The afternoon was horrifically hot. The temperature in the desert of Iran immediately to the north of them spiraled past one hundred and forty degrees Fahrenheit in the shade and the air there superheated and began to rise as quickly as the temperature, sucking more air up the narrow channel of the Gulf of Oman. So the south wind intensified, blowing into their faces with almost storm-force pressure, unremittingly, as though physically trying to keep them back.

It was a gloomy, dangerous wind bringing no relief from the heat, merely moving northward the parched intensities of the Ar-rab al Khali, that great sand sea to the south of Saudi. Such cooler air as might have been tempted north out of the Indian Ocean was turned aside by the cliffs of Oman and kept well away to the south. But before it crossed the furnace of the Al Khali, that south wind had once been over the Gulf of Aden, and so it brought with it just enough moisture to cause a high scud of cloud. The cloud danced mockingly around the unforgiving, shapeless blaze of the sun and then began to thicken as that indescribable afternoon wore on, causing Hood, and even the cheerful Weary, to become narrow-eyed and worried.

In the face of that foul wind, they had no choice but to zigzag across the gulf from east to west, clawing their way a little farther south with every tack. But this procedure, hardly one unknown to yachtsmen, was complicated immeasurably by the fact that they were crossing and recrossing the tanker lanes. "Steam gives way to sail" says the old adage of the sea, but in the unlikely event of any tanker captain feeling like obeying it, there were too many pressures forbidding him to do so. The great ships were too unwieldy to turn quickly or easily. The progression of them, a seaborne caravan, was so closely packed here that to attempt any variation of course or speed would be criminally dangerous. Even to try to stop was a process that would take five miles to complete, such was the power of the forces acting on those gigantic bodies. No: Weary never expected to be given an inch. From side to side of the Omani gulf they skipped, therefore, in the teeth of the wind, close hauled as the broiling blast of it intensified, slipping between those great black hulks like *Argo* between the Clashing Rocks.

The atmosphere aboard reflected the atmosphere in the air. Chris said nothing to her father about her conversation with Sam. Indeed, she was still unsure how best to interpret it. Martyr could see clearly the way Sam Hood looked at his daughter, however, and he did not like it. Sam himself felt almost adrift, powerless in the grip of forces he could not comprehend, let alone control. He was repulsed by what he had seen the girl do and yet he could not keep his eyes off her. In the stultifying heat of the afternoon, the three men were wearing as little as possible but Christine remained fully

dressed, armored against Hood's gaze, which seemed to
her to be hotter than the wind.

At four they were off Rass al Kuh, a low, sandy point
backed by depressing-looking mangroves and the helpless shrug of the Kuh i Mubarak rising three hundred
feet behind. Jarshak Bay lay before them as the Iranian
coast turned almost due east. "Helm alee," called Weary
and spun her onto the new tack. Sailing upwind like
this, he preferred to keep the con himself. The configuration of the sails moved smoothly as the computer
followed his orders. The foresail and main thundered
onto new curves as the blade of the mast swung round
on the joint at its foot, and everything clicked into
place. *Katapult* leaned the opposite way. The coastline,
dead ahead, wheeled majestically and began to fall away
behind. At once they were back among the tankers and
as they gathered speed down the new leg, so one of the
monsters gathered itself out of the wind haze and began
to ooze across their bows. Weary narrowed his eyes,
judging the convergence of their courses, not wishing
to let her head fall off even by as little as a point toward
the north. Quite the reverse, in fact. So they clawed
across and up the wind, pulling over fifteen knots, directly toward that black iron wall nearly a quarter of a
mile long, low and formidable in the water ahead of
them.

The tanker was fully laden and sat nearly twenty feet
lower in the water than the empty *Prometheus*. Her
decks were less than twenty feet above the sluggish water, therefore. *Katapult*'s damaged mast would be level
with the rust-yellowed bridge-wings when they got
close enough. Nor would they have to wait long before
measuring the comparison. Weary, still in the midst of
calculation, brought her head up one more degree to

the south, putting more speed on her but bringing her
course dangerously convergent with the tanker's. The
rest of them gathered automatically to windward. *Kata-*
pult had no trapezes, indeed her whole design was calculated to minimize the need for acrobatics from the
crew—but her weather outrigger showed alarming
signs of lifting out of the water, so it was natural that
they should try to lend support. Christine, indeed, every bit as intrepid a sailor as her friend Robin Heritage,
jumped out onto the outrigger itself. There she stood,
holding on to the singing shroud while her father sur-
reptitiously strengthened his hold upon her lifeline.
The steady pressure of the gale whipped her hair loose
from its ponytail. It tugged at her shirt, ballooning it
one minute, molding it to her torso the next. The calculated danger excited her, taking her mind off Hood
for a moment.

The supertanker's massive hull was moving south
past their course incredibly slowly while at the same
time closing with them dangerously fast. Chris watched
it dreamily, her mind lazily echoing the calculations
Weary had already made. Most of her consciousness,
however, was simply overwhelmed by the sensation of
speed derived from being up here, reading the strain
of *Katapult*'s movement through the wide-spread soles of
her feet and the vibrato of the shroud in her hand. In
spite of the fact that *Katapult* was nowhere near full
speed, the tension formed between herself and the con-
flicting forces around her gave Chris the most exhilarating sensation she had ever experienced.

The raucous bellowing of the men's voices spoiled it.
Her eyes sprang open to discover the rear of the tanker's
bridge-wing sweeping by. Weary had judged the line
to a nicety, but at the cost of bringing them almost
within touching distance of the tanker's stern. And it

seemed that all the crew were there, pressed up against the after-railings, leaning over, many with binoculars, looking at Christine's erect, romantic, eminently feminine figure. Yelling incomprehensible but clearly pointed messages to her.

It was too much. The weight of her memory crashed back down upon her and she reacted, as she had trained herself to do, with anger. With a rage as powerful as the sensation they had just defiled. "Bastards!" she yelled up at them. She leaped easily inboard, her hands busy with her lifeline. As she tore it off, she found herself confronted by Hood, his hand half extended to steady her. "Don't you touch me!" she spat, far beyond rational control. "Don't you even look at me again." The strength of the emotion on her face made that gentle man fall back, and she was gone, pushing past him, down the companionway.

"What've you done to her?" bellowed Martyr, replacing his daughter, dangerously close to Hood.

"Nothing!" But somehow the word didn't seem true even as he said it. What he had seen made him feel guilty and that guilt colored the denial, making it a lie.

Without another word, C. J. Martyr reached for him. The huge New Englander would have taken him by the collar but neither man was wearing a shirt so he took him by the throat instead. Hood hesitated for a split second, tricked by the possibility that the old man had a right. What they had been through probably gave the Martyrs the right to punch the lights out of one guy in every five. But not him, he realized at last. Not Sam Hood. He brought his hands up between Martyr's forearms, knocking them aside. The gesture of resistance, slight though it was, drove Martyr wild. He hurled himself forward.

The whole sequence of events from the moment

Martyr first attacked had taken up scant seconds. Sam
was preoccupied by his part in the action. Weary, caught
off guard by the whole matter, was still trying to bal-
ance what was happening in the cockpit with what was
happening to *Katapult* as a whole. And the latter still
demanded his attention, for the multihull was creaming at eighteen knots straight under the massive stern of
the tanker, less than fifty feet from the churning maelstrom above its single screw. But then rational thought
stopped altogether as the forces that controlled them all
took over.

Just as they hit the first high swell of the tanker's
wake, newborn in that restless cavern below her overhanging counter, the twisting bodies of Hood and Martyr hit Doc and knocked him across the cockpit. As he
fell, he tried to keep hold of the wheel and so he tumbled awkwardly and struck his massive head upon a
stanchion. He fell back into the cockpit beside the two
writhing bodies, rolled over, and lay still.

Katapult pirouetted madly out of control. She spun
into the tanker's wake, outriggers threatening to tear
themselves out of the water. The blade of the mainsail
swung this way and that, threatening to rip its boom
out of the mast. And, with a sound like a whiplash, the
foresail tore free and flew overboard until brought up
short by the last ten feet still firmly attached to the far
end of the forward telescopic boom. The whole mast
shivered to come down and only the steel shrouds held
it together.

The bulk of the tanker, less than forty feet away now,
began to suck at the helpless craft. It had created a vacuum in both wind and water because of its massiveness,
and already *Katapult* was slewing over toward the suction of the thrashing propeller blade, preceded by the
billowing dacron of the foresail. In all too few mo-

ments, it seemed, first the sail and then the craft herself would be sucked in and pulled under and chopped to bits.

This was the situation Christine found when she ran back up the companionway. Weary was out cold. Her father and Hood seemed to have fallen on top of each other, and neither of them could be counted on to help. The actual sequence of events never occurred to her. It simply looked as though something catastrophic had thrown them into confusion. She was in action at once. The foresail was gone by the board. Should she try to jettison it? She didn't know how. Her first priority in any case was to get *Katapult*'s head round and force her out of the vacuum here. How quickly would she answer the helm? Especially with the sail out there? Again she didn't know. Only one way to find out, she thought.

Katapult's momentum had carried her partway across the tanker's wake and even as she reached the wheel, Chris could see the foresail begin to spread out down the back of a wave, as it slipped even farther toward the propeller, pulling *Katapult*'s head round after it. Without any more thought, she hit the sail furl buttons and both mechanisms kicked into life at once. Some very strange noises indeed began to come from the leading edge of the mast where there was no sail to be furled, but, good as gold, the boom began to telescope inward, pulling the floating sail along with it. But this of course only served to turn *Katapult*'s head more quickly. She needed power to put a stop to that. Chris spun the wheel over hard aport and hit the big red button to start the diesel. As soon as it kicked to life, she pulled the telegraph handle to full astern. Like a motorcar going into reverse, *Katapult* began to inch back and into the dead air, away from the suction of that great screw, along the line of least resistance.

As *Katapult*'s forward motion toward destruction slowed, Chris rose onto tiptoe, looking around for other shipping that might pose a threat, already planning ahead. If they went under, there was nothing she could do. But if they pulled free, she would need all the information she could get. The next tanker down the line was a good three miles behind. There was a big one inbound coming up, however, and she didn't want to end up under that. If she did get them out of danger, therefore, she would have to turn around and motor back the way they had just come. She allowed herself one quick glance at the useless bundle of humanity on the cockpit sole. Jesus, she thought, men were a bloody nuisance. All over you when you didn't want them, but the moment you needed some help . . .

Then she forgot them and concentrated on keeping *Katapult* easing back as the forward boom telescoped slowly down, pulling the heaving, twisting sail back out of harm's way.

Her dad was the first one to make it to his feet, but he was still dazed and wasted time hanging on to her shoulder saying, "What . . ."

"Come on, Dad, snap out of it. Go and see to the foresail, will you?"

"What . . ." There was a bright streak of blood on his forehead at his hairline. She would have liked to have had time for sympathy. "Come on, damn it! We're not out of this yet! Jesus!" She hardly ever swore. She didn't smoke or drink. She held herself down hard all the time. But not now. She couldn't afford to be quiet and controlled now if she were going to get them out of this alive. And, all of a sudden, she was surprised to discover how much she did want to survive. "Damn it, Dad, will you wake the hell up?"

But then Hood was there and his eyes were at least

clear. "The foresail," she yelled at him. "Get the foresail out of the water before it gets tangled in the tanker's screw!" He didn't even pause. He saw as clearly as she did that this was their only hope. *Katapult* was almost dead in the water now while the pull of her own propeller fought the power of the tanker's. "As soon as we have it in," he yelled, grabbing her father and pushing him up onto the foredeck, "you hit full ahead and come to starboard."

"I know what to do, for God's sake! I just can't do it until the sail is out of the fucking water!"

But she called it after their retreating backs and within moments they were both at the end of the retracted boom, pulling in the sodden sail, hand over hand. As the weight of it came out of the water, so *Katapult* at last began to make a little sternway. Chris took in a great juddering breath and kept it in, watching through slitted eyes as the wringing bundle on the deck grew and grew, straining to know the first moment she could ease the throttle slightly. *Katapult*'s diesel did not like running full throttle in reverse like this and was beginning to run dangerously rough. A little more sternway. She eased back slightly. The wild note dropped out of the engine sound, but the multihull hesitated again. Damn! If they would only hurry! Then she felt her head spring free and Hood, unnecessarily, shouted, "Go!"

As *Katapult*, at Chris's command, began to move forward, starting to swing right as she moved, so the two men heaved the last of the sail out of the water and swung it up onto the running deck. The whole pile of it tumbled backward as they did so, exploding against the mast-foot and drenching Chris at the wheel. She was so busy spinning the helm hard over that she didn't even notice. Oblivious to the fact that her shirt was clinging to her like a second skin, she was completely caught up with the necessity of bringing *Katapult* round in the tightest possible U-turn and heading her, innocent of canvas now, back under the tanker's stern toward the long shallow bay they had just tacked out of between Rass al Kuh and Jask.

Once again they came near the tanker. Once again the air was filled with the sound of male voices shouting indistinctly. But as they passed back into the wind shadow exactly astern of her, the quiet air suddenly made the sounds clearer. And Christine looked up, surprised to discover that there were no wolf whistles this time, only cheers.

CHAPTER TWELVE

Weary exploded awake jerking and writhing on the sole of the cockpit with such force it took two of them to hold him down. His huge, leonine head thrashed from side to side. His startlingly blue eyes rolled, empty of any knowledge. It was as though he were having a seizure. Christine wasn't repulsed or disturbed at all. Quite the reverse. She had done this sort of thing before, helping the other inmates of the detox clinic. She wrapped both her arms round his right arm and hugged it to her, frowning with concentration while Sam went through what was clearly a ritual, reminding him who he was.

"Who're you?" Doc's bright blue eyes were suddenly fixed on Christine's green ones. The massive head rose off the deck. His fist closed on her shirtfront, screwing it up until it seemed as though he would tear it off. He pulled until their faces were scant inches apart. She felt herself being sucked in. The irises shaded from the near white of the sky at dawn to the indigo of evening behind the first bright star.

"I'm Chris, and you're Doc," she said gently, calmly, joining in the therapy. "You're Doc Weary." And Doc knew who he was again.

And who they were: "Hi, Chris," he said. "What's up?"

"Hit your head."

"Did I? I don't remember. Jeez!" He began to struggle up. "What's going on?" They let him go and he was on his feet at once, striding over to stand by the wheel, looking past the sodden mass of the foresail to the dun-colored coast of Iran. Ras al Kuh was back on their port bow and the whole bay stretched out before them. Behind the flat water, a low series of sandbars elevated themselves into dunes before collapsing into swamps beyond. It was a dangerous lee shore, shallow and poorly charted; but it was all they had. Yelling explanations, recriminations, congratulations one to the other, they dropped the anchor, letting *Katapult* swing until she faced the wind and the hook took firm hold, leaving a couple of fathoms of clear water beneath them.

It was late afternoon by now, nearly five local time. They had little more than an hour of daylight to complete their damage check. The fiercest heat was going out of the day and the wind beginning to die down, but this was no cool evening nor any sort of an atmosphere for heavy work. Yet the work had to be done, and so they set to it.

First Doc climbed the mast using footholds so cleverly designed that those few visible seemed to perform an aerodynamic function. After a few moments' close inspection he called down, "Sam, it looks quite fair up here."

"No more damage?"

"Not even from switching it on after the sail ripped out?" Chris couldn't believe it. She had had visions of the complete mechanism being destroyed by her desperate action.

"No. That wouldn't do this system any harm."

She started checking over the jumble of drying sail with her father, trying to put it into some kind of order for ease of further handling. She had changed back into the bikini and if anyone had noticed, no one had made any remark. Up and down the front of the mast went Doc, peering into the thin vertical opening at the mechanism inside. At last he crouched down beside the joint with the telescopic boom. Chris moved up and crouched beside him, fascinated. No sooner did she do so than she felt a firm touch on her upper thigh. She jumped like a startled colt. Her whole body flinched. She looked up, eyes wide. But it was only Doc, preoccupied, trying to catch her attention, with no idea at all of the effect he was having on her. He was holding a stub of metal out for her to see. "Main masthead retaining clip," he said. "What holds the top of the foresail in the furling mechanism. If it fails, the sail falls down. And look at it."

He crouched closer, his left knee thrust between her thighs, to brush the front of her bikini. All his attention on the clip, moving it so that she could see how it was cracked from side to side.

"Design fault," she said. "I'd sue the builder to hell and gone."

"Too bloody true!" The grip on her thigh intensified; then it was gone as he levered himself erect. "Sam," he called, striding past her. "Look at this. Ten-dollar clip nearly cost us a quarter-of-a-million-dollar boat. Can you believe it!"

By sunset he was back aloft, sitting in a makeshift boatswain's chair secured by block and tackle to the damaged masthead. By 18:45, he was satisfied, and they rethreaded the sail back into the front of the mast, securing it safely into a spare set of clips. By 19:45, they were ready to sail again and by then the unusual meteorological physics of the day had been reversed by the relative coolness of the night. The Iranian desert, under clear skies, was little short of freezing; a brisk "northeaster" sprang up to push them quickly south. In moments, Weary had plotted the rhumb line to the dumping ground and they were off again on a course slightly to the north of it, trusting the tide and weather to drift them safely into position above the explosives. Somehow, during all of this, the watches had changed their composition so that when Hood went below to prepare supper, the watch mate who accompanied him was Martyr.

Chris stood by Doc, shoulder to shoulder. Her eyes followed his in the practiced sweep from instruments to water ahead. And they needed to keep a keen-eyed watch. They were showing running lights, as were most of the other ships in the dark gulf, but there might be some coastal craft in the vicinity who didn't bother with such niceties. The tankers, every one of them showing the legally required running lights and additional lighting, nevertheless posed a more subtle threat. They were so large, and were, as usual, following in such close sequence that it was possible—no, disturbingly easy—to become confused by the distance between bow and stern lights, and try to sail through the middle of the tanker itself rather than before or behind it. This danger was compounded by the absence of deck lights or any lights visible in the heavily curtained bridge-houses except the dimly illuminated navigation bridges themselves. And, of course, almost all the tankers' hulls were black, making them absolutely invisible in the dark.

Total concentration was needed at all times. But in the way of practiced sailors, they kept up a conversation at the same time.

"What's it like when you can't remember who you are?"

Doc paused before answering. No one had ever dared ask him this question before. "When you were a kid, did you ever wake up in the middle of the night all alone and afraid of the dark?"

"Sure."

"I mean really terrified for no reason at all. No nightmares, no monsters, no nothing: just the dark."

"I guess. Sometimes."

"Well, it's like that. Only the darkness is inside, somehow. And I don't know where the light switch is."

"The light switch with your name on it."

"Got it in one. When I know who I am, everything comes back to normal. But . . ."

"Yes?"

"But my memory's not always there. You know what I mean? One minute I'll be looking at something familiar, a knife, maybe, or a spoon, and the next I'll be thinking, well this is really great but what is it called? What does it do? A *spoon*, mind you, and I can't remember what it's for."

She stood in silence, weighing it up. Which was worse? Too much memory, or not enough?

"What's your problem?" he asked, like her, going to the heart of the thing with childlike directness.

"What problem?"

"Start with Sam. What's that all about?"

"He . . . I don't know how to explain it. He knows something about me. . . ." She could feel herself blushing in the dark, her cheeks burning with embarrassment.

"Go on," he prompted gently. "You can tell Doc. I won't hold it against you. Chances are I won't even remember it when I wake up in the morning."

She began to laugh, but then with a strange kind of emotional lurch she realized he meant it seriously. Literally. Her whole body began to shake. She held on to the low windscreen in front of her and took a deep, deep breath. "Okay. It started when I was just a kid in high school. Ninth grade. There was this guy selling drugs . . ."

When Martyr brought his daughter up a cup of soup, he found her so deep in conversation with Weary that he just left it convenient to her elbow and went away again, feeling like an intruder. He joined Hood and heard, much as Robin had done five hundred miles south of here, the story of their meeting. At once he saw the dangers to the boat and to his daughter of a man whose memory did not work, but Sam put his mind at rest. "Funny thing, Mr. Martyr," he said in that deep, gentle, strong bass of his, "I've never known him to switch off in action, you know? Unless he hits his head, like this afternoon, he's always clear as a bell when there's anything to do. But if he's resting, say, or just sitting around, then it can sometimes slip away from him. I remember we were anchored off Silhouette just a couple of weeks ago . . ."

"*Sam!*" Doc's voice interrupted the conversation.

"Yeah, Doc?"

"I think we're coming up on the right spot. You want to start checking with the echo-sounder?"

They dropped anchor just after 23:30 and decided to go down at once. Richard had described the box he wanted in careful detail, especially after his bad luck with the original. As long as there were no unwelcome visitors down there to disturb them as he had been disturbed, they should get the thunderflashes up and stowed within half an hour. Then they could all get some rest and sail again at dawn.

Sam and Doc suited up. They would dive while Chris and her father pulled the boxes carefully aboard and checked them, leaving them on the afterdeck to drain. Robin's wetsuit was too small to fit either man, so they split Richard's. Doc got the leggings and Sam the top. Both men had their own flippers for snorkeling, and the masks and tanks were standard size.

Vividly aware of Richard's warnings about marine life in this area, they both took spear guns and powerful torches with flotation chambers, designed to rise quickly to the surface if they were dropped. Quietly, tensely, they went over the simple routine they had worked out, then it was time to go down into the warm, inky water. They rolled off the back of the lazarette, side by side. Christine put the bright waterproof guiding lights in the water, the beacons that were designed to vector them back to *Katapult*. For a moment Chris could see them, two bright yellow beams shading to green as they went deeper. Then there was only an occasional, secretive glimmer and the sound of the bubbles among the other restless sea sounds in the night.

Chris and C. J. Martyr sat at *Katapult*'s stern, legs dangling, close together and silent. So much had happened since they had boarded the Concorde at JFK that they felt a little like new people, like strangers starting a new relationship. Chris was at the heart of the change, changing herself, swiftly as a chameleon today alone. Her own head was spinning so much that she had no idea how the changes might seem to an observer, but she was aware of nothing special except that she had somehow come to terms with the look in Sam's eyes. She was pleased she had handled *Katapult* well in a crisis. Had her father asked her, she might also have admitted that she proposed to wear bikinis more often in the future. And that she wanted Doc to come back, safe and sound and soon.

He exploded out of the water at their feet so unexpectedly that they both jumped. There had been no warning of his approach because he had switched off his torch while swimming toward the brightness of

Katapult's guiding lights. "They're there," he gasped. "Sam's sorting out the ones we want. It's a mess down there. I'd like to meet the criminal bastards who mixed that lot all up and then dropped it overboard. I know Richard only asked for one box, but we'd better bring a couple up in case there are more duds." They threw him down the line to secure to the first of the chosen boxes and he caught it easily. Then, with a wave and a wash of water, he was gone.

This was not Doc's idea of fun. As he switched on his flashlight and powered back along *Katapult*'s sleek hull toward the anchor chain, pulling the rope behind him, he turned over in his mind what it was he had become involved in. He liked the Mariners. He respected them, both individually and as a team. He wanted to help them and he wanted them to help him and Sam. But the thought of charging around a supertanker armed with Kalashnikovs and thunderflash grenades really had to give him pause. He thought he had left that sort of thing in Vietnam. And yet. And yet, the more he thought about it, the more he had to admit that it excited him. The prospect of action. Of going back to the edge one more time before settling down to build boats and make babies and grow fat and happy.

The first box was sitting waiting by the anchor as agreed. No sign of any others yet, or of Sam. He hung there, secured the rope to the handle at its side then pulled twice. The line tightened, the box stirred and began to slide across the sea bed. He turned to follow it up.

Sam Hood was swimming purposefully in the opposite direction, carrying another of the boxes close to his chest, trying to get out over the long drop where he could get rid of it safely. It was one of the broken ones, one of the ones Richard had warned them to be particularly careful with. But the warning had been in vain. There was something going on inside it Sam did not like at all. There was something hot in there. Something trailing a thickening stream of bubbles behind it. Although smashed, the box remained stubbornly impenetrable, its lid locked, its sides damaged with cracks too narrow to admit prying fingers. God knew what was in there. Some grenades for certain—he had just been able to make them out in the beam of his torch. But there was something else there as well. Long pipes, like candles: flares of some kind, maybe. And one of them had ignited, he had no idea how or why. It just had, a cloud of bubbles giving it away. As soon as it became clear the thing was not going to explode at once, he decided to take the calculated risk of moving it. This was a small box. Light. He reckoned his chances were okay. And anyway, if it went off close to all the other stuff it would probably set off a chain reaction that would blow them all out of the water.

Dare he drop it yet? Not really. Heaven knew what the detonation would do to Doc's head if it went off too close. Especially after this afternoon. Hood felt sorry about that. His reaction to the girl and her father had resulted in Doc getting it in the head once more. Well, not again. Not again today.

It must be coming up to a minute now and nothing had happened except that the flare had started the plastic round the grenades to melting. He shone his torch down, the beam powerful enough to show him the sea bed, still close at hand. Littered with boxes and piles of rubbish. But close beyond, a cliff edge, and over that a bottomless abyss by the look of it. Another thirty seconds away. Another thirty seconds couldn't hurt.

Weary broke the surface and handed the box up as though it contained eggs. Fabergé eggs. Chris leaned forward to take it, eyes like emeralds shining in the dark.

And the sea seemed to catch fire. A brightness spread through it, white at its heart, shading through the color of Christine's eyes to black again. And above it, the surface heaved up so that Weary found himself looking at a hill of water. Not a wave. A hill. Then the shock hit his body like a charging horse.

Chris and C. J. acted in concert and like lightning. Even as the hill of water was forming, they reached down so that when the shockwave threw him back, they caught his arms and tore him up out of its grip onto the deck. Then, as *Katapult* rushed forward to swing, rocking round on her anchor chain, the three of them were huddled together beside the box of grenades on the afterdeck. The sound was like the slamming of a huge door close by.

None of them spoke. First they held each other and the box. Then they prayed the anchor would hold them. Then, when it had done so and the water was dark again, Doc hurled himself back down into the seething blackness.

Swimming with manic speed, he followed the anchor chain down, only to pause. Coming up toward him in the dark distance was Sam's torch, its beam shining purposefully upward in the darkness. With a grunt of relief, he swam toward it, waving his own torch to signal. But Sam, probably stunned by the blast, just kept coming steadily upward. Doc pumped his legs until they popped and creaked, swimming toward his friend marveling that even the torch had survived, supposing that Sam must have found some shelter from that blast.

But then, something made Doc pause and hang motionless in the water. He had been swimming back along *Katapult*'s length. The brightness of the lights at her stern was striking down through the water more powerfully than his own torch beam. And yet it failed to reveal anything behind the circle of brightness Sam's torch was throwing. More slowly now, and with a sinking heart, he swam down toward that puny light. It was surprisingly close at hand, shining dazzlingly into his face. At last he gripped it and his fist closed around Sam's wrist behind it. "Ha!" he shouted, in an exultant cloud of bubbles, and he pulled his friend toward the light. Only to find himself falling backward in the water, fighting to understand why Sam's bulky body moved so easily.

But then he understood fully. Even as he saw, in the brightness behind the boat they had built together, the torch, the hand, the arm.

And that was all.

The rest of Sam was gone and the torch had floated upward alone, still gripped by that dead hand.

They pulled him out of the water and on to the lazarette together. He had brought nothing back with him. He had simply reared out of the water, clearly in terrible distress, and come toward them, fighting to get aboard. They pulled his twisting, shaking body up onto the afterdeck. Then, three abreast, they had guided his stumbling frame down into the cabin. Once there, Martyr left them, going back to secure all aft.

Chris took off his face mask, and the headband came with it. The cowlick of hair lifted to show that great, scarred forehead.

His eyes were everywhere except on her eyes.

"Doc," she said gently. "Tell me, Doc. Is Sam dead? Is that it?"

"Sam?" said Doc. "Who's Sam? Who're you? Who am I? *Sweet Christ almighty, who am I?*"

CHAPTER THIRTEEN

The shots rang out down the length of *Prometheus* and Richard was in action at once. He rolled forward to the edge of the forecastle head and swung easily down. The pipes that ran along the center of the deck did not end abruptly. They plunged into the tank system below like plumbing for giants. He had to turn sideways to squeeze among them but then he could hurry forward, as Salah had done, at a slight crouch. The stench of oil was overpowering down here, and, with the shadow so deep in contrast to the sunlight, he had the crazy impression he was wading through crude. But even this failed to slow him. He ran on, fearing the worst.

Midships, he met Salah coming the other way and they took the risk of pausing for a hurried conference. "What were those shots?"

"Warning fire. Making a point. Not as bad as it sounds, Richard. They were shooting over their heads."

"Why?"

"I don't know. They're all in the gym, just as you reckoned. All twelve terrorists are in there with them. I can't find out anymore. Something's going on but I don't know what. I get the impression it won't take much longer, though, and when it's over the terrorists will all be out again. Back on watch."

"What makes you think that?"

"I checked their watch stations. Bridge, engine room, where you suggested. There were cups of coffee still warm. Stuff half eaten, half done. They'd just gone into the gym when we came onto the scene. They'll be coming back out soon."

"Right, That's it. Let's go." As they turned, Richard checked his watch. "We'll be on our way back here, in thirty-six hours. I hope it stays calm until then!"

They got off in the same way they had boarded and set sail as soon as possible. If Salah was correct, they had been lucky to get this far unobserved, and it would be a pity to hang around too long and make the terrorists suspicious after all. But they had been successful. They had confirmed *Prometheus*'s position and the disposition of the enemy. It had been a worthwhile reconnaissance. With all of them in high spirits, they motored back to Bahrain as quickly as they could. After an idyllic day's cruising across the Gulf, which even that stiff, hot southerly could not spoil, they arrived just before sunset and went ashore at once.

This time there was no polite policeman awaiting them. In fact nobody seemed to remark their arrival at all. They went straight to Angus's apartment. Here, Salah, who had become very quiet during the day, abruptly requested the loan of a djellabah and some robes. Within moments, the Palestinian had transformed himself into an innocuous figure who would blend with the local populace. "I have a visit or two to make tonight," he said. "I will be back by dawn."

"Anything I can help with?" asked Richard at once. "Need a good man to watch your back?"

Salah wavered. He was bound for the Soukh and had meant to go alone. He had contacts in the ancient market—or used to have contacts there—who might give him some information. Especially as he had found two further clues on *Prometheus* that he had definitely not discussed with the Mariners yet. But going into the Soukh alone was dangerous for a man such as himself. Especially if he had to reveal his true identity to too many people. There were many in the Soukh who would happily see him dead. Or who would also quite happily inform the authorities that he was there. In either case, Richard would prove invaluable. On one hand, a face-less, dangerous bodyguard. On the other, a powerful friend who would not easily let him vanish into some hellhole prison without making a fuss about it. But there were dangers for Richard as well. The Palestinian's wise eyes glanced across to Robin, who was studiously look-ing out of the window. Angus stepped into the breach at once. "Robin," he said quietly, "let me take you out to dinner. I will find you the finest meal Manama can offer."

And she turned to him with a brittle smile. "That would be lovely," she lied.

Like the Medina and the Kasbah, the Soukh was effec-tively a medieval walled city. A huge labyrinth of tiny, twisting streets leading into and out of each other in seemingly endless profusion. High, forbidding walls, windowless, featureless, alternated with bright shopfronts selling all kinds of wares, for this city within a city was dedicated to one thing only: commerce. The two men, apparently unremarkable Arabs, arrived just after the sunset prayer. And they did so just in time, for soon the gates would be closed to outsiders so the night's business could begin. Richard had been here before but was over-whelmed anew by the intensity of the place. As he was in disguise, he was not pestered by boys demanding alms or offering wares for sale. Instead, he had some leisure, though not much, to look around himself.

The gates to the Soukh were huge, carved in wood and adorned with black iron. They would fill the high stone arch of the entrance completely when closed, forbidding entry to all the rest of the world. Inside them the clamor began at once. A clamor that threatened to overcome ears, eyes, and nose alike. A million voices, it seemed, trapped by the walls and the buildings within them, demanded, demurred, cajoled, chatted, begged, and bargained. Radios and televisions mingled conversations, car chases, high, wailing songs, and occasional gunshots with the noise. Livestock bleated, bellowed, neighed, lowed. Cars revved their engines threateningly and hooted their horns imperiously. Dogs—a great profusion of dogs—barked, snarled, yapped, whined, and howled.

The odors of the place varied constantly according to the vagaries of the heavy breeze. The stink of camel dung would be replaced in a breath by the scent of sandalwood; the carrion stench of open butchers' shops piled with offal would give way to the aromas of simmering curry or the fragrance of bread baking in roadside ovens. The eye-watering fumes of dye from boiling vats or great hanks of vivid yarn hanging to dry would, in a single step, be replaced by the perfume of fresh dates and green figs. The putrid emanations from leather being tanned in shallow baths of urine would mingle with the bouquet of oleander, japonica, mimosa.

His eyes were at first dazzled by the kaleidoscope of color, shape, and movement, which slowly resolved itself into the visual counterpart of all he could hear and smell. Immediately within the gates was a square from which many roads led off in all directions. In the center of the square stood a great water trough. All round it clustered animals drinking and pens for those that had drunk. Camels he saw at once, and goats and a few lean

sheep. No cows or pigs. Oxen. Donkeys. Horses. Around
the patient herds swirled people. Light-skinned and
tall, dressed in dark blue and black. Dark and wiry,
dressed in plain white djellabahs and multicolored kaffiyahs, as they were themselves. Boys in little more than
vests. Stately gentlemen in fine sleeveless overrobes.
Shy women in black abbahs with gold filigreed chadors
over their faces, gold chains falling from beneath their
headdresses to hang above their huge, kohl-dark eyes.

"Come," said Salah at his side in whispered English.
"We'll start in the Street of the Carpet Makers."

Together they crossed the busy square and dived into
the dizzying swirl beyond. The Street of the Carpet
Makers led away to the right and it was as though the
throng from the central square had simply been
squeezed into it like toothpaste. On the pavements,
such as they were, and on the narrow roadway, lay carpets. Individually, flat. In piles, in hillocks. In bundles
rolled like logs or standing erect like multicolored for-
ests against tall walls. In shopfronts that were little
more than stalls open to every passerby. In exclusive
establishments that would not have disgraced Knights-
bridge or Fifth Avenue. Here the smells were of dye
and dust, of rope and of age. The sound remained overwhelming save that no cars drove here and the rumble
of footsteps was muffled by millions of pounds' worth
of rugs. At the most exclusive-looking of the shops,
Salah paused. There were no customers in evidence
within, nor anyone paying particular attention to two
more shoppers thinking of entering.

"Wait by the door. Pretend to look at the carpets, but
keep an eye on the street. Say nothing." Salah spoke in
a barely audible whisper and they were in.

The air-conditioning hit Richard like a bucket of ice
water; he was surprised his breath did not come in

clouds on the air. A tall man came forward and sa-
laamed. The two of them performed the same courtesy,
then Salah was escorted into the dark recesses within
and Richard found himself alone. He began to exam-
ine the exquisite workmanship on those carpets nearest
the door, keeping a careful eye out through the plate
glass. Soon he became fascinated by the way in which
the carpets were thrown into the road. When he had
first come across the practice, he had assumed that only
the cheapest rugs were put there as a sort of advertising
gimmick. But later he discovered that this was not so.
Sometimes the most expensive carpets were put out for
anyone to walk on because the constant motion of so
many feet tightened the knots in the carpets' weave and
made them stronger and more priceless. In fact, some of
the most priceless carpets in the world, tradition had it,
were left in the roadways outside villages near Bokhara
or Tabriz for the better part of a year so that the footsteps of passersby could finish the weavers' work in the
summer, and then the winter snows lift out the dirt to
leave them fresh and clean.

"Richard!" He spun round. It was Salah, holding two
small shoulder bags made of carpet. Richard had seen
many people carrying them here this evening, for traditional robes had no pockets. He took the one offered
and, feeling its weight, looked inside. His eyes flicked
up to meet the Palestinian's calculating gaze.

"They are necessary. Vital. We have come to do
business. We must be seen to mean business. And if we
do not need them for tonight, we will find a use for
them soon enough."

With a sudden imperative sense of danger, Richard
slung his bag over his shoulder. If he let his hand hang
casually inside it he could easily grasp the butt of the
machine pistol it contained.

Then they were out in the suffocating miasma of the street. Richard felt his whole body prickling with sweat and resisted an urge to scratch. A man immediately in front of him felt no such inhibition, however, and luxuriously scratched his right buttock. The result was a huge damp patch on the crisp white cotton, through which could be seen the garish patterns on his underwear.

"Where next?"

"Let's try the Street of Gold."

As with the Street of the Carpet Makers, the name described the trade. Every piece of pavement, stall, shop, emporium, was given over to the smithing and selling of gold. It could be seen molten in crucibles, being stretched into wires or being beaten into silver-gilt; being etched, stamped, filigreed, set with precious stones. Made into finger rings, toe rings, earrings, nose rings. Anklets, bracelets, armlets, necklets, waistlets, and belts. Chains, bangles, medals, medallions, stars, shapes of a thousand different sizes and significances. The place reeked of the smelting fires, of the seething metal. It rang with the tintinabulation of the goldsmiths' hammers. The jingling of golden bracelets and bells; the ticking, striking, and chiming of all those golden clocks.

"We'll be quick here. It's just a hunch. We've only got an hour for the whole thing."

"Why that little?"

"That's how long it'll take them to find us."

"Them?"

"The police. You've met Captain Suleiman?"

"Yes."

"You'll be seeing more of him soon."

On that word "soon" they entered not a shop but an alleyway between two shopfronts. It was narrow—Richard's broad shoulders brushed the walls on either side—and dark. They reached a recessed doorway, a deeper shadow in the shade. "You are my bodyguard," whispered Salah. "You speak no Farsi!"

Too bloody true! thought Richard, and they were in. Five men sat drinking fragrant coffee on rugs more beautiful than any Richard had just seen. Three big bodyguards almost as tall as Richard stood around them. They all looked up as Salah entered, not unduly surprised to see him.

"*Salaam*," he said, and launched into a dialect Richard did not understand. He stood motionless, right fist closed on the gun, ready for action. Only his left hand might betray him. He had hidden it in the folds of the robe, for it was not the right color at all. And his eyes, narrowed in his tanned face half hidden by the kaffiyah.

But then, he thought, as his racing mind explained Salah's last, cryptic remark, only an Aryan Iranian would have such blue eyes in any case. And such a man would be bound to understand Farsi, the language of other Aryan Iranians. He looked around the room more closely.

The conversation switched from Salah to the others. Their accents were no more comprehensible than Salah's had been, but their body language was universal. We'd love to help, but . . . Sorry.

Out in the alleyway he inquired, "Waste of time?"

"Not at all. They seemed to be telling the truth. That was the point." He glanced either way. They were alone. "The PLO know nothing of the people who took your ship and your wife's father. I bought the guns from a man with Libyan contacts. Khadaffi had nothing to do with it. The men we have just seen represent the current government of Iran. They, too, know nothing."

"So, three simple negatives have wiped out almost all the possibilities."

"Yes. Whoever is doing this to you must therefore be small, independent, and probably unsupported."

"Just twelve men? No backup . . ." Richard was shaking his head with disbelief even as he spoke.

"You are right of course. It cannot be quite that simple. There are risks in taking the cover and reputation of terrorists. These cannot simply be criminals in disguise."

"And there can't only be twelve of them. There may be twelve on *Prometheus*, but who has Sir William? And where?"

"Well, let us be off. Time is short."

"Where now?" asked Richard as they hurried on down the alley, away from the Street of Gold.

"To the Street of Pearl."

"Why there?"

"To get wisdom." Salah chuckled in the shadows. "You have a saying, do you not? Wisdom comes in pearls?"

The Street of Pearl was the oldest and narrowest of all; the deepest in the whole market and the closest to its heart. It twisted from its opening at the corner of the Street of Silver down to a gate only slightly smaller than the gate into the Soukh itself. On the pavement sat tubercular-looking men of indeterminate age with hollow cheeks and great bony chests; displayed before them were scraps of silk piled high with the fruits of their difficult, dangerous labor. These were the pearl fishers. In the stalls and little shops there were more pearls, varying in size, shape, color, setting. There was mother-of-pearl, shell of all kinds, coral of every description. And in the window of the greatest of the shops, a display to take the breath away. Seed pearls drifted like dunes of white sand on saharas of black silk. Cultured pearls clustered in piles like tiny tennis balls. Natural pearls, round, translucently white, from the size of a pinhead to the size of Richard's thumbnail, scattered on beds of black velvet. The huge misshapen pearls they gathered from the sea beds here, twisted into fantastic shapes: drops, vortices, clenched fists; bigger than the others by far. Then, resting on white silk, pink pearls from the Orient. And, placed reverently upon white velvet at the pinnacle of the display, legendary black pearls, from the South Seas and beyond.

A glance was enough to fix it forever in his memory, then he was following Salah, dazzled, down toward that massive door. In the right wing of the great portal there was a smaller entry. Here Salah knocked, and here they were admitted. If Richard had been dazzled before, now he was stunned. They had stepped out of a busy, noisy, smelly street, into a haven of absolute peace. As the tiny door closed behind them, the bustle of the street became muted and a tinkle of falling water replaced it. The hot odor of thronging humanity was alike excluded and in its place a zephyr laden with the scent of flowers. The courtyard must have measured seventy feet on each side. It was paved and colonnaded with marble. At its center stood an oasis in miniature. Above on every side the building rose, story after story, each level having balconies to overlook this quiet, fragrant place. The tall sides of the building were further augmented by towers that Richard could just make out as silhouettes against the star-bright sky. Their domed tops scooped in the high, cool air and funneled it down here.

"Up," said Salah and they crossed to a stairway and climbed.

The room they entered a few moments later was dimly lit and silent. Empty, except for a frail old figure seated in a tall wooden chair. From the way he moved his head toward them as they entered, Richard suspected

at once that he was blind. Proximity confirmed his
guess. The old man's eyes were as white as the pearls in
the street below.

"*Salaam eleikum*," Salah greeted the old man with
something akin to reverence. And received a nod in
return.

The two of them stood, hesitating for a moment,
until the old man said, "Please be seated, gentlemen."
With a hiss of surprise, Richard snatched out his machine pistol and whirled. This had to be a trap. A micron
behind him, Salah mirrored his action. The old man had
spoken in English.

Now he chuckled with delight. "No, no. Put your
weapons away, please. You have not been betrayed.
That is, you will have been by now of course, but not
by me. It was a simple trick. A trick, no more."

They began to relax. The old man continued to speak
calmly and quietly. "I have been expecting you of course,
Salah. I am not surprised that you have brought your
English friend to me. This is, after all, my area of expertise. No one knows the truth of what is going on, so you
have come to me for a story."

As they sat, cross-legged at his feet, Richard asked,
"How did you know I was English?"

"European. That was easy enough. Your walk, your
shoes, the odor of your body. Your nationality and identity beyond that, Captain Mariner, simple intelligence.
Intelligence of both kinds: my informants told me you
were here soon after you arrived—and why. So when
Salah comes through my door accompanied by a tall
man of European extraction with a sailor's walk, who
else could it be? But this is childishness. And arises, I
admit, from a liking for the tales of your Sherlock Holmes in my youth."

The blind eyes smiled again. The voice continued, frail but clearly audible, sibilant, like sand sliding on silk. "And, expecting you, as I was, I have found a story that I hope will be of interest to you. Though I myself, of course, cannot vouch for its relevance or truth."

Richard glanced over at Salah. The Palestinian was listening, apparently rapt. Richard began to do the same.

"Some thirty years ago in the city of Dahran, a rich young man fathered twin girls. These were the earliest days of the European "swinging sixties," when London seemed to beckon the rich and the young of all the world. And so the rich young man took his one wife and his two daughters and he went. In London he became seduced by Western ways and at last he sent his girls to an English school, where they were educated after the English fashion. The girls were very close, as is often the way with twins, and the schooling made them closer than ever. In fact they did not separate at all until they went to university, which is, I believe, the natural end of such schooling. One studied to become a doctor, the other to become a journalist, or so I have been told."

Richard was growing restless. He would be damned if he could see the relevance of this, but he trusted Salah, and Salah was still hanging on the blind man's every wheezing whisper.

"And then an accident occurred. The car in which they were driving was run off the road by a drunkard and the wife was killed. The man was lucky to survive. Increasingly sickened by life in London and sure that he owed his own survival only to the direct intervention of Allah, blessings be upon Him, he returned to the bosom of his family in Dahran. Once there, he realized the enormity of his mistake. For the women in Dahran had not been infected by Westernism. They behaved modestly and correctly. How different were his own girls. How soiled had they become. How far had they been seduced from the true way.

"At once he commanded that they return. But one was a doctor now, and married against his wishes. The other was a reporter of some kind. They both made excuses and refused. Duty and obedience were things he had paid a fortune to have educated out of them.

"So he resorted to a stratagem. He announced that he was dying and begged them to come home so that he could divide his fortune between them. The reporter came at once. The doctor, in the middle of a divorce, did not. As soon as she arrived in her father's house, the reporter was locked away. Her life as a Western woman was over, she was told. All outside contacts were broken. She was given an abbah and a chador and she became like the other women. Slowly she acquiesced. It was difficult for her, no doubt, but she adapted. Tried to please her father. Worked to become as he wished her to be. And eventually he trusted her enough to let her entertain some acquaintances, for she was lonely, and the father was not a cruel man, merely a misguided one. These were acquaintances that he had selected for her, of course. But then, his indulgence of the girl betrayed him yet again. He found an Englishman whose friendship he thought would make her happy. This man was not a young man, but he was newly turned to the way of Islam. A man of great potential with business contacts all over the Gulf, from Syria and Iran to the Emirates. A seafarer. A captain. A merchant of some consequence and standing."

"Forgive me," interrupted Richard, courteously, "but did you say an Englishman?"

"I did. But like yourself, perhaps, looking less English than he really was. Looking more than he was in every other respect, however. For behind the foolish father's back, he seduced the girl away, stole her from her father's house, and they vanished into the night. It is said they went to Benghazi or Trabulus. And not as lovers, but as revolutionaries. She, they say, was afire to release all women from what she saw as the thrall of men. And he, too, had his own *jihad*. They vanished and they trained. I know nothing precise beyond these things. But within a year a new group had sprung up. The Dawn of Freedom, they called themselves. Thirteen in number. Owing no direct allegiance. Admitting to no known paymaster. Following no dogma. And remarkable in this: that they were led by an Englishman and a woman."

Richard sat silently, arranging his thoughts. The story's relevance remained elusive. Its credibility was suspect, in his mind at least. Oh, the English papers were always full of stories about Islamic fathers taking back their sons and daughters after their mixed marriages had failed. And he remembered reading of at least one terrorist who had turned out to be English. He had no doubt that the International Maritime Bureau could furnish him with more cases if he asked. But both situations merging like that. Was it possible?

He was still deep in thought when Salah heaved himself erect and began to make their farewells. Somewhere an electronic watch alarm went off and the old man smiled. "You set it as you left the carpet-sellers. For three-quarters of an hour, I hope. You still have to leave the Soukh."

"I was hoping to rely on your hospitality," said Salah quietly. "I would assume the gates are closed to us now."

"I assume you are correct as always. And yes, you may rely on my hospitality. It has yet to be violated, even by the importunities of this execrable century."

He turned his head toward Richard. "All true courtesy died many years ago. Everything now is rush and demand. Nothing is duty or correctness. Truly, this is a terrible time to be alive."

A man appeared in the shadows at the back of the room, ready to conduct them out through some hidden way. Richard paused, wondering how best to frame his thanks. The old man, sensing his stillness and divining the reason for it, raised a hand. "Come back and thank me later," he whispered, his voice like snake on tile. "You may ask for me anywhere in the Soukh. Ask for . . ." He paused, perhaps for dramatic effect, and smiled his secretive smile. "Ask for Sinbad."

"What was that all about?" asked Richard in the back of an old Lincoln Continental, working out its final years as a taxi. It was completely indistinguishable from the rest of the traffic, multilighted, bright chromed, high finned, and bald tired, blasting its way across Manama.

"He is the most reliable source I have," answered the Palestinian. "And he has yet to let me down. The one thing I didn't tell you about the terrorists aboard *Prometheus*. I heard most of them speak. Yelling orders. Having discussions. I listened outside the doors of the gym. I couldn't see their faces, or the color of their eyes or skin. But of two things I am certain." He turned to Richard and lowered his voice dramatically.

"One of them was a woman. . ."

"And one of them was English . . ." whispered Richard.

CHAPTER FOURTEEN

Richard climbed out of the taxi immediately outside Angus's apartment block and walked across the narrow strip of pavement toward the door. As he pressed the button on the entry phone, a figure stepped out of the shadows in front of him and he found himself face to face with Captain Suleiman. "Shall we go in?" asked the policeman, sliding a passkey into the security lock.

"Certainly."

Even this late—it was well past ten—the heat outside was such that the air-conditioning shocked Richard. But he showed nothing except polite interest in his questioner.

"You have been to the Soukh?" asked Suleiman as the door closed behind them. Richard glanced back. The taxi was still outside, surrounded by policemen. How wise they had been to split up before he returned.

"The Soukh? Indeed I have!"

"Alone?"

"No. An old friend acted as a guide."

"Salah Malik?"

"That's right."

Suleiman paused for an instant, weighing things up. "What was your business there?" he asked eventually.

"We were trying to find news of my father-in-law. And my tanker *Prometheus*. Or who's holding them."

"You did not go to a shop on the Street of the Carpet Makers?"

"We did."

"And bought there?"

"Two bags made out of carpet and, I believe, two Heckler and Koch MP-5 machine pistols. I didn't do the buying myself and I didn't inspect the guns too closely, so I can't be absolutely certain about that."

"I see. You realize that the unlicensed sale of fire-arms is forbidden in Bahrain?"

"Of course. Though I should emphasize that I was not myself involved in the purchase. In fact I had no idea there were any guns in the shop." On that slightly pompous, mentally rehearsed note, Richard paused at the lifts. "Are we going to continue this in the common parts? Or would you prefer to use Mr. El Kebir's flat?"

"The flat. They are not back from dinner yet."

Richard made no comment on the fact that Suleiman had Angus and Robin under surveillance. Nor on the fact that he had a key that fitted Angus's door. Instead he switched on the lights, crossed to the bar, poured two fruit juices, and offered one to the captain. Then they sat.

"Yes, Captain?"

"After the carpet seller's where did you go?"

"The Street of Gold. I'm afraid I can't be more spe-cific. There was an alleyway. In the house we ended up in, everyone seemed to speak Farsi. I'm afraid I didn't understand much."

Suleiman nodded. So he already knew about that, too, thought Richard. They had made the right deci-sion then. "I'm going to tell him everything," he had told Salah. "There are no secrets in the Soukh."

"'There are no secrets in the Soukh.' It could almost

be a saying of Omar Kayyam," Salah had said. "And so true."

"And then, Captain Mariner?" Suleiman called him back to the present.

"The Street of Pearl. There's a big place at the end. We talked to a blind man there. Liked Sherlock Holmes. Called himself Sinbad. Not much more I can tell you than that, I'm afraid."

"It is something, Captain Mariner. I had no idea that . . . ah . . . Sinbad, as you call him, had such tastes." He paused. "And then?"

"We left. Salah said something about running out of time."

"Just so. And the guns?"

"Salah has them. He is taking himself and them off the island, I believe."

"*Alouette* is being watched."

"Of course she is."

"Not much of an adventure for such a night."

"Really, Captain, I don't know. I didn't go for adventure, but for information. And all I got was two bags I don't like, two guns I don't want, and a story about twins and English Muslims I don't understand. Do you have anything more?"

"Nothing. But if Sinbad told you the story, it will be relevant. More so than anything I could tell you."

A silence fell and the two men, apparently casually, took the measure of each other. That final, weary admission that the blind storyteller had been of more use than the police softened Richard and he let the mask slip a little.

"What I have done tonight, with Salah. Is it highly illegal? Will our activities embarrass you?"

"Not unduly so. The fact that Malik has been here,

perhaps a little. It is like a joke. He comes and goes as he pleases—a man with contacts like that, it is hardly surprising. Today it is I who am the laughingstock. Tomorrow it will be another." He paused. Sipped. Watched Richard.

"The buying of the guns is another matter. Now I could make that unpleasant for you if I chose to. You were right, by the way. They were MP-5s. Either you looked more closely than you admitted, or you know guns."

Richard refused to be drawn on that point. "I knew they could be a problem as soon as I saw them," he admitted. "If you chose to make them so."

"But I do not."

"Why?" asked Richard at once, alert to the philosophy of the East whose poor—utterly inadequate—translation was, "I'll scratch your back . . ." The ubiquitous quid pro quo that ruled some people here.

"Because, as you say, you did not buy them. And if I chase the man who did, I shall be pursuing a chimera, a ghost. And if I prosecute the man who did not, everyone will know, and . . ."

"You will be even more of a laughingstock?"

"Perhaps."

"So, what do you propose to do?"

"Nothing."

"Nothing?"

"For the time being."

"I see. And what might we have to do in order to make you take action against us?"

"You wish me to take action against you?"

"Of course not. And I'm not being facetious, Captain. I really do not want to break your laws and upset your professional conscience."

"I believe you, Captain Mariner. That is why we are

having this conversation, and having it here. I see you—and please correct me if I am wrong in this—I see you and your wife as being law-abiding citizens, caught up in a situation where you feel you must take action."

"Yes."

"Because if you do not, then no one else will."

"Yes."

"Even if that action contravenes the law."

"It's more complex than that."

"Even if you find yourselves associating with people who are outside the law."

It was not a question. Richard did not answer it. He had nothing to say on the point.

"Even if you have to put lives at risk. Starting with your own lives."

Richard remained silent a little while longer, watching Suleiman. "Do you know the saying," he asked at last, " 'Needs must, when the devil drives'?"

Now it was the policeman's turn to be silent. Then he tossed back the rest of the drink. "So what you are telling me is this. You and your wife are caught in a situation over which you have no control. But you are people of action, let us say, and so you try to take control. And you call upon anyone you know who can help you in this. It is understandable."

"Given that we know the right kinds of people: murderers, terrorists . . ." Richard tried to keep the irony from his voice. With limited success.

"Yes. I was, perhaps a little heavy-handed yesterday." Suleiman did not sound unduly contrite.

"Your concern is understandable, Captain. But I have no intention of doing anything on Bahrain that would cause you or the Bahraini government any embarrassment."

"I think I believe that, Captain. And, of course, the real object of your actions is to punish the people who have already embarrassed the government. And myself. By taking Sir William from our airport. That is why I am content to remain a laughingstock. In the short term." He put his empty glass down with a decided click on Angus's coffee table and stood. "In the *very* short term."

The other two came in at 11:30, Robin running to Richard at once, laughing with relief at seeing him safe and well. Angus left them in each other's arms and went upstairs. In this apartment he had two spare bedrooms as well as his own. In one of them Richard and Robin were camping. In the other he had set up the radio equipment so that they could stay in contact with *Katapult*. They hadn't set up a proper routine yet, but Angus, in charge of communications, reckoned that Martyr, Chris, Sam, and Doc would just have dropped anchor. If they were all asleep, he would probably get no reply, but if they were up and about, Richard would want to know before he went to bed. Well, he'd see. He glanced at his watch as he sat down. 23:45. Give it fifteen minutes. No reply by midnight and he'd turn in himself. He turned to *Katapult*'s frequency and pressed TRANSMIT.

"*Katapult*, *Katapult* this is base. Are you receiving me? Over . . ."

Robin's kiss of welcome had changed into something else entirely and after the blunt danger of the Soukh followed by the knifepoint negotiation with Captain Suleiman, Richard was more than ready to respond.

Just as Robin's body had felt full of fat and ugliness to her as she had walked beside her friend in the airport, now it felt full of heat and yearning. The extra curves

her imagination kept adding to her still-slim frame
were no longer those of sagging, stretched ugliness:
now she saw her body in her mind as being full of vibrant voluptuousness, like the bodies of Indian maidens
carved into the erotic friezes of pagan temples. The
thought inspired her almost to a frenzy of passion. Every square inch of her skin glowed. Her right hand
found the hair on the back of his neck and curled it
around her fingers, raising her need almost beyond controlling. Her breath was coming in gasps as though she
had been running. Her cheeks burned, her head swirled.
The rest of the world withdrew very far away indeed.
All that seemed important—immediate—was in her
head and in her arms. She had never felt quite so full of
desire before. It was glorious.

Richard swept her up off her feet and carried her
across the room, her face still pressed against his; her
lips still burning against his own, slightly swollen and
silky with desire. He fumbled with the door handle,
impatient to be out. Her hand slipped down his neck to
massage his tense shoulder beneath the crisp cotton of
his djellabah. She had been eating fresh pomegranates
and with every gasp she filled the air with their perfume. When he found the handle, he paused and risked
another kiss, pressing his lips down onto her waiting
mouth. The tips of their tongues touched with a sensation like an electric shock. The door opened outward
and he stepped through it, pressing her to him closer
still to keep her shoulders clear of the frame.

That action crushed her breast against his chest and
even through the layers of cotton and silk, it was as
though their hot skin touched.

He strode across the hall and paused at the foot of the
stairs, glancing up to make sure they were clear. Where-
upon she twisted lithely, fluidly against him and pressed

her mouth to his neck below the lobe of his ear. The tip
of her tongue traced languorous lines in the fine hair
there working upward—as he mounted the first steps—
to the lobe itself where her gentle teeth took over.

By the time he reached the landing above, he was
gasping with breath every bit as short as hers—winded,
like her, with desire. Her tongue lazily followed the
folds of the outer ear, pausing in its erotic exploration
only to whisper the secret endearments that had become a most potent part of their lovemaking during the
last ten years. Her golden curls filled his face as she
moved her lips against him, full of the warm incense of
her perfume. Glancing quickly at the spare room where
Angus's voice monotonously repeated *Katapult*'s call
sign, he crossed to their bedroom door. It was open.

Pressing her against him again, reveling in the feeling of her firmness, he carried her into the bedroom
and released his hold on her legs. Her grip on his neck
did not slacken—it intensified and he took her gently
but firmly under the arms with broad, strong hands,
holding her head level with his as that fragrant cloud of
hair was replaced again by the burning beauty of her
face. Her eyes were closed, her mind at once far with-
drawn and utterly immediate. Her lips were hot and
silken, her tongue wantonly probing. The heels of his
hands pressed round her ribs into the resilient firmness
of her breasts and, with every lithe muscle in her long,
strong body at full stretch, she slid down the front of
him, out of that fetal position he had held her in, to a
full trembling pressure down his entire length. He
felt—as she made him feel—every curve of side and hip
and thigh as though they had been naked, oiled. And
when she was there, her feet still inches from the warm
Bokhara carpet, her arms still tight around his neck,
her honey-slick lips sucking at his, she moved against

him again, with every liquid fullness and hollow of breast and stomach and belly. And as she did so, deep in her throat, she began to purr, like a great golden kitten.

One gold-strapped evening sandal fell to the floor.

And,

"Richard," called Angus, his voice tense with alarm. "Richard, it's Martyr, speaking from *Katapult*. There's something terribly wrong. . . ."

They spread the chart on the bedroom floor and crouched over it, planning with desperate speed while Angus relayed ideas and suggestions feverishly back and forth, stunned by the massiveness of the blow.

"They're here." Robin's finger marked the spot deftly as Angus rattled off the figures. Richard was already calculating. "Four hundred and ten miles as the crow flies. Over five hundred by sea. Fifty hours flat out in *Alouette*. Out of the question. We need a plane."

"Or a chopper," said Robin.

"Or both."

"Not tonight," said Angus. "I can scare you up whatever you need in the morning, but not tonight."

"Right, ask them if they can hang on until the morning." Angus spoke into the radio.

"Martyr says he can do more than that. Once Doc's quiet, he and Chris can sail *Katapult* out of there."

"Right. That's good. We'd have had to board her at sea in any case. Can they get round Hormuz and into the Gulf?"

Angus spoke into the radio.

"He says they got her out. Back should be easier."

"Right. Then it's just a case of time and rendezvous point."

"I can get you in the air by nine. In whatever you want going wherever you want."

"Okay. But if we fly east in a small jet for speed we want to be able to pick up a helicopter somewhere along the line to get us aboard *Katapult*."

"Like that Navy chopper from the *Mississippi*," said Robin.

"Can you do that, Angus?"

"Get the air-sea rescue boys? Yes, in an emergency."

"So we're definitely up at nine. Down and in the helicopter by twelve. Looking for them somewhere by one. That's near as damn it twelve hours' time. Where can they be in twelve hours?"

"Shall I ask?"

"No. Martyr hasn't got the chart, has he? Not by the radio. And from the sound of things, Chris's got her hands full. Jesus, what a mess."

"They could get here in eighteen hours. Maybe less," observed Robin, pulling him back onto line. Her long finger, with its short-cut, boyish fingernail, rested squarely on Fate. As it did so, a single, huge teardrop splashed down onto the sea beside it. "It's a good rendezvous anyway," she persisted. "Bloody great oil rig in the middle of the sea lanes. Hard to miss even in the afternoon, from *Katapult* or from the air. That's where I'd meet them. Unless," she offered, "you want them to go into harbor somewhere."

"And give the whole thing up?" He tested the suggestion. Examining her true meaning. Had they gone too far? Should they call a halt now? Hand everything over to the authorities after all? All they had to do was tell *Katapult* to head for the nearest port and it was all over.

"No . . . you can't." Oddly, it was Angus who spoke. "You can't do that. We're too close. You can't chuck it in now. Robin's right. Get on to Salah. Tell him what's happened. Then you can all go at dawn and meet them at Fate sometime tomorrow."

"Right." Richard slapped his hand down onto the Gulf chart. "That's it, then. We contact Salah, then get a jet first thing in the morning to take us down to Sharja. Air-sea rescue helicopter out to Fate. We'll meet them there in eighteen hours' time. Just before sunset tomorrow."

"Martyr," said Angus at once into the microphone, completely unaware of any double meaning, "it's Fate. . ."

CHAPTER FIFTEEN

Chris ground the whole length of her body down against Weary's tossing form, arms and legs spraddled, trying to control him. "It's all right," she said soothingly. She felt like screaming at him but she knew that would do more harm than good. She imagined strength into her spread limbs, therefore. Believed weight and substance into her long frame, and pinned him to the bunk by the simple force of her will. And as she did so, she fever-ishly searched her memory for the magic litany of phrases Sam Hood had used to bring him out of this.

Sam Hood. The thought of him brought tears to her eyes and she blinked them fiercely away. She had only known the man for a day and had spent much of that time hating him for what he knew about her. So why was she crying for him? Above and behind her, she heard her father speaking urgently into the radio but had nei-ther the leisure nor the inclination to listen to what he was saying.

"It's all right. Don't be frightened. I'm here. It's okay. Try to remember. You're Doc. Doc Weary. Born Hal-loween, in Perth, Australia." No, that simply wasn't right. And a name. Hood had called him a full name. What was it?

She couldn't bear to look into those hurt, terrified little boy's eyes of his. Instead, she buried her face into the hot angle between his shoulder and his neck, whispering like a lover while her mind raced.

"You're Doc Weary. Born Sydney, Australia, November fifth, nineteen forty-eight . . ." That was better, she thought. It was coming. "William Weary, born Sydney, Australia, November fifth, nineteen forty-eight."

But still he twisted and bucked beneath her. She rose against him, forcing him down with her hips, arching her back and breathing deeply. And so it was she noticed that his hair had fallen back, revealing the great scarred dome of his forehead. The sweatband! It came to her in a flash. The sweatband was his security blanket. Like her old plaid shirt and tatty jeans. He would never come back without it! It was in the bundle of gear under the bunk. She reached down for it.

At once his freed hand was round her neck, forcing her down until mere inches separated their eyes. "Who am I?" he screamed.

And, in the midst of the crisis it came to her. The answer. "Albert Stephen William Weary. Born Sydney, Australia, November fifth, nineteen forty-eight. Don't be frightened, I'm here with you. You're Doc and you're going to be fine." Her hand scrabbled among the rubber, fingers searching for that discarded strip of elastic toweling. Terrified instincts telling her to scream, struggle, tear free of his overwhelming power, and run. Cool, calm mind delivering the words gently to her softly whispering lips. And something started stirring in the lost depths of his eyes.

Pain.

Of course, it would be. He had run away into his nothingness because of the pain of Sam's death, and here she was calling him back to face it. To suffer it. But she had no choice. Things needed to be done that only he could do. And he couldn't stay away forever.

Her fingers found the sweatband and she let go of his other arm, rearing up again against his weakening grip, thrusting both elbows into the mattress just above his shoulders. Still speaking soothingly, the calm tone never faltering, even as that second arm whipped around her waist, crushing her down again, she stretched the headband carefully and slid it gently over his head with shaking hands.

And suddenly the pressure on her was lessened. Suddenly his lips were moving in a silent echo of hers. "Albert Stephen William Weary . . ."

Until his eyes came to life again.

For a time they lay as they had been, bizarrely like lovers, crushed against each other on the bunk. From who knows what hidden recesses deep within her, a terrible warmth washed over Christine Martyr then. Affection that she had kept dammed within her for nearly fifteen years burst its barriers at last and flooded out of her long green eyes in tears. So, as the pressure of his arms about her neck and waist slackened away at last and his strong, broad body lay absolutely still beneath her, she pressed her lips down on his lips and she kissed with all her might. She did not know if he responded. For now she did not care.

After unnumbered, delirious moments, she broke away, gasping for breath. She looked down into the blue eyes that were watching her quizzically. Into a face as soaked in tears as her own. And when she spoke, her voice was broken, husky, as though she had been screaming for hours. "Welcome back, Doc," she said.

And he said, "Welcome back, Chris," as though he knew how long she, too, had been away. Now it was her turn to look quizzical, and his turn to reach up and move gentle fingers across her forehead into the long spun gold of her hair. Then her father came down the companionway and so she rolled off him and sat up.

Martyr hesitated in the doorway as they looked up at him. He was slightly confused for a moment, almost disoriented. Something seemed to have changed during the last few minutes. Something beyond Sam's death. Something almost as crucial. He felt certain of it but he could see no evidence of it. Only Weary, back to normal, sitting beside Christine on the bunk.

"They'll meet us at the old Fate platform in about eighteen hours," he said. "We'll have to get moving if we're going to be there."

They had two important duties to perform before they could up anchor. They had to stow the box of thunderflashes and they had to find some way of saying good-bye to Sam. Sam had been a preacher's boy. He kept a Bible and a service book with him at all times. So, after they had put the box of grenades beside the Kalashnikovs in the lazarette, they read a prayer over Sam. It was as simple as that. Unreal. Pack away the thunderflashes, read a prayer over Sam.

They pulled up the anchor and got under way at 01:30 local time.

The south wind that had been coming and going over the last few weeks was a phenomenon related exclusively to the fierce heat of the day. At night the prevailing wind returned, blowing stiffly from the north. For the next nine hours, they cut across this at speed until it began to falter in the midmorning. But by that time they were well north of Sirik. When the wind died, they tacked easily in the dead air and waited for the southerly to spring up as it had done at this time every day. And it didn't let them down. While Martyr was checking on the radio with Angus at base, Chris and Doc set the sails and waited for the first furnace gust. It came within minutes and built to that steady rush of air they had grown used to. *Katapult* leaned steadily away from it and sped southwest across it, her automatic knot meter clicking up from fifteen knots through twenty to twenty-five. It was exhilarating sailing, and, but for the dark cloud cast by Sam's death, they would have been ecstatic. Even so, Weary called across the keen song of the wind, "You wait till we put the spinnaker up. Then you'll see something!" They hit a long comber and white spray exploded back across the cockpit, soaking them.

She stripped her shirt off and let the spray hit her flesh, completely at ease in the bikini now. And yet the fact of this caused a twinge of memory and guilt. She looked across at Doc and he was frowning. Of course he was, she thought. She was herself, now. Well, let him mourn. There would be time enough to make him smile. Then, having nothing else to do, she leaped up to her favorite perch, on the weather side, by the shroud. "Put on a safety line," he called at once. "We'd never be able to stop in time if you went over." She was happy to do so. Especially as she realized that, for all his sad preoccupation, he had been watching her all along.

As they sailed back in through Hormuz without even deviating from the rhumb line that would take them down to Fate, Martyr reported in again that they were running tight to time.

They sighted the old platform at 16:15 local time and were beside it in ten minutes. They were all exhausted after the long, exhilarating run and, as Doc hit the buttons controlling the automatic sail-furling equipment, they looked around themselves, as if surprised to be here. *Katapult* began to pitch in the chop as the way came off her, that damaged mast moving in jerky arcs across the hard blue sky. A sense of anticlimax gripped the three of them as they stood gazing about at the empty sea.

But then Chris's sharp ears heard, above the slapping of the water on the hull, the whine of the wind in the minimal rigging and the distant surf-rumble of the waves against Fate's great hollow legs, the rhythmic throbbing of a helicopter engine. At once she was searching the sky with shaded eyes. And there it was, high in the air almost due south, riding the wind toward them. It was overhead within minutes and the first figure was being lowered onto the afterdeck. It was Richard, and after he had landed, he paused there to guide down first Robin, then Salah. Then the Mariners ran forward while Salah oversaw the lowering of their luggage, boxes, and bags.

The six of them assembled briefly in the cockpit while the helicopter thundered away. But they split into teams almost at once. Salah, uninvolved with the planning of the course, took the con—more as lookout than steersman because they weren't going anywhere yet. Martyr, in charge of the radio in Sam's place, reported safe arrival to Angus in Manama. The other four went below.

No sooner were they in the cabin than Richard had the chart on the table. "The current weather pattern is set to hold for the forseeable future," he began. "So it seems we can rely on southerlies during the day building up to gale force in the late afternoon, and northerlies at night. We really want to head west and we can get across either wind fairly efficiently." He glanced down at his watch. "If you agree to my rough sailing plan, Doc, then we can be away at seventeen hundred hours on the dot. Now here's what I propose." They all leaned forward as he gestured over the sand, purple, aquamarine, and white of Admiralty chart number 2858 spread out flat before them.

"Here we are at Fate. Here's where we want to be, at Bushehr. There is no direct course we can sail because the Iranian coast comes out so far down here, but it is three hundred and fifty miles as the crow flies. Clearly we have to dogleg round the coast of Iran, so we have to go west and then almost due north. But if we simply do that, then we lose a great deal of advantage from the wind and *Katapult*'s speed.

"So what I propose is this. First, we set a course southwest down to Zarakkuh here. That's one hundred and eighty miles. We'll have this southerly to run across for another hour or so, but then we should have that northerly at our shoulder until we're there. By my calculations that should be at oh two hundred hours tomorrow morning.

"At Zarakkuh we tack into a northwesterly course, which gives us a second leg of three hundred and thirty miles to a point out here about twenty miles southwest of *Prometheus*. From the moment we tack until dawn we'll be going across this northerly sailing upwind, but from dawn onward we'll have the downwind reach, and we can really get up some speed. I've allowed twelve hours for that and so we should be in position for our final tack at fourteen hundred hours tomorrow.

"About twenty miles from *Prometheus*, we make that final tack. It won't be much of one—just enough to bring us in at full speed. We'll have that southerly, at near storm force, steadily under our tails and, knowing *Katapult*, we can get across those last few miles in no time at all. They won't be expecting us. Even when they see us they won't suspect anything. What will we be, after all? A pleasure boat only just in control, running down the wind far too fast. We'll go alongside her at full speed, showing off, and get tangled in her anchor chain. While Chris and Robin make a meal out of freeing her, the rest of us go up the way Salah and I went up last time. Then we move down the deck under cover of the pipes."

He looked around at their faces, trying to read the thoughts behind them. Martyr's lean figure suddenly cut out the light from the companionway. "All clear with Angus," he said.

"Right," said Richard. "Seventeen hundred hours local. By this time tomorrow *Prometheus* will be free. Let's do it."

Salah stood almost at the top of the mast, looking out into the gusty afternoon. He had climbed up the footholds at the front and then turned so that the raked upright leaned back behind him and the shrouds stretched out from their junction just above his head, convenient to his hands. The boat's motion had moderated as her head swung into the wind, and now he found himself staring up and out at Fate. The huge platform towered above him, all rusty sands and russets and reds. A spider's web of girders stretched between its four great limbs and there the wind sang even more loudly than the surf thundered against the hollow iron members. With the power of the sinking sun throwing brightness and shadow starkly across it, the disused platform looked solid, businesslike, threatening.

And it felt to Salah, looking up, that there was someone hidden up there, looking down at him.

Then the others came cascading up into the cockpit. "Seventeen hundred hours," sang out Martyr, the log keeper. "Under way at seventeen hundred hours."

CHAPTER SIXTEEN

They tacked in the darkness off Zarakkuh at 2 A.M. precisely, having established their position by dead reckoning and checked it by the stars. As they settled into the long upwind reach, their speed fell off initially, but the northerly was steady at about force five on the Beaufort scale, more than enough to keep them creaming along until the first few gusts from the south came over their shoulders soon after dawn. It had been obvious from the outset that they had three watch teams of two. Richard and Robin took charge of their progress from Fate to Zarakkuh, then woke Salah and C. J. The four of them oversaw the tack and then the English couple went to bed.

Weary and Chris were up with the dawn, refreshed by a long sleep. Doc came-to knowing who he was, even after the better part of twelve hours' rest, though Chris, at his side even before his eyes opened, was haunted by the way he kept looking for Sam Hood. They did not relieve Malik and Martyr at once, preferring to do odd jobs around the boat and double-check everything that might let them down at the last moment.

As soon as the southerly puffed into existence, Weary retrimmed the sails, and the multihull took off like an express train. The wind rapidly built to force seven, twenty-seven knots without variation, and *Katapult*'s knot meter raced past thirty as she exploded joyfully through the white-backed waves. It was only then that the two senior watchkeepers retired, salt-rimed and soaking, to get what rest they could below in a hull that reverberated like a gong as she smashed through every comber. It was exhilarating sailing, the kind *Katapult* was built for—and she still had not reached the limits of her specifications. Richard and Robin rose for lunch and the four of them spent an exciting couple of hours as though they were boating off Portland Bill with no dangers approaching and no deaths at their door.

At two, twelve hours after the tack at Zarrakuh, they tacked again onto the other side of the downwind reach. Weary spent five minutes fine trimming the sails while Richard held the con, then suddenly, Doc hit Chris on the shoulder and they were off, agile as monkeys, about some business they had secretly planned. Chris passed down the side of the forward boom while Doc vanished momentarily from Richard's dazzled sight, only to reappear halfway up the mast, climbing rapidly, a block and tackle over his shoulder, trailing ropes.

"Good God, they're . . ." He turned, speaking, to Robin, but she had guessed what they were up to at the same moment as he had, and was gone to help them.

High on the mast, Weary made the block and tackle secure at the base of the damaged section, then shinned back down again at top speed, to career across the bucking, spray-washed deck. Chris ran back and hit a button on the dashboard that Richard had hardly noticed, and from the forecastle head, a jib boom began to telescope outward. Robin was laying out the ropes ready. Lazy sheet, after-guy, fore-guy down the midships; the sheet and the lazy guy. It was all ready with amazing rapidity, as though the four of them had crewed round-the-world racers together for years. Then they were back in the cockpit again, Weary beside Richard at the helm. "Now, Captain, you just keep your eye on the knot meter, please," yelled the Australian over the sound of the wind and the sea. "I want a witness to this. *Go!*" And the three of them were heaving on the ropes as Richard fought to keep the wheel from chucking him overboard. Miraculously, breathtakingly, beyond the luff of the foresail, reaching out on that new boom and spread across the wind at once, soaring up to that straining tackle high on the mast, bloomed the spinnaker.

Katapult flew.

Her attitude changed. Her head lifted. It felt as though the whole of her central hull jumped out of the water and soared from wave crest to wave crest leaving only the outriders in contact with the sea. And the knot meter, *Katapult*'s speedometer, clicked up remorselessly. Thirty-five knots. Thirty-seven. Thirty-nine. Forty. At forty knots she held steady and Richard felt her settle into it. The exhilaration was complete. The captivation of his senses total. It was an experience so real, so super-real, it had a dreamlike quality. It was impossible that such ecstasy should last. But last it did, with the wild spume flying; the rigging howling; the winches, cleats, plates, and blocks that held it all together, all groaning to break free; the slap and thunder of the waves against her; the ecstasy of holding the thrilling helm-spokes in his fists: all of it lasted and lasted.

Martyr and Salah came up, dazed, into the grip of it and stared about themselves in dumb wonder. All of them stood or sat, lost in the wonder of it, for fifteen minutes, twenty, thirty; until *Prometheus* came into view.

Instantly the mood changed. Martyr and Malik leaped up onto the afterdeck and opened the hatch. Martyr went down, and, within minutes, the guns were being handed up. Then the thunderflashes. Malik passed them forward and down to Chris and Robin, who put them on the cockpit sole to keep them dry. Then the two men came forward again and began to fit the long clips of ammunition into the guns. Loosening the harnesses so that the light, robust assault rifles could easily be slung across their backs. Salah disappeared down into the forward cabin to reemerge with the Heckler and Koch MP-5 machine guns.

Robin went to relieve Richard at the wheel. Chris took the spinnaker ropes from Doc. They had talked it through. They all knew what to do. The men went down into the forward cabin and quickly changed into shirts, jeans, and silent-soled footwear. Grimly they began to arm themselves. Each slung a Kalashnikov across his shoulders. Richard and Salah also took a machine pistol each. They had been up before. They were going first now. Martyr and Doc took portable radios. They all took thunderflashes and went up on deck. Last out, Weary took *Katapult*'s handgun and laid it on the table, beside the last two Kalashnikovs, in case the women needed an extra edge. Then he changed his mind and put it instead beside the radio where they were due to be monitoring transmissions while the four men were aboard the tanker.

He got up into the cockpit just in time to hear Richard ask, "Did you ever get a chance to test these out?" He was holding a thunderflash.

Martyr shook his head. In all the confusion, it was the one thing they had forgotten to do.

Richard looked up at the rapidly closing hulk of his tanker, then he twisted the top of the grenade he was holding and dropped it overboard. Three seconds later, the sea behind them lit up for an instant soundlessly.

Richard nodded once, in terse satisfaction. The attack had effectively begun.

The reality of it hit Robin like a truck. That gigantic hull bearing down on them at more than forty miles an hour held twelve trained killers, armed to the teeth, each one of them ready and able to kill any or all of the four men going in against them. And what of those men? Weary at least was a trained combat soldier, but how his damaged brain might function on the firing line, there was no way of predicting. And Salah—dear Salah—what was he capable of? If his reputation was anything to go by, he was battle hardened and every bit as fearsome as the other terrorists aboard. And yet he had always seemed to her the gentle diplomat, never the wild-eyed fanatic. And C. J., like a father to her: she had seen him move like a panther along dangerous decks before. But never against men like these.

And Richard. What she thought about Richard was dictated by heart, not head. Never in all the years she had known him had he let her down. She had fallen in love with him at the age of sixteen when he had appeared like a film star beside her father's yacht in St. Tropez, and she had loved him ever since. The thought that he might fail was completely foreign to her nature. But the odds against him were so high.

Then she thought of John Higgins and Asha Quartermaine; Bob Stark and all the rest. The men and women on *Prometheus*, pirated, kidnapped, terrorized. Of her own father, perhaps aboard with all the rest. And her rage gave her new determination. They would break free at the first chance, she knew. No matter who stood against them. As soon as they realized help was at hand, it would no longer be four against twelve, but twelve against forty-four. And God help the terrorists then!

"Easy . . ." said Weary, fussing.

"We're going to the downwind side of the hull," she said. "We have a quarter of a mile of wind shadow, Doc. I've got to keep her speed up." Even as she said it, they flashed past the stern and *Prometheus* came between them and the wind like a fifty-foot-high wall.

Inertia took them past the absolute stillness of the bridge-house—the wall rising to more than a hundred feet there—then some light air refilled the top of the spinnaker, enough to stop it flapping as *Katapult*'s speed picked up again. "Wait for it," called Robin, in charge now, as the men lurked on the companionway.

"Nobody on the port bridge-wing," called Chris softly, not quite as preoccupied with the spinnaker ropes as she might have seemed.

The Sampson posts flashed by and they were halfway along the deck.

"Wait for it," called Robin again. "Just a little longer . . ."

"Keep saying to yourself," hissed Weary, " 'This boat is worth a quarter of a million. This boat is worth a quarter of . . ."

"Let go!"

". . . a million.' "

The spinnaker flapped up, whipping clear of the boom in a trice, anchored only by the block at the top of the mast. As the way came off *Katapult*, Robin spun the wheel and the starboard outrigger slid neatly under the anchor chain and stopped. The loose spinnaker floated like a magic cloak a hundred feet above, hiding the forecastle head completely under its billows. Both women were on the afterdeck at once, presenting an eye-catching display of maximum distress and minimum clothing. "It had better be worth it," said Chris grimly. "I swore I'd *never* do this sort of thing again!"

★ ★ ★

Richard went up the chain first, sliding through the hawse hole and rolling back against the pulpit wall, machine gun at the ready in case there was a watch up here after all. There wasn't. He waited where he was for an instant until Salah came through. Salah rolled over the other way, and the two of them knelt tensely, waiting for Martyr and Doc. Richard's mind was racing, adapting to the situation at lightning speed. They could afford to get sorted into teams up here instead of on the main deck as planned because the spinnaker, one of the flying guy ropes wrapped around the flagpole at *Prometheus*'s head, continued to protect them from prying eyes.

The wait was not long. Both Martyr and Weary came through quickly and quietly. *Prometheus*'s forecastle head was massive but it was packed with equipment. The two anchor winches were here. The spare anchor. Bollards. Housings. Vents. Cover of every sort. Richard raised his hand, and they paused for a micron more. Richard gestured. Weary fell in behind him. Martyr joined Salah and Richard led off.

The four of them slid out from under the after edge of the spinnaker and into the forest of hiding places. Guns at the ready, they worked their way forward toward that avenue of clear foredeck concealed from the bridge by the pipes and the walkway above them. Then they ran forward in single file, lowered themselves down to the main deck, and plunged into that avenue of cover. There was no point in being shy about their movements here. It was highly unlikely that they would be spotted. They ran forward quickly, therefore, careful only to pace themselves to avoid arriving exhausted at the other end.

The pipes ended twenty feet in front of the bridge-house. Under the last of the cover they paused again.

Then Richard gestured and the two teams went in opposite directions. Each team consisted of two men iden-
tically equipped: one man with a Kalashnikhov and a
machine gun, the other with a Kalashnikhov and a radio to keep in contact with the other team and with
Katapult. Ten seconds later, Richard flattened himself
against the wall outside the port door onto A deck. He
had rounded his back carefully so that the Kalashnikhov slung over his shoulder made no sound against the
white-painted metal. His mouth was open so that he
could breathe silently. His eyes followed Doc's balletic
movements as he whirled and crouched, covering the
door with his gun. Richard held his Heckler and Koch
MP-5 ready in his right hand and grabbed the handle
with his left. A nod to Weary and he swung it wide,
and they both leaped over the high metal sill, into the
corridor, side by side.

It was bright. Cool. Almost silent.

The generators were throbbing. The power was on.
Weary slapped his radio to his mouth. Pushed SEND.
"IN!" he whispered.

"In," it said in return: Martyr's voice, whispering in
answer. There was a stairwell immediately to their left.
Richard went up first, freezing to a crouch in the angle
of the turn, MP-5 machine gun pointing up. Weary
went past him like a ghost, freezing just in sight above,
rifle pointing up. Richard ran past him into the threshold of the B deck corridor. He thrust his head out at
foot level. Look left. Right. Nothing. Out he went into
the corridor itself, whirling round at once, MP-5 pointing up. Weary slipped past him noiselessly.

C deck was empty as well. The doors to all the cabins and suites stood ajar.

Next deck up was the bridge-deck. There had to be
a watch here. He checked the safety and tightened his

hold on both the machine gun's grips. Arms straight, letting the gun lead, he went. Fast and silent up to the first angle. Crouch. Freeze. Empty steps, linoleum covered, reaching up to a corner. And suddenly Weary was on that corner, still, Kalashnikov rifle pointing up.

Bridge-deck corridor. Left. Right. Empty. Silent. Doors ajar. Bridge door opposite. All along the rear of the bridge, windows onto this corridor. At each end of those windows, doors out onto the bridge and bridge-wings. Ajar. Not a movement. Not a whisper.

Weary at his shoulder. One meaningful glance. Weary nodded: understood. Off they went, one each way. Pause at the bridge door looking in. Instruments, chart table, nothing more. Whisper of sound. Stirring of air. Weary gone out onto the starboard bridge-wing. Count of three.

"Three!" said Richard to himself as he rolled in. The room was empty. He stood up. Weary came in off the starboard bridge-wing and they both ran left, guns at the ready. But the port bridge-wing was empty, too.

Weary put the radio to his mouth. "Bridge empty," he whispered, and waited.

Richard stood behind him, eyes slitted against the glare of the sun reflecting off the water, looking down the whole length of *Prometheus*'s deck to that irregular white patch made by *Katapult*'s spinnaker on the forecastle head. Not a stir of motion. Not a flicker. Nothing.

And yet . . .

"Engine room empty," whispered Martyr's voice from Weary's radio.

Richard slapped him on the shoulder and gestured with his thumb: going down. They moved off like a ghost and a shadow.

They used the same routine going down they had employed coming up. At the A deck level they deviated, plunging back into the rear sections of the bridge, silently exploring the warren of corridors that led back to the recreation areas overlooking the afterdeck with its swimming pool and helipad. Where the gymnasium was.

The gym was constructed so as to extend the rear of the bridge-house into a balcony looking aft. It had four doors. Two opened down onto the afterdeck by the pool. And the helipad where *Prometheus*'s little Westland Wasp was anchored. Two opened in from the bridge corridor. All of these doors had glass pannels in the top. So that Martyr and Malik coming in from the deck knew a second after Richard and Weary that it was empty. The four of them stood facing each other in the deserted room, looking about silently. The big room showed every evidence of recent occupation. There was bedding on the floor. There were tables and chairs. The ship's televisions had been moved in here, each with its video player below. But there were no people. Richard looked up, vividly recalling the sound of automatic fire that had echoed behind his last departure from the ship. Sure enough, the panels of the suspended ceiling were splintered, scored, and pocked with bullet holes. But no other damage had been done.

They paused in the gym until Richard had finished that first, rapid inspection, then he led them to somewhere less exposed for a conference. Close to the gym was the doctor's surgery. Unlike the exercise area, it had no windows. One thick-glassed porthole was the only way of seeing in or out, and the door was solid. Here they grouped, gulping in great lungfuls of air, stilling muscles all quivering with tension, whispering a conversation between ragged gasps. Three of them stood in the middle of the room while Weary stood guard at the door.

"Empty!" said Richard first. "Abandoned! Did you see any sign of life?"

"Not a thing. Not a soul." Martyr shook his head in wonderment. Then he flicked the SEND button on his radio. "No one aboard, Chris. She's deserted."

"Where are they all?" Salah looked almost spooked. "There ought to be fifty-two people aboard. But not a whisper. Not a sign."

"Not quite," said Weary quietly. "There's someone here all right. Or has been, recently." He slid downward, his back against the doorframe, eyes busy through the inch he had left open. He put his left hand on the floor palm down, then lifted it like an American Indian saying "How."

It was covered in blood. Liquid. Oozing. Fresh.

Chapter Seventeen

"No one aboard," said Chris in wonderment. "All that performance on the afterdeck to an empty theater." She laughed ruefully and rose, flicking the radio to OFF. She stretched and Robin eyed her lithe form enviously.

"I think I'll go up and join them. You want to come, Robin?"

"D'you think I could get up that chain with my all-day morning sickness?" Robin sounded uncharacteristically low since her earlier fright.

"Sure you could," said Chris bracingly. "The men got themselves up there so it has to be a cinch. Tie her up tight and let's go. You know if we stay down here we'll just get bitched at for not having put the spinnaker away."

"I suppose you're right."

"You know I am."

It only took them a moment to dress—shirts and jeans over bikinis, and docksiders on bare feet. They made *Katapult* fast to one massive link, then climbed onto the chain itself.

Like the men, half an hour earlier, they arrived on the forecastle head under the light awning of the spinnaker. But, unlike the men, they saw no need to use it for cover. And no need at all to go creeping among pipes when there was a catwalk convenient to their feet. "It is

odd, though," Chris was saying as they started along
the narrow path above the pipes. "Where could they all
have gone?"

"I don't know." Robin was actually deeply concerned. She had wanted so desperately to find her father
here among her kidnapped friends and to release them
all together. But finding no one only deepened the
mystery and renewed the pain. And put them back in
that position of being helpless bystanders. She hated that.
Then, half ruefully, she admitted to herself that in this
case it was simply impossible to please her, for, while
she hated inactivity, she had found the action so far not
at all to her taste because it had put either her husband
or her unborn child at risk.

As she and Chris strolled along, fifteen feet above the
deck, her mind was preoccupied but her eyes were automatically busy. She was a fully qualified ship's captain
after all, and part owner of everything she surveyed.
All at once she called to Christine, "Look. The accommodation ladder's down."

The ladder was halfway along the ship on the starboard side, just opposite the midway set of steps leading
down from the catwalk to the deck. Both Chris and
Robin ran easily down these at once and set out across
the expanse of green deck toward the ladder's head.
Down here, the heat was intensified, reflecting back up
off the deck, which was soon singeing even Robin's
callused feet through the thin soles of her lightweight
footwear. They ran across as fast as they could, therefore, and stood looking bemusedly down. The steps
were almost at full extension, falling to within five feet
of the water. They stirred slightly in the steady south
wind and banged dully on *Prometheus*'s side. "This is
odd, too," said Robin. "All of it is bloody odd."

She turned, absently running her fingers through

her golden curls. And her eyes lit on something else odd.

Just inboard from the top of the ladder was a hatch. It was a low inspection hatch that consisted of a simple trapdoor, hinged and clipped, on a raised rim some eighteen inches high. It led down to a system of tunnels that wove around and between the tanks so they could be inspected from without as well as within.

The hatch cover should have been secured by two quick release clips at all times. The clips on this one were open. Her mind still preoccupied with the mystery of the accommodation ladder, she crossed to this and automatically stooped to snap the catch closed. Then she saw the stains on the deck. Crouching carefully, too wise to think of kneeling, she drifted the tips of her fingers over the brown mark nearest to the hatch itself. They came away sticky. She put them fastidiously to her nose. Even granted that it came from an iron deck, there was no mistaking the iron smell of the sticky stuff on her fingers.

She straightened at once, looking around narrow-eyed. Chris was still staring down at the ladder, unaware of this new development. Oblivious of the sudden purposefulness of her friend's movements. With her right foot, Robin snapped the nearest quick-release down. "Chris," she called quietly. "Let's go. Now!"

At first, Chris failed to understand the reason they ran down the remainder of the deck but the instant they were in the A deck corridor, Richard came pounding down the stairs, MP-5 at the ready, and Robin supplied the explanation.

"I don't know who it is," said Robin as her eyes met Richard's, "but there's someone down in the midships inspection area. Someone bleeding pretty badly."

★ ★ ★

"Okay," snapped Richard ten minutes later, "unclip it."

Weary's toe moved upward infinitesimally and the clip sprang open. The two men stood tensely, awaiting developments.

Nothing happened.

Weary sidled round to the hinge side of the raised cover and, holding his Kalashnikov upright on his right hip, he leaned across the metal disk and took its handle from behind. Then he straightened slowly, bringing the cover up to protect his body like a heavy iron shield.

On the far side of the deck, Salah had just done the same thing. Richard put his radio to his lips. "Going in."

"Going in," said Martyr in a hiss of static.

Both men carried radios, MP-5 machine pistols, and torches. No thunderflashes. Not down here. The guns were more for effect than anything else. To rupture a tank even with a single bullet would probably be to detonate the ship.

At Richard's feet, an iron-runged ladder led down into a tunnel dimly lit by low-wattage bulbs heavily protected. Nothing that could ignite stray pockets of gas was allowed down here. Even the leads between the lights were specially sheathed. Richard checked the gun's safety, then let it hang from his shoulder. He let the radio hang from one wrist and the rubberized torch from the other. They would slide from elbow to wrist depending on what he was doing.

He glanced across the deck one last time, then down he went. As soon as he stepped onto the ladder, Weary was there above him, Kalashnikov pointing down. Unlike the exploration of the bridge-house, this was a job for one man on each side. One man who knew the tunnels well.

Richard stepped down off the ladder into the first dim gallery and turned, holding his breath. No sound. He allowed the torch to slide down his right wrist and slap into his hand. He flicked it on without moving his feet and shone it on the iron-grating floor. At first nothing. He flashed it farther afield. And there it was, like Ariadne's thread in the Labyrinth: a bright drop of blood. He put his radio to his lips. "Level one, corridor A," he breathed. "Going aft. Blood."

He moved off at once, torch beam on the floor, look-ing for more blood. Whoever was in here now must have been in the surgery when they boarded. The fugi-tive had been disturbed by their arrival and fled to this bizarre hiding place. If he realized he had left a trail of blood, then he could use it as a trap. If he wished to at-tack instead of hiding. If he had the strength after los-ing all this blood.

"Don't try to imagine who it might be," Weary had warned them. "You want it to be one of your people hiding from terrorists. Fine. It might be. Or it might be a terrorist wounded and hiding out himself. Look, Richard, we don't know what's gone on here. For all we know, the SAS could have come aboard while we were off Zarakkuh and sorted it out like they did the Iranian Embassy in London."

"SBS more likely, but I see what you mean."

"Right. We'll all have time to think this through properly later. But for now, just see what happens and react accordingly. Fast. Remember: no presuppositions. They'll get you killed every time."

Another drop of blood. He went on down the tun-nel, every nerve tense. As he proceeded, a memory began to stir. There was something down here. On this level. Something slightly unusual. Hardly worthy of note and yet he had remarked upon it once. What?

When? Good God, yes. There was a little room down here. One of those tiny pieces of fun the occasional marine architect likes to add to a design. A useful little store place among all this maze of tunnels for the equipment one might need down here. Just the sort of place to keep all the sorts of things you were liable to leave on deck or up in the bridge-house by accident. By God, there was a *room* down here.

That's where he was.

"And don't be fooled into thinking there's only one of them either," Weary insisted in his memory, rehearsing the things his combat sergeant had told him out in Vietnam. "There's only one wounded by the looks of things, but maybe he's got a friend."

"C. J.," whispered Richard into his radio, "I think I know where they are."

Five minutes later they converged from either end of that long, midships tunnel to the head of the ladder going down. Silently, and without the aid of their torches, they looked down into that secret little room. They could see and hear nothing. Except, when Richard knelt and slid his finger along the top rung, there was the telltale sticky wetness of the track he had been following. That was it. Here they were.

No way out for their quarry.

No way in for them except down that ladder.

Richard held up his fingers, just visible in the dim, yellow light. THREE . . . TWO . . . ONE . . .

Both torches blazed their powerful beams down into the darkness. The stub barrels of the machine pistols clashed against the ladder.

"All right," called Richard. "We have you covered. Come out with your hands up!"

"Is that you, Richard?" replied a woman's voice,

hoarse with fatigue but rich and familiar. "Thank God! I thought you were those bloody terrorists coming back!"

And out into the pool of light stepped Asha Quartermaine, supporting the fainting, blood-drenched figure of Captain John Higgins.

"Help me get him back up to the surgery, would you? If I don't stitch him up again soon, he's going to bleed to death."

CHAPTER EIGHTEEN

The Gulf. Off Kharg Island. 08:15 hrs. Local Time.

As the body of First Officer Cecil Smyke collapsed onto the deck, Captain John Higgins strode forward, totally overcome by rage. The moment he moved, there was a series of sharp clicks as the terrorists across his deck cocked their weapons, and a hoarse, icy voice called out in English, "It won't be you, Captain. It will be your crew, one by one, like the lieutenant."

John froze at the threat, looking suspiciously around. Which of the anonymous figures had spoken? It was impossible to tell.

"What do you want here?" John demanded.

"At the moment, nothing more than your coopera-tion. Order your crew below, please. They seem reluc-tant to move without your permission."

"Where below?"

"The ship's gymnasium, please. All of them. *Now!*" The final word rang out like the crack of a whip. John was about to tell him to drop dead, but a sense of his own ultimate responsibility overcame his hot head. Whoever these people were, they had not boarded with-out a plan. They knew what they were doing and were ruthlessly willing to enforce their orders. The death of Smyke proved that. "Very well," he said quietly. "All of

you, please go below at the direction of these gentlemen."

In the gymnasium, they were at once split into work
parties. One began to empty the big room of its sport-
ing equipment. Another brought in bedding. A third
carried in tables and chairs. Throughout this bustle,
John, Asha Quartermaine, and Bob Stark stood restively
under the guns of two men assigned to watch them
alone. Both the captain and his American chief engineer
were active, dominant men and they reacted to this
situation uneasily. They were not alone in this. Asha
was pale with outrage and every line of her, from deep
red hair to ill-laced shoes, loudly signaled her defiance.
Among the crew, Chief Petty Officer Kerem Khalil and
Chief Steward Twelve Toes Ho both moved with surly
obedience, looking to the senior officers for confirma-
tion before obeying any orders. The atmosphere was
tense. Dangerous.

But at last the tasks were completed to the satisfaction of the anonymous terrorist leader. "Sit down," he
snapped. They sat. The terrorists ranged themselves
shoulder to shoulder across the room. There were eight
of them here, though John suspected there would be
more in strategic positions elsewhere about the ship.
They all looked similar—in many ways identical. They
were all wiry men, thin but strong looking. From the
way they moved, they seemed fit. Battle trained. They
all wore the same uniform—camouflage fatigues and
checked kaffiyah headdresses. The kaffiyahs were folded
across their faces so that only their eyes were visible.
The skin color on their hands varied slightly, but they
all had fierce dark eyes.

Standing all together like that, with seven of them
silent, it soon became obvious which one of them was
speaking. He could not quite disguise the movements

of his lips and jaw behind his kaffiyah. He could not control the tiny gestures of his hands. And the instant he gave himself away he became their target. Unnumbered eyes within the room searched that speaker's body for any sign that would single him out for special attention later.

At first sight, there was nothing to distinguish him from the others apart from the fact that he spoke English with an English accent in a hoarse, broken voice, but eventually Asha's quick, trained eye noticed a thin scar that writhed across the back of his left hand to disappear under his sleeve, and so, even as he threatened them he was marked.

"You will all spend most of your time in here for the next few days. There will be at least two guards here with you at all times. If you fail to obey them they will shoot. If you even so much as threaten them, they will shoot. I have no doubt that forty intrepid men and women could overcome two guards, even if they are armed with automatic weapons, so remember this: beyond the doors will be more guards and beyond them, more still. If you try to escape you will all die like your first officer.

"Now, as to the next few days, the routine is simple. You will remain in here. You may sleep, sit, or walk about. But you may not talk. Anyone who talks will be locked in one of the cabins and will receive no food or water for two days. In this heat, they will suffer greatly, I promise you. You all will, in fact, for to make this punishment effective I will be forced to switch off the ship's air-conditioning. You will be taken out to the ship's toilet facilities in small groups twice a day. You will be fed twice a day. Teams of cooks and stewards will prepare food, serve, and clear away under our direction. That is all you need to know."

"Now look here," John began.

"Captain Higgins," said the terrorist leader, crossing to him on swift, silent feet, "I just knew the first one would be you!" and he hit him with his rifle butt on the side of the head.

John came to in the ship's surgery with Asha by his side. "You did that on purpose," she whispered.

"Well, I'm no use cooped up in there."

"Not so loud! There's a guard outside the door."

"Where do you think they'll put me?"

"Don't count on them putting you anywhere. As we were carrying you out of the gym I heard him say that you got one chance—they got none."

"Damn! Well, we'll just have to see what happens next, I suppose. Ouch! That stings."

"Iodine. When you've got a plan worked out, let me know."

"You'll be part of any plan."

"Yes, but I won't be in there with you. They're moving me out. Keeping me apart."

"That's nasty."

"Logical. I'm the only woman."

"Yes, but . . ."

"Don't worry about me."

The door slammed open and the two of them whirled guiltily. One of the terrorists stood frozen in the doorway. Something in the room seemed to have come as a great shock. The gun dangled in limp hands. The kaffiyah mask moved from side to side as the terrorist's head shook. Both John and Asha tensed, sensing a chance. But they were too slow. The gun snapped up again to point unwaveringly at the captain. Then the barrel gestured: move.

Back in the silent gym, John considered that last

terrorist. A slighter figure than the rest. A different way
of walking. A woman? He filed the thought away for
future consideration.

During the days that followed, beneath the stultifying
boredom of the routine a kind of war was fought. It was
the type of war a class of schoolboys might declare on a
hated teacher—but it was no less serious or deadly for
being so. In the enforced silence, observed to break down
communication, communication flourished. Notes were
passed until all paper and writing implements were
confiscated. Sign language developed. Codes. And every message successfully passed bolstered the crew's morale and undermined the guards' authority. These games
centered around John and Bob Stark. There was no
situation that these two could not turn to some subver-
sive advantage, to the delight of their men and the dis-
comfiture of their captors. They became past masters in
the art of dumb insolence. They time-wasted in a thousand ways. They became stupid, clumsy, disruptive.

As time passed, the campaign had its effect beyond
questions of morale. The guards became tired, snap-
pish, dangerous. As the endless days dragged by, a tense
situation was escalated toward the explosive. And all
the pressure settled upon the head of one man. The
man responsible for the whole situation. The leader of
the terrorists.

They singled him out for special attention. They
never missed an opportunity to challenge his authority
or undermine his power. They gestured silently behind
his back. They reacted more slowly to his orders. They
were more stupid, clumsy, childish when he was around.
They exercised their ingenuity to the utmost trying to
destroy him in ways that would not cause him to destroy them first. And, indeed, as four days passed, then

five, the strain on him did seem to be intensifying beyond bearing. Almost as if he were waiting for something. Something that should have happened some time ago, but had not.

That was another objective of their endless communication games—speculation. Who were these people? What did they want? How could they be defeated? The regimen they imposed made anything other than guesswork extremely difficult, but in those early days speculation was rife. John and Bob collected it, sifted it, and filed it. Both of them knew with increasing certainty that the only way to get hard facts was to run the risk again that John had taken at once—to get thrown out. Only outside the gym was there a real chance to gather solid information. Only out there, in the little Westland helicopter, was there any real chance for escape. But the Westland had no fuel aboard, and only Bob knew how to fly it.

Kerem Khalil and Twelve Toes Ho became part of the central committee too, for they could begin to supply some information about what was going on outside. Their men were doing the cooking, cleaning, and other odd jobs required by the terrorists. Anyone who went out of the gym for whatever reason was thoroughly grilled on his return. Were there guards outside? How many? Had they seen one set relieve another or were they all on duty all the time? Where were the terrorists sleeping? Eating? Keeping watches? Even visits to the latrine became like sorties into enemy territory.

Life for Asha Quartermaine was very different. She was given much more freedom to move around the bridge-house from her quarters, to her surgery, to the library. Whereas the others filled their days with their games to ward off that terrifying boredom, she caught up with her reading and plotted alone.

She saw no one from the crew at all after that first tending of John's bruised skull. When the stewards were preparing or serving food she was kept well away. Her own meals were always brought by the slightest of the terrorists—the one she suspected of being a woman—and eaten alone. She had her own small shower and toilet in her quarters so she never needed to use the crew's. When the crew went to the toilet or the showers she was again kept clear so that not even the most intricate planning on her part could bring about an apparently accidental meeting with John or Bob. She began to feel more than lonely—she began to feel distanced. Deserted. No matter what John had said about including her in any plans they made, she began to feel that they had abandoned her.

And so she worked on her own plans.

Her whole reason for being here, the outcome of nearly a year's work and planning, was to contact her twin sister. She was the elder by a matter of minutes, but that fact colored her relationship with Fatima. Asha was the maternal, paternal, strongly protective half. The reliable one. The caring one. The doctor. Fatima had been wild, mischievous, adventurous. The romantic. The political activist. The reporter. The thought of her Fatima, trapped in a foreign society, that brave soul of freedom caged by the whim of a born-again Muslim father, was more than Asha could stand. She blamed herself for allowing Fatima to go to his bedside. She tortured herself with the thought of what it must be like for the flamboyant feminist to be held in the most repressive of conditions. Alone and friendless after her divorce from Giles Quartermaine, she had become almost morbidly worried about Fatima. And then the first letter had arrived. Posted during her flight through Dahran immediately after her escape from their father's house, it told of Fatima's life there and how she was now free.

That first letter had begun the transformation of Asha's life. For a start, it had emphasized how much had already changed since Fatima had been taken away— her young sister had no idea she was now divorced from Giles Quartermaine. Indeed, part of that turbulent missive proposed that Asha should get Giles to run a series of programs for Western television about the terrible injustice of forcing liberated women into conditions she described as medieval servitude.

Giles Quartermaine, in fact, featured largely in Fatima's early proposals, for that first letter was followed by others. The tenor of the letters changed as time went by, and Asha came to suspect the truth: that Fatima's offers of journalistic contacts within various terrorist cadres actually included Fatima herself. Asha's divorce from Giles Quartermaine had been reported quite widely, but nowhere Fatima could read about it, and the reason for her ignorance became disturbingly clear: freedom fighters such as she had become no longer read Western gossip columns. So her little sister continued to refer to her ex-husband, relying on him to guarantee her worldwide publicity as soon as she required it.

The letters did not arrive regularly or often. There were by no means many of them tucked in Asha's writing case in her cabin, but there were quite enough to give the elder sister a firm idea of her twin's rough whereabouts. With nothing to lose, therefore, Asha had handed in her notice at the small hospital she had been working in since the divorce and started to plan how she could get to the Middle East—preferably the Gulf— to look for Fatima. Becoming a ship's doctor aboard tankers filling at Kharg Island gave her just what she needed—a feeling of being close to Fatima and a steady

job into the bargain. She would probably have drifted
onto Heritage Mariner's ships eventually in any case—
after BP they were the largest British tanker fleet—but
for some reason she could never quite fathom, they featured once or twice by name in Fatima's letters. She
came onto their fleet on purpose, therefore, and found
the friendly atmosphere aboard was very much to her
taste. And so, amid the companionship so sorely lack-
ing in her life since the double blow of the kidnap and
the divorce, she began to let time slip by.

Then the last letter arrived: the one that had brought
her here. It was another one for Giles, really, though
addressed to her at their old home and forwarded, like
the others, by her bank. In it, Fatima offered her dazzling brother-in-law the veiled promise of a scoop. All
he had to do, she hinted, was to keep an eye on the
Gulf in general and on Heritage Mariner's flagship in
particular. At first, Asha thought of handing the letter
to the authorities or even to Richard Mariner himself—
but in the end either action seemed too much like a
betrayal of Fatima. So she simply folded it up, put it
with the rest, and contacted the ship's doctor on *Prometheus*. Would he mind swapping berths for a trip or
two? Of course not. And so it had been done. Her mo-
tivation was as uncomplicated as it had been since she
had lost Fatima: to get her little sister back again. Or to
see her—perhaps talk to her—at the very least. She had
been almost relieved to come out of the hold behind
John Higgins and find the deck crowded with terrorists.

The excitement died the moment she saw Cecil
Smyke. It was replaced with a sort of dull horror she
had been at great pains to disguise from the others,
indulging it only after her separation from them when
she was alone. But she was not the sort of woman to
give in to weakness and she soon began to use her rela-

tive liberty to put together a cache of the sort of equipment she would need if and when she tried to make her
escape.

At last, the only thing keeping her here was the cer-
tainty that she had not been mistaken in her first hopes:
Fatima was on *Prometheus* somewhere. But how could
Fatima have been party to the murder of Cecil Smyke?
And why hadn't she made some sort of contact?

The fifth night of captivity was literally hellish. The
air outside the bridge was so horrifically stultifying that
even in the coolness of the air-conditioned rooms,
something of that fierce Gulf heat intruded. Certainly
the thunderous atmosphere in the dark air above caused
fractiousness, short tempers, and colossal headaches in
everyone aboard. Asha was prone to atmospheric mi-
graines and fought this one by standing under a shower
set exactly at blood heat for the better part of an hour.
At about seven she emerged, cool enough to feel a slight
chill from the air-conditioning, and consequently she
caught up a towel to wrap around herself even though
she knew she would regret it later when she became too
hot to sleep. The action was providential because otherwise she would have been naked when she walked
into her cabin and found the terrorist leader there.

She froze, thunderstruck by his presence here. Automatically she opened her mouth to scream. But the instant she did so, the window behind his shoulder was
filled with an explosion of lightning like Armageddon
and the immediate havoc of thunder was like Judgment
Day. The deafening pyrotechnics of the storm gave
them pause and some semblance of calm had returned
to the situation before communication became possible.
He made no move toward her as the thunder rolled on
and on, so she walked past him to her wardrobe and put
on a long silk dressing gown.

As she did so, a second claw of lightning pounced down toward the desert. This time the thunder was, if anything, louder. She kicked her bare feet into open sandals and, sweeping her hair back over one broad shoulder, she confronted him again.

"Is this a social call?" she demanded as the echoes rumbled into silence. And their eyes locked. Hers beneath imperious brows, tawny; his deep-shadowed under the folds of his kaffiyah, dark brown, almost black. Not quite sane.

Lightning crackled down outside and an odor of ozone permeated the unquiet air. Had he answered, it would have been lost in the avalanche of sound outside. Instead, he raised his scarred hands to his shirt collar and began to unbutton it. At once she drew herself up, eyes busy around her cabin, looking for a weapon. But when she looked back into his mad black gaze, something she saw there stopped her. And the thought that rapists usually start with their trousers, not their shirts. She looked down at what he was doing and understood. By the time he pulled the shirt off altogether, she was total professionalism, concentrating absolutely. Her mind focused so that even the cataclysm outside receded until nothing existed but her expertise and his poor, twisted body.

He seemed to have been crushed. That was the only explanation that sprang to mind. She could only see his torso, of course, but nothing else could explain what she was looking at. The left side of his body seemed to have been crushed beneath some unimaginable thing or force. Something so massive that it should have killed him. Would have been far more merciful if it had killed him. Crushed him until his broken bones had cut their way out through his flesh. Then they had simply been tucked back into him and allowed to heal that way. He held himself erect. He seemed to move freely, normally. How he did so, she could not think: by the exercise of indomitable will. The twisted, tortured muscles stretching over the strange angular bones should not have worked at all. The bones themselves should not have held together. The joints, those many joints between ribs, breastbone, spine, shoulder, arm, hand, should not have worked. He should not have been able to breathe or move. This body should not contain life.

Looking at it in dumb wonder, she was reminded of a haunting story she had once read where the survivor of a space crash in some far distant galaxy had been saved by kindly alien surgeons who had sewn her back together—but they did so without ever having seen a human body before. The result must have been something like this, she supposed.

He did not flinch when her fingers probed gently down the twisted columns of his trapezius and latissimus dorsi, that long range of muscular hills astride the valley of his spine. The skin itself was not extensively scarred here, but from shoulder to knuckle on the left arm there was a network of scars the smallest end of which had served to distinguish this man from the other terrorists. He could have been crushed in a road accident, she supposed. Or trapped under a collapsing building.

"There is nothing I can do for you. You know that."

"You can give me something for the pain."

She watched in fascination as the muscles writhed into awkward but effective motion. He must have been tended by someone with no medical knowledge at all. "Oh, I can do that all right, but I don't think anyone could make this better."

"It was the hand of Allah, blessings be upon Him: it would be a sacrilege to make it better. But sometimes at night I weaken, for He asks me to bear more than I can endure. And I need . . . I need . . ."

Thunder drowned out what he said, but she knew what he needed well enough. "You'd better come down to the surgery."

On the way down, her mind worked rapidly, trying to turn the situation to her best advantage. The scope for action was large. Ultimately she could kill him if she wanted: he would have no idea what she was actually giving him, after all. But that was a course of action she could not contemplate for long, even under these circumstances. She could try something that might yield long-term rewards without causing immediate reprisals, however. She could try for information.

"You should keep a supply of pills with you," she told him when they arrived. "But for now, I'll give you an injection that will act more quickly. Only one injection. Then you'll have to rely on the pills." She paused, half hoping he would take the tablets and go. But he sat obediently on the examination table and rolled up his right sleeve.

Asha slid the long needle into his pale flesh and depressed the plunger. The porthole lit up dazzlingly and instant thunder roared. She held her breath and slid the needle out. John, Bob, and the rest were just next door. She felt their proximity acutely. God! How she wanted to help them. "Just stay sitting down," she advised gently. "It will make you feel a little sleepy, I expect. I'll stay with you. Don't worry. Lie down if you'd like to."

He swung round at her suggestion and lay back. His hands went to the folds of his kaffiyah but then hesitated. He had no intention that she should see his face. "Switch off the light," he croaked.

Sitting in the dark beside him she waited until the rhythm of his breathing told her he was asleep.

"How did it happen?" she asked quietly.

". . . ship . . ." His voice was sleepy. Dreamy. The drug she had given him had killed his pain. Put him to sleep. Left him susceptible to suggestion, like sodium-pentathol. He would answer her questions quite freely for a while if she was careful what she asked.

"A ship . . ." she prompted.

"The bastard killed my father. He deserved everything he got. God, he was so easy to fool. Me. The owner. The Afrikaaners. Everybody fooled him. No oil. No problem. But she had to sink, you see. No evidence. No comebacks. Full insurance. Had to sink. Ask old Ben. Good old chap. Shift the ballast, tank to tank. Break her back."

"Break whose back?"

"Easy? Christ, you'd think they'd know. Takes years of training to make sure we don't break their backs every time."

"Whose back?"

"Broke her back. Middle of a storm. Middle of the Channel. Perfect."

"What did you do?" she demanded, with all the force she dared, leaning as close to him as she could without touching him.

Just at that moment, another bolt of lightning filled the room with intense light for a micron and established every detail of his face on her retinas. He was turned toward her, kaffiyah open, eyes wide but blind with sleep. The right side of his face, nearest the brightness, was perfectly illuminated. The left shaded mercifully into shadow. The right side showed an open, cheerful, almost boyish countenance with high cheekbones, deep laugh lines, broad, square chin. The left side, beyond the crushed nose, twisted away into a ruin to match the ruin of the left side of his body.

"Oh, God!" she said, startled.

"Oh, God," he echoed at once, speaking incredibly quickly, "she's breaking up. Must get away. I'll never get off alive if I don't . . . No don't . . . Don't get in the way! Leave me alone! I'll kill . . . *Kill* . . . KILL . . ." He slammed upright. She saw him outlined against the porthole, arms reaching out as though holding something. As though pointing at something. "Good-byeeeeeeeee . . ." he sang. Like the old song. Triumphant. Insane.

He slammed back onto the table, rigid. "Nooooo . . ." A little boy's voice, sad and disappointed.

"Noooo . . ." squeezed out of him. He hadn't even breathed in.

"NOOOO . . ." Crushed out of him with the last of his air. The last of his life—or should have been. He was spread out against the table, shaking, in the grip of the ghost of whatever force had done this to him. During the breakup of whatever ship.

He was gone. Far beyond Asha's ability to recall him. She slowly got to her feet and crossed to the door to escape his cries of pain. She was disappointed to have missed the opportunity, for on the face of it she had learned nothing of any use. Except the depth of the madness gripping the man in whose power they lay.

She had to contact Fatima and get them both out of this situation at the earliest possible instant. But for the moment she had better go into hiding herself—if this man remembered anything of this when he woke up tomorrow then Asha was as good as dead. This was, after all, the man who had butchered Cecil Smyke without a second thought.

On the sixth day, things in the gym changed. Early morning saw the arrival of the books from the ship's library. Then the televisions and videos were wheeled in. Restrictions on talking were relaxed. "I don't like this," were John's first words to Bob Stark.

"Neither do I," said the big American. "Looks like this is shaping up to be a long stay after all."

The pressure was on them now to regulate the crew's amusements carefully. They did not want the team they had built up so painstakingly in adversity to fall apart now. They still had work to do. It remained obvious that the only way forward lay outside. But how to get out there? Able to talk now, they started to plan in detail.

Only to find that on the seventh day things had changed again. The leader came in at dawn, backed by a phalanx of five heavily armed men.

"Where is she?" he screamed, his scarred hand tight around the stock of his rifle. *Prometheus*'s crew, just coming awake, looked at him in dazed confusion. Only John and Bob had the wits about them to realize what he was talking about.

"Where is she?" he screamed again.

Silence.

"Very well then. Up and out. All of you. Line up at this end. We are going to search the ship. *You* are going to search the ship, under the direction of my guards."

The search revealed nothing, but such was the leader's rage that he made one major miscalculation. He allowed John, Bob, Kerem, and Twelve Toes to form a group together. As they pretended to search for Asha, they put together their final escape plans. Clearly whatever the terrorists were waiting for was not likely to happen soon. On the other hand, the fact that *Prometheus*'s complement had been here this long with no sign of help from the outside probably meant that no help was coming soon either.

There were ways of getting out, however: Asha had proved that. And there were places aboard to hide in. The terrorists seemed to know the layout of tankers very well indeed, but the fact remained that no two tankers are identical, and *Prometheus* had nooks and crannies only her crew knew about. But escaping from the gymnasium and hiding aboard would not be good enough. It would only be the first step. The prime objective would be to get clear away. To cross the Gulf, if a big lifeboat could be stolen, or to contact local shipping if the people who escaped had to take a liferaft or swim for it. And there did seem to be a lot of local shipping. From the main deck, they could see a fishing fleet out in the Gulf, and one neat little thirty-footer cruising inquisitively close at hand. It was even near enough for them to read its name: *Alouette*.

But then the terrorists' patience ran out. They were all herded back into the gym where they were made to stand, guards clustered threateningly around them, and listen to another speech. The speech went on for twenty minutes and was completed by an enraged gesture from the speaker. Immediately the guards opened fire, spraying the ceiling with bullets. Glass from the shattered light fittings, dust, and splinters came raining down. It was a mercy, thought John, that the gym had been added as an afterthought, that it wasn't iron plate up there, as it was in the rest of the bridge-house, or the room would have been full of lethal ricochets.

"Let that be a lesson to you," snarled the leader in the echoing silence after the shooting had stopped. "This is not a game. If you forget that, then you are all dead men. Now clear this mess up and get the books and televisions out of here. No more talking!"

So the silent boredom was resumed. But this time

the number of people willing to join in the games was sharply reduced. Many were genuinely frightened by the terrorists' display. Waverers were further disturbed as the heat of the day began to move into the crowded room and they realized the leader had made good another of his earlier threats and switched the air-conditioning off. But those threats made the escape committee even more determined to get someone out as soon as possible. How to do this remained problematic, for they were watched ever more closely by the grim guards. There was only one wild card: Asha. John and Bob moved their beds nearest to the doors out onto the afterdeck. If she was going to make contact she would do it here during the night.

At about two the next morning, John was dozing uneasily in the humid heat when he became aware of the faintest tapping noise. The regularity of the sound jerked him awake and he realized it was Morse code. Someone was tapping in Morse code on the door by his head. It could only be her. An emotion welled up in him which made it hard for him to breathe. It took him a moment to get control of himself, and then he was tapping back.

Once they had established a dialogue, she made a brief report, telling him what she knew of numbers, dispositions, watches, and patrols. He did not interrupt with the questions he was burning to ask—How was she? How did she escape? Where was she hiding? Instead he waited until she finished by saying she thought she could get one person out safely.

—Bob, he tapped. He can try to take the helicopter

—Tomorrow

—Yes

—I will get this door key

—Yes

—Tomorrow same time
—Same time
She was gone.

Asha arrived at the door at 02:30 the next night. The same gentle sounds alerted the two men who had been wide awake since lights out at eleven. Once more, there was a brief burst of Morse code, then Asha took the greatest risk of all so far. She stood up. Outlined against the glimmer of the stars, visible through the glass top of the door should either of the guards look her way, she stood up to slide the key silently into the door's lock. All three of them held their breath as she turned it, but the tongue slid back without a sound. The door opened a fraction. All three of them breathed easily.

And the lights went on. The far door was suddenly full of terrorists, the leader calling, "Get up! Get up!" in that raucous voice of his. There was an instant when Asha was plainly visible in the brightness, then she dropped to her knees and rolled away into the shadows of the deck. The crew sleepily began to sort themselves out as ordered. The captain and his chief feigned confusion, too, but they stayed by the open door and when that moment came that the better part of forty men were standing between them and their captors, they stepped out into the darkness on the deck.

Once out of the glare shining from the gym, the two of them felt liberated by the shadows. They walked upright. They briefly discussed the possibility of stealing fuel for the helicopter and getting away in that. They called out Asha's name dangerously clearly, and it was not until she materialized at their side and hissed a warning, that they began to take proper care again. Silently she led them down the side of the bridge-house,

flat against the dew-damp metal walls, forward toward
the main deck, their only obstacle a rack of BMX bikes.
As they came past the big bulkhead door onto A deck,
they hesitated by the ship's office on the corner, before
they dared go out onto the main deck. The curtains of the
office were closed, but the windows were open—they
probably had been since the air-conditioning was
switched off. And an argument was going on inside. In
English.

"But why?" demanded a woman's voice. Both men
were so busy eavesdropping they didn't notice the expression on their companion's face. "Why now? It is
too early. We must wait until the message arrives."

"No. It is taking too long. They are getting impossible to control. Moving them now will disorient them.
Give us a few more days before we have to start executing troublemakers."

"It is departing from the plan."

"I know. But the plan is only of use when it serves
our ends. And anyway, the doctor is doing too much
harm. I am sure *she* took the chart. She is still aboard.
Still a threat. If I can't find her or kill her, I must move
the others before the situation gets out of control."

"But . . ."

"That is enough. No more discussion. I have decided. We go now, as I have arranged."

"That is *not* enough! We have a plan. It is agreed
with our friends on the high seas. It is agreed with our
friends in Iran. We must stick to it."

"No. There are aspects of this situation beyond even
your knowledge. I have already contacted Iran . . ."

"Beyond my knowledge! *What is there beyond my
knowledge?*"

"I will tell you in due course. I promise. We have no

time to argue now, we must act before it is too late. The transports from Queshm are on their way. We have to move *now*!"

The sound of the door slamming galvanized the three of them into action. They moved as one person, Asha taking the lead. She ran out toward the shadowed deck keeping low. Forward of the bridge-house they went, sprinting past the pump-room hatch, past the first tank tops, toward the accommodation ladder. "Where are we going?" gasped John at her shoulder.

"To my hiding . . ."

As she spoke, the deck lights came on, trapping them out here, yards from cover. The instant the brightness blazed, a disorienting roar of sound washed over them. Shouts in a mixture of accents, far off and disturbingly nearby. The pounding of running feet. The rattle of safeties coming off guns.

"This way," yelled John, diving to his left. Three seconds of frantic movement brought them halfway to the shelter of the central pipes, but as they continued to run wildly forward, so the first shots rang out.

"Christ!" yelled Bob, "they're going to blow us all to hell . . ." Then he was gone, spinning away with a howl of frustrated rage as a ricochet clipped his left calf and blew the leg from under him, sending him tumbling across the deck. John turned as Asha dived into the safety of the shadow beneath the pipes. "Bob," yelled the captain, blinded by the light. And a single shot blasted him round, chucking him back into Asha's arms.

And she was off with him at once, half carrying him, using the strength lent to him by the shock, moving him as fast and as far as she could, before he realized how badly he was hurt. Down the length of the pipes they went, toward the bow of the ship. "Not the fore-castle head," he called. "There's no way off . . ."

"Don't worry," she told him. "I know where I'm going."

She took him to the farthest hatch connecting to the inspection tunnels beneath the deck. She led him down and guided him back, until, after nearly fifteen minutes, they were above her secret room, almost exactly beneath the spot where he had been shot. By this time, the numbness of shock had worn off and she could tell from his movements that pain had set in. And yet he refused even to slow up. Grimly he swung onto that last ladder, and down he went, and down. He almost made it to the bottom before his legs gave out.

She pulled him away from the foot of it and across her secret room. How he had kept going for so long before passing out she would never know. Clearly, behind that boyish blend of exuberance and diffidence there lay a good deal of unexpected grit. She felt herself fill with warm affection for him. He was, after all, quite a man. Having rolled him onto her makeshift bed, she knelt at his side, busily undoing the buttons of his once-white shirt, pulling it away from his red-matted chest.

As she did so, she gasped. The damage was even worse than she had feared. The bullet had gone in at the back, followed the curve of the ribs, ripped through the muscles of the upper thorax by his left armpit, and exploded out the front, leaving quite a severe exit wound. These facts, accepted numbly at first as she worked to render rapid first aid, abruptly triggered off a vivid memory. John had been looking for Bob when he was shot. Looking back toward the bridge. And yet he had been shot in the back. That should have been impossible. The terrorists never ventured out onto the deck, let alone this far down it.

Therefore . . .

Then the memory came. Bob falling, a small wound in the calf, blood flying, bright in the blaze. John turning back for him. And out of the darkness behind John, another figure rising up out of the ground. Seemingly through the steel of the deck. But no. Of course. If they were beyond the light then they were beyond the deck. And that meant they were coming up the accommodation ladder. Up from a boat below. Her hands froze. She sat for an instant trying to work out the implications. But they were incalculable. The situation was too new; the alternatives utterly unknown. Only observation would tell her anything now. And, as it happened, she would have to go back to the surgery in any case. John required much more than she had here.

She took the greatest care as she planned her return to the bridge, caught between the urgency of helping John, simple curiosity, and the certainty that they would be looking for her now more than ever. The leader seemed a fundamentally unbalanced person, holding himself on a path of relative sanity only by the exercise of massive self-control. She wondered what he would be like without the firm hand of Islam to control his actions. Deeply disturbed and disturbing, she thought, and she had no desire whatsoever to fall back into his hands. How had Fatima become involved with him? With this whole horrific mess? And *why* hadn't Fatima contacted her? She felt like screaming.

Feeling a little like the Phantom of the Opera, she used the steel tunnels below the decks, showing herself only at the hatch covers she had left unlatched for this purpose. Only that one closest to the accommodation ladder itself was near enough to the action to be of any use and, having tried another farther away without success, she returned to this one, hoping to hear something of the terrorists' immediate intentions. She approached it with a great deal of care. On the deck above her she could hear a confused rumble of footsteps and, when she eased the hatch up an inch, she was confronted with a forest of booted legs. It was instantly clear what was happening: the captive crew were being taken off *Prometheus*.

Hope swelled. Perhaps a ransom had been paid: perhaps they were going home.

Reality intruded: perhaps not.

"That's the last of them," a man's voice called, in Arabic.

"Wait a moment," answered the Englishman's voice in the same language. "I want a last look around."

"What about the two that are missing?"

"Forget them. Get ready to cast off."

"Very well."

Asha closed the cover silently and went back down the steps. Good. It seemed that her fears were unfounded. If he was content to have a last check around and then to leave, then she would be free to tend John. When he was comfortable, she would see about contacting the outside world. Her mind busy with plans, she crawled out onto the deck and ran for the bridgehouse. With hardly a second thought she sprinted down the corridor and in through the surgery door, straight into the arms of the terrorist waiting there.

Asha stood, paralyzed with shock, utterly incapable of movement. All for nothing, she thought. It was all lost now. She would have to take them to John or he would bleed to death. A sense of frustration swept over her. It was so acute it felt like fury.

"He knew you would come here!" snapped the terrorist. "You fool, Asha, how could you think he would not know?"

Asha stood, unable to breathe as the familiar voice went on.

"You hang around here risking your freedom to release your captain. Then you all but throw your life away to rescue him when he is wounded. Of course you will come back here the moment you think it is safe, to get what you need to tend him!"

"Fatima. It is you! Your voice, I . . ."

"Get down! Down on the floor."

"Fatima. Darling . . ."

"Now!" The barrel of the rifle in her twin sister's hand drove into Asha Quartermaine's stomach and she dropped to the floor at once, winded. Then sturdy legs rolled her over and over as though she were a big beach ball and she was under the examining table, concealed by the cotton sheet upon it.

"Has she come yet?" enquired the harsh voice of the Englishman suddenly, from the doorway.

"No," lied Fatima at once. "I told you she was too clever to fall into such a simple trap."

"Well, never mind. We still have enough hostages to ensure no action will be taken against us until it is too late. Come on, then. It is time to go."

CHAPTER NINETEEN

"That was last night," Asha said. "Just before dawn. I did some work on him then and let him sleep. When he was well enough to move, I brought him up here. Then you arrived and I thought they had come back. I made him move too quickly and we opened up his wound again."

John sat, pale but wide awake, on the examination table in *Prometheus*'s surgery, listening to the last of the story. Richard, Robin, and the others clustered, spellbound, around them. While she talked, Asha continued to work. The wound in John's back had been stitched, the track of the bullet disinfected and cauterized. Now the ragged pit of the exit wound at the front was being dealt with.

Richard hardly knew where to start. The fact that Sinbad's story had been so close to the truth disturbed him most, pulling him away from a clear view of the problems that now confronted him and the further action needed to overcome them.

It was a damn nuisance that, apart from John and Asha, the rest of *Prometheus*'s crew had slipped through their fingers, spirited away to some other location as the second part of the terrorists' plan began. But if Asha's account of the conversation between her sister and the Englishman was correct, then things were not going right for the terrorists either. They had held their hostages here unwillingly, for so long, because they had been awaiting the signal to begin part two. But that had never come. So they had gone ahead without it. Of all the welter of detail their story had revealed, this fact seemed the most important. But where had they gone? And with what purpose?

"First things first," he said. "Let's radio in. We've a fair number of people to inform about this . . ."

"I tried that," said Asha quickly. "The radio doesn't work."

"I'll go and take a look at it," said Martyr at once.

"If you can't fix it, we'll call in from *Katapult* when we get back aboard," called Richard after him. The central system for the handheld radios and the big transceiver Admiral Stark had donated to the cause of greater safety in the Gulf were still aboard *Katapult*, the heart of their simple communications system: perhaps it would be as well to move it all up here, thought Richard. And that, by association, took his mind to the multihull. "Better get *Katapult* shipshape," he suggested to Weary.

"Too right, Captain. Don't like having my spinnaker draped over your forecastle head, for a start," said the Australian. He and Chris left together, almost like twins themselves.

An instant after they departed, Salah was gone, to prowl about the ship, looking for clues.

"Anything we can do for you?" Robin asked Asha, too well aware that Richard, lost in thought, would be like an automaton until he had sorted out whatever was on his mind. Where his men were and what to do next, she guessed.

Oh God, if only Daddy were here, she thought. The poignancy of his absence brought tears to her eyes. "I beg your pardon?" Poor Asha had been talking to her in response to her question, and she hadn't heard a word.

"When I'm finished here, there are some things I want to bring up from that hole I've been hiding in for the last few days."

"Of course. I'll give you a hand."

"Thanks."

"I don't have to stay here, do I?" asked John.

"No. If you're careful, you can move around."

"Good," said John. Asha had filled him full of pain-killers, so that he felt quite well and was itching to get up onto the bridge. The fact that Weary had assumed Richard was the captain of *Prometheus* galled him. He, John Higgins, was the captain. And his place was on the bridge. So, as soon as the last layer of bandage was firmly round his chest, he went. After an instant, Richard followed him. The two women exchanged glances and went out onto the deck.

"It's just impossible even to guess where the murderous bastards are," said John, easing his stiff frame into the captain's chair on the port side of the bridge. Richard stood restlessly by the tiny helm, looking down toward the accommodation ladder, then out beyond it into the afternoon haze of the Gulf. Robin suddenly appeared, popping up out of the tiny hatch halfway down the deck, her golden curls glinting like guineas as the south wind tossed them in the sunshine.

"No clues at all?"

"Nothing. We can go through the story again later in case we've missed anything important, but it all happened like we told you in the surgery just now, and I don't think they gave anything away. Whoever this Englishman is, he's damned clever. This thing has been carefully planned to make sure that nothing they've said or done has given anything away at all."

"They've taken Bill Heritage too, you know."

"No!"

"Yes. They're holding him somewhere. Near here, I'd guess. Wherever Bob, Kerem, Twelve Toes, and the rest are bound for, probably. Poor old Bill will have been sitting there for a week now, waiting for them. But not knowing, I suppose. Kept as much in the dark as you all were."

"Bastards! It fair makes your blood boil, doesn't it?" John absently fumbled on the shelves by his chair and pulled out a briar pipe. Without thinking, he slipped the stem into his mouth and started chewing on it morosely.

In the distance, two tiny figures were sorting out the spinnaker on the forecastle head. Abruptly *Katapult*'s ruined masthead became visible. Richard watched the activity absently, his mind going over the cold ground of the events so far like a bloodhound searching for a scent.

"So, what do you want to do first?" asked John.

"The obvious thing is to get *Prometheus* out of here. Up anchor and move into safer waters. We're too close to Iran here."

"Anchor off the Saudi coast. Bring a new crew out. Get her back into business?"

"She'll have to go back into business in the end. Though the thought of replacing her crew while they're still . . ." Richard all but choked with frustrated rage.

"Perhaps, now that stage two of their plan has started, someone will actually hear from them."

"I expect someone will. I just wish to God there was some way we could make sure they heard from us first. I'd give a lot to know where they've gone. If only Asha's sister . . ."

"That's so strange," mused John, sidetracked. "Such a strange situation."

"All too common these days."

"Asha's quite a woman though, coming out after her sister like that."

"She is."

Martyr appeared. "No chance of fixing the radio I'm afraid."

"We'll bring the big set from *Katapult* aboard," said Richard. "Any chance of starting the engine?"

"I'll go look," said the American amiably.

Richard looked back out into the afternoon glare. Robin and Asha were carrying bits and pieces from Asha's hideout back along the deck. Two tiny figures, deep in conversation, all but lost on the immensity of the deck. That was what they all were, thought Richard bitterly: pygmies at the mercy of giant forces. Powerless. Helpless. And it simply was not good enough.

Salah prowled in, his long, dark eyes everywhere. "There's nothing," he reported quietly. "Not a hint. Not a clue. It's as though they were never here. I've never seen anything like it."

I have, thought Richard.

"They were a strange lot anyway," mused John. "I mean, who's ever heard of a terrorist cell being led by a woman and an Englishman?"

We have, thought Richard. He and Salah exchanged lean smiles.

Just at that moment, Robin arrived. "Here we are," she said. "We've moved most of Asha's stuff back to her quarters. But we thought we'd better bring this back up here."

"What is it?"

"It's the chart she stole. You know she was going to jump ship and go across the Gulf in an inflatable. At night. Alone. Daft."

"Here . . ." began John, leaping to Asha's defense, for all that he agreed with Robin.

"Asha said they were upset about losing that," said Richard. "Let's have a look at it."

Within seconds, the big British Admiralty chart 2858 was spread out in front of them and five pairs of eyes were scrutinizing it carefully.

"What's that?" asked Robin at once. There was a design in flowing script written in the margin.

"It's Arabic," answered Salah. "It means Dawn of Freedom." He looked across at Richard. "So Sinbad got that right as well."

But Richard wasn't listening. He was staring at the chart, thunderstruck. The Arabic script was written beside their present position. Then a long line charted a course away down the whole length of the Gulf. But the same script was written at the far side of the paper, right by the purple writing that said, "Adjoining Chart 707." And this time a course was charted back across the Gulf of Oman then in through Hormuz.

To a rendezvous, where the two courses met.

"My God!" he breathed.

He blinked. Frowned. Concentrated. He had to be certain about this.

But he *was* certain. There could be no other explanation. It all made too much sense. It all made too much terrifying sense.

He knew where the terrorists were heading. And he knew what they had been waiting for. And he knew why they had waited in vain.

With shaking hands, he took his wallet from his pocket and opened it. The paper was there among a wad of old photographs, cards, receipts. He emptied them all out on the chart and spread them out until he found what he was looking for. A simple piece of white

notepaper onto which he had painstakingly traced what
he could remember of the pattern written on that flimsy
he had taken from the dead radio officer a week ago.
Taken and then lost in the waterspout. The writing that
had been the name of the burning ship. He slid it across
the chart until it was beside the writing that meant
Dawn of Freedom. It was identical.

"Where did you get that?" asked Salah, awed.

Richard told him.

So the terrorists had been awaiting an arms shipment.
One that would never come. And rather than wait here
any longer for news, they had gone early to their rendezvous. That point on the chart where the two lines
crossed.

Fate.

But even as Richard's mind switched into lightning
calculations of the impact of this information, his thoughts
were interrupted by a gasp of shock from Asha. Suddenly
she was sorting through his personal belongings spread
out across the chart beside his empty wallet.

"It's him," she said, lifting a photograph of a smiling,
open-faced young man. "It is *him!*"

They all turned toward her, Richard last. She was
holding a photograph of a man who had been dead for
years. Lost in the breakup of the first *Prometheus*. A
photograph of his godson, Ben Strong. Over the top of
it she looked at Richard with horror on her face. "What
are you doing with a picture of the terrorist leader?" she
demanded.

CHAPTER TWENTY

Fate.

As soon as he was certain that the distant voices were not just another trick of his imagination, Bill Heritage started beating on his door and yelling at the top of his lungs. During the time he had been in this dark, silent room, he had come to know it so intimately that he could see it in his mind's eye almost as clearly as if the light were on. He moved about it unerringly now, for learning it had been what had kept him sane so far. Or nearly sane. So far.

When he awoke each morning—he called it morning when he woke up, though he had no idea what time it really was—he stripped altogether and did a long, complicated series of exercises. By the time he had completed these, he was always running with sweat, so, cosseting himself exactly as he would any of his thoroughbred racehorses, he walked gently round the room until he was dry. Only then did he dress. It was important to his self-esteem that he keep his clothes as clean and odorless as possible. Dressed in his shirt and trousers, he would then go for a tour of his room. He would explore it thoroughly, every bit as minutely as he had on the day of his arrival. He would test his memory by predicting what lay within a hand's breadth of his fin-

gers. He would take risks, gamble with himself, by walking rapidly in any direction then stopping, to find himself within an inch of the slop bucket, the bed, a wall. Every irregularity on these walls he knew by touch, but especially well he knew the doorway that never let in light or coolness or draft of fresh air. Whose round metal handle turned easily enough, but uselessly. To no avail.

In this way Sir William Heritage lived out some of the strangest days of his long life with nothing to do but to feel his way about the tiny room, await the daily rituals of feeding and slopping out, and rack his brains to think where he might be. It occurred to him he might be in a water tank, or something of the sort underground, for the warm walls felt more like metal than plaster to him, and the stale air smelled of iron. He imagined he might be aboard ship somewhere, moored in Beirut Harbor—but there was no movement of water beneath the keel; no grumble of generators for power.

Never during those long days and nights, in all his reasonings and thoughts and deductions, did he ever dream that he was aboard a disused oil platform at the mouth of the Persian Gulf.

"Hey!" He hammered on the door, yelling as loudly as he could. "In here! In here!"

And his cries were answered at once by the sound of the bolts going back. He stood back, eyes narrow, expecting blinding light. But the door opened to reveal a tall figure dimly silhouetted. "Ah, Sir William," it said, incongruously, in punctilious English. "So there you are! Come along. I think we'll put you in with the others now." Something in the man's tone warned Bill that this was not the SAS, come to set him free.

It must be a ship of some kind, he thought as soon as he walked out into the corridor. The combination of

white-painted, rust-streaked metal and bumpy, frayed linoleum had a decidedly maritime feel about it. The impression intensified as they climbed almost naval companionways. And yet the whole structure was rock solid. And he could hear traffic in the distance . . .

Light dawned, actually as well as metaphorically, when they came to deck level. They rounded a corner, and a window let in a shaft of light so fierce it had discrete edges as though it were a column of golden crystal. And outside, the unmistakable lines of an oil platform with the tanker-filled Gulf, sullen in the heat, equally unmistakable beyond. The rumble of traffic resolved itself into the sound of surf upon hollow iron legs.

"My God!," he said, his voice rusty from disuse. "It's Fate."

"Oh, Sir William," said the tauntingly familiar voice of his guide. "It's so much more than that!"

But then all conversation between them stopped. The guide opened a door and Sir William found himself on the threshold of a large lecture hall, where, under the guns of a dozen armed terrorists, stood the crew of his tanker *Prometheus*. At once his eyes were searching for the faces of John Higgins, Asha Quartermaine, Bob Stark. Only Bob was there, pale but defiant, leaning on Kerem Khalil. There was blood on Bob's leg.

"You will have time to greet our other distinguished guest in a moment," said the Englishman to them all. "In the meantime, listen to me. You know the rules. Keep to them. The guards may allow you to talk at their own discretion, but this is a privilege easily revoked. You will find life here a little harder than it was on *Prometheus*. There is no bedding or air-conditioning or videos or books. But I am sure you can adapt. Your discomfort is likely to be temporary. There will soon be

enough for all. In the meantime, remember this. The watchword is *obedience*. Your lives depend upon it."

"Who is that chap?" was Bill's first question, a moment later.

"Your guess is as good as mine, Sir William. Mind if I sit down? This leg hurts like a son of a bitch!" Kerem helped Bob down onto the floor. "Only a scratch, and bandaged at that, but just at the stage of stiffening up. You know how gunshot wounds can be." Tersely, he explained how he had come by it, putting Sir William's mind at rest about the two missing faces. Then he asked, "How long have you been here?"

"As near as I can estimate, since the day after you were taken. I'd come to Bahrain to try to get you out. They took me at Manama. Drugged me. Brought me here. I thought I was in Beirut."

"Thanks for coming to help us. Appreciate that." The two friends looked at each other long and hard. Then Bob continued, "But if you were out here alone working to free us, that means State doesn't want to know."

"That's the way it was when I came out. Even the President seems hesitant on this one. The Gulf is a powder keg at the moment. They say Iran is near to civil war: navy versus air force."

"My father must be going mad with worry!"

"That he is. Or was when I flew out."

A pause.

"Any idea what these people are actually up to, Bob?"

"Not really, Sir William. They were waiting for something, a signal or something, on *Prometheus*. I don't think it ever came. Then they brought us down here anyway. Just ran out of patience, I guess."

"Must be more than a signal, Bob. From the way that

chap was talking just now, they're expecting supplies, not messages. And that means . . ."

"A ship. God Almighty! Put terrorists together with a ship and what do you have?"

"Arms smuggling."

"Right! So what we have here is a small group of hard-line terrorists on an abandoned platform at the mouth of the Gulf with enough hostages to make sure that no one's just going to sashay right up and blow them away. We know they don't need small arms because, as we can see, they are well supplied with those already. So they have to be waiting for something heavier. Rockets, maybe. Wire-guided missiles. What does this picture look like to you?"

"My God, Bob, they're going to blockade the strait. They're going to sit here threatening to destroy any tanker that tries to get past. And they could do it, too! They're going to close the Gulf!"

CHAPTER TWENTY-ONE

They moved the admiral's big radio up onto *Prometheus*'s bridge and left the smaller communications center on *Katapult*. Richard had decided not to contact anyone— not even Angus, yet. But clearly, if they were going to fit into the pattern of Gulf shipping without arousing unwelcome interest until they reached Fate, they would have to be able to talk to other ships and coastal stations at the very least.

Two things obviously counted against their hoped-for anonymity, thought Richard. Firstly, who they were. The moment they told anyone that they were the Heritage Mariner tanker *Prometheus II* heading from Bushehr to Hormuz, alarm bells would start ringing from here to the White House. God alone knew who would come sniffing around then. Secondly, *Prometheus* would stick out like a sore thumb to the men on Fate even before they saw her name, because she would be the only unladen tanker going out of the Gulf. But that situation was not insurmountable either, for the tanker carried pipes that could be lowered over the side. She had pumps that could suck sea water aboard once she was under way, and distribute it evenly among the tanks until she appeared to be fully laden.

Just as Ben Strong had done on the original *Prometheus* ten years ago, to conceal a missing cargo of oil.

Ben! Richard drove his fist against the helm. He gazed out along the darkening length of *Prometheus*'s great green deck, but he saw nothing of the pipes, tank tops, hatches, Sampson posts, winch housings, pumps, steps, and walkways before him. Saw nothing of the early sunset beyond. Instead he saw the face of Ben Strong, his godson. He saw it as he had last seen it, mad and murderous, behind the handgun he was an instant away from firing. An instant before his ship broke in two and hurled the madman to his death, insanely singing out, "Good-byeeeeeeee."

And now here was the nightmare resurrected, his madness almost subsumed in Muslim fundamentalism, still at war with the world, and with Heritage Mariner. Able to lay his hands on all the weapons in a modern terrorist's arsenal. The thought was absolutely chilling. Never in his wildest dreams would he have guessed that the mysterious Englishman and the unfortunate twin in blind Sinbad's story should have been so closely related to themselves. It was as though Fate truly had a hand in this: the force, not the platform. Though who could tell the difference any more?

The lift doors behind him opened and John gasped in pain as he turned in the chair to see who was coming. "We can get her started," called Robin. She and Martyr had been looking at the engine.

"We can get under way whenever you want." The American's deep bass replaced Robin's warm contralto, and Richard turned to meet their expectant gazes at last.

Chris and Doc were on *Katapult*. Asha was in the surgery. Salah was checking the stores. The others were here, waiting for orders.

"Right," said Richard. "We sail at sunset. It will take us twenty-two hours to get down the Gulf. If we move out of the lanes and slow down a little toward evening tomorrow, we can get everything set up and arrive

with the last of the light. We'll have three watches on the bridge but none in the engine room. Set that on auto and leave it. It should be all right for a day. Starting at eighteen hundred, John will be on watch up here with Salah and Asha. C. J., you will relieve them at oh-one hundred tomorrow with Chris and Doc."

"Fine," agreed Martyr. "What about *Katapult* if they're up here?"

"I've thought about that. We'll have to tow her. It's the only way. We need constant watches. If they sail her, they'll have to keep twenty-four-hour watch themselves while we'll be doing six hours on and six off. We'd all be exhausted by the time we hit Fate."

"Yeah. I can see that. Okay, I'll go tell them to batten down . . ."

"No. I'll go in a minute. You and Robin had better go and get the engines ready. John, I'll find Asha and send her up here. Then I'll get the others out of *Katapult*. Secure her to the stern and see if the three of us can get the hook up."

"Tall order for half an hour's work," observed John.

"It's going to be bloody hard work for all during the next twenty-four hours, on watch and off. Can you work at the chart table, without too much discomfort?"

"Yes," lied John cheerfully, heaving himself up out of the chair.

"Good. I need our best route to Fate worked out ready for when we set sail."

"Consider it done," said John. "In fact it has been done. I'll check his workings if you like, but I'll bet you that what Ben Strong has marked there will be just the ticket."

"Perhaps," said Richard dryly. "But he must have been laying for a smaller ship. The one that took them off last night."

"I hadn't thought of that."

"It'll probably be the same. He was a good seaman."
Richard paused. "Then we'll just have to hope," he
added as he went, "that whoever is steering *Prometheus*
can follow the madman's course."

Richard found Asha in her surgery and sent her to the
bridge. She was pleased enough to go, knowing that
John would need her there if he was going to do much
moving around. Salah was in the ship's refrigerator,
checking provisions as ordered. Richard sent him up to
the bridge as well. He knew John would need an experienced helmsman the instant they got under way. He
had designed the watches carefully so that there would
be an experienced officer and helmsman available to
each as well as a third person for lookout and emergency backup. Robin and he would take the last watch
themselves, starting at 09:00 hours in the morning,
while the others caught up on sleep or made final preparations. And after the end of their watch, at sunset tomorrow, *Prometheus* would either have a full complement
once more, or she would be in no condition to need
any watchkeepers at all.

These reflections were quite enough to take him out
onto the baking foredeck where he came face to face
with Chris and Doc, who had just finished securing
Katapult at the foot of the accommodation ladder. Suc-
cinctly, Richard explained to them what he had told
the others and the Australian nodded his agreement.
Ten minutes later, *Katapult* was resecured on a long line
to *Prometheus*'s afterdeck and the three of them were on
the way to the forecastle head, racing like children on
BMX bikes.

It was by no means a difficult or a lengthy task to
winch *Prometheus*'s great anchor up off the shallow,

sandy seabed, and, in the absence of tide, it made no real difference to her disposition whether the hook was up or down. Not even the south wind would move the inert mass of the tanker. Only her great screws could do that. And sure enough, as they sped back up toward the bridge, the deck began to throb beneath them and the steady blast of the southerly seemed to swing around the quarters so that as they returned the BMXs to the rack under the awning aft of the A deck door, a steady headwind blew in their faces along the deck. *Prometheus* was under way.

Five hours later, Richard sat back, massaging his tired eyes. Completed on the worktop before him were all his notes and contingency plans rendered into manageable form. He patted them with grim satisfaction. They would go into the log so that if anything went wrong in eighteen hours' time . . . At the thought he glanced at his watch: 23:05 local time. Damn! He had run over the hour. He flicked a switch on the big transceiver beside him and caught the tail end of the World Service news.

". . . the worst plague of recent years still moving north destroying millions of acres in the Ethiopian Rift Valley and on the Danakil plain in Eritrea. Experts hope that the strong southerly winds will blow them across the Red Sea and into the desert of Ar-rab al Khali where they will perish. This seems to be a faint hope and in the meantime, the people of Saudi Arabia are bracing themselves for the onslaught. And finally, cricket. The English batting collapsed at the Oval this afternoon in the face of an unremitting onslaught from the West Indian pace attack. England's top scorer, with a total of seventeen runs, was . . ."

Richard made a peculiarly Scottish sound of disgust

and turned it off. Time for bed, he calculated. A busy
day over and a busier about to begin. He sat back in the
spare chair on the bridge, the image of John's captain's
chair except that it was on the starboard side. Salah Malik stood at the helm. John sat, half asleep, in the captain's chair. Asha, her face green and ghostly, divided
her scrutiny between her patient and the collision alarm
radar that watched the waters around them, alert for
danger there.

"I'll just set this to an open emergency channel. Then
I'll leave you to it," he said. But he showed no sign of
moving. For the first time since coming aboard he had a
little leisure to luxuriate in the simple fact of being back
aboard. *Katapult* had been like a holiday, vivid and exciting. But this was like coming home. All his senses
were attuned to the familiar sensations around him,
from the steady throbbing of the engines coming
through the floor to the sight of a star-bright, calm Gulf
night distanced by the clearview. The smell of the conditioned air. The taste of it on the back of his tongue.
The sheer size of his bridge. Of his vessel.

Home.

Humming a little tune to himself, he went off to
look for Robin. When he found her, he would take her
to the officers' pantry and they would make a cup of
cocoa, drink it, and go to bed. It was what they did at
midnight every night when they were at sea together.
The prospect of it made his contentment complete, almost as though he were insensible to the danger they
would be in tomorrow.

In eighteen hours' time every single one of them could
be dead.

They were up again before six, well aware that it would
take the better part of twelve hours to get sufficient

water aboard to make *Prometheus* seem like just another laden tanker outbound through Hormuz.

As the swift dawn broke into yet another stifling day, so they worked, with Richard firmly in command and—typically—the most active. To pipe heads standing three feet high, they attached great hoses that reached left and right across the deck before the bridgehouse. The deck railings were opened, and the ends of the hoses rolled overboard to fall thundering against *Prometheus*'s high sides, down into the sluggish sea. The ends of the hoses plunged deep beneath the surface, dragged back toward the stern at once by the tanker's steady progress through the water.

Richard ran to the cargo control room at once. Its long window looked forward to where the pipes were attached. Here Robin was just completing the programming of the computers according to the plans they had agreed on last night. Now the Mariners stood shoulder to shoulder as she punched in the final instructions. The computers immediately communicated with the pumps in the pump room three sheer decks below. The main pumps thundered into life, sucking in water past the filters at the pipes' ends. As it came aboard, the filtered water was fed immediately into a system of smaller pipes controlled by secondary pumps that passed it in carefully measured increments evenly into the tanks along *Prometheus*'s massive length.

In the cargo control room, displays automatically monitored the disposition of the cargo. Schematics of the ship lit up, each tank represented by a safe green box, as strategically located sensors read the forces unleashed by the movement of the liquid through the system. The greatest danger came from the shear force, that terrific tension that could arise at the junction of improperly laden tanks where the upward force of a

buoyant empty tank ran up against the downward force
of a full one. Mistakes in lading could tear—had torn—
tankers apart in seconds.

But Robin was far too competent a cargo-control officer to allow anything of the kind to happen. And in
any case, the task of controlling the oncoming water as
it passed relatively slowly along two basic channels was
not one she would find particularly hard. She was used
to calculating the shear forces unleashed when six or
eight tanks were being loaded all at once. They stood
side by side in silence until it was clear that the programs were coping successfully with the work. Then
Richard looked at his watch. "The automatic alarms
will ring here, in the engine room, and on the bridge if
there's a problem," he said. "Let's go."

They took the watch at once, early. Richard crossed
to the helm and relieved Weary with a clap on the
shoulder that made the big man jump and look around,
bewildered.

"Time for some rest, Doc," he said.

The sound of his name stopped the frown of confusion on Doc's face and he turned away with a grin to
shamble over toward Chris, who was dozing on her feet
by the collision alarm radar. Robin went over to C. J.
Martyr, the only one of the watchkeepers truly awake.
When she put her hand on his shoulder, he automatically rubbed it with his steel-stubbled jawline, a piece of
easy intimacy as though she were as much of a daughter
to him as was Christine.

"I'd never have believed he could have survived," he
rumbled, talking to Richard as much as to her. "And
given that he did, I'd never have thought he would
come back like this."

The first *Prometheus* had been breaking up, splitting in
two halfway down her long deck in a storm in the En-

glish Channel. Martyr and Robin had been out on that doomed deck together in pursuit of the man who had masterminded poisonings and murders to cover the illegal sale of her cargo, and the lethal attempts to have her sunk for insurance. That man had been the first officer, the captain's godson, Ben Strong. When the ship had broken up, Richard, Salah, and the others had saved the two of them. And they had all seen Ben Strong, splayed on the forward section, whirled away to destruction as it had sunk. How could a man trapped in such a cataclysm, sucked down to such an end, return ten years later to take his mad revenge? Or, more correctly from the look of things, to make the settling of his account with Heritage Mariner a part of his larger plan.

For it was clear enough, and had been from the outset as they looked back on it, now wise with hindsight, that the pirating of *Prometheus II* was almost incidental to the overall plan. A ruse to keep the eyes of the world on one end of the Gulf while the real work went on at the other. Preoccupied with the drama at Bushehr, who had given a second thought to Fate? The planning behind it, the preparation, and the cunning were deeply disturbing. Perhaps the cunning most of all. While they were on Fate, waiting for a lost ship, unaware that she would never come, the terrorists' defenses were at their lowest, and Richard's plan stood a chance. But the moment they realized that *Dawn of Freedom* was not coming, the instant that they realized that something had gone wrong—anything at all—such a well-prepared, clever team as Ben Strong had assembled would be bound to come up with an equally effective alternative. And once they did that, the whole world was likely to be helpless, as it had been in the affair so far. And then what hope would the team on *Prometheus* stand? Eight desperate people undermanning a half-empty supertanker.

At the helm, Richard glanced up at the chronometers above his head. 08:59 local time. Good. Caught it this time. "Log on, Robin, will you? And, just as you do, get the radio please."

They crossed to the chart table where the logbook lay, then Martyr stayed, tidying up his entry before he signed over to Robin. She hit the switch on the receiver and a quiet voice filled the bridge.

"This is the BBC World Service. Here is the news at six o'clock A.M., Greenwich Mean Time . . ."

"You think we're going to be on it?" asked Robin, her voice brittle, caught between playfulness and grimness.

"If we are, I hope it hasn't been updated recently. If I were Ben, I'd be tuned in to it. It might just be a useful early warning. Best he'll have, unless he has a satellite receiver down there and a television for the twenty-four-hour news stations." Richard's voice, unnaturally gruff, was beginning to show the strain. She couldn't read his expression, outlined as he was by the blinding glare.

". . . news from Tehran of the continuing power struggle within the Iranian armed forces. Sources close to the Iranian government suggest that it is the officers in the Iranian Air Force who are loyal to the regime. Officers in the Iranian Navy, however . . ."

"This is getting close," said Robin. "Wait for it!"

"The United States Sixth fleet continues to perform maneuvers in the Gulf of Oman but has yet to pass through the Strait of Hormuz. The White House reiterated yesterday that, while the current climate persists, the fleet will not . . ."

"No, it's too long," said Robin with some relief. "I don't think they'll mention us. . . ."

"There is no doubt however, that the taking of the Heritage Mariner supertanker *Prometheus Two*, with its full complement of forty men and women, has considerably worsened an already tense situation. There is no further news of Sir William Heritage, chairman of Heritage Mariner. And still no official reaction from Heritage Mariner itself."

"Quite an item!" spat Martyr, his voice heavy with disgust.

"Nothing compared to what it would be if they knew what Heritage Mariner's reaction actually is," observed Robin dryly.

"And now the rest of the world news. Remaining in the Middle East, it is now reported from the city of Ubaylah in Saudi Arabia . . ."

"Well, so far so good," said Richard, much relieved. "Nobody seems to have noticed that we've gone. Still nine hours to go, though. And we're likely to stir up a hornets' nest when we report in. . . ."

"But we haven't been challenged by any of the coastal stations yet," said Robin matter-of-factly. "After all, what are we to them? One more blip on their radar going the same way as all the other blips, like one more freight car on an infinite train. What do they care?"

"They'd care quickly enough if they realized."

"But they haven't. And they won't unless they get in contact directly. They wouldn't even expect to hear from us until we get close enough to Hormuz to start asking for a pilot. And anyway, if anyone does contact us, why tell them the truth? Unless they come out here and look us over, how are they going to know? I've got all the Heritage Mariner sailing schedules in my head. So have you, Richard. *Neptune* should be in the Gulf now. We'll just say we're *Neptune* if anyone asks us. At the very least it'll confuse the hell out of them for a while. Christ! We only need nine hours."

In the silence, the bulletin continued, ". . . scientists

have recently discovered they do not fly directly down-wind. The configuration of their wings is such that they actually fly across the wind at an angle dictated by the sun. The southerly winds presently dominating the region during the day, therefore, mean that a northeast-erly course is more likely. The citizens of Dubai . . ."

"Well, let's not worry about it until it happens," decided Richard.

"As the actress said to the bishop," quoted Martyr.

"Can I smell coffee?" asked Robin.

". . . as far as Bandar Abbas and Zahedan in Iran."

Salah came in through the door with four steaming mugs. Robin's nose wrinkled. One of the side effects of her present condition was super sensitivity to smells which, on the one hand meant that she could smell the coffee coming long before the others, but on the other hand meant that she couldn't actually face it when it came. And she thought she had been getting over morning sickness. What she really fancied, actually, was a morsel of cheese. . . .

And so the day proceeded. Richard had the con. Robin kept watch on the collision alarm radar and slipped out onto the bridge-wings with binoculars whenever she got the chance; checked their position on the satellite navigation system against the notes on the course in Ben's neat handwriting; ran down to the cargo control room during the quieter moments to check that the tanks were filling all right, and every time she did so, she popped into the galley for just one more sliver of cheddar cheese.

The others had a rest, or pretended to, each lying alone and tense in his or her cabin. Only Christine and Doc shared each other's company, he sleeping like a baby while she kept watch beside him, watchful for when he awoke. And when he did spring awake, at a quarter to four, she was still there, still watching, wide-eyed. But he knew who he was and remembered what was going on.

By four they were all on the bridge, waiting for Richard's final briefing. For the last two hours, Richard had been cutting speed and pulling north so that now they were dawdling along the very top edge of the one-way, east-bound channel just southwest of the island of Tanb e Borzog. Now he swung north again and cut power altogether. *Prometheus* continued to coast forward, dominated by the massive momentum of her fully laden tanks, out of the shipping lanes altogether until she came to rest, still facing east, safely behind the shallows stretching down from Tanb.

While the way was slowly coming off her, Richard took them over the plans for one last time, and the moment she was dead in the water they all hurried away to start assigned tasks. By five to five only Richard and John were left on the bridge. Richard stood by the helm, staring morosely down the deck. John sat in the right-hand chair—not the captain's chair—by the radio, with one of the walkie-talkies by his side. During the next five minutes it squawked almost continuously.

"Asha here, John. Ready."

"Martyr here, Captain. Ready. Over."

"Robin here. Ready but out of cheese."

"Weary here. Ready when you are. We'll hold as planned for as long as possible."

Seventeen hundred hours local time clicked up.

"They're all ready, Richard."

"World Service News, please, John. One last time."

"And here is the news at two o'clock. . . ."

"Fingers crossed, eh, Richard?"

"Fingers crossed, John."

"It has just been reported from the Arabian Gulf that the Heritage Mariner supertanker *Prometheus* has vanished. . . ."

"Hell's teeth!"

"The tanker, taken over by terrorists recently, has been anchored for over a week off the Iranian coast at Bushehr. . . ."

"Martyr. Martyr, can you hear me? Engine room. Come in!"

". . . but unconfirmed reports started arriving this morning that the ship had been moved during the night. . . ."

"Engine room here, Richard. . . ."

"The story's broken on the world news, Chief. They're broadcasting it now. . . ."

". . . Iranian authorities have just confirmed that *Prometheus* is no longer at Bushehr, although news from that troubled state . . ."

"Chief, I want full speed ahead, as fast as you can give it to me." Richard's hand moved on the engine-room telegraph, confirming his words even as he spoke: FULL AHEAD. Immediately he felt the whole ship begin to shudder as the twin screws thrashed the seas behind her. He felt life come into the tiny helm beneath his sweating palms as she began to gather way. The low gold shoulder of the island began to move across his vision and he swung *Prometheus* onto her new heading southeast, choosing the shortest route between themselves and their target little more than fifteen miles away across the quiet, unsuspecting Gulf.

Aiming to hurl her like a great javelin across the slow-moving, humdrum eastbound sea lanes, to hurl his command at Fate, at flank speed, no matter what the risks or consequences.

CHAPTER TWENTY-TWO

"An urgent search is currently being carried out all through the Arabian Gulf to try to discover what has become of her. . . ."

"Ben! Ben, can you hear me?" Fatima spoke feverishly into the walkie-talkie, praying that Ben was listening in somewhere close at hand. Not for the first time, she cursed the old platform for being so big. It was a long way from their center of operations to this lookout post down here.

"Fatima? What is it?"

"It's gone, Ben. *Prometheus* has disappeared. It's on the news."

"They've moved it. Someone's gone aboard and moved it. It must be Mariner. I'm on my way down. Don't tell the others yet. I'll have to think this through."

Fatima sat back, breathing deeply, trying to calculate what this might mean. The words of the rest of the bulletin whispered meaninglessly in the background.

". . . over Dubai. Observers say it is among the largest ever seen and reports speak of the sun being obscured . . ."

She could not sit still. She left the radio on but she could not bear to stay beside it. Long before the bulletin was finished or Ben arrived, she had begun her restless prowling. She was in the rig foreman's office, the

equivalent of a ship's bridge. It was a long, spacious
room, chosen to be their forward observation post because it gave such excellent views north across the shipping lanes to the Iranian island of Queshm twenty miles
away. But the shipping lanes were nowhere near that
wide, for there were seven miles of shoals and shallows:
the Flat, they were called, and *the Mariner shoal* . . .

"Mariner!" Ben exploded into the room, almost
hobbling in his hurry to get up here. When he walked
at his own pace, in careful control of the wreck of his
body, he could move normally. But let him rush, or try
to run, as now, and his rebellious muscles twisted and
turned him until he became almost hunchbacked. In
their early days together, when his body twisted thus,
she would sit for hours massaging him and listening
dreamily to the story of how he was picked up, thinking himself dead, by a freighter in the English Channel.
The little ship was crewed by Iranians. They never told
him where they had been loading in Europe, but they
were returning with war supplies to Bandar Komenhi
at the north of the Gulf, and they were happy to take
him with them. How he had come to be there, afloat in
that stormy sea, how he had been reduced to the state
he was in, he also never revealed. He treated his rescue
as though it had been a new birth. He had been born
again into Islam. As the freighter made its slow way
back to Bandar Komenhi, he had been re-created,
physically, spiritually, mentally. The gentle crew had
adopted him, nurtured him, educated him in all aspects
save one. He was when he came aboard, and he remained, an outstanding seaman. And, when Bandar
Komenhi had been attained, he revealed that he knew
the Gulf like the back of his hand. To the Iranians, it
was little short of a miracle. And one of which they
made increasing use, for the Bandar ports were hard up

against the border with Iraq and, as the war between the two of them intensified, so the mysterious English convert joined the fleets of dhows who were doing for Iran what the little ships at Dunkirk had done for England forty years before. And there he made the contacts who now supported his personal *jihad*.

Romantic stories they had seemed to her then. Now she asked herself more often what really lay behind them since the murder of First Officer Smyke; especially since he had told her there was more to the plan than she knew.

"I know Mariner," fumed Ben. "I know that murderous bastard of old. He won't be sitting still for this. He'll be up to some scheme or other. God, how I wish I'd killed him. Him and his bitch of a wife!"

Fatima had never seen Ben like this before and she stood aghast. A feeling of helplessness swept over her. A familiar feeling that had never been far away since that terrible day when she had stepped off the plane in Kuwait to find her father waiting for her, not dying after all. She was not a weak or subservient person, but she was beginning again to feel like the victim of forces far beyond her control. Once more she was feeling used.

She should have trusted her better instincts and stayed with the one person she knew for certain she could trust—Asha. But that was in the past now, far beyond recall, like those pointless letters she had written. Asha hadn't even recognized her until she had revealed herself. No, she was utterly alone now, so she had better get a grip.

"Calm down, Ben," she said quietly. "You know it makes the others nervous if we speak for too long in English and they cannot understand. And to see you like this as well . . ." She looked meaningfully across to where Ali was seated, dutifully staring into the bowl of their smaller radar set, his body unnaturally tense.

"It is bad enough that *Dawn of Freedom* is late and we are trapped here with the hostages and so few weapons. If you begin showing too much strain as well, you may sow the seeds of panic." In her passion she pulled her kaffiyah open and frowned at him, her face naked, willing him to be calm. And her action shocked him: she could see it in his eyes. So traditional had he become in the ways of his new religion, that he saw a woman's face unveiled in public as a sin. She turned away bitterly, rearranging her headdress, too well aware that her days as an equal member of the group were numbered. Soon he would find a convenient prison to condemn her to, just as her father had.

So the time for her own holy war was running short indeed: no matter what he demanded when the sea lanes had been closed, she must be sure her voice was heard as well, demanding freedom for all the sisters who found the yoke of submission too heavy to bear. Freedom from the abba, yashmak, and chador. Equality under the law.

"So the tanker has been moved, according to the unbelievers' news," she said, speaking in Arabic.

"What difference does it make to us?" Ben's ruined voice had regained its icy calm. His twisted body came erect. Their leader had returned. "It is just another tanker now. Just another easy target as it tries to move through Hormuz." He strode across to the window and positioned himself so that he could watch the tanker lanes and see into the radar over Ali's shoulder. The light blips in the green bowl registered themselves as dark, funereal shapes, moving in dolorous series before him. High sided and empty, away in the distance close to Queshm. Low and fully laden, scant miles away, each one filling even this huge window as it passed. What targets they would make when *Dawn of Freedom* arrived. "The last few," he said, calm now. "The last few to pass by Fate without knowing we are here."

His black eyes looked down from the window into the radar bowl watching the radial line sweep round like the second hand on a clock, lighting up all the obstacles between themselves, at its center, and Queshm to the north, with its naval base to which he could look for help as the situation progressed. Counting the chain of tankers—each vessel a link—passing in and out in regular, predictable series.

Behind him, the woman turned the radio to Hormuz frequency and the room filled with the quiet communication between the coastal station and the ships. She had not asked his permission to do that. She was becoming unreliable. And as for that shameless display just now . . .

Something was wrong.

He forgot about the woman and concentrated on the radar.

Something was very wrong.

"What is that?" he snapped, his finger stabbing down.

"I don't know," said Ali, uncharacteristically hesitant. "I've never seen . . ."

"Fatima. Look at this. What do you make of it?"

It was not in front of them but behind them. Not over the tanker lanes at all but sweeping north along a line stretching from Rass al Kaimah to Sharja. Not from the coast, either: from above the coast. Whatever it was, it was airborne. He went cold. This had been his nightmare.

"Do you think it could be planes?" asked Fatima. "It's difficult to tell."

"Then let's go and look. Quickly!" He was in motion at once, moving rapidly enough to twist himself all out of shape. His left arm curled up by his chest. He began to hurry crabwise to the door.

For once, the pain of his rapid movement was as nothing. Inside he was raging with tension. It had to be an airborne attack. It had to be. He had always reckoned that the hostages would be an effective barrier against such a thing—against any sort of attack at all. He had chosen them carefully, his contacts with that greedy fool Cecil Smyke allowing him full knowledge of the crewing of the Heritage Mariner ships. And their flagship *Prometheus* had furnished him with so much. English, Chinese, Pakistanis, Palestinians. The American, son of a senator, nephew to an admiral. He had hardly needed to bother with a Knight of the British Realm. But he owed Sir William Heritage, and taking him would hurt Robin and Richard most. All in all, they had seemed perfect protection even against the hysteria a closed Gulf would bring. But not against one of the emirates or sultanates if they decided to go it alone, and hang the consequences. Not against some madman in the Iranian Air Force with a squadron of fighters and blood in his eye. The struggle for power in the Iranian forces could not have come at a worse time for him. But recognition for his naval friends and supporters would just be another demand, when the time came, and they knew it. Unless this was the Iranian Air Force now.

All it would take was one concerted rocket attack. Fate was not as solid as it looked.

With these thoughts threatening to burst his head as his heart threatened to tear itself from his mutilated breast, he hurled himself out onto the flat roof of the tallest prefab facing south and, with binoculars jammed almost painfully into his eyes, he looked out into the evening sky.

Five miles due east, heading west at twenty knots, Robin Mariner was also studying the southern sky. She was standing on the afterdeck of *Prometheus*, between the swimming pool and the helipad. Behind her, the tanker's little Westland Wasp was uncovered, unfettered, fueled and ready to go. Robin was of two minds about her part in Richard's plan. She understood everything he had told her about the importance of total surprise—that was elementary. And she saw that it followed logically that he had to be careful how he used the radio, therefore. Ben would know by now that *Prometheus* had vanished. He would realize that the people most likely to move her this fast were her owners. He would be expecting them to be up to something, listening for clues of their whereabouts, ready to start executing hostages at the first whisper of them. It was absolutely imperative that the first solid indication of her presence would be her bows bearing down on him at full speed, so close that he had to start defending his command at once, for only then did the hostages stand a chance. And again, it followed from that, that the only way to get the help they so desperately needed was to go and ask for it. Only she, in the Westland, could do that. But all along she really knew what this was all about: Richard wanted her and the baby well clear of *Prometheus* and Fate when the two of them came together.

So she stood, calculatingly, beside the little helicopter, looking south and thinking. But then her thoughts began to be disturbed by what she was looking at. Even without the aid of binoculars, it was clear something was wrong down there. The sky between here and Sharja City was black. Not with early evening. Not even with clouds. With something more. It chilled her to look at that roiling black mass even when she had no clear idea what she was seeing. Some atavistic memory buried deep in her bones made her blood run cold as she watched it sweeping toward her, high in the last of the south wind. She hesitated. What should she do? Should she depart from the plan in the last instants before it got properly under way? Should she go up onto the bridge and warn Richard? Pop into the surgery and tell Asha before she took off? She had put her personal radio in the Westland when she was getting it ready. It was on the pilot's seat. She could sit inside and talk to the bridge from there. A couple of quick words about this strange biblical phenomenon then off to get help. As she turned to climb into the helicopter's little cabin, something landed on the deck behind her and hopped into the pool.

"Steady as you go," said John from behind the collision alarm radar. "I've got a clear echo. You should be able to see it now. Dead ahead, five miles."

"The light's going pretty quickly," answered Richard, concern creeping into his voice. "What's the time?"

"Eighteen hundred. Dead on sunset. You should be all right for light."

"There's some kind of cloud or fog coming in from starboard. Damned if I can make it out. Strangest thing."

Richard's personal radio buzzed. He lifted his left hand from the helm and raised the black box like a telephone handset, never taking his eyes off the sea ahead. "Yes?"

"It's Robin. There's some kind of cloud coming up out of Sharja . . ."

"I see it. It's reaching right round to Hormuz by the

look of it. You'd better steer clear ôf it when you take off."

"Don't worry. I will!"

"And Robin . . ."

"Yes?"

"I love you. Take care."

"I love you too, Richard. *Oh, my God!*"

"Robin! Robin, what is it? Robin!"

Asha was busy in the surgery, tensely preparing her medical equipment to receive the wounded. She had talked it over with Richard and they were both of the opinion that she had better get ready for gunshot wounds. And she knew exactly what she would need to treat those, after her recent experiences with John.

Her personal radio buzzed.

Richard's voice said, "Asha! Come in, Asha!" He sounded worried.

"Yes, Richard?"

"Something's the matter with Robin. Check for me, would you?"

Asha glanced through the porthole. It was too murky out there to see anything clearly. She thought of opening it, but it was secured by four butterfly bolts. Instead, she crossed to the door, went out into the corridor, turned right and right again, into the gym. It was dark in here, even this early. The lights had been smashed when the ceiling had been riddled by terrorist bullets. She looked up, expecting to see starlight through the holes in the roof. Nothing. Except . . .

She reached the glass-paneled door through which she had released Bob and John and paused with her hand on the handle looking out. Darkness was snowing down. Physically. It was as though the blackness of the sky had been broken into pieces like strange snowflakes and was settling here in a blizzard.

The helicopter was gone, the sound of its departure lost under the thunder.

Then the noise registered, and its significance, just as the weakened ceiling of the gym started to collapse under the weight of them.

"Locusts!" Fatima yelled at him. "It's a plague of locusts!"

Ben stood, transfixed, looking up at them as the rays of the setting sun abruptly shone from beneath them. In that instant, the black, swirling mass of them was transformed into an infinity of burning dots. Wings flashed like sword blades catching the light, bodies glittered, hard-shelled legs glinted. Multifaceted eyes glowed. And the light vanished.

"They ate the light," whispered Ben, awed by them.

But Fatima did not hesitate. She took him by his good arm and pulled him back inside. For she had seen what he had not. The locusts were coming down. Within an instant of the door closing behind them, the first massive grasshopper body thudded onto the thin, prefabricated roof above them. And that first, isolated noise was soon followed by others, pattering down onto the pale surfaces like the outriders of a storm.

They ran back down to the foreman's office as quickly as Ben could go, strangely disturbed by the invasion of the creatures, but hardly counting them as having any effect on their plans. They could secure the doors and windows well enough. What did it matter to them what landed on the outside?

But as Ben had observed, the locusts had all but eaten the light. Already the tankers heading to and from Hormuz were almost invisible, except for on the radar. In fact, over all the Gulf it seemed, darkness gathered at the beck of the creatures until nothing remained visible except the last of the sunset on the upper works of one final tanker, coming west, out of sequence, farther south than all the others. Seemingly heading straight for the platform itself.

"Three miles. Can you see it now, Richard?"

"Barely, John. I'm looking straight into the sunset now, but it'll be gone in another minute. There's something else, though. I still can't make it . . ."

The radio buzzed again. "Yes?"

"Locusts, Richard. It's a huge cloud of locusts."

"Asha. How's Robin?" He asked almost automatically. Asha's words had made scales drop from his eyes. As though he had put on spectacles, he saw what was happening clearly.

"She's gone. The helicopter got clear."

"Thank God."

"The locusts are settling back here, though. The weight of them is making the gym cave in."

Of course they would be settling! The thought appeared out of nowhere, The ship was green. The horde of insects probably thought it was edible.

He hit the deck lights. They flooded on. Their glare was soaked up by the swarm and the very air seemed to catch fire as their bodies reflected the beams.

"Two miles, Richard."

Only eight times their length to go. "Guide me. The deck lights have helped, but I still can't see. I'm going in blind." His eyes whirled with the confusion of insect bodies dancing in front of him. They were all he could see; they were the last thing he needed to see. His right hand was like rock on the helm.

He thumbed SEND on his radio again. "Two miles, *Katapult*. Watch out for the locusts. Good luck."

Fully laden, *Prometheus* rode low in the water, her deck only twenty feet above the surface. Only the narrowest part of her cutwater showed at the bow, cleaving through the flat sea at twenty knots. Fifty feet above the water, her white bridge-wings thrust out on either side, clear of the hull itself, overhanging it by ten clear feet. Above the bridge, another thirty feet of housing supported the tanker's communications equipment, dishes, and aerials. Above that stood her funnel, the smoke it was giving out lost to view immediately among the clouds of locusts there. For a moment after the lights came on, the locusts hesitated. Only their weakest had settled so far, a curtain of bodies like a rain shower beneath the thunderheads of the swarm. Between the water and the mass of the locusts just above *Prometheus*'s funnel was about a hundred feet of uninfested air. The wind came relentlessly from the south at little less than gale force.

Katapult darted out from behind the stern of the great tanker, shuddering in the force of the wind. As she heeled across the steady blast, her mast top came clear of the stratified bodies and she fitted into the low, clear air. Sails at full stretch, spinnaker billowing in front of her, she rode across the wind at twice the tanker's speed, leaping down toward Fate. She would reach the platform in two roaring, thundering minutes while those aboard her prayed they could get in behind the terrorists as planned, while their attention was still on *Prometheus*.

"She's going to ram us!" yelled Fatima.

"It's Mariner!" screamed Ben.

"Five minutes," called Ali from the radar, computing her course and speed.

"Get the others, Fatima. Get them all."

"But the hostages."

"All right. Leave two guards. And one in the main control room. Get the rest. Get the guns. Get everything."

In front of the manager's office, the deck of the platform stretched forward across an area about the size of a tennis court before it ended in a low rail and an eighty-foot drop to the sea. It was designed as an observation area, nothing more, like the outside bridge-wings on *Prometheus*. Ben tore open the office door and ran out onto it without further thought. His feet skidded out from under him. His whole side tore agonizingly. He plunged headlong into a writhing, hopping, buzzing mass of insects. Howling with rage, he pulled himself up and stumbled forward to the rail. In an instant, he was alive with locusts. Like a living shroud they clustered round him, piling themselves precariously on his shoulders, even hanging, one layer upon another, down his back. Only his kaffiyah kept them out of his hair and face. Their feet scratched the skin on his hands as they crawled. He could feel the weight of them, caked thickly around him. The humming, buzzing thunder of them was overpowering. The dead, earthy stench of them like vermin droppings. The wind of their wings was more powerful than the south wind in this sheltered place. He skidded to a stop by the rail, lucky not to slither under it, and leaned forward with its crawling crosspiece at his waist. He had to keep shaking the binoculars to keep their slow, fat bodies off the lenses.

And there she was, low in the water. That was what had fooled him at first. Closing at flank speed, her bow coming straight toward him, a bone in her teeth, kicking up a bow wave like a cruiser. Then the blaze of her deck lights with the hellish clouds of locusts dancing there, gathering on her, swarming over her, masking her lines and angles under curves of sandy, writhing, faintly glistening bodies. And her bridge-house. The white of it gone under the carapace of insects. The shape of it swollen, bloated, unwholesome. Only the windows uncovered. And behind the bridge windows, a glimpse of movement.

"I know you, you bastard. You've got the con yourself."

A blow on the shoulder spun him round. He was confronted by a shapeless monster made up of twisting, writhing things. More shapes loomed, amorphous, in the humming gloom beyond.

The sound of hammering started and it took him a moment to realize that one of them was already firing at the ship. The others joined him at the rail, firing wildly. Ben shook his head with frustration—his kaffiyah stayed still and his cheeks moved unsettlingly against it—shooting an AK-47 at the forecastle head of a supertanker was as pointless as throwing stones. They needed their heaviest weapons giving concerted fire at the bridge if they were going to stop *Prometheus*. He doubted they had more than a couple of weapons powerful enough to do her serious damage at all. But they could kill the men and women aboard: they had more than enough for that.

"One mile. Keep her at that. Due west."

"It's bloody difficult to see anything at all. How many of these damn things do you suppose there are?"

"Millions."

"Right. Remember. I don't actually want to ram it."

"Okay."

"Good. Cutting speed now." He rang down on the

engine room telegraph ALL ASTERN. The automatic equipment began to obey at once. It wouldn't actually stop them for another five miles at this speed, but stopping wasn't the real intention.

Suddenly, beyond the dancing brightness of the deck the forecastle head seemed to explode. Richard flinched, dazzled. A column of fire and smoke belched up fiercely from the head of his ship. "Here we go," he said grimly. "That looked like a mortar round to me."

"Three-quarters of a mile."

Katapult lay dead in the water under the southern side of Fate. Her spinnaker was down now and her sails were furled. The aerodynamic column of her mast rocked metronomically in the swell and as it did so, it almost touched the back of the platform. "Now!" yelled Salah, already on Fate, and C. J. Martyr jumped. He seemed to hang in the air for a moment between the masthead and the railings, but then the safe iron slammed into his chest and Salah's strong hands gripped his shoulders until he scrambled over onto the still, flat metal of the deck. At once he turned, unlooping the rope from his shoulder and dropping its weighted end down to Weary's waiting hands below. The locust infestation was not as heavy here, but still there was a layer of insects clinging to everything vertical and hopping on anything flat. The two men fought to disregard the almost nauseating sensation caused by the insects crawling on their skin as they went into their carefully planned routine. While Martyr was pulling up the first bundle of weapons from below, Salah scouted forward, checking their route. There seemed to be no guards on this side of the platform at all. Good. Richard's diversion was working well. Now all they had to do was get the weapons up, find the hostages, and give one to the other.

He glanced down, surprised by the weight of the Heckler and Koch MP-5, and found it was completely hidden in an amorphous mass of insects reaching down in a club from his elbow. His skin crawled, as though the foul things were inside him as well as out.

Martyr pulled up the first bundle of weapons and dropped the line for the second. So far, so good, he thought.

The manager's office had a flat roof that overlooked the observation platform where the mortar was. Up here, at an elevation slightly higher than the bridge windows that were its target, Ben put the general-purpose machine gun. It was the heaviest piece he had here apart from the mortar, but that only had four rounds left and it wasn't big enough to be accurate down the length of the tanker's deck. One lucky hit on the forecastle head had been enough to set it on fire, but the tanker was still powering toward them, chopping through the curtains of dancing insects. The blazing bows were a quarter of a mile away at most, halfway between here and the bridge. "Fire!" yelled Ben. He was so preoccupied, he spoke in English, but the meaning was clear enough. A bright line of 7.65mm tracer arced out toward the bridge-house less than half a mile away.

"One minute to impact," sang out John.

Richard was already spinning the helm, able to see the platform quite clearly now, and able to judge things for himself.

He moved the engine-room telegraph from FULL ASTERN to STOP.

It had never been his plan to ram the rig. That would have been far too dangerous for all concerned. The mathematics were something he must work out when he had leisure, but the force that would be released by the impact of a quarter of a million tons of water moving at twenty knots, with all its attendant momentum, against one immovable object like the platform would be colossal. It would certainly be enough to destroy Fate and all upon it. And probably the tanker too: her steel sides would be split apart like tissue paper.

Having taken the attention of the terrorists and held it while *Katapult* crept in, it was now his job to graze his ship gently along the platform's side and try to do some damage with the overhanging bridge-wings.

"Thirty seconds!" called John.

The center of the deck between the Sampson posts erupted like a volcano and Richard, who had decided the mortar had ceased firing, jerked right back in shock. The movement saved his life, for just at that moment, the bridge windows exploded inward, and he was overwhelmed by tracer bullets, shards of glass, and whirring, panicked insects.

The tanker's blazing forecastle head began to swing away. Fatima, crouching beside the mortar team, clapped her hands with relief, sending up a cloud of crippled insects. "Well done," she yelled in raucous Arabic. "It's time to try one more."

Above her head the long hose of tracer reached out toward the bridge. As it moved in a lazy snake of light, so it cleared the air around it and the mortar was inundated with smoldering pieces of locust. But the air was clearing anyway: miraculously, it looked as though the whole swarm had settled on the tanker, seemingly forcing it down more deeply into the water by the weight of their deep-piled bodies. It was as though she had come through some living sandstorm, with great dunes piled high on her decks. Dunes whose every grain was a locust. "Let's put one right in the middle. *Now!*" she ordered. The round rattled down the tube and thumped onto the firing pin. They leaned back as the explosive lobbed it over the heads of the rest of the men, still firing their assault rifles from the railing in front.

The middle of the tanker's deck burst open. The front of the bridge-house seemed to shiver as though a hurricane wind swept across it.

Prometheus's burning forecastle head began to swing back in.

The bridge was a shambles. The equipment at the front was in ruins from the combination of blast and tracer fire. The helm was in splinters. The only piece of equipment still functioning seemed to be the collision alarm radar, which was shrieking out its most urgent warning. There was glass everywhere littering the floor, the work surfaces, the chairs. Smoking tracer rounds, still red hot, lay on the deck. The radio was a total wreck. And everything was covered with locusts, most of them dying or dead.

Richard, on one knee, looking around the wreckage, softly called out, "John?"

"Behind the chart table. Fifteen seconds to impact, I'd say."

"I can't control her anymore. They've destroyed the helm."

"You mean, we're actually going to ram Fate?"

"Looks like it."

"Good God."

Ben reckoned they had about ten seconds before the tanker hit. He looked down over the edge of the roof he was kneeling on. Fatima was already clearing the observation platform down there. Good. Up here he had four men, all lying belly down. Three of them were firing their relatively useless assault rifles at the bridge; the fourth had the exceedingly effective general-purpose machine gun. "Stay here as long as you can," he ordered. "Keep firing at the bridge." As he stood up, the bow of the supertanker, still belching a column of flame, came level with the edge of Fate. The whole platform began to shake and a deep bass note, so low and powerful it made his eyeballs tremble in their sockets, seemed to come from every plate of it. "Now it really begins," said Ben to himself and ran to the steps that would take him down to the deck. He was on his way to the main command post in the central buildings.

Prometheus's flank ground along Fate's great metal legs. The observation platform slowly bent upward as its edge caught the tanker's deck railing. Then it folded back and tore away altogether. Beyond it, the second column of fire rose from the tanker's deck, guttering now as the mortar bomb dissipated its force in the water in her hold. A protruding beam of metal caught on the nearest Sampson post. Fate seemed to stagger round. The whole manager's office shook, threatening to tumble free.

It was at this point that Ben's men stopped firing at the bridge and retreated, follow-my-leader. Thirty seconds after they had gone, the scythe of the starboard bridge-wing, ten feet wider than the ship, crushed into the shuddering platform, destroying what little was left there before it ground to a juddering halt.

The second that it did so, Richard's long body dropped down from its after edge onto Fate, and rolled into the shadows of the wreckage.

Christine stood at the base of *Katapult*'s mast, looking upward. The last bundle of arms and grenades destined for the hostages had gone. Salah and her father were waiting at the platform's edge for Doc to climb up to them. He went up the swaying mast like a monkey, then paused at the top to look down at her. He waved. The mast swung. He leaped.

And the whole platform began to jump and shake. The two men on it fell to their knees as she watched in horror. Doc, flying toward it, never stood a chance. He hit it but he could not hold it. Chris watched, riven, as his body bounced back off it and began to fall. Then she, too, was in motion, running down the hull's length, some half thought of catching him in her mind. But he fell free. Into the water, just in front of the sleek bow of his creation. She was there, reaching down, pulling him aboard the instant he came to the surface. But it was not until he was on the deck that she noticed his headband was gone.

She had seconds, if that, before the inevitable seizure began. She ran him back toward the cockpit and just about made it. The spasm hit him on the coaming and he tumbled in. She was beside him at once, cradling his head in her arms, looking down into his huge, lost eyes. "It's all right," she screamed over the horrific noise of the impact. "It's all right . . ." But she was screaming into a sudden silence.

Then she saw something in those eyes she had never seen before and glanced involuntarily up over her shoulder.

And saw the massive metal section immediately above their heads tear itself loose from the platform and fall.

"*Chrissie!*" screamed Martyr, looking back like Lot's wife; like Orpheus to lose his dream.

Salah and he had pulled themselves to their feet the instant after Weary fell, and stood for long enough to see Chris pull him aboard. Then they had run across the bucking steel to the relative solidity afforded by the first of the buildings. Salah kicked the door in and they slung the bags into a long corridor, jumping in behind them. As they did so, the shaking stopped and a sudden, stunning silence replaced it. They knelt, gasping. And a tearing, screaming roaring overwhelmed them. A fountain of spray deluged them. A cold wind fanned them.

And Martyr looked back.

The metal platform they had just jumped onto, sixty feet by sixty, more than a foot thick, undergirdered for added strength, weighing God knew how many tons, was gone. *Katapult*, beneath it, was gone. The corridor they were kneeling in now looked out onto a heaving, foaming maelstrom where the multihull used to be. Where Doc and Martyr's daughter used to be.

"*Chrissie!* I've got to go down after her, Salah."

"It's no use, Chief. They're gone."

"But you don't understand. She's all I've got! She can't be gone. I've got to go down after her!"

"Look! We've got a job to do! I can't do it alone. The others are relying on us. *Martyr!*" He used his most brutal tone. It shocked the man and he hated to do it. But what he had said was true. Without their effort, the whole enterprise was doomed. Martyr flinched. Some semblance of reason returned to those deep green eyes. "We'll look for her later," said Salah and they were off.

Behind them, the last of the bubbles rose out of the tossing water and the sea slowly returned to a calm, as though it had never swallowed anything at all.

Richard had the other Heckler and Koch MP-5 held out at arm's length in front of him, pushing it forward along the deserted corridors. He left doors open behind him; the locusts followed him into the buildings, hopping along the passages he had vacated. He was looking for Ben. He found no one. Nothing.

Behind the buildings ruined by the collision, there was an open space. In its center stood the rusting remains of the drilling equipment. Beyond it stood the hill of prefabs that had housed the rig's crew in the days when it had been in service. Richard looked up at it, calculatingly. If he were in charge here, he would put his headquarters at the top. Better communications. Overview of everywhere around. And there were lights to be seen up there, strengthening his supposition. So, if the HQ was up there, that was where Ben would be. Ben was his prime objective. Ben was his responsibility: being a godfather counted for something, after all!

He ran to the rusting derrick and paused, looking around. The upper works of his ship peered over the destruction she had caused. Her lights lit up this part of the rig, showing it to be empty. He turned, then turned back, thinking that something was wrong. He saw what it was: the air was clear. The locusts had gone. He gave a lean smile and ran forward toward the illuminated shantytown of the prefabricated huts, crunching the last of the insects beneath his feet.

Salah went through the first doorway and entered the prefabricated building like a ghost. There was no one immediately to be seen, but the corridor ahead led to a stairway that was certain to be guarded. He paused for an instant, mind racing, then he slid out again, grabbing the bundle of bags Martyr was guarding. Together, they slung them through the doorway he had just checked. With his chin, Salah gestured toward the stairway. Martyr nodded. They left the bags of weapons where they were and raced forward on silent feet. If there was a guard there, he would have been alerted—

they had by no means come silently through the door that second time. And sure enough, when they reached the foot of the stairs, a hail of bullets greeted them.

So much for silent surprise, thought Salah, as he reached for a thunderflash.

Richard rolled through the doorway and into a massive room. At first, he paused, disoriented, trying to make sense of what he could see. Then the figures of his crew became part of the background, as someone started to shoot at him. He had been looking for the headquarters, expecting it to be up here, but instead he had stumbled into the lecture hall where the hostages were. This was not going according to plan at all. A wiry figure in battle fatigues spun toward him; he fired automatically, without even thinking, and the man spun away. At the corner of his vision, someone else stood up, aiming at him. He scrabbled round feverishly, trying to draw a bead, and the figure was gone under a pile of erstwhile prisoners. Inundated, without a further shot being fired.

He picked himself up, overcome. And they were gathered around him at once, wanting to shake his hand, thump him on the back. . . . "No!" he called, above their cheering. "It's not over!"

They quieted at once.

"Bob, you can't come with me, not with your leg like that. You and Bill stay in charge in here, please. Kerem, you and Twelve Toes take the guns from the guards. We're looking for the other terrorists. Watch out, the rest of you. If we don't find them all, then some of them will be coming back in here."

You could have heard a pin drop. Thirty-five unarmed men silently weighing up their chances if the terrorists did come back. So near yet so far after all.

"But Salah Malik and C. J. Martyr are on their way up with guns for you, too," he added, and left them cheering again.

At the sound of the first thunderflash, Ben sent two more of his men hurrying toward the rear of the platform. That left four more in here with himself, Fatima, and Ali, who was trying to raise Queshm naval base on the radio. The main command center was the highest of the buildings on the platform, towering even above the lecture hall where the hostages were. It had been the rig's communications center, much larger than the radio rooms Ben was used to even on supertankers. It had windows looking east, west, south, and north. Ben had brought tables and chairs, cooking equipment, as well as radios and the main radar in here. There was a cot in the corner for the watchkeeper and another one for Ben, who habitually slept here. For the little that he did sleep.

He was now using the room as his defense post. His defensive plan was simple and dictated by circumstances. He and his command team would remain here until he had contacted Queshm and called the Iranian gunboats in. As his enemies approached, so he would send out men to support the ring of guards already out. He was working on the assumption that Mariner could not have brought more than half a dozen with him; he could even list their names. As soon as he had talked to Queshm, he would move down to the lecture hall where he could make full use of the hostages.

As the door closed behind the first two, who unknowingly were going out against Salah and C. J. Martyr, Ali swung round in his chair triumphantly. "I have Queshm," he announced.

Ben's hand reached for the microphone, but stopped in midgesture. In the distance, he could hear cheering.

"Take two men down to the lecture theater," he said quietly to Fatima. "Two men and the machine gun."

Salah stepped over the body of the boy at the stair-head and glanced around the corner into a long, broad corridor. A flash of movement at the far end was followed by a burst of fire. He jerked back as the corner of the wall exploded into splinters. Then Martyr was there beside him, face white, hands shaking. It might have been fear but Salah knew better. "We're pinned down here," he whispered. "Long corridor. Good man at the far end. We'll have to look for another way up."

"Why bother?" asked Martyr. "Chuck a grenade."

Salah slung another thunderflash around the corner and Martyr was gone after it on a count of three. He departed, seemingly, into the thunderous glare of it and Salah wasn't far behind. Martyr was halfway up the corridor, AK-47 at his hip, hosing the far corner with fire. The thin wood of the prefabricated wall turned into a smoking colander and the terrorist using it for cover collapsed into view. Martyr ran over to him and kicked his weapons away. "Let's get going," he said.

Salah ran back for the bags with the American at his shoulder and a frown on his face. He was paired with a man who had decided he had nothing left to live for, and that was very worrying indeed.

Fatima flattened herself against the wall just outside the control center and listened as though her life depended upon it. Her men ran on before her with the general-purpose machine gun as Ben had ordered, but she was slower to obey. Ben spoke tersely to the Iranian naval officer at Queshm, the same man who had overseen the movement of the hostages from *Prometheus* to Fate; the man who was relying on Ben and the rest of them to close the Gulf and save his bacon before he became another victim of the ruthless purge going on in Iran at the moment. This part of the plan she knew all about and understood. But from the moment Ben had let slip that there was *more* going on—about that other timetable he had mentioned aboard *Prometheus* while they had been waiting for the gunboats to move the hostages— she had been on guard. It had been the final piece in a pattern of growing mistrust she could now see stretching back for a surprisingly long time.

At every opportunity she had spied and watched and listened, trying to discover what this man whom she had trusted with so much for so long was keeping hidden from her. And now, at this last moment, her efforts were rewarded. For, the moment Ben broke contact with Queshm, he was ordering Ali to contact someone else—and Fatima's blood was running cold at the sound of his calm, hypocritical, lying voice.

"Get me Dahran now," said Ben. "Here is the wavelength and the call sign."

"Through," answered Ali almost at once.

"This is the *Dawn of Freedom*," said Ben, in English, which only he and Fatima understood, clearly speaking into the microphone. "I wish to speak to His Excellency Prince Assad."

There was the briefest of silences and then Ben's voice continued, dripping unctuousness, "Your Excellency, we are ready. Everything is at last complete. Please transfer the payment now. Yes, now is the time for you and your associates to move in Aqaba, before the story breaks worldwide. My payment: as you rightly recall, one hundred thousand American dollars a day into the Swiss account. No, it has not gone absolutely smoothly, but we have nothing to fear. The reinforcements are coming in from Queshm as arranged. Yes, it will look like an Iranian affair as planned. Yes, of course the Americans will continue to hesitate, everyone will, and the Gulf will stay closed for as long as possible. *Only through Aqaba*, yes . . ."

Fatima turned away and ran on down the stairs after her men, only a moment or two behind them, so briefly had she needed to pause. She had eavesdropped for such a short time, but what she had learned was such a complete reversal of everything she had believed. She felt an overwhelming urge to stop and scream but she ran on in a daze of shock, her lean body moving by instinct. Her mind could feel itself thinking, so deep was the shock. It was like the moment she had realized the truth about her father's so-called illness and his actual plans for her. She could hardly believe it was happening to her all over again. Blindly she ran on, her breath coming in ragged sobs, something deep inside her crying, "Trapped, trapped, trapped; betrayed, betrayed, betrayed."

Ben's plan stood fully revealed and so easy to understand now. The greed behind all that cant about liberating their brothers and sisters in the great international army of freedom fighters. The lies he had told about his friends in Iran—the lies he must have told *to* his friends in Iran. All so he could close the Gulf, as he was just about to do, not in the cause of freedom or in the cause of justice, but for a hundred thousand dollars a day. American dollars. In his own Swiss bank account.

To be paid by the men in Dahran who controlled the refineries at the port of Aqaba. *Aqaba*, at the far end of the longest desert oil pipeline of all. Aqaba, on the *Red Sea*. Aqaba, the only way left to get crude out of the whole of Arabia when the Strait of Hormuz was closed. And how much would it be worth then to be the only people in the Middle East able to supply any oil at all? Compared with the likely profits of such a scheme, one hundred thousand dollars a day was less than nothing.

And then, there was the source of the money to be considered, too. That certainly bore careful thinking about. For Ben's blood money was due to be paid by His Excellency, Prince Assad.

His Excellency, Prince Assad: *her father.*

Two terrorists came round the corner at a run, without having checked ahead. It was such a gross mistake under these circumstances that it all but beggared belief. Certainly the confrontation was so unexpected that everyone froze. Richard, Kerem, and Twelve Toes had been moving forward so carefully in case their enemies were waiting in ambush, that to have two of them jump out like this was, to say the least, surprising. The five men stood there for an instant, about three feet apart. Then Richard hit the nearest on the side of the head with the stock of his gun. It was a roundhouse right hook, and would probably have felled the man even had Richard not been holding the MP-5. As it was, the first terrorist, instantly unconscious, flew into the second one, knocking him down as well. Kerem's desert boot finished the almost silent exchange. "More presents," said Richard lightly, as they stripped the men of their weapons. "Kerem, take these back to the others. Make yourself up a little commando unit of three. Look for Salah and C. J. Then come looking for me."

Kerem was gone almost at once. "Now, remind me," said Richard to the chief steward, "How should a turkey be trussed?"

* * *

The cheers that greeted Salah and C. J. were almost as loud as the cheers that had greeted Richard. Within moments the guns they brought had been distributed and the hostages were surging toward the doors like the mob assaulting the Bastille. None of the men notionally in charge could hold them and they dashed out into the corridor, looking for terrorists to kill. They found three immediately. Fortunately for *Prometheus*'s crew, Fatima, just catching up with her men, did not have time to deploy the machine gun properly, or she would have killed most of that first wave, if not all of them. The man holding the GPMG opened fire at them with it at once and all but blew himself off his feet. The tracer shots went high and wide, tearing prefabricated walls and ceilings into smoking ruins before it jammed. Fatima and the second man flicked the safeties off their assault rifles, and the shouting mob was gone.

"Set that up to cover the doors. Get it unjammed, fool." Fatima ordered. "We will guard you from here."

But even as she spoke, the head of the man she was addressing exploded. She whirled, searching for her enemy. The second man, beside her, staggered back crazily fast, as though this were a speeded-up film, throwing his rifle away. But Fatima could see him now, a tall Palestinian at the far end of the corridor, familiar from the captive crew. Kerem, they called him. Kerem was standing even as she was standing, looking down an assault rifle at her. She fired first and he fell.

Then she was swinging round incredibly quickly, knowing what had to happen next. The first man out through the lecture hall doors was tall, gray-haired, distinguished looking. She shot him in the chest. The second man out was another Palestinian.

But this time he shot her.

Salah crossed swiftly to the terrorist woman who had

shot Martyr all but through the heart and knelt briefly at her side as he moved her gun away. She lay still as death, huge dark eyes staring upward. They were running with tears and for a moment the tall Palestinian thought they were tears of shock or pain. But then he saw how wet her cheeks were and realized she must have been weeping all along. Then, for some time, he found his mind returning to her, wondering what in the world could have caused her to cry like that.

Ben was beating madly on the rim of the radar, howling with joy. There, in the bright green bowl, weaving their way through the slow tankers, coming to his aid at more than thirty knots, were the four gunboats his naval friend had promised him.

"Ben!" The voice called quietly from nearby. And from far away, down memory lane, Ben stopped what he was doing, as though carved in rock. Uncle Dick was just outside the door. Uncle Richard bloody Mariner was here.

Immediately at Ben's right hand sat Ali, also looking into the radar bowl. Ready, one on either side of the door, were two more guards. Four in here. Now how many did his godfather have?

"Hello, Uncle Richard. What are you doing here?"

"I've come to take you home, Ben."

"But I don't want to go home, Uncle Richard. I want to stay here with my friends." He put on the lunatic singsong voice, thinking like a fox.

"But I'm afraid we can't have that, Ben. They're waiting for you at home."

Ben began to turn, slowly, looking out through the door at his back. "But who'll be waiting, Uncle Richard? My mummy's been dead so long. . . ."

At the far end of the corridor, he could see his enemy

standing looking in. Mariner's hands were by his sides, but he seemed to be holding a pistol. Ben squinted. It was a short corridor, but dark. The light was coming from behind Richard, where another corridor went across. Why, it was a Heckler and Koch MP-5. Now where did you get one of those? wondered Ben. Well, it doesn't matter now.

He raised his empty hands in a helpless, little-boy shrug. "My mummy's been dead for so long," he said. *"And my father went down with your ship kill the bastard!"*

The two men behind the door spun out, guns ready. They understood the English word *kill*. Ali leaped up, grabbing for a gun as well, and all hell was let loose.

Richard dived forward as the two men jumped into the door. Twelve Toes leaned round the corner above him and sprayed them with automatic fire. They didn't stand a chance. As they fell, Richard was looking beyond them at the twisting shapes farther in. A slight figure sprang forward. Richard squeezed off three. The figure stopped where he was, as though his mind had changed. Then Twelve Toes lobbed a thunderflash into the room and dashed past Richard's prone form. Richard picked himself up the instant after the explosion and leaped forward as though coming up out of sprinting blocks. They went in through the door shoulder to shoulder, firing as they went. Ben was thrown back against the radar and the gun he was holding flew away. Richard stood following his slow slide to the floor, every inch, with the MP-5. "Check him," he said to Twelve Toes, and the gun didn't move until he had.

"I thought you'd give me a bit of a chance." Ben's voice was little more than a whisper.

"You're out of your mind."

"I know."

Ben died with a smile on what was left of his face.

Richard frowned. He didn't like that smile at all. Alternatives whirled in his head. Was the place booby trapped? Rigged to explode and kill them all? What was Ben doing when they arrived here? Start with that.

Looking in the radar. Richard looked into the radar. Four fast-moving blips were coming out of Queshm, cutting through the shipping lanes. He looked at his watch. They'd be here in fifteen minutes. "Twelve Toes," he snapped urgently, "we've still got work to do."

"How many do you think, Richard?" asked Sir William Heritage, softly.

"Four boats. Maybe twenty-five heavily armed men in each."

"We don't stand a hope against a hundred. Look what it's cost us to fight thirteen!"

"You're right, Bill."

The others were clearing up below. Sir William Heritage, Bob Stark, Salah Malik, and Richard Mariner were in the blood-and-cordite-reeking mess of the command post. Through the north-facing windows, they could see the bright outline of *Prometheus* jammed against the side of Fate, but beyond that, there was only darkness.

Salah was looking down into the blood-smeared radar bowl morosely. "Five minutes, tops," he said.

And Bob Stark muttered, looking down at Ben, "I'd like to wipe the smile off this bastard's face!"

"It must always have been a part of his plan," said Sir William. "Take over the platform. Close the Gulf. Hand it over to his friends in Iran."

"They could always close the Gulf if they wanted to," Salah reminded him. "Or close Kharg. The Iranian government has that right without going to these lengths."

"But this isn't the government," said Richard. "This

is just some people from the navy in the middle of a power struggle. And getting pretty desperate, too."

"They're here," said Salah.

And even as he spoke, the blustering roar started. Massive searchlights lit up every nut and bolt around. A huge, disembodied voice boomed, "Stay calm. Everybody stay calm, please. This is Admiral Walter Stark of the United States Navy. Our forces have been invited into the Gulf to help with this emergency. Our frigate *Hazard* will be here to oversee any danger arising from this collision in a matter of moments. I would like to thank the Iranian gunboats for their prompt offer of assistance but assure them we have everything under control . . ."

"Now, what is that," said Sir William. "What in Heaven's name is that?"

Richard crossed to the window and looked out. "That's a couple of Kaman Seasprites," he answered. "It looks like Robin is back."

Nobody else knew where he had gone, but Salah and Richard did. They followed the bloodstains down the corridor to where it opened onto nothingness above the quiet sea. He was lying there, face down, with one arm hanging over the edge, as though he had tried to go down and join them but had run out of strength just here.

Richard turned him over. His face was like wax.

"Christ, Richard. It hurts."

"I know."

Neither of them was talking about the chest wound.

The American took a long breath. Richard could feel it bubble through the thin walls of his chest. "She was a good kid, you know? Best daughter a father could ever wish for."

"I know."

"But now she's gone, I don't feel much like hanging around."

Richard looked up at Salah. In the face of so much grief, he simply did not know what to say.

Salah crouched down. "You should not give up," he told his old friend. "I, too, had a child once, remember. And he was taken from me."

Again, that long, rumbling breath. "Have you had one happy day since then, Salah?"

Salah's silence was answer enough.

Martyr started to cough. Richard held him until the fit was over. "That'll just about finish me, I think," whispered the American like a ghost.

"Wait for Robin," pleaded Richard. "It'll break her heart if you don't say good-bye."

"I'll try to hang on for Robin," said Martyr. "But she'd better not take long."

But Robin never came. She was tending the other wounded, Fatima among them, with Asha on *Prometheus*. Instead, an explosion of gasping and splashing suddenly came upward through the night.

And a voice, loud and triumphant: "What a hull, Chris, what a hull. Damn near impossible to break. Enough air still trapped in it to last for a perishing week. We designed it and we built her. Me and old Sam Hood."

✂

☐ **YES!**

Sign me up for the Leisure Thriller Book Club and send
my FREE BOOKS! If I choose to stay in the club, I will
pay only $4.25* each month, a savings of $3.74!

NAME: _____

ADDRESS: _____

TELEPHONE: _____

EMAIL: _____

☐ I want to pay by credit card.

☐ VISA ☐ MasterCard ☐ DISCOVER

ACCOUNT #: _____

EXPIRATION DATE: _____

SIGNATURE: _____

Mail this page along with $2.00 shipping and handling to:
Leisure Thriller Book Club
PO Box 6640
Wayne, PA 19087
Or fax (must include credit card information) to:
610-995-9274

You can also sign up online at **www.dorchesterpub.com**.
*Plus $2.00 for shipping. Offer open to residents of the U.S. and Canada only.
Canadian residents please call 1-800-481-9191 for pricing information.
If under 18, a parent or guardian must sign. Terms, prices and conditions subject to
change. Subscription subject to acceptance. Dorchester Publishing reserves the right
to reject any order or cancel any subscription.